IAIN M. BANKS
FEERSUM ENDJINN

www.orbitbooks.co.uk

ORBIT

First published in Great Britain by Orbit in 1994
This edition published by Orbit in 1995
Reprinted 1997, 1998, 1999, 2001, 2002, 2004 (twice),
2005 (twice)

Copyright © Iain M. Banks 1994

The moral right of the author has been asserted.

A CIP catalogue record for this book
is available from the British Library.

ISBN 1 85723 273 9

Printed in England by Clays Ltd, St Ives plc

Orbit
An imprint of
Time Warner Book Group UK
Brettenham House
Lancaster Place
London WC2E 7EN

www.orbitbooks.co.uk

14.41

Iain Banks came to widespread and controversial public notice with the publication of his first novel, *The Wasp Factory*, in 1984. *Consider Phlebas*, his first science fiction novel, was published under the name Iain M. Banks in 1987. He has since gained enormous popular and critical acclaim and in 1993 he was acknowledged as one of the Best of Young British Writers. Iain Banks lives in Fife, Scotland.

Find out more about Iain M. Banks and other Orbit authors by registering for the free monthly newsletter at www.orbitbooks.co.uk

'The standard by which the rest of SF is judged' *Guardian*

'A mordant wit, a certain savagery and a wild imagination' *Mail on Sunday*

'Spectacular . . . the field needs his energy, skill and invention' *The Scotsman*

'Gripping, touching and funny' *TLS*

'Dazzlingly original' *Daily Mail*

'Sharp, witty, comprehensively terrifying' *Observer*

'Banks is a phenomenon . . . writing pure science fiction of a peculiarly gnarly energy and elegance' William Gibson

'There is now no British SF writer to whose work I look forward with greater keenness' *The Times*

'Banks has rewritten the libretto for the whole space-opera genre' *The Times*

'Poetic, humorous, baffling, terrifying, sexy – the books of Iain M. Banks are all these things and more' *NME*

'Staggering imaginative energy' *Independent*

For the Daves

ONE

1

Then, it was as though everything was stripped away: sensation, memory, self, even the notion of existence that underlies reality – all seemed to have vanished utterly, their passing marked only by the realisation that they had disappeared, before that too ceased to have any meaning, and for an indefinite, infinite instant, there was only the awareness of something; something that possessed no mind, no purpose and no thought, except the knowledge that it was.

After that came a rebuilding, a surfacing through layers of thought and development, learning and shape-taking, until something that was an individual, possessing a shape and capable of being named, woke.

Buzz. Buzzing noise. Lying on something soft. Dark. Try to open eyes. Something sticking. Try again. Light flash shaped 00. Eyes feel open, un-gummed, but still dark. Smells; at once vital and decadent, lush with death-life, stirring some memory, recent and forever-far at the same time. Light comes; a small . . . searching for the name of the colour . . . a small *redness* hanging in air. Move arm, hand coming up; right arm; noise of skin on skin, feeling coming with it.

Arm, hand, finger: rising, positioning, eyes focusing. Red patch of soft light disappears. Press on it. Arm shaking, feeling weak; falls back to side. Skin on skin.

Click.

Noise of buzzing, something sliding again but not skin on skin; harder. Then light from behind/above. The small red light has disappeared. Then movement; darkness above/around sliding back, face neck shoulders chest/arms trunk/hands in light now; eyes blinking in light. Light grey-pink, shining down; blue-brightness through hole in curved cliff above/around.

Wait. Rest. Let eyes adjust. Songs around, wall around/above (not cliff; wall), curving round, curving over (ceiling;

roof). Hole in wall where the brightness is called a window.

Lie there, turning head to one side; another hole, glimpsed over shoulder; goes down to ground, and called doorway. Daylight there beyond, and the green of trees and grass. Floor beneath where lying; pressed earth, light brown with a few small stones set in it. The song is birdsong.

Get up slowly, arms back, resting on elbows, looking down towards feet; woman, naked, colour of the ground.

Ground is quite near; might as well stand up. Sit up further, swivel (dizzy for a moment, then steady), then feet/legs over side of . . . of . . . tray thing that has appeared out of hole in wall of building, tray thing lying on, and then . . . stand.

Hold onto tray, legs feeling funny, then stand properly, unaided, and stretch. Stretch feels good. Tray slides back into wall; watch it go, and watch part of wall slide down to cover hole that was there, hole came out of. Feel . . . sadness, but feel . . . good, too. Deep breath.

Breath makes noise, then cough makes noise, and . . . *voice* is there. Clear throat, then say:

'Speak.'

Slight startle. Voice makes a feeling in throat and face. Touch face, feel . . . smile. 'Smile.' Feel something building up inside. 'Face.' Still building. 'Face smile.' And still. 'Face smile good alive hole red wall me look door doorway sun garden, ME!'

Then the laughter comes, bursting out, filling the little stone rotunda and spilling out into the garden; a small bird hurtles into the air in a commotion of leaves and flies away upon a wake of song.

Laughter stops. Sit on floor in the building. Feeling empty inside; hunger. 'Laughter. Hunger. Me hungry. I am hungry. I laugh; I was laughing, I am hungry.' Get up. 'Up.' Giggle. 'Giggle. Get up and giggle, me. I learn. I go now.'

But turn and look at inside of building; the curved walls, stamped-earth floor, the polished rectangular stones with lettering on them which are set into the walls, some of them with little cups/baskets/holders. Not sure which one was the one with the tray and the little red light now; not sure which one came from, now. Sadness, a little.

Turn again and go to door and look out over shallow valley;

trees and shrubs and grass, a few flowers, stream in bottom of valley.

'Water. I thirst. I have thirst, I am thirsty; I will drink. Go for drink now. Good.'

Leave the birth-place vault.

'Sky. Blue. Clouds. Walk. Path. Trees. Bush. Path. Other path. Sky again. Hills. Oh! Oh; shadow. Fright. Laugh! Bigger bush. Flat grass. Thirsty; mouth dry; think stop talk now. Ha-ha!'

2

On the morning of the one hundred and forty-third day of the year which by the new reckoning was called second-last, Hortis Gadfium III, the chief scientist to the pan-alignment clan Accounts/Privileges, sat on a steel girder and looked up at the almost-finished bulk of the new Great Hall oxygen plant number-two liquifier unit, and shook her head.

She watched a crane swing a palleted load of steel-plate towards the workers waiting on the summit of the structure, while above the crane's delicate web-work the ponderous mass of a lufter drifted, engines droning, delivering a new batch of supplies. She looked around at the swarm of human-scale toil that was the new oxygen works, where engines laboured and variously puffed, grumbled and hummed, where machines crawled, floated, rolled or just sat, where chimerics sweated, strained, lifted and pulled, and where humans too laboured, shouted or simply stood scratching their heads.

Gadfium drew one finger through the layer of dust on the girder beneath her, then held the begrimed finger up to her face and wondered if in that smudge there lay a nano-machine capable of creating within the day machines which would create machines which would create machines that would give them all the oxygen they would ever need, and by the end of the season, not by the end of next year. She wiped her finger on her tunic and looked up again at the number-two liquifier unit, worrying whether it would ever work properly, and, if it did, whether there would be any workable rockets for it to supply.

She gazed towards the Hall's three vast windows, where – beneath high, rainless ceiling-cloud – sunlight shone slanting down in great broad bands of dust-struck radiance, illuminating a swathe of landscape a few kilometres away and sparkling on the towers and domes of Hall City, two thousand metres beneath the pendulously extravagant architecture of the Lantern Palace.

It was bright outside, and on such days you could deceive yourself that all was still well with the world, that there was no threat, no shadow on the face of the night, no remorseless, system-wide, approaching catastrophe. On such days one might persuade oneself that it was all a huge mistake or mass hallucination, and that the view last night, when she had stood outside the observatory dome above the darkened Palace, had been a figment of her imagination, a dream that had not vanished or been properly sorted by her waking mind, and so which lived on, as nightmare.

She stood up and walked back to where her junior aide and research assistant were waiting, conversing quietly in the midst of the oxygen works' constructive chaos and looking about occasionally with a kind of disparaging indulgence at the undignified physical clamour such mere technology required. And, Gadfium didn't wonder, probably amusing themselves discussing what the old girl was doing, not wanting to linger any longer than absolutely necessary at this building site.

There probably had been no need for her to attend the site conference at all; the science in this project had long been settled and the burden of effort passed to Technology and Engineering; still, she was invited to such meetings out of politeness (and her rank at court), and she attended when she could because she worried that, in the rush to recreate technologies and processes which had been obsolete for thousands of years, they might have missed something, forgotten some simple fact, overlooked some obvious danger. Such an oversight might be quickly dealt with, but they had anyway so little time that any interruption at all to the programme might prove disastrous, and while in her lowest moments she sometimes suspected such an interruption was almost inevitable, she was determined to do all in her power to ensure that if it did befall them it would not be for want of any diligence on her part.

Of course, it would all have been a lot simpler if they had not been at war with the clan Engineers, headquartered (and besieged) in the Chapel, thirty kilometres away on the far side of the fastness, and three kilometre-high floors higher than the Great Hall. There were Engineers on their side – just as there were dissident Cryptographers, Scientists and members of other clans on the other side – but too few, and like so many Scientists Gadfium had had to shoulder the extra burden of trying to think on an industrially practical scale.

As for her desire simply to sit and look at the plant, that was probably a function of her doubt that what they were doing here was going to make any difference to their plight even if it went exactly according to plan; she suspected that subconsciously she hoped the sheer presence and scale of this industrial enterprise – and the physical energy of its creation – would somehow convince her there was a point to it all.

If that had been her wish, it had not been granted, and no matter how much of the oxygen works filled her field of vision, always lurking at the edge of her sight she seemed to see that hazy spread of darkness, rising from the night's horizon like an obscene inversion of dawn.

'Chief Scientist?'

'Hmm?' Gadfium turned to find her aide, Rasfline, standing a couple of metres away. Rasfline – thin, ascetic, stiffly correct in his aide's uniform – nodded to her.

'Chief Scientist; a message from the Palace.'

'Yes?'

'There has been a development at the Plain of Sliding Stones.'

'A *development*?'

'An unusual one; I know no more. Your presence there has been requested and the relevant travel arrangements made.'

Gadfium sighed. 'Very well. Let's go.'

The piker swept out of the oxygen works and headed for East Cliff along a dusty, winding road filled with heavy traffic both machine and chimeric. The groomed, carefully landscaped park-land that had graced this part of the Great Hall for a thousand generations had been ripped up without a second thought when the Encroachment's implications had – apparently – been driven home to the King and his more sceptical advisers; normally any such industry would have been banished to the inner depths of the fastness, where there was little natural light and objectionably ugly or effluent processes could safely be housed without disturbing either the view or the air, and where only the desperate or outlawed would ever choose to live.

Still – for all the outrage, and the suicides of a number of gardeners and foresters – when the King had decided such a plant must be built, and must be built quickly, and under the eye of the Palace, the earth-movers – themselves newly constructed for the purpose – had been sent in, and woods, lakes and glades which had delighted all castes and classes for millennia were levelled under their ploughs, scrapes and tracks.

The chief scientist watched the oxygen works disappear behind a wooded hill, until the construction site was marked only by a haze of smoke and dust hanging in the air above the trees. It would reappear as they headed out across the plain to East Cliff; the oxygen works was sited on a small plateau and so visible from almost everywhere throughout the ten-kilometre length of the Great Hall. Gadfium wondered again whether the real reason the King had had the works built here was to impress upon his subjects the full gravity of their situation, and give them a preparatory hint of the kind of sacrifices that would need to be made in the future. Gadfium shook her head, tapped her fingers on the seat's wooden armrest and opened a vent by the side of the window to let the warm air in. She looked at the man and woman sitting opposite her.

Rasfline and Goscil had been with her since the start of the present emergency, ten years ago, when science had started to matter again. Rasfline epitomised the officer caste, and seemed to take pride in making himself as much like a machine as possible; in all those ten years he had never called Gadfium anything other than 'Chief Scientist' or 'ma'am'.

Goscil – plump-faced, wild-haired, and whose tunic never seemed to quite fit properly or ever be entirely free from stains – had seemed to grow more dishevelled over the years, as though in response to Rasfline's severe tidiness. She had uploaded some files from the oxygen works, and sat with her eyes closed now, reviewing this information and occasionally making small involuntary noises; tutting, hissing, snorting, humming. Rasfline set his jaw and looked away out the window.

'Any more details from the Plain?' Gadfium asked him.

'None, ma'am.' Rasfline paused, making it obvious he was communicating, then shook his head. 'As before; the observatory there has reported something unusual and the Palace has granted their request that you attend.'

'Plain of Sliding Stones?' Goscil said, opening her eyes suddenly. She blew hair away from the side of her face, glancing at Rasfline. 'I heard some gossip on the science channel about the stones doing something weird.'

'Really,' Rasfline said drily.

'And how did this weirdness manifest itself?' Gadfium asked.

Goscil shrugged. 'Didn't say; there's just a filed report from some junior timed about dawn that the stones were moving and something strange was happening. Nothing since.' She glanced at Rasfline again. 'Probably been clamped down.'

Gadfium nodded. 'Has there been much wind and precipitation up there lately?'

Both Rasfline and Goscil went still for a moment. Goscil answered first: 'Yes. Enough melt for them to move, and some wind. But . . .'

'Yes?' Gadfium said.

Goscil shrugged. 'The way that junior reported; said there was a . . . may I repeat it verbatim?'

Gadfium nodded. 'Go on.'

Goscil closed her eyes. Rasfline looked away again. 'Umm,' Goscil said, '. . . Usual identifiers; Plain of Stones Observatory, etc., then, quote:' – her voice changed here to something like a chant – 'something odd going on. Something very odd. Oh shit. Let's see, right, general data first: wind blowing; north-west, force four, precip; three mill yesterday, plain friction factor; six. Oh, look at them! Look at that. They can't do that! They've never done that, have they? Wait till – (*unintelligible*) – I'm calling the chief observer . . . filing this as is. Signing off.'

Goscil opened her eyes. 'Unquote. After that, nothing. People have been trying to get in touch with the observatory since, but there's no reply.'

'When was the report timed?'

'Six-thirteen.'

Gadfium looked at Rasfline, who was smiling thinly. 'Has the Palace been in touch with the observatory since?'

'I cannot say, Chief Scientist,' the aide replied, then, as though seeking to be helpful nevertheless, added: 'The message I received requesting your presence was timed at ten forty-five.'

'Hmm,' Gadfium said. 'Kindly request that the Palace furnish us with more details, and allow us to speak directly with the observatory.'

'Ma'am,' Rasfline said, and took on the glassy-eyed look of someone making it politely obvious they were communicating.

Gadfium's status decreed that she was above the need for an implanted direct status link, being one of those valued souls whose mind must be left free from the distractions of constant inter-communication to concentrate on undiluted thought, unless they chose to access the data corpus by some external means. She knew she must accept this, but even so oscillated between a guilty pride in her privileged position and an intermittent frustration that she so often had to rely on others to furnish her with so many of the details her work required.

'We're to take a clifter up the East Face,' Goscil announced after a moment's pause. 'The King's own machine, just for us,' she told the chief scientist. 'They must want us there very quickly.'

3

The caisson-train lumbered across the broken landscape of the collapsed Southern Volcano Room; a line of huge, cylindrically rotund, multi-wheeled heavy carriers interspersed with smaller vehicles and chimerics. Some of the larger chimerics, all of them of the incarnosaur genus, carried troops; most of the other make-beasts were considered at least semi-sentient, and were themselves soldiers, variously armoured, impedimented and armed.

The other ground vehicles were all-drive holster-buggies, armoured scree-cars, one- or two-gun landromonds and the huge multi-turreted tanks known as bassinals. The struggling convoy accounted for a good sixth of the King's military transport, and represented either a brilliant flanking manoeuvre to supply the beleaguered garrison of troops guarding the workings in the fifth-floor south-western solar, or a desperate and probably forlorn gamble to win a war that was not only unwinnable but anyway pointless; Sessine had still to decide which.

The Count Alandre Sessine VII, commander-in-chief of the second expeditionary force, looked up and away from the slow-moving convoy of beasts and machines in his charge to gaze at the gaping shell of ruined walls around them, and the revealed topography of mega-architecture and cloud beyond.

Standing waist-high in the turret of the command scree-car, shaken this way and that by the rough, trackless ground the convoy traversed, his body armour clunking dully against the inside rim of the hatch, it took an effort to focus on the vast and sullen grandeur of one's surroundings, and a further effort to dismiss the apparent irrelevance of such scale to the more immediate task at hand (or rather at foot, and paw, and wheel and track).

All the same, it pleased him to do so every now and again when the steam and smoke-clouds cleared sufficiently, and he judged it no extravagance upon his supposedly valuable attention; keener eyes and more extrapolated senses than his would mind the progress of the convoy over such increments of time as he chose to allow the wider view, and – after all – what was his silent, self-solitary mind left so for (by the King's good grace) if not to attend to the greater world beyond the vulgar intimacy of the immediate?

The collapsed Southern Volcano Room was really many rooms, and several levels of them, too; the walls still standing formed a huge extra curtain of cliff in the shape of a C between ten and thirteen kilometres in diameter and one and six kilometres in height. The crumpled ground the convoy moved across with such exquisite slowness was the wreckage of five or six floors, compressed by the cataclysm that had befallen this section of the fastness to a height of less than two great storeys, and was still shaken every year or so by smaller earthquakes. Steam and smoke drifted from a hundred different cracks and fissures across the crazily tilted geography of the room, and when dispersing winds did not whip whorling through the vast cauldron, the air was filled with the smell of sulphur.

It was a moderately calm day now, and the clouds of yellow-tinged smoke and brightly white steam that drifted over this tortured legacy of landscape provided cover for the convoy's painstaking progress, even if they also sporadically prevented one from witnessing the full majesty of the great castle beyond.

Sessine looked behind him, through the high hanging valley that was the breach in the fortress structure created by the buried volcano. The curtain walls made a wavy line on the landscape, blue with distance beyond the hazily glimpsed forests, lakes and parkland of the outer bailey. Beyond was only the vaguest hint of the hills and plains of the provinces that made up Xtremadur.

It looked warm down there, Sessine thought, imagining the smells of summer pasture and woodland, and the feel of pool-water on his skin. Here, though the snow-line was still a good kilometre above, the air was chill when not heated with the rotten smell of the semi-dormant volcano beneath the convoy. Sessine felt himself shiver, for all his armour and furs.

He smiled as he looked around. For the privilege of being here in this gelid hell risking his last life on a mission the point of which even he did not entirely understand, he had indulged in the sort of prolonged and strenuous string-pulling he normally quite thoroughly disapproved of. Perhaps after all I am a masochist at heart, he thought. Maybe it had merely lain latent (he glanced at the pitched upheaval of ground they were crossing) – dormant – these last seven lives. The idea amused. He continued his sweep of the panorama briefly available through the shifting clouds.

At one end of the vast C bitten from the castle a single great bastion-tower stood, almost intact, five kilometres high, and casting a kilometre-wide shadow across the rumpled ground in front of the convoy. The walls had tumbled down around the tower, vanishing completely on one side and leaving only a ridge of fractured material barely five hundred metres high on the other. The plant-mass babilia, unique to the fastness and ubiquitous within it, coated all but the smoothest of vertical surfaces with tumescent hanging forests of lime-green, royal blue and pale, rusty orange; only the heights of scarred wall closest to the more actively venting fissures and fumaroles remained untouched by the tenacious vegetation.

Above, trees grew on the summit of the serrated ridge, which grew haphazardly, jaggedly, as it swept around the huge bowl of the Volcano Room, gradually lifting above the tree-line until directly in front of them it merged with the intact structure of the fastness Serehfa, where the walls – some pierced by enormous windows and clerestories, some plain, some shining sheer and some roughened sufficiently to be coated with snow or the blue-green strain of high-altitude babilia – climbed through the clouds and into the sky.

Sessine was looking almost straight up now, trying to glimpse the summit of the fast-tower itself, the mightiest of Serehfa's mighty towers, standing glittering in its solitude above all but the most vestigial traces of atmosphere, fully twenty-five kilometres above the surface of the Earth and almost in space itself.

Clouds hid the mysterious summit of the castle, and Sessine smiled ruefully to himself as another veil of steam and foul-smelling smoke drifted across the view, obscuring. The Count held the image of those enormous distant walls for a moment and wrinkled his nose as the vapours and gases wrapped themselves round the slowly moving car. He lifted a pair of all-band field glasses from a hook inside the hatch and scanned his surroundings again, but the effect, and particularly the sense of scale, was not the same.

Still, there was a little added safety in the mists. He wondered – as he always did at some point in one of these recreational panoramas – whether his inspection had been in any way reciprocated.

He knew the King had his own spyers, dispatched to towers and high walls to watch the open areas beneath them and report to Army Intelligence, and he had never entirely believed that the Engineers seemed never to have thought of the same idea. He put the field glasses back. The volcanic mists did not appear to be dispersing; if anything they were growing thicker and more noxious.

There was a crackle of noise from inside the car, then someone spoke. It sounded like a signal-burst had been received. The convoy had to observe complete communicative silence, though the Army could still contact them through broadcasts. It meant that all the men were alone in their own heads, or at least in their own vehicles. To join the Army was to lose the ability to have unrestrained access to the data corpus; everything had to go through the Army's own network.

Being unable to contact distant loved ones was bad enough for troops unused to war and brought up from childhood with the ability to reach anybody they wanted through the corpus, but at least in most of the rest of the Army they could talk so to each other. For the duration of this mission they were forbidden even that, lest they betray their positions, and only encapsulated within their closed transports could they use their implants.

Sessine glanced back at the bulbous snout of the provisions caisson immediately aft – it was all there was to be seen behind, just as all he could see in front was the rear of a weapon-laden chimeric – then ducked back inside the scree-car, closing the hatch cover after him.

The scree-car's interior was warm and smelled of oil and plastic; in the two days since they had quit the newly built hydrovator at the breach lip opposite the bastion-tower he had come to regard its humming, machine-scented interior almost with affection. Perhaps there was something womb-like about its hermetic, humming redness.

Sessine settled into the commander's seat and took his gloves off. 'Hatch down,' he said.

'Hatch down, sir,' the car's captain called out, calling back over her shoulder. The driver at her side twisted the scree-car's wheel, his eyes fixed on the clear image of the ground ahead produced by the all-band display.

'Communication?' Sessine asked the comms operator. The young lieutenant nodded, trembling. He looked frightened, his skin grey. Sessine wondered what the news was, and felt his guts start to knot.

'We got it too, sir,' the captain called, still watching the screen. 'Gistics update code: routine.'

'Routine?' Sessine asked, staring at the lieutenant's stricken-looking expression. What was happening?

'I – I heard some— ' the comms operator began, then swallowed. 'I heard something more, sir, over the machine's hard channel, from Intelligence,' he stammered. He licked his lips and rested one shaking hand on the comms console.

The captain twisted round in her seat, frowning. 'What?'

The lieutenant glanced at her, then told Sessine, 'They have a spyer on the north rim-wall, sir; he reports . . . a . . .' the young man hesitated, then blurted, 'an air attack.'

'*What*?' yelled the captain, twisting in her seat and punching at the car's sensor controls, then sitting back, one hand to her ear, eyes closed.

'A . . . an air attack, sir,' the lieutenant repeated, tears in his eyes, glancing up at the hatch.

The captain muttered something. The driver started to whistle. Sessine could think of nothing to say. He jumped up onto the observation platform and threw the hatch open again, remembering to shout, 'Hatch open!' as he rose into the steams and smokes above. He lifted the field glasses.

As he put them to his eyes, he heard two shots from beneath him, inside the car, followed quickly by two more. The car lurched and swung right.

Sessine dropped through the hatch, and as he did so realised that he might have made a terrible mistake.

His hand went to his own gun; he registered the sick-sweet smell of burnt flesh, and found himself looking into the tear-streaked face of the comms operator, pointing his gun straight at him.

The two bodies in the front of the scree-car jiggled slackly as the car thumped over some obstruction. The lieutenant braced himself against the car's ceiling with his free hand and sniffed hard. Sessine held his hand out to him, leaving his other hand on the butt of his gun. 'Now— '

'I'm sorry, sir!'

Then the world lit up, and a terrible blow struck Sessine's lower face. He fell, knowing he was dying, falling surrounded by smoke to hit the floor, beyond pain with a noise past sound in his ears, no breath left in him and no way of breathing, and lay there for some terrible suspended moment before he sensed the young lieutenant over him and felt the gun at the back of his head and had time to think, *Why*?, and he died.

4

Woak up. Got dresd. Had brekfast. Spoke wif Ergates thi ant who sed itz juss been wurk wurk wurk 4 u lately master Bascule, Y dont u ½ a holiday? & I agreed & that woz how we decided we otter go 2 c Mr Zoliparia in thi I-ball ov thi gargoyle Rosbrith.

I fot Id bettir clear it wif thi relevint oforities furst & hens avoyd any truble (like happind thi lastime) so I went 2 c mentor Scalopin.

Certinly yung Bascule, he sez, i do beleave this is a day ov relativly lite dooties 4 u u may take it off. ½ u made yoor mattins calls?

O yes, I sed, which woznt stricktly tru, in fact which woz pretti strikly untru, trufe btold, but I cude always do them while we woz travelin.

Wots in that thare box yoor holdin? he asks.

Itz a ant, I sez, waven thi box @ his face.

O this is yoor litil frend, is it? i herd u had a pet. May i see him?

Iss not a pet, iss a frend; u woz rite thi furst time, & iss not a im iss a she. Luke.

O yes very pretti, he sez, which is a pretti strainge thing 2 say about a ant if u ask me but thare u go.

Duz it – duz she ½ a naim? he asks.

Yes, I sez, sheez calld Ergates.

Ergateez, he sez, thatz a nyce name whot maid u call her that?

Nuffink, I sez; itz her reel name.

A I see, he sez, & givs me 1 ov thoze lukes.

& she can tok 2, I tel him, tho I doan xpect yule b able 2 here hir.

(*Shh*, Bascule! goze Ergates, & I go a bit red.)

Duz she, duz she now? mentor Scalopin sez wif wunna them tolerint smylez. Very wel then he sez, pattin me on thi hed (which I doan much like, frangly, but sumtimes u jus ½ 2 poot up wif these things. N-way whare wer we? O yes he woz pattin me on thi hed & sayin), off yugo (he sez) but b bak by supper.

Ritey-ho, I sez, all breezy like, nevir thinkin.

Swing doun past thi kitchins 2 see mistriz Blyke 2 flash my big solefool Is & giv hir thi soppi smile all shy & bashfool & skrownj sum provishins. She pats me on thi noddil 2 – what is it wif peeple?

Leev thi monstery about $1/2$ 9 & lift 2 thi top; thi sun iz shinin in fru thi big winders acros thi grate hol strait in2 ma Iz. Dam shure it dozen luke like itz gettin dimmer 2 me but evrybody sez it is so I spose it muss b.

Grab a ride on a waggin heddin 4 thi souf-west hydrovater along thi clif roade, hangin on 2 thi bak ov thi truk abuv thi x-ost; bit steemy when thi truk stops @ junkshins, but beets havvin 2 ride in thi cab & tok 2 thi dryver & probly get pattid on thi bonce aggen like as knot.

I like thi cliff rode cos u can luke ovir thi edge & c rite doun 2 thi flore ov thi hol & evin c thi big rownd bobbly bits what wood b thi handils ov thi drawerz ov thi bureau if this woz a propir size place instead ov being BIG like it is. Mr Zoliparia sez ov coarse ther wernt nevir no jiants & I bileev him but sumtymes u can luke owt ovir thi hall wif its mountins like cuboardz & mountins like seets & sofas set agenst thi wall & thi tabils & poofs & so on skaterd about thi playce & u fink, Whenz them big bags cummin bak then? (Bags is my own koinin & am qwite proud ov it – meenz Boys & GirlS. Ergates sez its called a nacronim. N-way whare woz we? O yes hangin on 2 thi bak ov thi truk rolin along thi clif rode.)

Ergates thi ant iz in hir box in thi left brest pokit ov my jakt-wif-lotza-pokits, all saifly butinned down. U alrite Ergates? I whispir as we bownse along thi rode.

Am fine, she tellz me. Whare r we rite now?

Um, weer on a truk, I sort ov $1/2$-lies.

R we hanging off thi bak ov a veehikl? she asks.

(Blimey you get nuffink past this ant.) Wot maiks u think that, I asks, stollin.

Muss u always maximise thi dainger ov any givin moad ov transpoart? she asks, ignorin me stollin.

But am Bascule thi Rascule, thass whot they call me! Am yung & am onli on my furst life I tells her, laffin; Bascule thi Teller

nuffink, that's me; no I or II or VII or any ov that nonsins 4
yoors truly; am good az immortil 4-all intense & purpusses &
if u cant act a bit daff when u never dyed not even 1nce yet,
when can u?

Well, Ergates sez (& u can juss tel she's tryn 2 b payshint),
aside from thi fact that it is folly 2 fro away even 1 life out ov 8,
& thi eekwilly sailyent poynt that in thi present emerginsy it mite
b fullish 2 rely on thi effishint funkshining ov thi reeincarnative
prossess, ther is my own safety 2 think about.

I thot u woz indistructibil 2 a fol from any hite on acount
ov yoor scale & mass-to-surfis area givin thi relativ sighz ov air
mollycules? I sez.

Sumthing like that, she agreez. But if you landid thi wrong
way it is conseevabil i might b krushd.

Ho, Id like 2 kno whotz thi rite way 2 land from this hi up,
I sez, leenin out ovir thi drop wif thi wind in my hare & gayzin
doun thi way @ thi treetopz ov thi forist-floor, what must b a
gude cupil ov hundred meetrs blo.

Yoor missing thi point, sez Ergates thi ant, soundin sniffy.

I fot 4 a momint. Tell u wot, I sez.

Yes? she sez.

When we take thi hydravatir up thi clif, this time weel go on
in thi inside; howzat?

Yoor mewnifisince astonishiz me, she sez.

(Sheez bin sarcastic, I can tel.)

Thi hydravater car is 1 ov thi old wooden 1s wot kreeks a
lot & it smelz ov rope-oyl & varnish & thi emty watir tanks
unnerneeth thi deck maik big boomy spooky noyses as it
climes up thi wol ov thi hol. Thi flor ov thi car is mostly
taken up with six big militry veehikls witch look like airships
wif wheels. Thair garded by some armi ladz hoor havin a game
ov pinkel-flip & am thinkin ov joinin in coz Im a pritty good
shot @ thi old finkel-plip & I probly cude stand 2 make a deel
ov gambil-toakins on account that Im so yung & innosent lookin
& yet a bit ov a huslir reely but then Ergates sez, Dont u think u
shude make those callz like u promised bro Scalopin? & I sez O
I spose so.

Am a tellir, so thi callz $1/2$ 2 b made, I spose.

I find a qwiet spot neer thi gaits where thi wind rufflz in, &

I sidown & leen bak & let ma Is go moasly closed & I tap inter thi kript whare thi ded peepil r.

From thi top ov thi hydravater I cros thi marshalin yard on thi freize neer thi rufe ov thi hol & hed in2 thi wol thru varius passidjways & tunils & take a tube along thi inside ov thi wol 2 thi far end ov thi great hol. I get off @ thi cornir stayshin & climb up sum steps; I cum out in a galleria on thi outside ov thi wol what xtends out from thi greenery & bluery & etcetery ov thi babil plants. From heer I can look down on2 thi terisses & litil villiges on thi roofs ov thi parapet merlons wif thi litle feelds on thi crenels & if I look rite down I can c thi flat green valey that is thi alure but I xpect nun ov this terminoloji meens much if u doan no mutch about cassils.

N-way, iss a pretti impressive view, & sumtimes yule c eegils & rocs & simurgs & lammergeiers & uther big funny-lookin burds wheelin about juss 2 add a bit ov lokil culur, + further blo thers moar wals & towrs & alures & steep roofs – some ov them terrissed 2 – & blo that thi forists & hilz ov thi bailey, then thi curtin wall in thi distince & furthir away stil thers thi haizi seenery ov thi far beyawnd. (They reckin u can c thi c from thi veri hiest hites ov thi habitabil castle, but tho I seen this screend I nevir seen it wif ma own Is.)

A rikiti ole chare lif takes me up & along, through a sort ov tunil in thi hangin babil plants, & b4 long I arive @ thi corner ov thi grate hol & thi playce under thi eaves whare thi Astroligers/Alchemists hang owt, & hang out is xactly what they do, espeshilly Mr Zoliparia, who bean an importint ole jent ov sum noat has got 1 ov thi prime posishins in all thi town 4 his partments, viz thi right eyeball ov thi septentrynil gargoil Rosbrith.

Thi gargoil Rosbrith lukes out 2 thi north, but coz its on thi cornir & therz nuffin in thi way, you can see east 2, whare thi sun is proan 2 rise ov a mornin & thi nastines ov thi approachin enkroachin is poppin up sayin High thair foaks itz lites out soon bi thi way!

I hit a snag; Mr Zoliparia dozent apeer 2 b in. Am standin @ thi top ov a rikiti ladder inside thi bodi ov thi gargoil Rosbrith abangin & abashin on thi litil sircular doar ov Mr Zoliparia's partments but 4 ol my hammerin therz no anser. Therz a woodin landin blo me wot thi laddirs perchd on (its rikity 2, by thi way. Cum 2 fink ov it moast stuff in thi Astrolidjers/Alchemists town seamz 2 b pretti rickiti) but nway therz a old lady scrubbin thi dam landin wif sum horibil bubblin stuff thatz bringin thi wood on thi landin up a treat evein if it disolvin most ov it & makin it even moar rikity, but thi poynt is this stuffs makin fewms go up my nose & cozin my Is 2 wotir.

Mr Zoliparia! I shout. Iss Bascule here!

Perhaps u shood 1/2 told him u were cumin, Ergates says from her box.

Mr Zoliparia doan hold wif moderin like inplants & that sort ov stuf, I tell her, sneezin. Heez a disidint.

U coud 1/2 left a messidje with sumbody else, Ergates sez.

Yes yes yes I sez, ol anoid bcoz I no sheez rite. I spose now I 1/2 2 use my own bleedin inplantz & Ive been tryin not 2 apart from contaktin thi wurld ov thi ded coz I want 2 b a disidint like Mr Zoliparia.

Mr Zoliparia! I shouts agen. Ive got my scarf up round my mouf & noze now cos ov thi fumes cumin up from thi landin.

O, bugration.

Is sumbody using hidrokloric asid? Ergates sez. On wood? She sounds mistified.

I doan no about that I sez but therz sum ole girl down thare scrubbin away @ thi landin wif sumfin pretti nockshis.

Odd, Ergates sez. I woz sure heed b in. I think u bettir get down – but then thi door opins & thares Mr Zoliparia in a big towel & what ther is ov his hares ol wet.

Bascule! he shouts @ me, mite 1/2 noan it woz u! Then he glares down @ thi ole lady & waves @ me 2 come in & I scrambil ovir thi top ov thi laddir & in2 thi I-ball.

Take yor shooz off, boy, he sez, if u stept in dat stuf on di landin yule b rotten me carpets. When uve dun dat u can make yoorself usful & warm me up some wine. Then he pads off, hoistin his towl up around him & leavin a trale ov watir behind him on thi flor.

I start 2 take me shooz off.

You bean havin a baf Mr Zoliparia? I asks him.

He juss lukes @ me.

*　　*　　*

Mr Zoliparia & me & Ergates thi ant are sittin on thi iris balconi ov thi gargoyle Rosbrith's rite I-bol havin respectivly mulled wine, t, & a mikeroscpic morsil ov stale bred. Mr Zoliparias in a chair wot lukes a bit like a I-bol isself, suspendid from a Ilash abuv; am on a stool sat b-side thi parapet whare Ergates is tukkin in2 thi bred Mr Zoliparia gave her (& whot I moysined wif sum spit) – iss a hoal huge lump ov crust & far 2 much 4 her reely, but she tares crums off & works them wif her moufparts & front feet until she can swollo them. I herd Ergates say Thanku 2 Mr Zoliparia when he gaiv hir thi crust but I ½ nt told him she can tok yet & he didn seem 2 heer her.

Am watching Ergates carefully coz its a bit windy out heer & tho thers a sort ov net under thi balconi & Ergates woodnt b harmd by a fol, shed probly go strait thru thi net & evin if she woznt harmd shed b lost; blimey, sumfing as lite as hir could get blown rite inter thi bailey from this hi up & how wood I ever find her then?

U wury 2 much, Ergates sez. Im a hily racehorseful ant & i wood find u.

(I doan say nuffink in return bcoz Mr Zoliparias tokkin & it wood b inpolite.) Nway thi point is kwite frangly Id rather Ergates woz stil in my pokit but she sez she wishis 2 take thi air & bsides she likes thi vew.

. . . simbil not ov potency or invulnrability but ov a kind ov sultifing *in*potenz & xtreem vulnrabiliti, Mr Zoliparia is sayin, bangin on about thi cassil agen as he is offin want 2 do.

We live in a folli, Bascule, nevir forget dat, he tellz me & I nod & sip ma t & wotch Ergates eat her bred.

Iss no coinsidins di ainshints usd 2 refer 2 di kwick & di ded, he sez, swalowin sum more wine & burrowin in2 his cote (iss a bit coald out here). 2 liv is 2 moov, he sez. Mobiliti is all. Tings like diss (he waves his han aroun) r a kind ov admishin ov dfeet; Y, de dam tings litil betir than a hospis!

Wots a hospis? I ask, not recognizin thi wurd & not wantin 2 yous inplants (& wantin Mr Zoliparia 2 no this, it has 2 b admittid).

Bascule, u mite as wel uze di fasilitys yoov been given, Mr Zoliparia sez.

O yes, I sez. I forgot. I made a show ov closin my Is. Haven dun this 4 a while, I sed. Lessee; ah yes, hospis . . . place whare you go 2 di, basikly.

Yes, Mr Zoliparia sed, lookin annoid. Now uve made me go & forget; Ive loss de flo.

U woz sayin thi cassil woz like a hospis.

I remember *dat*, he sez.

Well am veri sori, I sez.

No mattir. Di burdin ov mi argumint, Mr Zoliparia sez, is dat 2 set lself up like dis in such a defeetinly vast & intimidaytinly inhumin structyir is meerly 2 anounce di cumin 2 rest ov 1s progress, & witout dat we r lost.

(Mr Zoliparia is big on progress tho from what I can gathir iss a pretty old fashined idea these daze.)

So ther definitly wernt never no jiants then? I sez.

Bascule, Mr Zoliparia sez, cyan, wot is dis obseshin wit thi idea ov jiantz? He fillz his glas wif more wine; it steamz in thi cold air. I wotch Ergates 4 a bit while he duz this, zoomin in 2 look @ her face; I can c hir Is & feelers & wotch her mouth-parts needin & tayrin @ thi gummy-lookin bred. Pull back as Mr Zoliparia sets thi wine jug bak down on thi tabil.

Thi ting is, he sez, & size agen, der *wer* 1nce jiants. Not jiantz in di sens dat dey wer fizikly bigir dan us, but bigir in der powrs & abilitys & ambishins; bigir dan us in der moral curidge. Dey made dis playce, dey bilt it from rock & materielz. Weave loss di art ov makin & workin. Dey bilt it 4 a purpis in a sens, but itz ludicrisly over-desined 4 itz suposid funcshin. Dey bilt it di way dey did 4 fun. Juss bcoz it amyoused dem 2 do so. But dave moovd on, & we r all dats left & now di plaice teems wit life but den so duz a magoti corps; der is much moovmint but no qwicknis in uz; dass all gon.

Wot about thi fass-towr? I sez. That soundz pretti qwikish 2 me.

O Bascule, he sez & lukes up @ thi ski. Fass as in hold-fass or stuck-fass. How meny more times muss I tell u?

O yes, I sez. So all theez qwick tipes leff 4 thi starz did they Mr Zoliparia?

Yes dey did, he sez, & y shoodint dey? But wot puzzils me is y dey shood abandon uz so compleetly, & dat y we shood 1/2 given up di abiliti evin 2 keep in tutch wit dem.

Int that in nun ov yoor books & stuff, Mr Zoliparia? I asks him. Int that noware?

Duzent seme 2 b, Bascule, he sez; duzent seme 2 b. Sum ov uz $1/2$ bean lookin 4 di ansers 2 dose qwestions 4 longir dan weave been abil 2 record, & we seem 2 b no closir now dan wen we startid. Weave lookt in books & films & files & feeshes & discs & chips & byos & hollers & fomes & cores & evry form ov storidge noan 2 humaniti. He drinx his wine. & iss oll from b4, Bascule, he sez, soundin sad. Oll from b4. Ders nuttin from di time we want 2 no about. He shrugz. Nuttin.

I dont no wot 2 say when Mr Zoliparia sounds all sad & sorri like this. Peepil like him $1/2$ been tryin 2 wurk this sort ov fing out 4 jenerashins, sum thru thi old stuf like books & so on & otherz by usin thi kript, whare supposidly everithin iz but u jus cant find it. Or if u find it u cant get bak wif it.

I 1nce sed 2 Mr Zoliparia it soundid a bit like lookin 4 a needil in a haysack & he sed Moar like lukin 4 a partikulir wattir molicule in a oashin & evin thats probly unnerestimatin thi task by sevril ordirs ov magnetude.

Ive thot about bein thi 1 2 dive inter thi kript propir – reely deeply – & bring bak thi seekrets Mr Zoliparia wants, but apart from thi fact that meens serius inplant work & I wan 2 sho Mr Zoliparia I only yous mi inplants 4 tellin & nuffink else as a rule, iss also been attemptid & proovd pointliss.

Iss kaos in thare, u c.

Thi kript (or kriptosfear or data corpis – iss ol thi saim fing) iss where everfing reeli happins heer, & thi deeper u go thi less likeli u r 2 com out; iss like iss a oashin & conshisnis is solubil, like divin in2 asid, beyawnd a certin depf. It scarz u 4 life if u go 2 deep, u cum bak as sumfink shrivild & dyin if u go deeper stil, & u juss doan cum bak @ ol if u go reely reely deep; u juss disintigrate toatily as a distink personaliti & thass that.

Ov coarse u persinally r still alive & kikin, back in fizzikil reality & nun thi wurse 4 ware (usuly; unles u $1/2$ a bad trip like they say & get feedbacks & deedbacks & flashbacks & flashforwids & nitemares & daymares & troma & stuf), but thi kript-copy u sent in thare, thass juss gon 4evir u can kiss its ass by-by, & thass factule.

Ergates is playin wif her food; sheez moldin thi bredy-bits in2 funny shapes wif her mouf-parts & front legz & not botherin

2 eat it @ oll no moar. Rite now sheez makin a tiny bust ov
Mr Zoliparia & I wundir if he can c her doin that or if heez
so ded agenst inplants & inproovments in jeneril that he haz
ordniry old-tipe Is & cant zoom in on details like I can.

Do u think iss a gude likeniss, Bascule? she asks me.

Mr Zoliparia is lukin thotful & starin in2 space, or in2 thi
atmisfear nway; buncha birdz circlin way in thi distinz over a
bartizan – maybi heez lookin @ them.

Nway I dcide 2 risk whisprn 2 Ergates: Ver gude. Now u
wan get bak in yoor box?

Wassat Bascule? Mr Zoliparia sez.

Nuffink, Mr Zoliparia, I sez. I woz juss cleerin my frote.

No u werint; u sed sumtin about gettin bak in yoor box.

Did I? I sez, stollin.

U werint referin 2 me I truss, he sez, frownin.

O abslootly not Mr Zoliparia, I tell him. I woz actuli adressin
Ergates heer, I sez, dcidin 2 make a clean brest ov it. I luke @
hir sternli & wag mi fingir @ hir & say Get bak in yoor box
now, u notty ant. Sori about this, Mr Zoliparia, I tel him, while
Ergates qwikly changes thi bust sheez wurkin on 2 1 ov me with
a enormis nose.

Duz she evir tok bak? Mr Zoliparia asks, smilin.

O yes, I sez. Itz qwite a talkativ litle crittir actule. & veri
inteligent.

Duz it reely tok tho, Bascule?

Ov coarse, Mr Zoliparia; iss not a figmint ov my majination
or a invisibil frend type ov fing, onist. I had a invisibil frend but
he lef when Ergates caim on thi seen last week, I tel him, feelin
a bit embrasd now & probly blushin.

Mr Zoliparia laffs. Whare did u get yoor litl pal? he askz.

She crold out thi woodwurk, I sez, & he laffs agen & Im evin
moar embrasd & gettin qwite swety now. That dam ant! makin
a full ov me. & makin my face all big & bloted in that bust shees
workin on now & still not goin bak in hir box Ither.

She did! Mr Zoliparia I sez. Crold out ov thi woodwurk in
thi refectori @ suppir time lass Kingsday. She came heer wif me
thi next day 2 c u, but hid in my jakit that time on acount ov
bein shy & a bit okwird wif strainjirs. But she reely toks & she
heers whot I say & she uzis wurds I dont no sumtimes, onist.

Mr Zoliparia nods, & lukes wif new respect upon Ergates thi

ant. Den sheez probly a mikro-construct, Bascule, he tellz me;
dey crop up now & agen, tho dey doan yously tok, lease not
inteligibly. I tink di law sez yure supposd 2 take such tings 2
di otorities.

I no that Mr Zoliparia but sheez mi frend & she dont do
no 1 no harm, I sez, gettin hottir still coz I doan wan 2 luze
Ergates & am wishin I hadnt sed nuffink 2 bro Scalopin now
coz I didn think peepil botherd wif such finiky roolz but heers
Mr Zoliparia sayin they do & whot am I 2 do? I luke @ hir but
sheez still workin on that infernil bust & givin me big buck teef
now, ungratefil retch.

Cam down, cam down, Bascule, Mr Zoliparia sez; am not
sayin u *ot* 2 turn hir in am juss sayin dats thi law & u bettir
not tell peepil she can tok if u want 2 keep her. Thass ol am
sayin. Nway sheez juss litil & so nice & eezi 2 hide. If u luke
aftir hir yule b fine. May I—? he starts 2 say, then he stairz abuv
me & his Is go wide & he sez, Wot di fuk? & am qwite shokd
bcoz Ive nevir herd Mr Zoliparia sware like that & then therz a
shadow over thi balconi & a nois like a snappin sail-wing & a
gust ov wind, & – b4 I can do anyfink cept start 2 turn roun
– a hooj bird, grey & bigir than a man, suddinly clatirs down
on2 thi parapet ov thi balconi, grabs @ thi box & thi bred &
whaps its wingz down & lonches away agen skreetchin, while
Ergates goze '*Eek*!' & am up on mi feet & sos Mr Zoliparia
& I can see thi bird lowerin its hed as it beets away & peckin
@ what its got in its talons & iss eatin thi bred! & Ergates is
stuck in thi birdz talons! cot between a talon & a bit ov bred,
hir litle anteni wavin & 1 leg out wavin 2 & thas thi lass I see
ov hir coz thi distince gets 2 grate, & ah heer Ergates screamin
'Bascuuule . . .!' meewhile am shoutin & Mr Zoliparias shoutin
2 but thi big bird lifts away & disapeers up ovir thi edje ov thi
roof & Ergates is gon & am bereft.

TWO

1

'Face.'

She stared at her reflection in the pool, then drank some more, then waited for the water to settle and looked at her face, then drank some more.

'No more thirst. Stand up. Look around. Blue. White. Green. More green. Red white yellow blue brown pink. Sky clouds trees grass flowers bark. The sky is blue. The water is not colour, is clear. Water shows thing on other side. Of angle. This is. Reflect. Shone. Reflection. Redflection. Blueflection. Hmm. No.

'Time to walk again.'

She followed the path along the floor of the little valley, the sound of the water in the stream never far away.

'Fly-thing! Oh. Pretty. Is called bird. Birds.'

She walked through a small copse of trees. A warm wind rustled the leaves over her head. She stopped to look at a flower on a bush by the stream bank. 'More prettiness.' She put her hand over the flower, then bowed her head, sucking in its scent. 'Smell of sweet.'

She smiled, then gripped the flower at the top of the stem and appeared to be about to tear it from its stem. Then she frowned, hesitated, looked around and finally let her hands fall back to her sides. She patted the blossom gently before resuming her walk. 'Bye-bye.'

The stream disappeared into a hole in the side of a grassy slope; steps carried the path winding upwards. She looked into the darkness of the tunnel. 'Black. Smell of . . . damp.' Then she took the steps to the top of the slope and found a broader path leading between tall bushes and small trees.

'Crunch crunch. Ow. Gravel. Feet. Ow ow ow. Walk on green. Walk on grass. Not pain . . . Better.'

In the distance, beyond a tall hedge, there was a tower.

'Building.'

Then she came to something that made her stop and stare for

some time; a huge square hedge in the shape of a castle, with four square towers, crenellations cut into its parapets, a raised drawbridge of exposed, intertwined tree-trunks and a moat of sunken, silver-leaved plants.

She stood at the side of the pretend moat, looking down at the ruffled silver surface, then up at the castle walls, rustling quietly in the breeze. She shook her head. 'Not water. Building? Not building.'

She shrugged, turned on her heel and walked on, still shaking her head. Another minute along the grassy margin of the long avenue took her to where a series of huge heads faced each other across the gravel.

Each head was two or three times her own height and made up of several different bushes and other types of plants, producing dark or light complexions, smooth or lined skin and varying hair colours. The lips were formed by leaves of a dusty-pink colour, the whites of the eyes by a plant similar to those impersonating the waters of the moat surrounding the castle-topiary further down the avenue, while the irises took their colour from clusters of tiny flowers of the appropriate shade.

She stood and looked at the first face for some time, and eventually smiled. She walked on in the direction of the distant tower, and only stopped again when one of the heads started to talk.

'. . . says there is no need to worry, and I think he is right. We are not primitives, after all. I mean, in the end it's just dust. Just a big dust cloud. And another ice age is not the end of the world. We shall have power. There are already whole cities underground, each full of light and heat, and more are being built all the time. They have parks, lakes, architecture of merit, and no shortage of facilities. The world might be different for the duration of the Encroachment, and doubtless altered considerably after it has passed, as it surely will; many species and artifacts will have to be artificially preserved, and the glaciers will affect the planet's geography, but we will survive. Why, if the worst came to the worst, we might enter suspended animation and wake to a newly scrubbed-clean planet and a bright fresh spring! Would that be so terrible?'

She stood, only half-understanding the words. Her mouth

hung open. She had been sure the heads were not real. They were pretend, like the hedge-castle. But this one had a voice; a voice deeper than hers. She wondered if she ought to say something in return. Somehow she did not think it had actually been talking to her. Then the head used another voice, more like her own:

'If it is as you say, then no. But I've heard it may be much worse than that; people have talked of the world freezing, of every ocean becoming solid, of the sunlight reduced to the strength of moonlight, of this lasting for a thousand years, while others have said the sun will dim and then brighten; the dust will cause it to explode and all life on Earth will end.'

'You see,' said the first, deeper voice. 'Some say we shall freeze, while others maintain that we shall roast. As ever, the truth will lie between the extremes and so the result must be that nothing much will change and things will remain largely as they are, which is exactly what tends to happen most of the time anyway. I rest my case.'

She thought she ought to say something. 'I rest my case too,' she told the head.

'What?'

'Who—?'

'Crisis! There's somebody—'

There were some noises from within the head, then a face appeared within the hedge-face, sticking out from the middle of one cheek. The face looked altogether heavier and thicker than her own; thin hair covered its top lip.

'Man,' she said to herself. 'Hello.'

'Grief,' the man said, his eyes wide. He looked her up and down. She looked down at her feet, frowning.

'Who is it?' said the other voice from within the head.

'A girl,' the man said, speaking over his shoulder. He grinned and looked her up and down again. 'A girl with no clothes on.' He laughed, looking back again. 'Bit like you.' There was a slap and he said, 'Ow!', then he disappeared.

She leant forward, wondering if she ought to look inside the head, while whispers and rustles came from within.

'Who *is* she?'

'No idea.'

The man and woman came out of the head. They wore clothes. The man held a light brown jacket.

'Trousers,' she said, pointing at the woman's brightly coloured pantaloons as she tucked her blouse in.

'Don't gape, Gil,' the woman told the man, who was standing smiling at her. 'Give her your jacket.'

'My pleasure,' the man said, and handed her the jacket. He brushed some leaves off his shirt and out of his hair.

She looked at his shirt, then put the jacket on, awkwardly but correctly. She stood there, her hands covered by the cuffs of the light jacket, which smelled musky.

'Hello,' she said again.

'Hello yourself,' the woman said. Her skin was pale and her hair was gold-coloured. The man was tall. He bowed, still grinning.

'My name is Gil,' he said. 'Gil Velteseri.' He indicated the woman. 'This is Lucia Chimbers.'

She nodded and smiled at the woman, who smiled back briefly.

'What is my name?' she asked the man.

'Ah . . . I beg your pardon?'

'My name,' she repeated. 'You are Gil Velteseri, this is Lucia Chimbers. I am who?'

They both stood looking at her for a moment. The woman looked down and tried to brush a smudge from her blouse. In a quiet, sing-song voice she said, 'Sim-ple-ton.'

The man laughed lightly. 'Ah-ha,' he said.

2

The wind was a never-ending edge within the air, a knife-wire sawing back and forth in Gadfium's throat and lungs with each laboured, wheezing breath. The plain was a dead flat, almost featureless expanse of dazzling, eye-watering whiteness four kilometres across, splayed beneath a darkened purple sky. A thin, desiccated wind cut out of the bruise-coloured vault

and keened across the sterile salt-flats, picking up a thin dry
spray of particles which turned the air into a chill shot-blast
for exposed skin.

I am a fish, Gadfium thought, and might have laughed had she
been able to breathe. A fish, dredged from the fluid-thick depths
of warmth beneath us and dumped upon this high salt-crust of
shore; landed here to suck in vain at the parched air and die
drowning beneath a thin membrane of atmosphere where the
stars shine clear and unwavering in daylight, in half the sky.

She motioned to the assistant observer, and the woman
brought over the small oxygen cylinder. Gadfium gulped in
the mask's cold cargo of gas, filling her lungs to their depths.

This morning at the oxygen works, this afternoon sampling
their future product, she thought. She nodded gratefully to the
assistant observer as she handed the cylinder back.

'Perhaps we ought to return inside now, Chief Scientist,' the
woman said.

'In a moment.' Gadfium lifted the visor from her eyes and
squinted through the binoculars again. Salt dust and sand swirled
in twisted veils in front of her and the cold wind made her eyes
water. The grey-black stones nearest the observatory looked
like nothing more than giant pucks from some huge game of
ice hockey. Each stone was about two metres in diameter, half
a metre high and supposedly made of pure granite. They had
been sliding about this plain for millennia, riding the sporadically
slicked surface of the salt-bowl whenever snow had fallen and a
wind subsequently blew. Any snow and ice the plain collected
was turned to water by a combination of the pipework buried
beneath the plain itself and by the reflected sunlight of mirrors
shining from the twentieth level of the fast-tower, rearing bright
and solid to the north, three kilometres away.

The Plain of Sliding Stones formed the flat roof of a complex of
giant rooms on the eighth level of the fastness; these huge, almost
empty, barely habitable spaces were arranged in a wheel-like
formation, the exposed flank of which formed a great nave of
kilometre-tall windows facing from south-south-east to west. It
had always been assumed that the redundant systems of both
buried pipework and tower-mirrors were there to ensure that
no roof-destroying thickness of ice could ever accrue on the
plain, though the reason the roof had been left flat in the first

place had never been determined. Also unknown was exactly what the stones were there for, or how they contrived to move in ways that were subtly but undeniably at variance with the ways they should have moved according to both highly accurate computer models and carefully calibrated physical re-creations of their environment.

The mobile observatory – a three-storey sphere supported by eight long legs each tipped with a motor and tyre and resembling nothing more than an enormous spider – had been following the mysterious stones across the plain for hundreds of years, gathering vast amounts of data in the process but without really contributing anything of great note to the anyway rather exhausted debate concerning the origin and purpose of the stones. More had been learnt when one of the stones had been partially analysed centuries earlier, though as the crux of what had been learnt was that to start chipping bits off one of the stones was to draw down some highly focused and scientist-evaporating sunlight from the fast-tower's twentieth level (whether it was day or night), such a lesson was arguably something of a dead end.

Gadfium looked back out across the Plain of Sliding Stones, to the edge of the darkly livid sky. A chill gust of razor-wind stung her face and made her close her eyes, the salt like grit between orb and lid. She could taste the salt; her nose stung.

'Very well,' she said, dry-gasping in the meagre air. She turned from the balustrade and had to be half-led to the lock by the assistant observer.

'The circle began forming at six-thirteen this morning,' the chief observer told them. 'It was complete by six forty-two. All thirty-two stones are present. The distance between the stones is a uniform two metres – the same as their diameter. They have arranged themselves in a perfect circle with an accuracy of better than a tenth of a millimetre. The predicted-motion discrepancy factor for certain of the stones during the period they were forming the current pattern was as high as sixty per cent. It has never in the past exceeded twelve point three per cent and over the last decade has averaged below five per cent.'

Gadfium, her aide Rasfline and assistant Goscil, the mobile

observatory's chief observer Clispeir and three out of the four
junior observers – one was still on duty in the vehicle's control
room – sat in the observatory mess.

'We are in the exact centre of the plain?' Gadfium asked.

'Yes, again to an accuracy of less than a tenth of a millimetre,'
Clispeir replied. She was fragile-looking and prematurely aged,
with wispily white hair. Gadfium had known her at university
forty years earlier. Nevertheless, like the other observers she
was able to operate without extra oxygen and pressurisation,
which was much more than Gadfium felt able to do. That
she, Rasfline and Goscil were able to breathe easily now was
only because the observatory had been lightly pressurised
for their comfort. Still, she told herself, they had travelled
from barely a thousand metres above sea level to over eight
kilometres higher in less than two hours, and a human-basic
individual would already be suffering from altitude sickness
to which she was genetically resistant, which was some con-
solation.

'However the circle did not actually form around the observatory.'

'No, ma'am. We were stationary a quarter kilometre from
here, almost due north, waiting on the wind to rise following
the precipitation and melt last night. The stones began to move
at four forty-one, holding pattern T-8 with drift-factor one. They
veered— '

'Perhaps a visual display would be more . . . graphic,' Goscil
interrupted.

Embarrassed looks were exchanged around the mess-room
table. 'Unfortunately,' Clispeir said, clearing her throat, 'the
pattern formed during an observation-system down-time event.'
She looked apologetically at Gadfium. 'We are, of course, only
a very small and perhaps insignificant research station and I
don't know if the chief scientist is aware of my reports detailing
the increased incidence of maintenance-level-related breakdowns
and our requests for increased funding over the last few years,
but— '

'I see,' Rasfline said impatiently. 'Obviously you lack implants,
ma'am, but I assume one or more of your juniors recorded the
events in their habitua.'

'Well,' Clispeir said, looking uncomfortable. 'Actually, no; as it has turned out, the team here consists entirely of persons from Privileged backgrounds.'

Rasfline looked shocked. Goscil's mouth hung slightly open.

Clispeir smiled apologetically and spread her hands. 'It's just the way it's happened.'

'So you don't have anything on visual,' Rasfline said, contriving to sound at once bored and exasperated. Goscil blew some hair away from her face and looked crestfallen.

'Not of an acceptable standard,' Clispeir admitted. 'Observer Koir – ' the elderly scientist nodded to one of the two young male observers, who smiled sheepishly '– took some footage on his own camera, but— '

'May we see it?' Rasfline asked, tapping his fingers on the table surface.

'Of course, though— '

'Ma'am, are you all right?' Goscil asked Gadfium.

'I'm – actually . . . no, not— ' Gadfium slumped forward over the table, head on forearms, mumbling and then going quiet.

'Oh dear.'

'I think some oxygen— '

'I'm sorry; the observatory cannot be pressurised beyond this level, and we are so used to . . . we forget. Oh dear.'

'Thank you. Ma'am; oxygen.'

'Perhaps we should leave . . .'

'Let her lie down a moment first.'

'My cabin is at your disposal, of course.'

'I'm fine, really,' Gadfium mumbled. 'Bit of a headache.'

'Come; if you'd take her . . . that's it.'

'I'll bring the oxygen.'

'We should leave . . .'

'. . . always has to see things for herself.'

'All right really . . .'

'Down here.'

'Please don't fuss . . . How embarrassing . . . Terribly sorry.'

'Ma'am, please; save your breath.'

'Oh yes, sorry; how embarrassing . . .'

'Mind the steps.'

'Careful.'

'In here. Sorry, it is a little small; let me . . .'

Gadfium heard the voices of the others sounding loud in the

small cabin, and felt herself lowered into a narrow bed. The oxygen mask was put to her face again.'

'Let me stay with her. You take a look at observer Koir's recordings; I'm sure the others can answer any questions . . .'

'Are you sure? I could— '

'There now, dear; let one old lady look after another.'

'If you're certain . . .'

'Of course.'

When she heard the door close with a clunk and a wheezy hiss, Gadfium opened her eyes.

Clispeir's face was above her, smiling hesitantly.

Gadfium looked warily round the small cabin.

'It is safe,' Clispeir whispered, 'providing we don't shout.'

'Clisp . . .' Gadfium said, sitting up and holding out her arms; they hugged for a moment.

'It is good to see you again, Gad.'

'And you,' Gadfium whispered. Then she took the other woman's hands in hers and gazed urgently into her eyes. 'Now; old friend, has it happened? Have we made contact with the tower?'

Clispeir could not contain her smile, though there was a hint of worry within it. 'Of a sort,' she said.

'Tell me.'

3

The Count Sessine had died many times. Once in an aircraft crash, once in a bathyscape accident, once at the hand of an assassin, once in a duel, once at the hand of a jealous lover, once at the hand of a lover's jealous husband and once of old age. Now, it was twice at the hand of an assassin; a male one this time, for a reason he was unable to determine, and – most distressingly – for the last time. Finally physically dead, for ever more.

The venue for Sessine's first in-crypt resuscitation had been a virtual version of his apartments in the clan Aerospace's headquarters in the Atlantean Tower, it being normal for *primimortis'* rebirths to be conducted in familiar and comforting surroundings and closely attended by images of friends and family.

For his subsequent revivals he had stipulated an unpopulated, ambiently scaled version of Serehfa, and it was there he awoke in bed, alone, on what gave every appearance of being a fine spring morning.

He lay in the bed and looked around. Silk sheets, brocade canopy, oil paintings on the wall, rugs on the floor, wooden panelling, tall windows. He felt oddly neutral, washed clean.

He smoothed his hand over a fold of pinkly silk sheet, then closed his eyes and murmured, '*Speremus igitur*,' and opened his eyes again.

His smile was sad. 'Ah well,' he said quietly.

It had been a statutory requirement almost from the dawn of what had then been called Virtual Reality that even the deepest and most radically altered and enhanced virtual environment (indeed, most especially those) must include periods of sleep – however truncated – and that towards the end of each sleep event a dream ought to intrude upon the sleeper in which they were offered the option of returning to reality. Sessine, of course, had been aware of no such opportunity just prior to waking up here, and the repetition of his private code to instigate a complete wake-up merely confirmed that this was not part of some voluntary virtual scenario; this was already as real as he could get, and it was a simulation; he was incrypted, now, for good, as well as for good or ill.

Sessine got out of bed, went to the tall windows and stepped out onto the balcony. The air felt fresh and chilly; a strong wind blew. He shivered, raised his right arm to his face, watched goose-bumps rise under the hairs there, then imagined that the wind dropped. It did.

He imagined that it blew again, but that he felt no cold; in a moment the wind was sharp and clean in his nostrils and cool on his naked skin, but it did not make him shiver.

He went to the parapet. The balcony was situated in one of the higher reaches of the humanly-scaled fortress, with a view to the west. The shadow of the castle lay across the western inner bailey, the umbrous image of the fast-tower just touching the foot of the curtain-walls. As Sessine had ordered, there was nobody to be seen, and not even any wildlife visible. The sky, distant hills and the castle itself looked perfectly convincing.

He imagined himself on the fast-tower

/and was there, suddenly standing on a gaily painted wooden platform at the summit of the castle's tallest tower, with only a flagpole and a snapping flag – his clan's – above him. The view was better from here; he could see the ocean, far to the west. Just beyond the handrail the slates sloped away to the circular battlements.

He gripped the wooden rail of the platform, squeezing it until his fingers ached, then squatted and inspected the underside of the rail's inverted U near where it met a stanchion. The red paint under the flat surface was convincingly bumpy, with little bubbles of smooth, solidified paint near the angle the rail described with the post. He put his thumbnail against one of the bubbles and pressed hard. When he took his thumb away again there was a little groove impressed on the hemisphere of paint.

He ducked quickly under the rail and launched himself into the air. He bounced once off the steeply raked tiles, winding himself and hurting his shoulder, cleared the crenellations of the tower's battlements and hurtled towards the steeply pitched roof far below. The wind-roar screamed in his ears as the slates rose to meet him.

'Oh, this is silly,' he said, gasping against the storm of air.

He cancelled the injury in his shoulder and decided . . . to fly; the roof below slid to one side and he glided away, sweeping through the air above the castle.

Had he plummeted to his death upon that slated roof, it would have been also to another – almost immediate – rebirth in the same bed he had not long departed; just as in base-reality one had eight lives, so one had eight here. Choosing to end them meant that one would remain unconscious for the duration of the mourning period, and only be woken for a slowed-down real and subjective hour to converse with one's bereaved relations and friends immediately before disposal. This was not a common option, but remained available for those whose depression or ennui extended beyond their deaths.

Flying was exactly as he remembered it from his childhood dreams; it required some sort of willed effort in the mind, like pedalling a cycle even though one's legs did not move. If one ceased this dream-virtual effort, one sank slowly to earth. The harder one pedalled, the higher one flew. There was no fatigue and no fear, just wonder and exhilaration.

Sessine flew round the castle for some time, at first naked, then clothing himself with trousers, shirt and frock coat. He landed on the balcony outside the bedroom where he had awoken.

A light breakfast was waiting, on a table by the bed. At this point – in every other rebirth since that first one – he had eaten, then indulged in a full morning's dalliance with a maid he remembered from his late childhood who had been the first woman he had lusted after, as well as one of the few with whom he had been unable to requite such regard. On this occasion, however, he cancelled the breakfast, his growing hunger, and the maid's appearance. Nor would he spend the next few subjective months in the castle's library, re-reading books, listening to music, watching films and recorded plays and operas and watching or taking part in discussions with recreated ancients, recreated historical incidents or virtual fictions.

He imagined an antique phone by the bedside. He lifted the receiver.

'Hello?' The voice was pleasant and sexless.

'Enough,' he said.

The castle vanished before he could replace the handset.

There was ample time before his funeral.

At that point – like all the dead, whether they were high or low, and Privileged or not – he would face the final proof of the crypt's ferociously impartial judgment. As the saying had it: the crypt was deep and the human soul was shallow. And the shallower the soul, the less of it survived as any sort of independent entity within the data corpus; somebody whose only opinions were received opinions and whose originality quotient was effectively zero would dissolve almost entirely within the oceanic depths of the crypt's precedent-saturated data streams and leave only a thin froth of memories and a brief description of the exact shape of their hollowness behind, the redundancy of their beings annihilated by the crypt's abhorrence of over-duplication.

Should that personality ever be called back into existence in the base-level world, it could be recreated exactly from the crypt's already existing database of sentience types.

It was believed that the certainty of such a verdict provided the incentive for people to improve themselves in a society which gave every appearance of being able to function quite adequately with almost no human input whatsoever.

Sessine, if not as one of the Privileged then as a man who had over the course of several lifetimes assiduously cultivated his own cultivation, was in practice if not in theory guaranteed a continued existence within the corpus as an individual.

Even had he been due solely for the compulsory incorporation that was the fate of lesser mortals when the moment came, there would still have been time for what he had in mind. The three days in physical reality before his funeral equated to over eighty years in the quickened medium of crypt-time; time enough for another life to be lived after death, and easily sufficient to encompass the investigation a dead man might wish to mount into the reason for his murder.

'The data-set from the time of your death was recorded as a matter of course by your bioware and transmitted to the command car's event-recorder as well as its own computer; the latter was destroyed along with the car when your murderer turned the car's gun on the convoy and drew retaliatory fire. The event-recorder survived; it also squirted its primary function-suite state to the nearest convoy units when it realised the car was under attack and these read-outs square with the data in the recorder itself, so we may comfortably assume your final memories are accurate.'

The construct of the clan Aerospace's chief crypt-lawyer was configured to respond to its clients' personalities; for Sessine this meant that it appeared as a tall, highly attractive woman in early middle-age who wore her long black hair tied back, used little make-up, dressed in late-twentieth–century corporate-male clothes and talked with quiet authority; Sessine found it almost amusing how perfectly such an image demanded and received his attention. No bullshit, no unnecessary gestures or expressions, no false buddiness, no flimflam and no attempts either to impress or ingratiate. Even his short attention span and low boredom threshold had been catered for; she spoke fast. And in the pauses, he could imagine her unclothed (though, as she was a separate entity within the crypt, such imagining no more made itself immediately actual than it would have had they both been real people in base-reality).

He supposed that a male construct might have worked almost as well, but he *liked* smart, quick-witted, self-assured women, and he despised the off-the-peg models of such constructs just because convention demanded they must exhibit some hint of vulnerability, some girlishness that was supposed to make him feel that despite such obvious capability and presence, this woman was some kind of sexual pushover, or not really his equal.

They were sitting in a vault room of the Bank of England, in Edwardian times. Their seats were constructed of gold ingots and cushioned with layers of big white five-pound notes; their table was a trolley normally used to transport bullion. Primitive electric lights flickered on the metal walls and reflected off further piles and stacks of gold bars. Sessine had salvaged the image from an early twenty-first-century VR fiction.

'What do we have on the man who murdered me?'

'He was called John Ilsdrun IV, second-lieutenant. Nothing anomalous in his background or recent behaviour. His implants had been doctored and, if he survives in usable form anywhere, it is not in the general body of the crypt. We're running deeper checks on all his lives and contacts so far, but they'll take subjective days to complete.'

'And the message he received?'

'A code within the gistics burst: "*Veritas odium parit.*"'

'"Truth begets hatred." How cryptic.'

The construct permitted itself a smile.

Barely five minutes had passed in base-reality since his death, and he had spent the great majority of that time unconscious, the data-set that was his stored personality being updated with the rigorously cross-checked information from the time and place of his murder before being activated: the wreck of the command car he and the rest of the crew had been killed in was still burning on the fractured floor of the Southern Volcano Room, the convoy had yet to regroup properly after the young lieutenant's treacherous attack on it, his co-directors at Aerospace had been summoned to an emergency virtual meeting due to take place in a subjective half-hour and a base-reality physical meeting in the Atlantean Tower scheduled in two hours real – two years and three months subjective – time, while his widow had been contacted but had yet to reply.

'Backtrack on the coded message; how did it find its way into a hardened military narrowcast?'

'Still investigating. The jurisdictional protocols concerned are complicated.'

Sessine could imagine; the military would not easily be persuaded to open its data corpus to outside investigation.

'I want to request an audience with Adijine, priority.'

'Contacting the Palace, royal apartments . . . monarch's office . . . on hold . . . His Majesty's private secretary suite . . . your call-sign going through . . . private secretary construct on line real time now. Replace?'

'Replace.'

The woman disappeared, turning in a blink into a small wizened man in a black dress coat and holding a long staff. He looked briefly around the vault, stood and bowed slightly to Sessine, then sat again.

'Count Sessine,' he said. 'The King has already asked me to inform you of the profound shock he experienced at hearing of your murder, and to convey his deepest sympathy to you as well as to those you leave behind. He has also asked me to assure you that everything possible will be done to root out those responsible for this foul crime.'

'Thank you. I would like to request an audience with His Majesty, as soon as possible.'

'His Majesty can spare a short while between other appointments in twenty minutes real – approximately four months subjective – time.'

'I must ask for an emergency meeting before then.'

'I understand your distress and shock, Count Sessine. However, His Majesty is in an important meeting with representatives of the Chapel usurper forces, discussing peace; informing him of your death and giving him time to express the above-mentioned shock and sympathy has already, perhaps, used up whatever diplomatic slack we have with the Engineer delegation; we cannot possibly incur any further interruption without risking an apparent sleight and the breakdown of negotiations.'

Sessine thought about this. The secretary sat smiling patiently at him. Measuring his words, Sessine spoke again: 'My concern is that the message which appeared to instigate my murder was embedded within a military signal sent from Army HQ, and that this therefore implies either a serious signal-security breach or a traitor in at least the middle-level military.' He paused to let the secretary speak, then went on. 'Has the King authorised a full military investigation?'

'An investigation has been authorised.'

'At what level?'

'A level commensurate with your standing, Count; the highest level.'

'With full military access immediately?'

'That is not possible; the Army has operational reasons for not being able to reveal such matters precipitously; there are controls, checks and balances which must be negotiated over a minimum real-time scale if one is not to trip a series of automatic security-violation safeguards. The relevant authorisations are of course being sought, but—'

'Thank you, private secretary. Would you put me on to military High Command, level five, and replace?'

The construct had time to look distinctly annoyed before it was replaced with a young soldier in full dress uniform.

'Count Sessine.'

'Is this level five?' Sessine frowned. 'I thought—'

The young soldier stood, quickly drew his ceremonial sword and in the same movement brought it scything above the trolley-table and through Sessine's neck, parting his head from his shoulders.

What? he thought, then everything faded.

He awoke in the tower-bedroom of the ambiently scaled version of Serehfa, alone, on what gave every appearance of being a fine spring morning.

He lay in the bed and looked around. Silk sheets, brocade canopy, oil paintings on the wall, rugs on the floor, wooden panelling, tall windows. He felt washed clean, and distinctly unsettled.

He closed his eyes, said, '*Speremus igitur*,' and opened his eyes again.

His smile was troubled. 'Hmm,' he said quietly.

He got out of bed, dressed in the clothes he had been wearing earlier, and went out onto the balcony.

A dot in the distance, somewhere over the curtain-wall to the west, attracted his attention. A hint of light around it, a thin, hazy trail in the sky behind . . .

He watched the dot expand, then imagined himself on the fast-tower.

/He stood on the gaily painted wooden platform again; the flag snapped in the air above him. He watched the missile tear across the roof-tops below and disappear into the tower where he had been standing a few seconds earlier. The tower erupted; yellow-white flame burst outwards across the balcony, sundering the stones all around that floor and throwing back the tower's roof, releasing a cloud of slates like some flock of disturbed birds.

Straight through the balcony windows. Sessine felt both impressed and depressed.

He did not see or hear what hit him from behind, just glimpsed a searing light and felt the concussive blast.

He awoke in bed, alone, on what gave every appearance of being a fine spring morning.

He lay there for a second, then imagined himself to the summit of the fast-tower.

/He saw the first missile, crossing the curtain-wall to the west. He turned and saw the other, approaching from the east, level with him and approaching fast. He remembered the feeling he had had when he'd heard the shots inside the scree-car and ducked back in to see what was happening. He imagined the view from the middle of the inner bailey,

/then from a tower on the curtain-wall to the south,

/then from the north,

/then from the eastern gate complex,

/then from some low hills outside the castle altogether.

The whole edifice detonated, disappearing in a scattering series of explosions, flickering light, throwing stones and timbers high into the air, black amongst fire.

'Sessine?'

He turned, and the image of his first wife was there, standing on the path behind him, as lovely as on the first day they had met. *She never called me—*

She was upon him with the strangle-wire before he could move; gripping him, trapping him with a strength no human had ever possessed.

He awoke in the bed, alone. *What is this? What is going on? Who is—?*

Light at the window, something—

Fool!

Then light everywhere.

He awoke in the bed.

'Alandre,' the young maid breathed, alongside him, reaching.

/He was on the deck of the clan yacht, at anchor one evening off Istanbul; the Bosporus glittered darkly beneath, the twin bridges arced above. His heart thudded. He looked quickly around. Nobody. He looked up. Something falling from the rail-bridge . . . he started to imagine – then light again, atomically bright, lighting up all the city . . .

He awoke.

'Ala— '

/He was in bed, in his apartments in the clan Aerospace's headquarters in the Atlantean Tower.

The doctor looked down at him, his face somehow familiar, his expression regretful. The young doctor fired the gun straight between Sessine's eyes.

He awoke.

'Al— '

/He was in the nursery of the clan's Seattle stronghold. The nurse was above him; the knife came down on his mewls.

And something inside him screamed, *Seven!*

He awoke.

He was in a hotel room; it was small and tawdry-looking. The curtains drawn, the ceiling light on. He was sitting. His heart was hammering, his body covered with cold sweat. He cancelled the fake physical symptoms of his panic then started

to imagine being somewhere else . . . but he was out of places
to run, and as he did not know where he was, he suspected that
here was as good a place as any to stay a while.

What had happened? What had been going on?

He stood up and went to the window, carefully lifting one
corner of the curtains while staying behind the wall, half
expecting the arrival of a hail of bullets or another missile the
instant he betrayed his position.

He looked out onto a darkened town; a port within a huge,
dim space all speckled with small lights. Dark waters lay in
the distance beyond wharves and cranes. Spaced regularly in
the shadows across the inky glints of waves he could just
make out huge pillars, growing out of that broad, buried
sea like impossibly perfect steep-cliffed islands and sprouting,
spreading at their summits to meet a jet-black vaulted sky more
remembered than seen.

He was still in Serehfa, then, underneath it, within the cistern
level. The port was called Oubliette. The narrow street outside
looked quiet. A few lights showed behind shades on the tall,
narrow buildings opposite, and down in the port he could see
ships tied against the piers, container cranes swinging slowly to
and fro above them, and hints of movement within pools of dim
yellow light on the wharves themselves.

He let the curtain fall back, then looked around the room.
There was little to search; a small bed, a seat, a table, a screen,
a bedside cabinet. A notice on the back of the door said that the
room was room 7, floor 7, in the Salvation Hotel.

In the cabinet's drawer, he found a paper envelope.

On it was written, *Alandre Jeovanx.*

It had been his name before promotion. He tore open the
envelope.

There was a single sheet of paper folded inside. *Read Me*, it
said.

He read it.

4

Bascule, ah no dis hard 4 u, but goodness sakes bcy it only a dam ant.

It woz a most special & uneek ant Mr Zoliparia I tel him & I feel responsybil 4 what hapind 2 hir.

Weer inside thi Iball ov thi septentrynal gargoil Rosbrith, in Mr Zoliparia's study. Mr Zoliparia has a fing calld a telifone in his study u can speek in2 (didn evin no he had it – fink heez a bit embrased about it 2 tel thi troof). Nway, he juss got in tuch wif thi gard 2 report whot happind aftir Id insistid, tho heed only report that thi bird had stole a valubil anteik box, not a ant. (Actule, thi box isnt a anteik @ ol but that isn what matters.) Id 1/2 tryd callin thi gard myself soon as it happind but I no from past xpeeryins they wooden lissen 2 me cos Im yung.

Weed been hopin that maibe thi bird whot had stolen Ergates woz 1 ov them ringed 1s wif cameraz & stuf, or 1 ov them bein followed roun by little buzzir-bugs 4 a wildlife screen program or thi purpisses ov cyantific reserch but I gess it woz a bit ov a long shot & shurenuf thi ansir woz no 2 both. Thi gard took sum detales but Mr Zoliparia duzent hold out much hope ov them doing anythin.

U mussnt blame yoself, it woz a accident, Bascule.

I no that, Mr Zoliparia, but it woz a accident I cood 1/2 priventd if Id been moar observint & watchful & juss plain diligint in jeneril. What woz I thinkin ov lettin hir eat that bred on thi balstraid like that? Speshily when I seen them birdz in thi distins. I meen; bred! Evrbidy no birds luv bred! (I slap ma hand off ma 4head, finkin what a idiot Ive been.)

O Bascule, ahm sorry 2 on account ov me being di hoast & all; dis happin in ma hoam & ah shood 1/2 taken moar care 2, but wot's dun is dun.

Is it tho, Mr Zoliparia? U reely think so?

What u mean, yung Bascule?

Am a tellir, Mr Zoliparia, u mussnt 4get that. (I screws

up ma Is @ this point, 2 sho him I meen bizniss.) Them birdz—

Bascule, no! U cant go doin dat sorta ting! U crazi or sumtin chile? U onli go & scrambil yor brainz u try any ov dat sorta nonsins.

I juss smile.

I doan no whot u no ov whot a tellir duz but now mite b as good a time as eny 2 tell u if u doan no (them that duz can haply skip thi next 5 or 6 paragrafs & get bak 2 thi storey).

Basikly, a tellir fishiz in2 thi kript & pools out sum ole boy or girl & asks them qwestyins & ansirs there qwestyins. Iss kinda $1/2$ archilojikil reserch & $1/2$ soshil wurk if u want 2 look @ it coldly & r happy 2 ignoar whot peepil col thi spiritul side ov it.

Coarse its all a bit murki & weerd down thare in thi kript & moast bags (thas Boys & Girls remembir) get a bit spooked even thinkin about contactin thi ded let alone actuly welcomin them in2 ther heds & $1/2$in a natter wif them. 2 us tellirs tho iss juss sumthin we do as a mattir ov coarse & no bothir . . . well, providin u r carefil, naturily (admitidly ther arnt a lot ov old tellirs aroun, tho thas moastly coz ov whot they col naturil waistidje).

Nway, thi point is that tellirs yooz their natcheril skills 2 delv in2 thi kript, partly 2 find out things from thi past & partly 2 fulfill pledjes & bqwests whot thi relivint ordir has taken on. Mi order is calld thi Little Big Brothers ov thi Rich & we orijnaly jus lookd aftir thi inkripted soles ov peepil whot were very well off indeed thang-u-veri-mutch but our remit has brodind a bit sins then & now parrently weel tok 2 eny ole rif raf if they got sumfink inarestin 2 say.

Now, thi thing iz this; juss as thi deeper u go in2 thi kript thi hazier & more corosiv doun thare things get, so thi longir it is since u died thi moar kinda disoshiated u get from realty, &, evntule, evin if u want 2 stay in sum kinda hoomin form, u juss cant support that sort ov complexity, & 1 ov thi things that mite hapin after that is that u get shunted in2 thi animal kingdum; your personality, such as it is by then, is transferd in2 a panfir or a roc or cat or a simurg or a shark or eegil or whotevir. Iss aktuly considered sumfink ov a priviledge; loadsa bags fink thers nuffink betir than bein a bird or sumfink simla.

Ov coarse, theez animalz iz stil linkd in2 thi kript by ther own inplants, & thusly ther brains is potenshily availabil 2 a tellir, tho this is a pritti irregulir – not 2 say kinda daingerous – oakurinse. Irregulir bcoz nobody evir duz it. Dainjerous bcoz whot u r basikly tryin 2 do as a tellir in such a sircumstanse is try 2 fit yoor hoomin size mind inside a bird size 1. Takes sum finessin, but Ive always had this theery that bcoz my thots cum out wif a spin on them, so 2 speek, Im speshily good @ coapin wif 2 diffrint thot modes @ 1nce, & so moar than capabil ov takin on thi task ov becomin a bird & flyin in2 ther airea ov thi kript.

Thiss, u may 1/2 gatherd, is xactly whot I am proposin 2 do, & Mr Zoliparia is not 2 enamerd ov thi idea.

Bascule, pleeze, he sez, attempt 2 retain a sens ov proportshin. Iss onli a ant. & u r onli a junior tellir.

4shore, Mr Zoliparia, I sez. But am a tellir whot haznt evin bgun 2 b stretchd yet. Am a grate tellir. Am a tottil blinkin hot-shot tellir & I juss no I can fynd that bird.

& do whot? Mr Zoliparia shouts. De dam ant is probly ded! Dat birdz probly 8 it by now! Y u want 2 torture youself by findin dat out?

If so, I want 2 no, but nway I dont fink that's rite; Im bankin on her 1/2 in been dropt by that big bird & am hopin it mite remember whare, or—

Bascule u r upset. Y doan u juss go bak 2 di ordir & try 2 cam down & tink dis —

Mr Zoliparia, I sez qwietly, I thank u 4 your consern but I intend 2 do this no mattir whot u say. Cheerz oll thi saim.

Mr Zoliparia lukes @ me diffrint than he has in thi past. Ive always liked him & Ive always luked up 2 him evir sins he woz 1 ov thi peepil they sent me 2 when they reelized I tolkd farely normil but I thot a bit funy, + I tend 2 do whot he sez – it woz him sed Perhaps u wood make a good tellir, & him whot sujjestid I keep a jurnil, witch this is whot u r readin – but this time I doan mutch care whot he finks, or @ least I do but I doan mutch care how bad it makes me feel goan agenst his advice bcoz I juss no I 1/2 2 do this.

O deer Bascule, he sez & shakes his hed. I do bleev u do intend 2 do this & iss a sorry ting 4 eny persin 2 do 4 sumtin as insignifcant as a ant.

Iss not thi ant, Mr Zoliparia, I sez feelin ded grownup, itz me.

Mr Zoliparia shakes his hed. Iss u & no godam sens ov proporshin, dats wot it is.

Ol thi saim, I sez. It woz mi frend; she woz relyin on me 2 keep hir safe. Juss 1 try, Mr Zoliparia. I feel I O hir that.

Bascule, pleese, juss tink—

Mind if I juss hunkir down heer, Mr Zoliparia?

Givn u detrminded, Bascule, heer is probly bettir than lswhare but am not happi about dis.

Doan wury, Mr Zoliparia. Woant take a second, litterly.

Der anytin I can do?

Yep; let me boro that pen ov yoors. Ta. Now am goanta sit up here – I sqwatted on a chair, ma chin on ma nees, & put thi pen in ma mouf.

'en 'i 'en 'all ou' 'a 'ouf, I start 2 tel him . . .

Whot u sayin, Bascule?

I take thi pen out ma mouf. I woz juss sayin, when thi pen falls out ov ma mouf, let it hit thi carpet then shaik me & shout Bascule, fast awake!

Bascule, fast asleep, Mr Zoliparia sez.

Awake! I yelz. Not wide asleep; fast awake!

Fast awake, Mr Zoliparia repeats. Bascule, fast awake. He shakes his hed & heez shakin. O deer Bascule, o deer.

If yor that wurried, Mr Zoliparia, catch thi pen b4 it hits & then wake me. Now, just giv me a minit heer . . . I settil in2 place, gettin comfterbil; thisil onli take a sekind but u $^{1}/_{2}$ 2 feel settld & redy & @ peece.

Rite. Am prepaird.

Thisl all hapin very qwickli, Mr Zoliparia; u redi? I put thi pen bak in ma mouf.

O deer Bascule.

Here we go.

O deer.

& so its off 2 thi land ov thi ded 4 yoors truli 4 thi sekind time 2day, onli this time iss a bit moar serieus.

Iss like sinkin in2 thi sky on thi other side ov thi Erf wifout goin thru thi whole fing furst. Iss like flotin in2 thi erf & thi sky @ thi time, becomin a line not a point, plumin thi depths & assendin thi hites & then branchin out like a tree, like a plane tree, like a hooj bush interminglin wif every bit ov thi erf & thi sky, & then iss like every 1 ov those bits isnt juss a bit ov erf or a molicule ov air eny more, iss like ol ov them is suddenly a littl system ov ther own; a book, a library, a persin; a world . . . & yoor connectid wif ol ov it, ignorin barryers, like u r a brain sell deep in thi grainy grey mush ov thi brain all closed in but joined up 2 loadsa uthir sells, awash in ther communicashin-song & set free by that trapt meshin.

Boompf-badoom; slapadowndoodie thru thi topmost obvyis layers whot corrisponds 2 thi upper levils ov thi brain – thi rashinil, sensibil, easily understood layers – in2 thi furst ov thi deepdown floors, thi bit under thi cerebral, under thi crust, under thi fotosphere, under thi obvyis.

Iss heer u ½ 2 b a littl bit careful; iss like bein in a not-so-saloobrius neyborhood ov a big dark city @ nite – only more complicaitd than that; mutch moar so.

In here, thi trik is thinkin rite. Thas all u ½ 2 do. U ½ 2 think rite. U ½ 2 b dairing & koshis, u ½ 2 b ver sensibil & totily mad. Moast ov ol u ½ 2 b *cluvir*, u ½ 2 b *ingenius*. U ½ 2 b abil 2 use whotevir is aroun u, & thass whot it reely cums doun 2; thi kript is whot they col self-referenshil, which meens that – up 2 a poynt – it meens whot u want it 2 meen, & displays itself 2 u as u r best abil 2 understand it, so iss up 2 u reely whot yoos u make ov it aftir that; iss ol about injinooty & thass y itz a yung persins meedyum, frangly.

Nway, I new whot I wantid so I thot *bird*.

& suddinly I woz up in sum dark bildin abuv thi wee twinkly lites ov thi city, up thare wif big metalic skulptyirs ov feersum lookin birds & ther woz lots ov screetches & skwaks about thi place but u coudnt c no birds jus heer thi noyse they made & it woz sort ov crusty-soft under foot & smeld asidic (or alkline; 1 ov thi 2).

I snifd about, walkin qwietly, then hopt up on2 1 ov thi big metallic birds & sqwatted there, wings by mi sides, stairin out ovir thi lite-spekd blak grid ov thi citi & not blinkin juss lookin 4 movemint, & lowrin ma hed now & agen & pokin in under mi wings wif thi twig whot I held in ma beak, juss like I woz preenin or sumfin.

Noticd ma wake-up code in thi form ov a ring roun ma lef leg. Handy 2 no it woz thare, juss in case fings go rong an/or Mr Zoliparia flufs his line.

. . . Staid ther a while, payshint as u like, juss watchin.

Wot u wan then? sed a voice from abuv & behind.

Nufink mutch, I sed, not lookin. I woz aware ov thi twig in ma beak but it din seem 2 make speakin eny hardir.

U muss want somthen, u woodin b heer otherwyse.

U got me thare, I sed. Am here lookin 4 sumbodi.

O?

Loss a frend ov mine. Roost-mate. Like 2 trace her.

We all got frenz we like 2 find.

This 1 very recent; 1/2 hour ago. Taken from thi septentrynil gargoil Rosbrith.

Sep whort?

Meens – (this is complicated, referin 2 thi uppir data levil whyle am down here in thi furst circle ov thi basement, but I do it) – meens northern, I sed (blimey). Rosbrith. Norf-west on thi grate hol.

Taken by whort?

Lammergeier, I sed. (Didn no that neevir til now.)

Reely. Whot u given in return?

Am heer amn I? Im a tellir. U got ma eer now. Il not forget u if u help. Luke in me if u want; c whot I say is tru.

Not blynd.

Didn fink u wer.

This bird; u catch eny distingushin marx on it?

It woz a lammergeir, thas oll I no, but ther cant b oll that meny ov them aroun thi norf-west cornir ov thi grate hol 1/2 a our ago.

Lammergeiers r a bit funy theez days, but Il ask aroun.

Fanks.

(flutr ov wings, then:)

Well, u mite b in luk—

– then ther waz a mega-sqwak & a screem & I had 2 turn roun & luke & ther woz a huge grate bird beetin in thi air behind & abuv mi, holdin anuthir torn bird in 1 ov itz talons; thi big bird woz red-black on black & feerse as deth & I cood feel thi wind ov its flappin snappin wings on ma fayce. It hung in thi air, wingz spread beetin like somethin feersly crucified, shaken thi ded bird in its talons so that itz blud spatterd in my Is.

Y u askin qwestions, child? it screemd.

Tryin 2 find a frend ov mine I sed, keepin cam. I clumpd

aroun on mi perch 2 fayce thi big red-black bird. Twig stil in ma beak.

It held up one foot; 3 talons up, one down. C these three clawz? it sed.

Yup. (Mite as well play along 4 now, but Im checkin thi exits, finkin ov ma leg-ring wif thi wake-up code on it.)

U got 2 thi count ov 3 2 moov yoor beak bak 2 realty u skin job, thi red burd sez. U heer me? Am startin countin now: 3.

I juss lookin 4 ma frend.

2.

Iss juss a ant. Am only lookin 4 a litil ant who woz my frend.

1.

Wass thi fukin problim heer? Doan a creetch get no respect 4 – (& am shoutin now angry & I drop thi twig from ma beak).

Then thi big red birdz foot cums out like itz bleedin leg is telescopic & zaps itself 2wards ma hed & raps round it & sqwishes me down b4 I can do anythin & I feel maself trapt & sqwelched down thru thi fabric ov thi metalic bird am perched upon & down thru thi bildin its part ov & down thru thi city & down thru thi grid & down thru thi erf beneaf & down & down & down & whots wurse I can feel that thi ring roun ma leg that had my wake-up code on it has gon like that big red bird swiped it when it hit me an shurenuf I cant fink whot thi hel thi wake-up coad is meenwhile am stil goin down an down an down an am finkin,

O shit . . .

THREE

1

'Ah, this must be she. Good morning, young lady.'

'Good morning, young lady.'

'I beg your . . .? Ah, well, no, though I am half flattered.'

'You not young lady, no?'

'Neither young nor remotely lady-like. My name is Pieter Velteseri; I understand you may not know your own name, but— '

'No, I do not.'

'Quite. Well, first let me welcome you to our estate and to our house, both of which are called Jenahbilys. Please; do sit down . . . Well, I meant . . . Ah, perhaps the seat might be more appropriate? There; behind you. You see? Like this.'

'Ah, not floor; seat.'

'There you are. Just so. Now . . . Ah, would you excuse me? . . . Gil, I can see this young lady's pudenda, and despite my surfeit of years it is most off-putting, if more in the memory than in the tumescence. Might we clothe her in something more, ah, complete than what would appear to be merely your jacket and fundamentally nothing else?'

'Sorry, uncle.'

'. . . What are you looking at me for?'

'Come on, Lucia; you could lend her something of yours.'

'Tech. She hasn't even been *washed* or anything yet; have you seen the state of her feet? Oh, all right . . .'

'. . . My nephew's friend has gone to fetch you some further attire. I thought she might take you, and . . . well, never mind. Perhaps you would like to come to the window over here? The view of the formal gardens is particularly pleasing. Gil, perhaps our young guest would like something to drink.'

'I'll attend to it, unc.'

The second man – of course not a lady, which was to do with women, like herself (and she had to search for the word she now felt; it was *embarrassed*) – the second man, who was old and a little stooped and had a crinkled face, motioned to one of the windows, and they both walked there while the first man, the young one, closed his eyes for a second. The view from the window was of a gravel and flower garden, arranged in a strange, half-swirling, half-geometric pattern. Small tracked machines rolled amongst the blooms, clipping and sorting.

A little later a small wheeled thing appeared in the room, humming quietly and carrying a tray which held four glasses, several bottles and some small filled bowls. Then Lucia Chimbers appeared with some clothes and took her to a side room where she showed her how to put on shorts, pants and a shirt.

They stood looking at their reflections in a long mirror for a moment. 'You on something deep?' Lucia Chimbers asked quietly.

She looked at Lucia Chimbers.

'Because if you are, I'd like to know what it is.'

'On something deep,' she repeated, frowning (and watched herself frown, in the mirror). '*In* something deep, mean you? I mean; you mean?'

'Never mind.' The other woman sighed. 'Let's wheel you out there. See if the old man can get any sense out of you.'

'I believe she may be an asura,' Pieter Velteseri said, over lunch.

He had spent the morning patiently questioning the girl in an effort to determine what memories she possessed. From this he knew that she had appeared in the clan vault a few hours earlier, seemingly artificially rebirthed in the manner a family member might be were there no clan member suitably pregnant at the time of their scheduled reconstitution. Being born without warning, alone, and in adult form did make the girl unique in his experience, however. She had an extensive vocabulary but seemed uncertain how to employ it, though he had gained the impression that her linguistic skills had developed considerably just in the two hours or so of their conversation.

Gil and Lucia had sat in on his gentle inquisition for a while, then grown restless and gone for a swim. Lunch-time had reconvened them, though if he had been hoping to impress his nephew and Lucia with their guest's new-found articulacy it seemed Pieter was to be disappointed; the presence of large quantities of food seemed to have temporarily driven all thought of conversation from the girl's head.

They sat at one end of the dining-room table. The windows were open to the veranda and the curtains billowed slowly.

Pieter sat on one side of the table while the young lovers sat on the other, with their strange, fey guest at its head, a generously proportioned napkin tucked into the neck of her blouse and another spread across her lap while she frowned and sighed and dipped her head down almost level with the table while she attempted to manipulate a knife, fork and spoon to the end of eating the food on her plate.

Gil and Lucia exchanged looks. Pieter watched the young woman at the head of the table attack a lobster claw with the wrong end of a heavy spoon, and sighed.

'On reflection, perhaps seafood salad was a mistake,' he said.

Bits of red-white carapace spattered across the table; their guest made an appreciative growling noise at the back of her throat and after sniffing at the meat revealed, sucked it out and sat back, chewing open-mouthed and smiling happily while looking at the other three diners. A cleaning servitor hummed and clicked from under the table and busied itself on the floor, gathering up the bits of food and debris the girl had let drop. She looked down at it, grinning, and swept more shards of lobster off the table and onto the floor.

'What,' Lucia asked Pieter, 'exactly is an assurer?'

'I can't find it either,' Gil said, smiling at Lucia and squeezing her hand. Like her, he was eating one-handed.

'An asura,' Pieter said, secretly pleased, though wondering if the two young people really couldn't find the word in their habitua or were just being polite. 'A Hindi word, originally,' he told them. 'It used to mean a demon or a giant opposed to the gods.'

Lucia wore that annoyed look Pieter had come to recognise as her reaction to anything that was not expressed through implants and which she thought ought to be. It was fairly common for those in the first inflationary rush of infatuation, lust or love to embrace almost exclusively the inner voicelessness of implant-articulation in preference to the somehow physically off-putting and clumsy medium of normal speech, and although Pieter did not think Lucia jealous of their guest – any more than Gil seemed able to spare the girl more than the most cursory attention – she did seem to resent both the simple distraction she represented and the fact Pieter had suggested they communicate by speech in deference to the girl's seeming total lack of implants.

'Hindi, hmm,' Gil said, obviously having to look the word up. 'So what does "asura" mean nowadays?' He smiled at Lucia, squeezing her hand again under the table.

'A sort of . . . natural, one might say,' Pieter replied (mischievously, knowing they would both have to look that up too). He spooned a little crabmeat and ate contemplatively while watching the girl flick bits of shell further and further away across the floor so that the cleaning machine described a zig-zag course towards the windows. 'Something generated semi-randomly by the corpus or some separate system for reasons of its own,' he went on, dabbing at his lips with a napkin. 'Usually to do with some required change impossible to achieve from within. A non-predictable variable; a wildness.'

Lucia glanced at the girl. 'Why does she have to appear here, though?'

Pieter shrugged. 'Why not?'

'She's nothing to do with the clan, is she? She doesn't belong to any of our families,' Lucia said, her voice low, though the girl didn't seem to be listening, still throwing lobster-chunks towards the window. 'So why does she have to pop out of *our* vault; bit cheeky, isn't it?'

'I think it may have been sheer chance,' Pieter said, frowning a little. 'Whatever; she is here now and we must decide what to do with her.'

'Well what does one normally do with . . . asuras?' Gil asked.

'Gives them shelter and does not try to impede them when they want to move on, I believe,' Pieter said. 'Rather like any guest.'

The girl aimed and threw; a piece of lobster-claw bounced at the edge of the window between the softly blowing curtains, ricocheted through the rails of the balcony outside and disappeared down towards the garden. The pursuing cleaning machine trundled as far as the rails, and then stopped. It clicked a couple of times, then retreated into the room. The girl looked disappointed.

'Why, where's she going to go?' Lucia asked.

'I don't know,' Pieter admitted, nodding at their guest. 'Though she may.' He sipped at his wine.

They looked at her. She was holding another section of lobster above her, squinting up into it, one-eyed. Gil and Lucia exchanged glances.

'But what exactly is she supposed to *do*?' Gil asked.

'Again, I have no idea,' Pieter admitted. 'She may provide some fresh input for some section of the corpus, or possibly – indeed probably – she is what one might call a system test; a specimen signal-carrier whose only purpose is to ensure everything is in working order should the medium require to be used in anger – as it were – at some point in the future.'

Lucia and Gil looked at each other again.

'Could this have something to do with the Encroachment?' Gil asked, his expression serious. He squeezed Lucia's hand again.

'It might,' Pieter said, waving his fork while inspecting the oysters on his plate. 'Probably not.'

'Suppose she isn't just a signal test?' Gil asked with deliberated patience. 'What does she do *then*?' He refilled Lucia and his glasses.

'Why then, she will probably find her way to wherever she is supposed to find her way and deliver her message.'

'She can hardly talk in joined-up words,' Lucia snorted. 'How is she going to deliver a message?'

'She doesn't even have any implants,' Gil added.

'The message may be in an unusual medium,' Pieter said. 'It might lie in the precise pattern of flecks in the iris of one eye, or in one of her finger-prints, or in the disposition of her intestinal flora, or even in her own genetic code.'

'And this message is something the data corpus knows and yet doesn't know?'

'Quite. Or it may come from some system which isn't part of the main corpus and which can't communicate with it.'

The girl was watching Gil drink from his glass. She imitated the action and spilled only a little.

'*Machines* that can't *communicate*?' Lucia said, laughing. 'But that's . . .' she waved her hand.

'Diseases are communicated, too,' Pieter said quietly, folding his napkin. Their young guest seemed to be practising gargling.

'*So?*' Lucia said, with a contemptuous glance at the girl.

'Well, anyway,' Gil said emolliently, patting Lucia's hand while addressing his uncle, 'She's here and our guest; she may even prove amusing if she is so preternaturally naïve. At least she appears to be house-trained.'

'So far,' Lucia said. 'Anyway; isn't there somebody we ought to tell about her?'

'Oh, I suppose one might report her arrival to the authorities,' Pieter said easily. 'But there's no hurry.'

The girl sat back, belched, looked pleased with herself, then farted. She appeared slightly taken aback, then just grinned.

'Air,' she said, nodding to the other three people round the table.

Pieter smiled. Gil guffawed. Lucia stared at the girl for a moment. Then set her napkin down primly. 'I am going to lie down,' she announced, rising.

Gil got up too, still holding Lucia's hand. 'Me too,' he said, smiling broadly.

Pieter returned their nodded farewells and watched the two young people leave.

He turned to the girl. She wiped one bloused forearm messily across her mouth then thumped her chest hollowly with her fist.

'Asura,' she said, grinning triumphantly, and burped again.

Pieter smiled thinly. 'Quite so.'

2

'The signal came at noon yesterday,' Clispeir said quickly, quietly. 'The observatory was stationary. Gad,' she laughed gently, 'all our preparations and cryptography went for nothing; the signal came in light all right, but not in any ancient code or any fancy wavelength, and not in frequency or amplitude modulation; they just manipulated the beam to make actual letters appear upon the plain, shining lines like the reflections waves cast on a wall or ceiling.'

'What did it say?' Gadfium asked. They sat together on the small bed, curtains drawn, light dimmed, whispering like school girls conspiring a prank. She was not sure if it was some ancient memory that made her head spin, some genuine reaction to the impoverished air in the observatory, or the import of what they were talking about.

Clispeir laughed. 'At first it just said, "Move",' she said. 'Oh, Gad, you should have seen us. We stared at the letters on the salt for a full minute before we pulled ourselves together and decided that even if we *had* gone plain-crazy, and it was some mass hallucination, we might as well shift. So we did; we moved a couple of metres. The letters stayed where they were, then disappeared. When they reappeared it was as though they had followed us.'

'But what did they—?'

'Ssh! I'm coming to that!' She pulled on a chain round her neck and drew a slim pen from inside her tunic, unscrewed it and pulled out a piece of flimsy paper which she unrolled and handed to Gadfium. 'They came in groups every eight seconds. Here; read for yourself.'

Gadfium stared at the scribbled writing.

* (flash)
MOVE /
NOW MOVE BACK /
THANK YOU /
LOVE IS GOD / ALL ARE HALLOWED / * WE HAVE NOTED / THAT YOU ATTEMPTED / TO COMMUNI-CATE WITH / US IN THE PAST / HOWEVER STAND-BY / SYSTEMS THEN FUNCTIONING / WERE NOT ENABLED TO / REPLY OR INSTRUCTED / TO COM-MENCE / OUR REACTIVATION / THIS HAS NOW / OCCURRED DUE TO / SOLAR SYSTEM'S APPROACH / TO INTERSTELLAR / DUST CLOUD / WHICH EVENT YOU CALL / ENCROACHMENT / THIS CONCERNS US ALL / CURRENT ESTIMATES / OF EFFECT ON EARTH / GIVE CAUSE FOR / ALARM / WE HAVE NOT / RECEIVED NOR DO / WE BELIEVE YOU HAVE / RECEIVED ANY / COMMUNICATION FROM / OFF-PLANET THERE / FOR WE MUST ACT / ALONE TO SAVE / OURSELVES / ACTION OPTIONS / INCLUDE

CURRENT / LOWER-LEVELS / ATTEMPT TO CON-
STRUCT / ROCKETS FOR / EVACUATION / THIS IS
ALMOST / CERTAIN TO FAIL / IT IS KNOWN / SEC-
TIONS OF LOWER- / LEVELS COMPETE / AGGRES-
SIVELY FOR / SUBSIDIARY SPACE / TECHNOLOGIES
BUT THIS / TOO IS UNLIKELY / TO SUCCEED / ALSO
NOTE DANGER / WORKINGS IN L5SWSOLAR / * HAL-
LOWED BE / THE CENTRE THE / ABSENCE THAT /
GIVES STRENGTH / GIVES MEANING / * THREATEN
SIGNIFICANT / FABRIC INTEGRITY LOSS / CORRECT
ANSWER MUST / LIE IN CRYPTOSPHERE / OR AN
ASSOCIATED / BUT COMMUNICATIVELY / REMOTE
SUB-SYSTEM / WE BELIEVE AS / WE BELIEVE YOU
DO / THAT TECHNOLOGY EXISTS / TO SAVE US ALL
/ BUT ACCESS TO / DISCOVERY OF THIS / TECH-
NOLOGY EVADES / US AND WE ARE / UNABLE TO
CONTACT / CRYPTOSPHERE / DIRECTLY DUE TO /
CURRENT CHAOTIC / INFECTIOUS STATE / OF SAME
/ GIVEN RUMOURED / EXISTENCE OF EMERGENCY
/ META-PROTOCOLS / WE THEREFORE URGE / YOU
TO REMAIN / VIGILANT AS SHALL / WE FOR ADVENT
/ OF EXTERNAL DATA- / CARRYING EVENT OR /
SYSTEM-EMISSARY / (ASURA) / PLEASE ALSO NOTE
/ WE BELIEVE RULING / SECTIONS OR LOWER- /
LEVELS KNOW THEIR / APPARENT ATTEMPTS / TO
ESCAPE CERTAIN / TO FAIL / WHY IS THIS / WE
QUESTION / REPLY THROUGH / HELIO SEMAPHORE
OR / SIGNAL-LAMP ONLY / * LOVE IS FAITH / IS
UNKNOWING / BE ALL HALLOWED / IN THE EYE
OF / NOTHING / SHANTI / END *

She couldn't take it all in; she started, got half-way through,
lost it again, started more slowly, then read it in full a second time.

By the end of it, Gadfium was staring at the piece of paper;
she could feel her eyes bulging from her face and sense the
tension in the surrounding skin. Her head still felt as though
it was spinning. She gulped, looked at the smiling, shining face
of Clispeir.

There was a knock at the cabin door. 'Ma'am?' Rasfline asked,
voice muffled.

Gadfium cleared her throat. 'I'm alive, Rasfline,' she called, her voice shaking. 'Just let me rest. Ten minutes.'

'Very well, ma'am.' She could hear his hesitation.

'Yes, Rasfline?'

'We should not stay much longer, Chief Scientist . . . and also, there is an urgent message from the Sortileger's office. He would like to see you.'

'Inform him I'll be on my way in ten minutes.'

'Ma'am.'

They waited a few moments, then Clispeir seized the other woman's shoulders, glancing at the paper Gadfium held. 'I know some of it seems like nonsense, but isn't it just the most exciting thing?'

Gadfium nodded. She put one shaking hand to her brow and patted Clispeir's shoulder with the other hand. 'Yes, and very dangerous,' she said.

'You really think so?' Clispeir said.

'Of course! If Security hear about this, we're all lost.'

'You don't think if you could somehow get this to the King he'd, well, have a change of heart? I mean: realise that the best thing was for us all to work tog—?'

'No!' Gadfium said, appalled. She shook the other woman's shoulders. 'Clispeir! The message itself mentions the King and his pals seem to have some secret agenda; if we tell them we know they'll just silence us!'

'Of course, of course,' Clispeir said, smiling nervously. 'You're right.'

'Yes,' Gadfium said, 'I am.' She took a deep breath. 'Now, we have ten minutes – may I keep this?' She held up the sheet of paper.

'Certainly! You'll have to make your own copies for the others.'

'That's all right. Now, as I was saying; we have ten minutes to decide what to do.'

3

The Palace was situated in the Great Hall's central lantern, a tall octagonal construction protruding from the centre of the steeply pitched roof which in a humanly scaled version of Serehfa would have been open and hollow and have helped light the Hall's interior below.

The Palace filled a hundred tall storeys within the lantern and projected downwards into the Great Hall for another ten levels; those lower floors were mostly devoted to the Security services and their equipment. Lush gardens and broad terraces graced its outer walls, and within it were housed its own great halls, ballrooms and ceremonial spaces. Its summit was capped by further walled gardens and a small airfield.

His Majesty King Adijine VI sat in the great solar, at one end of a mighty table too long to be used for purely vocal discussion without amplification. He listened to the chief ambassadorial emissary for the Engineers of the Chapel as he forcefully outlined some subsidiary position on possible technological cooperation should the hoped-for peace be forthcoming. The emissary's voice boomed out across the hall. Possibly, thought the King, the emissary would not have required amplification.

The chief ambassadorial emissary was a fully sentient human-chimeric; a man in the guise of an animal – in this case *ursus maritimus*, a polar bear. Such creatures were generally frowned upon; animals were seen as the final resting place – or at any rate one of the last resting places – for the crypt-corroded souls of the long dead, but the clan Engineers had a tradition of such beasts. It had been something of an aggressive statement for the Chapel usurpers to make, appointing such a being as their main representative at the talks. Adijine didn't care.

He was finding the chief ambassadorial emissary's tirade tiring; certainly in the course of providing the bear's body with vocal equipment capable of reproducing human speech the Chapel scientists had created a powerful and profoundly bassy instrument, but one could grow weary of it all the same, and the man within the beast ought to leave the sort of detail he was now dealing in to his retinue. However, as well as liking the sound of his own voice, the chief ambassadorial emissary seemed unable to delegate effectively, and Adijine had rather lost interest in the substance of what was now being discussed.

He switched away.

Like the other Privileged, the King had no implants, save for those which would be used only once, to record and transmit his personality when he died. Unlike most of them he had access to technologies that allowed him the benefits of implants without the drawbacks, giving him unrestrained one-way access to all those with implants and – in the right circumstances – even those without them. It did mean he had to wear the crown to make it all work, but he had a choice of several attractive models of crown, all of which were tastefully designed and sat lightly on one's head.

In theory the regal paradigm best expressed the reality of modern power – better than a commercial, civil or military archetype for example – and certainly it seemed that people were happy enough with a kind of benignly dictatorial meritocracy which at any given moment looked somewhat like a real monarchy – with primogeniture and fully hereditary status – but wasn't.

Actually he suspected few people these days really believed that in the past kings and queens had been chosen by the accident of birth (and this when it really had been an accident and even their crude attempts at improving their bloodstock tended to result in in-breeding rather than regal thoroughbreds). Equally, though, the sheer grandiosity of the stage that Serehfa itself presented might be seen to demand an imperial repertoire.

The King entered the minds of the men behind the walls.

Twenty troops of his bodyguard were concealed behind the paper partitions lining the room. He scanned each quickly – on principle, really, they were thoroughly programmed – and then focused on their commander. He was watching the scene in the hall on a visor monitor. Adijine followed the man's slow sweep of the view and listened to quiet system chatter coming over his audio implants. Head-ups flickered on and off as the guard commander's gaze fell on individuals in the room.

His gaze settled on the King for a second, and Adijine had

the always rather strange experience of looking at himself through another's eyes. He looked fine; handsome, tall, regal, impressively robed, the light crown sitting straight on his curly black locks, and by his expression paying due but not deferential attention to what the polar-bear emissary was saying.

Adijine admired himself for a while longer. He had been bred to be King; not in the ancients' crude hit-or-miss interpretation of the words but in the literal sense that the crypt had designed him; given him the aspect, bearing and character of a natural ruler before he'd even been born, selecting his physical and mental attributes from a variety of sources to make him handsome, attractive, charming, gracious and wise, balancing wit against gravitas, human under-standing against moral scrupulousness and a love of the finer things in life against an urge towards simplicity. He inspired loyalty, was difficult to hate, brought out the best in men and women and had great but not total power which he had the sense and modesty to use sparingly but authoritatively. Not for the first time, Adijine thought what a damn fine figure of a man he was.

He looked like an absolute ruler, even though he wasn't; he shared his power with the twelve representatives of the Consistory. They were his advisers, or better, his board; he was managing director. He controlled the physical realm of the structure through the other clans, the personal loyalty he commanded from the masses, and the Security services (now including the newly formed Army), while the men and women of the Consistory spoke for the crypt itself and the élite body of Cryptographers who formed the interface between the data corpus and humanity. It was a nicely balanced arrangement, as was proven by the fact it had existed for multi-generations of monarchs. Nothing had disturbed the calm face of old Earth for millennia until that Nessian cloak of darkness had started to stain the heavens.

Adijine watched as the guard commander's gaze curved above his King, then around him, then resumed its slow sweep.

Adijine had hoped to find the man day-dreaming, but the guard commander wasn't thinking of anything at all; he was on automatic pilot, watching, listening, being professional. He did day-dream, very occasionally (it would have been suspicious in the extreme had he never done so) but he wasn't at the moment. Adijine switched again.

The colonel-in-chief of the Security services was herself

remoting into another mind, watching a meeting of clan Cryptography chief programmers through the mind of one who was trying to suppress thoughts of republicanism and revolution. Utterly boring. The colonel-in-chief had a robust, healthy and inventive sex-life and Adijine had spent many a happy hour with her and her partners, but everything seemed to be strictly business right now.

His private secretary was receiving details of a conversation his construct had just had with the shade of the late Count Sessine. Oh yes, thought the King; poor Count Sessine. He'd always felt a certain empathy with Sessine. The private secretary was eating lunch at the same time; anchovy salad. The King detested anchovies rather more than his private secretary adored them, and so switched again.

His seneschal was surveying the zeteticist team monitoring the Chapel usurper party for stray noetic radiations. Boring *and* incomprehensible.

His current favourite courtesan was remoting into the mind of a mathematician contemplating an elegant proof – the court retained many mathematicians, philosophers and aesthetes to provide this sort of vicarious epiphany – but Adijine found the third-hand experience less than absorbing.

How frustrating to attempt to pry on people only to discover they were in turn spying on others.

He checked that the ursine ambassadorial emissary was still talking (he was, and the King allowed himself a pre-emptive gloat at how the emissary was going to feel when the bomb workings in the fifth-level south-western solar came on line and he realised that this entire negotiation was just a matérielly inexpensive exercise in time-wasting), then the King dipped into minds elsewhere in Serehfa; a peruker in a tower-roof terrace-town, crouched over her latest extravagant creation; a cliometrician carrelled half-asleep in a bartizan high on the east fifth level; a moirologist petitioning in the sacristy of the northern upper chapel; a funambulist reaping babilia on the pyramid spur of a shell-wall tower.

Prosaic.

He checked on his spyers, clinging to ledges and lintels, shivering on shingles and cinquefoils, hooked and netted under hoardings and machicolations or just crawling like half-frozen fleas through the gelid vertical forest of hi-alt babilia while they watched the lofty, cold, snowy slopes and plains of the high castle for enemy movement, or just something interesting . . . Another one dead on the tenth-level northern pentice; the spyer-master Yastle insisted acclimatised men could survive at ten thousand metres, but the poor devils kept proving him wrong . . . A faller from the seventh level butry gable . . . One watching the black smoke drift inside the white, a tiny snow-scene within the cold cauldron of the Southern Volcano Room . . . One on the south side of the octal tower, snow-blinded and raving . . . Another in a mullion of the seventh-level western clerestory, holding his black, frostbitten fingers up in front of his face, crying, knowing that he would never get down now. Little wonder people thought spyers must be mad. Less dangerous to be a spy.

He examined the view from a few ordinary static cameras and avians; they'd been losing a few of those recently to real birds. Some blip in the crypt's faunastatus, possibly caused by the workings in the L5 SW solar, the Cryptographers said; they were sorting it out.

He looked in on the Palace Astronomical Observatory; they had instruments watching the sun. Radiation was ninety-one per cent of normal; still falling slowly and still decreasing more steeply in the IR-end of the spectrum. Boring and depressing.

He cast his regard further afield, and was briefly in the mind of a scrape-scrounge haunting the quiet ruins of Manhattan, then looked through the eyes of a wild chimeric condor, high above the southern Andes, then in the mind of a young woman surfing at dawn off New Sealand, before becoming part of a chimeric triple-mind within a sounding hump-back in mid-Pacific, then joining a chanting priestess in some midnight temple in Singapore, followed by a drunken night-guard at an ovitronics plant in Tashkent, an insomniac agronometricist in Arabie, a spanceled Resiler preaching unheeded in the smoky chaos of a traumkeller in old Prag, and finally a sleepy balloonist descending through the dusk above Tammanrusset.

All very mind-broadening, but still . . . ah; the Army colonel-to-the-court was thinking about his new mistress. This was more like it.

. . . Sessine's wife!

Now, wasn't that a coincidence?

You must have thought seven, *in the context of having used up seven out of your eight incrypted lives. Unless you are here for the trivial reason that you have been very careless with those lives, I assume you're in trouble and under direct – and directed – threat.*

So you're here, in the place you prepared for yourself a long time ago, in case. You're safest staying in the room, where everything works the way it would in reality. Using the screen may be risky, leaving certainly is. You're in the crypt's crustal basement, the last sane level before the chaos.

If you know of anybody who remains loyal to you back in the mortal world, you can try to contact them on the screen; it's a brand new address, never been format-collapsed, so the first call is safe. The rest can't be guaranteed.

If you think it's safe to sit and wait to be rescued, look inside the bedside cabinet; there's a book, a phial and a pistol. The book contains a general library, the phial will make you sleep until somebody comes to get you and the pistol will work on others within the confines of the room.

If you're going to leave, head west from here – that's away from the ocean tunnel, which is the direction the room's window faces – until you reach the walls and then turn left and walk until you reach the spill-sluice; take the steps up. There's a smoking-tavern called the Half-way House. The hopfgeist is friendly. I hope you never did tell anybody your most-secret code, or forget it. Or change it.

Remember that if you do leave this room, or transmit more than once from it, you are vulnerable, and that if you communicate openly with the crypt you will betray both your identity and location. You can ask information of other constructs you can trust, and you can move within the crypt. That is all.

You are an outlaw now, my friend; a fugitive.

I am – that is, you are – setting all this up in direct-link just after a snort of Oblivion, so if it works – worked – you may remember once waking up on the floor of your study on a Wednesday evening with a head-full of nothing, wondering what possessed you to take that stuff. And if anything goes wrong, that's because you were drunk when you had the idea.

I'm drunk now but I feel fine, in here. Anyway, Alandre; best of luck. I'll be with you all the way.

  Yours.

Sessine folded the sheet of paper and tore it into little strips, slowly and carefully, thinking.

He was in the level of the crypt just above the chaotic regions, where – apparently perversely – things worked much more according to the rules of the real world than they did elsewhere in the corpus. Throw yourself off a roof here and you wouldn't be able to decide suddenly to fly; you'd hit the ground and die. Here, knowing how literally things worked, it was difficult to make the kind of mistake that might lead one to enter the crypt's chaotic regions accidentally; it was the last safeguard the system provided.

He wasn't sure what to do with the sheet of paper he'd just read, so he shrugged to himself and imagined it gone, but of course it didn't go. He ate one of the strips but it tasted bitter and he felt foolish. He shook his head and put the paper scraps in one pocket of his jacket.

He looked at himself in the bedroom mirror. He was wearing . . . he tried to instigate a search but that, too, didn't work, so he had to resort to a laborious shuffle through his own memory . . . Grief, what did you call this stuff? And this stuff? A lifeless, ill-fitting, creased blue shirt, a jacket of . . . tartan? plaid? and the trous . . . Nimes, de Nimes . . . neams? Geams? Something like that.

Awful stuff; the shirt felt scratchy, the jacket had great hairy bits of fabric sticking out from it like mussed hair and the geams had enormous, crude, visible stitches. Late twentieth-century corporate dress would have been his choice, but then maybe that was what people would be looking for, if they were still looking for him.

He inspected the bedside cabinet. The items his note to himself had listed were indeed there. He hefted the pistol; an ancient automatic projectile weapon. It wasn't supposed to work outside the room. He put it down the back of his trousers anyway. He took the little glass phial, too.

He went to the screen. He thought of calling his wife but she was probably still busy fornicating. He was reasonably certain she had started seeing some courtier recently and round about now had always been her favourite time of day for sex. He hadn't bothered trying to find out who the fellow was; it was her business.

He smiled regretfully, thinking of his own latest affair. A girl in the air corps, keen on skiing and ancient flying machines; long red hair and a wicked laugh.

Never again, he thought. Never again.

Well, he could be her incubus, of course, but it would never be quite the same.

Perhaps if he appeared to her in the guise of an antique airman . . .

. . . Anyway, he would call Nifel, the clan Security chief; the man was ferociously efficient and he felt they had become friends over the years. Probably never have got into this mess if Nifel had been in charge; trust the Army. Nifel; just the man, Sessine thought. He turned the screen on, sound only.

'Nifel, Mika; officer clan Aerospace, Serehfa.'

'Nifel's agent-construct.'

'Sessine.'

'Count. We have heard. Commander Nifel is shocked and saddened. He— '

'Really? How unoriginal of him.'

'Indeed, sir. He wishes to know why you did not want the in-crypt support systems instigated around your data-set.'

'But I do,' Sessine told the construct, and felt fear. 'I always did. Kindly institute them immediately and tell Nifel the Army may be behind all this; Army intelligence, especially. I am down to my last life in here and whoever killed me the other seven times comes very well-equipped, very well-informed and with the ability to intercept calls from the crypt to specific Army high staff.'

'I shall inform Commander Nifel— '

'Never mind informing him; first get those support systems running and give me some back-up down here.'

'It is being done.' There was a pause. 'What is your location, sir?'

'I'm in . . .' Sessine hesitated, then smiled. He had died eight times today; seven of them in the space of about a tenth of a second, real time. He was becoming cagey at last.

'First,' he said, 'complete this phrase, if you will: *Aequitas sequitur* . . .'

'*Legem*, sir.'

'Thank you,' Sessine said.

'. . . your location, sir?'

'I beg your pardon. Of course. I am near the representation of a place called Kittyhawk, North Carolina, North America.'

'Thank you, sir. Commander Nifel, on your instructions— '

'Would you excuse me for a moment?'

'Sir.'

He switched the machine off and sat on the bed for a moment, his head in his hands.

So there was nowhere in the real world to turn.

Aequitas sequitur funera had been the more mordant version of the saying he and Nifel had settled on.

He stood, looked once around the room, then opened the door and left. The gun's bulk simply vanished from the small of his back as soon as he crossed the threshold. He paused.

Well now, he thought, for the duration of these real days I am like the ancients used to be; restricted to one careful life in a time of danger. Every instant might be his last, and the only memories he could access were those in his own mind.

Nevertheless, he told himself, he was still better off than those of purely mortal ages; he could hope that he would wake up again after his funeral, and rejoin the universe of the crypt for at least a little of eternity. Somehow, though, given the ferocity and apparent profundity of the forces ranged against him, he doubted that was really likely, and suspected he was indeed on his own, with one slim chance of survival. *Desperado*, he thought, and smiled, amused at his fall from power and grace.

He wondered anew how the ancients had endured such fragility and ignorance, then shrugged, closed the door and walked down the dim, deserted corridor.

Aequitas sequitur funera. Justice follows the grave, not the law.

It had not occurred to him he would ever employ that mutated phrase in circumstances that might give him the chance to verify it.

Or refute it, of course.

4

1nce thi sky woz ful ov birdz; used 2 go blak wif birds it did & birdz roold thi air (wel, apart from thi insectz) but thas all changed now; hoomins came along & startd shootin & trappin & killin them & evin if they've mostly stoppd doin that sort ov fing now theyr stil top ov thi roost partly coz they kild off so meny speesheez & partly coz they make stuf fly, witch when u fink about it duz kind ov spoil it 4 thi birdz on account they had 2 spend milyons ov yeers jumpin off clifs & out ov treez & crashin 2 thi groun & dyin & then doin it ol ovir agen & 1 time miby not crashin qwite so hard but glidin a bit & then a bit moar & a bit moar stil & so on & so on etc & juss jenerily paynstakinly evolvin in this incredibly complicatd way (I meen, lizird-scales in2 fevvirs! & holo bones, 4 goonis sakes!) & then theez bleedin hoomins theez ridicolos-lookin bald munkys cum along whot 1/2 nevir showd thi slitest inarest in flyin nor sine ov adaptayshin 2 thi air whot-so-bleedin-evir & they start buzzin aroun in flyin masheens juss 4 a laf!

Makes u sik. Din evin 1/2 thi decincy 2 do it slo; one minit theyr flyin mashines is made from paper & spit, then 1 evilushinary blink ov thi i & thi bastirds is playin golf on thi moon!

O, thers stil birdz around olrite but thers a dam site fewr ov them & a lot ov what u wood fink is birds iznt; itz chimerics, or machines, & even if it is thi case that whot looks like a bird is a bird if its a big one its probably not evin got its hed 2 itself but its been taken over by a ded persin. Can't evin 1/2 peece in yoor own bonce. Birdz av coped wiv tics & flees & lice ol ther evilushinary life but theez dam hoomins r wurse & they get evryware!

Am flapin & skwokin & wokin about ma perch & wishin Mr Zoliparia thi hoomin wude hury up & wake me coz thi moar I think about peepil thi less I like them & thi moar I like bein a bird.

Been almos a week now; whatz keepin thi man? Mi own folt 4
entrustin mi saifty 2 a old geezir. Thats thi trubl wif old persins;
slo reactshins. Probly dropt thi pen I askt him 2 catch & is evin
now scrabblin about on thi flor 4 it, forgetin thi importint thing
is 2 wake me, not get thi bleedin pen. But it must ½ been a minit
in reel time by now; shurely evin a old persin cant take that long
2 luke 4 a bleedin pen 4 gooniss sakes.

Howma goan wake up? Am blo thi levil whare u get askd in
yoor sleep otomaticly & mi own wake-up code woz taikin from
me by that big bastardin bird whot slapt me down heer in thi
furst place & evin tho Ive rimemberd it sinse it juss dozen seem
2 b wurkin no moare.

Mi goos, like they say, may wel b cookd.

Am on a perch in a sorta litl dark caiv.

If u can imagine a jiant black brain in a evin biggr dark space, &
then zoom in on thi brain & go down inamungst its corugayshins
& foldz & c that thi walls ov evry fold is made out ov zillions ov
litl boxes wif a perch in it, well, thatz whot this bit ov bird-space
is like, in thi kript.

Mi litl box lukes out on2 a uge hangin dark spaice oll fild
with shados & thi okzhinal passin bird flappin sloly past (we
oll flap slo – thi pretend graviti is less heer). Wel, am sayin
its all dark but maybe it iznt realy, maybe thats juss me coz
truth 2 tel Iv not been very wel; in fact Im ½ blind, but
thats betr than whot I woz a cupl ov days ago, which woz
½ ded.

Therz a dainti flutr ov wings @ thi entranse 2 mi box, & in
cums litl Dartlin, whos thi frend Iv made heer.

Ullo, Dartlin, howzit goin?

Fine, Mr Bathcule. I bin tewibwy bizzy, u no; tewibwy bizzy
bird i been. I flu thwu 2 thi paliment ov thi cwows & pikd up
sum gothip, wood u like 2 here it?

Dartlin is my spy, sort ov. When I imagind miself in heer
in thi furst place, bak in Mr Zoliparia's pad, I juss naturily
sumhow took on thi apperince ov a hok, which is whot I stil
am now. Dartlins a sparo, so in feery we shood b rapter & prey
respectivly, but it dozen actule work that way here, not in this
bit nway.

Dartlin foun me on thi flor heer. Id juss got bak from thi levil beneeth whare thi reel fun in thi kript starts & I woz in a sory state, let me tel u.

Thi furst cupl ov days wer thi wurst. When thi big burd slapt me down thru all them levils I thot mi time woz up; I meen, I new Id wake up in thi Iball ov thi Septentryinil Gargoil Rosbrith sooner or later, but I thot I woz goin 2 die in heer, & thats a helluva fing 2 take back 2 yoor waitin mind; scar u 4 life, that can.

Iss ver difficult 2 explain what its like when u go that deep in thi kript, but if u can imagine bein in a sno storm, *flyin* in a *fik* snostorm only thi sno is *multi-colurd* & sum ov it seems 2 b *cumin @ u from evry angil* (& each sno-flake seems 2 sing & hum & sizil & hold littl flashin images & hints ov faces in it & as they go past u heer snatchiz ov speech or music or u feel a emoshin or fink ov a idear or consept or seem 2 remembir sumfink) & if 1 ov thi sno-flakes hits u in thi I u r suddenly in sumbudy elses dreem & its a effort 2 remember who thi hel u r, wel if u can imagine xperyencin oll that when u r feelin a bit drunk & disoreyented then thas a bit like whot iss like, cept wurse ov course. & weerder.

I doan actuly remember much about that bit & I doan think I want 2, Ither. I lernd 2 navigate by thi flavir ov thi surroundin dreemz & graduly sortd sum sens out ov thi gibbersh & tho I got blindid by thi abraidin impact ov ol those sno-flakes & loss thi wordin ov my wake-up code, I fynaly broke bak thru 2 thi darknis & peece & qwiet here, & lay xosted on thi flor amungst lotsa scraggly ded fevvirs & solidifyd droppins & thass whare Dartlin foun me.

Heed been terifyd by sumthin & loss thi memry ov how 2 fly & so ended down on thi flor 2, but he could c & so lnce Id got my strenf bak he got on2 my back between my wings & gided me 2 whare thi sparos gather. They told him how 2 fly agen but they didn feel cumfterbil 1/2 in a hok around so they foun me this place down here & thass whare Ive been thi last 4 days, gettin mi site back wyle Dartlin flits about makin inkwyries & bein bizy & nozi & gossipin, which is whot sparos like doin nway.

Y I certinly wood like 2 heer whot u herd, litil frend, I tel Dartlin.

Wel, ith tewibwy intiwestin & i hope u doan get fwitened but, tho u r a *feerth* hok aftir ol & pwobibwy doan get fwitened . . .

o, ithn thith a dark ole place? I doan like perchin here on thi edje. May I hop up bethide u?

By ol meens, Dartlin, I sez, shufflin along a bit on my perch.

Thank u. Now; ah yeth, now i doan wan 2 make u nervith or anthin – like i thay, with u bein feerth i cant imagin u no thi meenin ov thi word – but it wood appeer that therth a bit ov a dithturbinth in thi air – o, it givth me a shiver juth lookin @ thoze big feerth talonth ov yourth – whot woth i thayin? – o yeth, a dithturbinth in thi air, affectin evwybody, neer enuf – u no i think i felt it begin mythelf evin tho i woz down on that hawwibl flor @ thi time with uthir thingth on mi mind – wothint hawwibil down thare? I hatid it. Nway, it theemth thi raptorth & carrion-feederth & moatht *ethpethyally* thi lammergeierth 1/2 been behavin thtrainjly – o! woth that a theegull jutht thare? I new a theegull 1nce, hith name woth . . .

Thas thi trubl wif sparos; they got a veri limitid tenshun span & r inclind 2 go witterin on 4 ages b4 they get 2 thi poynt, always flutterin off @ tanjints & keepin u gessin whot it is thare actuli tokin about. Iss veri frustratin but u juss ½ 2 b payshint.

Nway, I bettir parafraze or weel b here oll bleedin day listnin 2 this sparo-crap.

Furst, sum ov thi birdz is lookin 4 sumbody & I get a funy feelin it might b yoors truli. Thi song goes that thers a hunt on 4 sumbodi whoze loose in thi sistim, existin in thi kript &/or thi base-wurld & thers a pryce on ther hed. Apparintly this persins a furst-born, which fits me. Fits lots a peepil, u mite say, but apparintly this persins got sumthin a bit difrint about them; they ½ sum peculyarity, sum strainjnis, & thare a signil carryer, carryin a mesidje they mite not evin no they ½.

O I no itz probly not me, but u no how it is; I alwiz felt I woz speshil – juss like evrybodi els – but unlike evrybody els I got this weerd wirin in mi brane so I cant spel rite, juss ½ 2 do evrythin foneticly. Iss not a problim cos u can put eny old rubish thru practikly anyfin evin a chile's toy computir & get it 2 cum out speld perfictly & gramatisized 2 & evin improvd 2 thi poynt whare yood fink u waz Bill bleedin Shaikspir by thi langwidje. Nway, u can probly c y I got a bit paranoyd when I furst herd ol this, & it gets wurse.

Thi stori goze that this persin – mayb a burd, mayb not – is a contaminint from thi kript's nasti ole nethir reejins, a vyris cum 2 corupt evin more levils, which is qwite a thot & mite evin b a bit worryin juss in case it woz me, onli not evry1 seems 2 bleev this bit ov thi roomir coz its rekind that thi stori cums from thi palas & thi king & thi consisterians r behind it & thay can almost b garanteed not 2 tel thi trooth.

Sum flox rekin its oll 2 do wif thi approachin enkroachin; they fink thi kaotic levils ov thi kript $1/2$ sumhow woken up 2 thi fact that fings cude eventjulie get a bit hazardis even 4 them.

U c, evrybody's assoomed that thi kript's kaotic levils qwite liked thi idear ov thi enkroachmint; sumthin that ushird in a new ice age (@ thi veri leest) & cut off thi sunlite & kild off praktikly thi hole planitiry ecosfere & juss jenerili gaiv hoomins & byological stuf a hard time sounded rite up thi kript's tree thang-u-veri-mutch, but now that it lukes like thi enkroachmint mite b evin moar seryis than that & possibly fretin thi existins ov thi sun, thi planit, thi cassil & thi kript, well thi beests ov thi kaotic zones $1/2$ fynaly sat up & took notis & fings $1/2$ been stirin evir sins.

Y it shood b happenin in thi relm ov thi birdz spesifikly is a good qwestyin but thare u r; not much point tryin 2 figir out thi kript.

Xactly *whot* is goin on apart from thi fact that thare lookin 4 sumbodi isnt 2 cleer Ither, thers 2 meny conflickin roomirs (& nway this is ol bein tranmitd by Dartlin, who is a deer litl bird but wude not evin get a oneribil menshin if they woz givin out prizes 4 conversayshinil coherince) but thi poynt ov it ol is that basikly thers big doo-doo flyin aroun & ol thi flox is nervis & a bit histerikl & enybody whos a bit diffrent is bein sot out, roundid up, interogatid & taken away. Ol ov which mite sound familyir 2 eny studints ov history & juss goze 2 sho that sum fings nevir chainj, leest not when theez pluckin hoomins desined thi orijinil sistim.

So thare u r Mr Bathcule, ithnt it ol tewwibwy, tewwibwy interethtin?

O its inarestin ol rite, Dartlin, ole chum.

I think tho 2 – o look, i think i juss thaw a flee on yoor leg thare; may I preen u?

I feel like sayin, U shure its a flee not a ant? coz I stil think tendirly ov poor litl lost Ergates now & agen, but I juss sez, Preen away, yung Dartlin.

Dartlin peks roun thi fethery top ov my left leg & eventjulie crunches on a flee.

Yum. Thank u. Wel enway, i wonder whot on erth can b goin on? Who do u think they ah lookin 4? Do u think it cood akchooly b 1 ov uth birdth? I dont think tho, do u?

Probly not.

O, ith not u, ith it? Tee-hee. Tee-hee-hee-hee.

I doan fink so. I juss a poor blindid ole hok.

Well *I* no that, thilly, tho u r a very *feerth* old hok, & gettin less blind ol thi time. I woth jutht kiddin. O luke anuthi thee-gull. Or ith it? Lookth moar like a albino cro, akchooly. Well, i cant thtand awound hea ol day chattin with u; i ½ 2 fly, Dartlin sez, & hops down off thi perch. Ith ther anythin i can get u, Mr Bathcule?

No, Dartlin, am gettin bettir ol thi time, fanks. Juss u keep yoo eers opin tho; I like heerin about ol this stuf.

My pwezhir. Thure i cant get u somthin 2 eet, perhapth?

No, am fine.

Vewy well.

Dartlin hops 2wards thi edje ov thi box lukin out ovir thi dark canyin. It preens itsself a bit, then balansis on thi edje, lukes roun 2 say, Well, bye then . . . but iss litl voyce sorta trailz off, & it lukes bak roun 2 thi outside & then it stars shiverin & it jumps bak & almost falls ovir & keeps jumpin bak until iss underneef mi perch.

Dartlin! I shout. Whas thi mattir? Whot is it? & I luke down @ thi litl fellir & hees juss pressd bak agenst thi reer ov thi box & qwiverin wif frite, hiz tiny Is buljin & starin & not seein me, & meenwhile thers movemint & thi soun ov flutirn wings outside thi box & sum whisperd sqwawks. A cupil ov larje dark shapes flit past thi entrinse 2 thi box.

Dartlin shaiks like thi poor littl buggurs ½in his own pryvit erfqwake.

He lukes @ me & wails, Feerth, Mr Bathcule! Feerth! & then juss keels ovir on2 thi flor ov thi box, his Is stil opin.

Dartlin! I sez, not shoutin, but I doan fink this sparo's goan 2 b doin no more spyin nor flyin. I can c his flees gettin redy 2 move out ov his scrawny littl bod, & thas always thi wurst ov sines.

I luke up agen & thers more movemint & a rustlin sound

from outside & then suddinly thi noys ov uge grate wings flappin.

A crow pops itz hed roun thi side ov thi box.

It lukes @ me wif 1 beedy blak glintin I & croaks,

Yeh thass im, muss b im.

It disapeers b 4 I can say anyfin.

Then there's a face @ thi entrins 2 thi box, & I cant beleve it; its a hoomin face, a hoomin hed but its bin flayed, iss got no skin on it @ ol & its ol red with blud & u can c tendons & mussils & its Is r starin out wif no lids neethir but iss also got thi biggist smile u evir seen & its held in thi claws ov sum huge bird I cant c apart from its talons & lower legs; thi talons r holdin thi hed by thi eers & thi hed opins its mouf & starts makin this weerd noise, incredibly loud & gutteril & its tung comes out, but iss not a ordinary tung iss far 2 long 4 a start & iss flapin & lashin & thi hed's makin this screemin noise & thi tung is snakin rite @ me & iss got hooks & claws @ thi end ov it & thi tung flix 2wards me & I jump bakwards off thi perch & land almost on top ov Dartlin's body & thi tung is snappin bak & 4th ovir thi top ov thi perch tryin 2 get me & Im peckin & screetchin & tryin 2 get @ it with my talons but its 2 hi up & ol thi while this hoarse cacofoni ov noise is ringin in ma eers & @ furst I think its screemin Gimme gimme gimme but it isnt, iss moar like Gididibididibididigididigigigibididigibibibi ol run 2gether like that like iss a mashine gun or sumthin & thi tung lashiz bak roun thi top ov thi perch & down & now iss cummin strait 4 me & I slash @ it wif mi talons but it twists & grabs my rite wing & starts 2 pool & am scretchin & iss goin gididibibibigigigibigigigibibigigi & am tryin 2 hold on2 thi perch wif 1 talon & scratch thi tung wif thi othir & peck @ it 2 & its tearin ma wing off, brakin it & it snaps & it pools off a hole buncha fevirs & thi orribil face gets a moufful ov those & I hop bak agen 2 thi reer ov thi box, flappin & screetchin & trailin mi broken wing; thi tung fliks bak in & I kik littl Dartlin's body @ it & thi tung raps tite round it & pulls it bak but throws it away when it gets it outside & iss still hammerin away wif this gigigibididibibibigigigi stuf fillin mi eers & am juss about 2 die ov frite as thi tung cums snappin 2wards mi face when it goze gididibibibibibibigididibigiBasculefastawake!

– & am bak in thi study ov thi gargoil Rosbrith sqwattin on

thi chair & starin @ this hooj hoomin Mr Zoliparia holdin a pen & shakin my sholdir & goin, Bascule? U olrite?

It can b a bit ov a shok watchin sumbodi cum out ov a kript trip; if its only a minit in yoor time its a week in thers & a lot ov fings can happen in a week & if its been a bad 1 it tends 2 sho in yoor face, so 4 thi persin wakin u up its like they tel u 2 wake up & instantly yoor face goes old & paind & worn-lookin & thi persin finks O no, whot 1/2 I dun?

Am sqwattin on thi balustrade whare Ergates woz liftid from, hunkerd down takin moar t & biskits wif Mr Zoliparia. He's lookin a bit worryd coz Im sqwattin here facin thi drop like am about 2 lonch miself in2 thi air, but ther is thi safety net aftir ol & nway I juss feel cumfterbil perched here & I like thi vew & thi feel ov thi wind on mi face.

My left arm has that sorta echo-pain u get from a bad kript trip injury & I keep wantin 2 lift thi biskits wif my foot & eet them that way but I fink am graduly loosin mi birdishnes. I can tel Mr Zoliparia wants 2 ask me lots ov qwestyons but Im stil findin it a bit hard 2 tok.

Few, that woz a hard ole kript trip that 1. I supose u cood argu I shood 1/2 taken a bit more time & juss sent a send ov miself in; a image or construct whood 1/2 dun everyfin I did & felt everyfin I felt & in fact wude 1/2 been a dooplicate me, xcept meanwhile Id stil 1/2 been fooly conshis here wif Mr Zoliparia, but it takes much longir doin it that way; u 1/2 2 prepare furrily b4 u go & u 1/2 2 spend ages reeintigratin yoor 2 selvs when thi send cums bak, sortin memirys & feelins & caractir chainjes & so on; juss jumpin in & out wif thi 1 persinality is a lot qwicker; less than a sekind rather than up 2 1/2 a day . . . but ov coarse that supposid sekind dozent alow 4 thi persin whots supposed 2 wake u up gettin confused bcoz almost thi lass thing u sed 2 him woz, 'Juss giv me a minit heer,' & them totily misunderstandin whot u ment on account ov them bein old & confused, & so u spendin a week in thi kript insted ov a few ours, & thusly gettin so alterd by yoor kript-self that u fink yoor a blinkin hok 4 thi next cupil ov ours.

I c a flok ov smol birdz in thi distince & while 1 1/2 ov me's finkin, this is how this ol started, & rememberin that poor deer litl ant, thi othir 1/2 is goin, Ha! Prey!

* * *

No I doan fink it is ol a haloosinayshin, Mr Zoliparia, I sez (am missin out thi bits whare he keeps apologisin 4 what hapind). I fink its ol as tru as u & me sittin here. Thers sumfin happenin in thi kript; I coodin work out whot part ov its 2 do wif thi palas & whot part is 2 do wif thi kaotic reejins, but thers sumfin goan on, & thers a wotch bein kept 4 sumbody or sumfin unusual in thare & out here 2, + sumthin reely disgustin from thi hoomin relm has axsess 2 thi bird part ov thi kript & has sikured thi copperashin ov @ least sum ov thi birdz.

It ol sound moar like a nitemare, speshily thi lass part, Mr Zoliparia sez.

Weer boaf sittin now; I feel less like a hok ol thi time. Mind u, I stil need 2 b out here on thi balcony; doan like thi thot ov goin inside & bein trapt.

I saw it wif mi own Is, Mr Zoliparia. I no u doan hold wif thi kript & ol & fink its ol a dreem nway, but iss not that simpl, & whot I saw I saw, & I nevir seen nor herd ov nuffink like that fing like a flaid hed & makin that orribl noise; I meen, u heer stories ov goasts & beasties & stuf like that from thi kaotic relms cumin up & snatchin peepil & gobblin them up, but u nevir c it happen; that stufs juss mif; this woz reel.

U r sure dat bcoz it had a hoomin hed it wos sumtin from di hoomin part ov di kript?

Thas thi way it wurx, Mr Zoliparia. It woz sumfin that had 2 preserv hoomin form evin in its monstrisness or it coodin funkshin, or mayb bcoz it mite $1/2$ let thi birdz c whot it woz reely like, which givin that birdz doan much like hoomins in thi furst place, is sayin sumfin.

& it woz after u.

It shure woz. Am not sayin I am what thare actuli lookin 4 – doan xpect I am – but thare catchin & cajin evrybody a bit diffrint or suspishis & that hed fing seems 2 b involved in thi round-up.

Mr Zoliparia shakes his hed. O deer Bascule, o deer.

Nevir mind, Mr Zoliparia. No harm dun.

Thass tru, Bascule; lease u bak heer safe & soun, no tanks 2 me. Nway, i tink u shude keep away from thi kript 4 a bit, doan u?

Wel that mite b a idear, Mr Zoliparia, I sez. U certinly got a point thare.

Good boy, he sez. I no; why doan we play a game? Or mayb u wude like 2 go 4 a wok; take a constichewshinil roun sum ov thi terrices on thi roof, mayb stop off sumware 4 lunch – wot u say, Bascule?

Ol soundz good 2 me, Mr Zoliparia.

Less do boat tings, he lafs. Weel go 4 a wok but weel take di portibil Go board wif us & 1/2 a game ovir a nice long lunch @ a rathir nice restoront i no.

Good idear, Mr Zoliparia. Thas a fine ole complicatid game, that Go.

Rite! Ahl get di Go, den weel go! he lafs, & he jumps up & heds indoars. Drink up yoor t! he shouts.

I luke out @ them birdz again, circlin above a far towr. I doan want 2 tel Mr Zoliparia but am goan strait bak in thare 2 that kript juss as soon as I feel abil. I stil want 2 find out whot happind 2 poor Ergates, but I want 2 no whots goan on, 2.

Truth b told, it terryfys me 1/2 2 def jus finkin about it, but I got this feelin I lerned a lot while I woz in thi kript today & iss tru whot they say; iss like a addictiv game, & lnce u cum out ov it a bit brused & woondid, thi furst thing u want 2 do is get strate bak in thare & get it rite next time. I juss woan fink about that horribl hed fing.

I finish my t & tidy up thi cups & stuf (u 1/2 2 do this @ Mr Zoliparias cos he hasnt eny servitors) & take thi tray inside juss as heez puttin on his coat & stuffin thi portabil Go board in his pokit.

Redy, Bascule? he asks.

Am redy, Mr Zoliparia.

Redy ol rite. Big stuf happenin in thi kript & sum poor buggir bein huntid & me wif a hed start on thi peepil doin thi huntin.

Bascule thi rascule thas me & am moar than redy; am *feerce*.

A litl bird tole me.

FOUR

1

When she awoke there was a halo of light all around the circular bed; the light led up forever into and beyond the sky and shrank to a point that was both the source of the light and a calm, dark hole.

She wondered where the ceiling had gone.

The light was like nothing she had ever seen or even had any words for; it was at once absolutely smooth, uniform and pure, and somehow wildly various, composed of every hue there were words to describe and many more besides; it was every shade and intensity of every colour any eye or instrument ever born or made had ever been able to distinguish, and it was the utter un-colour of profound darkness too.

As she sat up, the tunnel of light moved with her so that she was always looking straight into it, until she was gazing down to the end of the bed over the little hills her feet made in the soft coverings. Now the tunnel of light led away across where the floor ought to be and out through the tall windows and over the balcony and the lawns outside. It was as though in that silent gloriousness she could see vague dim outlines of the earlier room around her, but the brilliant shining had made them the unreal world, not the real one.

She could remember waking and her journey through the garden and the hedge-castle and the talking heads and her conversations with the old man in this house; she could remember the two younger people and the lunch and supper they had taken together, and recall being shown to this room by the old man and the woman, and shown the bathroom by the woman, but all that was made as though into a dream by this utterly quiet cascade of light, so that now she could have believed that all of it had indeed been a fiction.

She crawled to the foot of the bed and slipped out of the covers. They had given her a beautiful nightgown of soft blue and she had worn it first then taken it off because it felt restricting, but now she reached back and slipped it on again.

They had given her slippers too but she stared into the light and could not bear to go back round the side of the bed to look for them, and so she set off into the light, walking gently with a flowing, measured tread, as though frightened her footsteps might bruise the fabric of this beckoning radiance.

The tunnel's floor was neither warm nor cold; it yielded to her soles but it was not soft. The air seemed to drift with her as she walked and she had the impression that with every step she took she moved a great but somehow natural distance, as if one could stand on a desert and look to a far mountain peak and suddenly be there on that summit, in the thin rush of cold air, looking at a line of hills on the horizon, and then be there too, and then turn and see a broad grassy plain in the distance and be there, standing on the warm earth with the tall swaying grass brushing at her legs and buzzing insects sounding lazy in the hot, damp air; she looked from there to a small hill where short grass grew around old, fallen stones and birds trilled overhead and from where she looked into a broad forest and then she was within the forest and surrounded by trees and didn't know where to go; everywhere she looked was the same, and she could no longer tell whether she was actually moving anywhere now or not and after a while realised that she was completely lost and so stood there, her mouth set in a tight line, her fists clenched and her brows furrowed as though trying to contain within herself the fury and perplexity she felt at still being enclosed by the night-dark jungle, until she noticed a cool shaft of soft light glowing through the branches, and was there, bathed in it but still surrounded by the green pouring weight of rustling foliage.

But then she smiled and lifted up her head and there in the sky was a beautiful moon, round and wide and welcoming.

She looked at it.

She went to the moon where a small ape-man tried to explain what was happening, but she didn't completely understand what he was telling her. She knew it was something important, and that she had something important to do, but she could not quite work out what. She set the memory aside. She would think about it later.

The moon disappeared.

In the distance there was a castle. Or, at least, something that looked like a castle. It rose above a blue line of hills in the far distance, castle-shaped but impossibly big; a blue outline painted on the pale air, flat- and even upside-down-looking, not because it was not the correct shape for a castle – it was exactly the right shape – but because the higher up you looked the clearer the castle appeared.

Its horizon-spanning, many-towered outer wall was barely visible through the heat-haze above the hills, while the bulk of its sky-filling middle section was more defined, although obscured by cloud in places; its upper storeys and highest towers shone with a pale whiteness that brightened with altitude, and the tallest tower of all, just off-centre, positively glowed towards its summit, its sharpness giving it the perverse appearance of proximity despite its obvious extreme height.

She sat in an open carriage drawn by eight fabulous black cat-beasts whose silky fur pulsed with muscly movement beneath harnesses of damascened silver. They rippled along a road of dusty red tiles, each one of which bore a different pictogram picked out in yellow, between fields of grasses and shining flowers; the air whistling past was thick, humid and perfumed and full of birdsong and insect buzz.

Her clothes were delicate and fine and coloured lighter than her skin; soft ankle boots, a long flowing skirt, a short gilet over a loose shirt, and a sizable, firm-surfaced but very light hat with green ribbons which flew out in the slipstream.

She looked behind her at the road stretching back into the distance; the dust of their passing hung in the air, slowly drifting. She gazed around and saw far-away towers, spires and windmills scattered across the cultivated plain. The road ahead led straight towards the wooded hills and the vast castle-shape hanging above.

She looked up; directly over the carriage a flock of large, sleek grey birds were flying in an arrow-head formation, keeping station with the carriage with purposeful, coordinated wing beats. She clapped her hands and laughed, then sat back in the soft blue upholstery of the carriage seat.

There was a man sitting in the seat across from her. She stared. He hadn't been there before.

He was pale-skinned and young and dressed in tight black clothes which matched his hair. He didn't look quite right; he and his clothes looked speckled somehow, and she could see through him, as though he was made of smoke.

The man swivelled round and looked behind him, towards the castle. He crackled as he moved. He turned back.

'This won't work, you know,' he said, his voice whining and cracked.

She frowned, staring at him. She tipped her head on one side.

'Oh, you look very cute and innocent, to be sure, but that won't save you, my dear. I know you can't, but just for form's— ' The young man broke off as several of the escort birds stooped screaming at him, talons spread. He batted one away with an insubstantial fist and seized another by the neck without taking his eyes off her. He wrung the bird's neck while it struggled, wings beating madly, in his hands. There was a snap. He threw the limp body over the side of the carriage.

She stared at him, appalled. He produced a heavy umbrella of darkest blue and spread it over his head as the keening birds attacked.

'As I was saying, my dear; I know you don't really have any choice in this, but for form's sake – so that when we do have to kill you we feel at least we gave you a chance – hear this; cease and desist, now. Do you understand? Go back to where you came from, or just stay where you are, but *don't* go any further.'

She looked over the rear of the carriage at the body of the bird the man had killed, lying crumpled on the roadway, already almost out of sight. The rest of the flock swooped and screamed and battered off the thick fabric of the night-blue umbrella.

Tears came to her eyes.

'Oh, don't cry,' he said tiredly, sighing. 'That was nothing.' He waved one arm through his own body. '*I* am nothing. There are things a *lot* worse than me waiting for you, if you continue.'

She frowned at him. 'I Asura,' she said. 'Who you?'

He gave a high, whinnying laugh. 'Asura; that's rich.'

'Who are you?' she asked.

'KIP, doll. Don't be silly.'

'You are Kayeyepee?'

'Oh for goodness sake,' the man said, with an exaggerated isn't-this-tedious roll of the eyes. 'Are you *really* this naïve? KIP,' he repeated, sneering. 'Cliché number one, you stupid bitch; Knowledge Is Power.' He grinned. '*Asura.*'

Then he opened his eyes wide, leant forward at her and made a funny face. He sucked in, his cheeks concaving and his eyes staring while the air went *sss* through his pursed mouth. He sucked harder and harder and his skin stretched and his lips disappeared and his nose came down to his mouth and she could see the pink skin under his eyes; then his skin ripped somewhere behind and suddenly it was all flowing in through his mouth; nose, skin, ears, hair; everything sucked in through his widening mouth, leaving his face bloody and slimed and his mouth fixed in a great broad lipless grin and his lidless eyes staring while he swallowed noisily and then opened his raw red mouth and between gleaming yellow-white teeth screamed at her, 'Gibibibibibigididibigigibididigigigibibigibibi!'

She screamed too, and covered her face with her hands, then shrieked as something touched her neck and jerked back.

The birds had clustered round the man's face; four of them had snagged the umbrella in their talons and lifted it away; the rest beat and keened in a storm of wings around the man's face, where something long and red lashed to and fro, beset by pecking, tearing birds.

She sat and watched, horrified, while the birds tore at the man's face and the long lashing thing; an awful bubbling scream forced its way out through the fury of thrashing wings, then suddenly the man was gone, becoming smoke again for an instant before vanishing utterly.

The birds lifted in the same moment and resumed their arrow-head formation above. No trace was left of the fight, not even a fallen feather. The same number of birds beat rhythmically over the carriage. The great black cats pounded on down the road, having taken not the slightest notice of the struggle.

She shivered despite the heat, looked all around, then settled back in her seat, smoothing her clothes.

Then there was a soft *pop*! and flying next to her face there was a tiny bat with a livid, skinned-red face.

'Still think it's such a good idea, sister?' it squeaked.

She grabbed at the bat but it flicked easily away from her grasp before side-slipping back towards her. 'KIP!' it hooted, giggling. 'KIP!'

She hissed in exasperation. 'Serotine!' she cried – surprising herself – and snatched the bat out of the air.

It had time to look surprised and to go 'Eek!' before she twisted its neck and threw it behind her. It thumped twitching onto the road. The last she saw, one of the escort birds had landed beside the body and started pecking at it.

She dusted her hands and looked through narrowed eyes at the vast, vague, unchanged shape of the castle above the distant hills.

The carriage bowled onwards, the thick warm wind whistled past, the birds stroked the air above and the giant cats swept along the dusty red road like a wave of night engulfing sunset.

She felt sleepy.

In the morning they found her dressed and sitting at the breakfast table.

'Good morning!' she said brightly to them. 'Today I have to leave.'

2

He took the Queen by the shoulders and pushed her back so that she had to sit upon the bed. 'You go not,' he told her, 'till I set you up a glass where you may see the inmost part of you.'

'What wilt thou do? Thou wilt not murder me?' she cried. 'Help, help, ho!'

Then from behind the arras came another voice, that of an old man: 'What, ho! Help, help, help!'

He spun towards the noise, shouting, 'How now! A rat?' He drew his sword, swinging it towards the tapestry. 'Dead, for a ducat— ' He swept the arras aside with the tip of the sword, revealing the quivering figure of Polonius. '– Or just trapped, and justly?'

'My lord!' the old man cried, and sank, stiffly, to one knee.

'Why then, not a rat, a mouse! What say you, good mouse, or hast the cat your tongue?'

– the King paused there.

It was always a moment to savour, in this branching of the improved story; the point where the Prince began to get his act together and behave neither tactically too rashly nor strategically too hesitantly. From now on you just knew he was going to prevail, avenging his father, marrying Ophelia, ruling wisely in a flourishing Denmark and living happily ever after (well, until he died).

The King liked happy endings. You couldn't blame the ancients for coming up with unhappy conclusions so often – they each spent all their single short life waiting either for oblivion or some absurd after-death torture – but that didn't mean you had to stick faithfully to their paralysed paradigms and ruin a good story with a depressing dénouement.

He sighed happily and got up from the bed, exiting via its foot so as not to disturb the voluptuous forms of the sleeping Luge twins, between whom he'd been lying.

Adijine had woken – still sated but desiring some form of diversion – a little earlier, in what might fairly be termed the middle of the night. His pillow contained a transceptor array similar to the device in his crown which let him access the data corpus; it made a pleasant change to dip into the crypt without that thing on his head. The revised inter-active *Hamlet* was one of his favourites, though it could still be a little long, depending on the choices one made.

He left the Luge twins breathing softly beneath their silk sheet and padded across the warm pelt of the bedroom carpet to the windows. He took some satisfaction in pressing the button that opened the curtains, rather than simply thinking them apart.

Moonlight spilled across the mountains that were the roofs of the fastness; the sky above was cloudless. Stars filled half the vault. The darkness of the other half was absolute.

The King stared up into that inkiness for a while. That was all their dooms, he thought, all their rash mistakes and compensating hesitancies, on the far side of the curtain. He let the drapes sweep back and – stretching, scratching the back of his head – returned to the bed.

The sight of the Encroachment had left him restless. He lay between the sleeping girls and pulled a cover over himself, unsure what to do next.

He glanced into the crypt, first at the paused *Hamlet*, then at the general security situation, then at the state of the war – still stalemated – and at the progress the bomb-workings were making in the level-five south-western solar – still struggling, still hoping to initiate in a few days, and still tightly controlled by Security – then swung through a few minds, finding various couples coupling and finding his own sexual interest piqued despite his earlier exertions with the almost insatiable Luge twins. He turned away from that for a moment, roaming through the accessible minds still awake in Serehfa, and looked for a moment into that of the Security agent they'd placed with the Chief Scientist Gadfium.

So, they were still up at this hour.

Adijine pondered the significance of the strange and unprecedented circular pattern the stones had formed, and wondered if Gadfium had come up with any explanations. Were the stones also linked into the crypt somehow? His Cryptographers seemed puzzled by some of the corpus' deeper-level behaviour as well as by some of the upper-level and even physical manifestations of those disturbances. Was the crypt preparing to intervene in the present emergency? If it was, he wanted to know. Gadfium was no more trustworthy than any other Privileged, but she had had a habit of making good guesses in the past, and if anybody was to furnish him with the first warning of the crypt's interference, it might well be her, one way or the other.

Gadfium. It had annoyed the King throughout his this life-time – and Gadfium's last two – that she had stuck with the male version of her name; why hadn't she changed it to Gadfia when he had become a she between incarnations? Wilful type, Gadfium.

He listened in, through the agent.

'I beg your pardon, Chief Scientist?' Rasfline said.

'I said,' Gadfium replied, sighing, 'I'd like the data on brand new births displayed related to each clan's vault, from five years before the new dating system came into use, compensated for clan size.'

'I beg your pardon,' Rasfline said, obviously embarrassed at seemingly being caught either day-dreaming or dozing. 'At once.' The wall screen cleared the previous three-dimensional display and replaced it with the new bar field.

'Hmm,' she said, scrutinising the display and realising she could not recall exactly why she had asked for it.

'I *do* apologise, ma'am,' Rasfline said, sounding mortified.

'That's quite all right,' Gadfium told him, still staring at the display. 'We're all tired.'

She glanced at Goscil, who was yawning again, though somehow still with a look of concentration on her face as she sat, eyes fixed straight ahead, unseeing, while she reviewed some other aspect of the Sortileger's files.

The same light tragenter that had taken them to the mobile observatory on the Plain of Sliding Stones had returned them to the elevator, which had dropped them through the thickness of the roof itself and the kilometre-deep space of the room below; a cold, gloomy, barren place where flutes of scree and bahada lay slumped against the walls and thin lancet windows cast mean slivers of light across a dark desert of broken stones where even babilia struggled to grow.

An Army scree-car had jolted them to where a hole let into one wall led to a tunnel and a restricted funicular; they exited to the sixth level on a broad shelf where subsistence farms made the most of the cold and still thin atmosphere and the light came from broad, full-length windows looking out onto a sea of air where little puffy clouds sat like white islands.

A hydrovator had lowered them to the floor and a piker swept them between machine-tended fields to the terminus of the clifter they had ascended in. The tethered balloon had vented gas and sunk quickly through the next three levels, their ears popping as they entered a sunny farm room, a shady suburb solar and then an artificially lit industrial chamber two concentrics in from the Great Hall. They had passed through dark, deserted, outlaw chambers beneath Engineer-controlled room-space in a fast armoured monorail and ascended to the Sortileger's office –

an old yamen housed within a piscina in the sunlit eastern chapel
– by airship.

The Sortileger Xemetrio met them at the dock, alone. 'Madam
Chief Scientist,' he said, taking her hands. 'Thank you for
coming.'

'My pleasure,' she murmured, smiling at him, then looking
down and taking her hands from his. 'I think you know my
staff; secretary Rasfline, scientific aide Goscil.'

'A delight, as ever,' the Sortileger said, nodding. He was a
tall barrel of a man, and another near-contemporary of the chief
scientist. His face was much lined but still firm and his hair was
a convincing jet-black.

Rasfline and Goscil returned the nod, Rasfline with a knowing
smirk to Goscil which she did not acknowledge.

'You seem to be much in demand, Chief Scientist,' Xemetrio
said as he led them to the doors.

'Indeed.'

'Yes, I understand you've been busy elsewhere today.'

'That's right,' Gadfium said, nodding.

'Ah.' The Sortileger looked like he wanted to inquire further,
but as they stepped through the doorway Gadfium asked:

'And what may we do here? Have you another of your . . .
glitches, Sortileger?'

Xemetrio nodded. 'It is the same problem, Chief Scientist, and
my staff seem unable to divine the source. Security maintain it
cannot be deliberate falsification by an operative, Cryptography
insist everything is in order at their end, therefore the problem
must lie here. Two days ago we predicted a cryptosauric event
which did not happen and today we failed to foresee the
assassination of a . . . well, somebody important. If this goes
on we'll soon be unable to forecast the weather . . .'

Goscil stood, her back stiff. She rubbed her eyes and stretched.
'No. If there's anything here, I can't see it.'

Gadfium turned away from the wall display. She watched
the other woman make circling motions with her arms. 'Well,'
she said. 'I think after this morning's rather pathetic faint-
ing fit I've regained a little self-respect, keeping you two
youngsters up this late.' She smiled, then she too yawned.
'There,' she laughed. 'Time for us all to head bedwards.'

She looked at Rasfline and nodded at the wall screen, which switched off.

They were in the display room of the Sortileger's office library, surrounded by records and accounts committed to almost every type of storage medium known to history.

'I'm not really tired, ma'am,' Rasfline said, sitting up sharply. 'I could continue to— '

'Well, *I'm* tired, Rasfline,' she told him. 'I think we'll all benefit from some sleep. It's been a long day. Perhaps in the morning when we're refreshed we might spot something.'

'Perhaps, Chief Scientist,' Rasfline said, reluctantly. He stood up, straightened his uniform and blinked rapidly, as though still trying to wake himself up.

Goscil rubbed absently at a stain on her tunic. 'Do you think the Sortileger is telling us the whole truth?' she asked, yawning. Rasfline shot her a look.

'I think we have to assume that,' Gadfium said reasonably, folding her note-file.

– The Sortileger, thought the King. He should be asleep by now.

Adijine left the chief scientist and her aides and shifted to Xemetrio's bed chamber. The old fellow was indeed asleep, and his head lay on a pillow which contained a receptor net.

... flying above a blue sea, blue wings beating on a warm wind; a green isle beneath, naked women languorous on the black sand, standing and pointing and shading their eyes at him as he wheeled and turned back towards them—

– Lucid dreaming again. Adijine had been in the Sortileger's sleeping mind before and always found the same thing: some erotic adventure, shallow, and ultimately more concealing than revealing.

He switched back to the others, and into Rasfline's mind, in time to hear him saying, 'Goodnight, ma'am,' and catch a fleeting, caricatured image of two old bodies coupling against a wall. Rasfline smirked at Goscil as they went to their separate rooms and Gadfium walked to hers. This time, Goscil returned the glance.

The King, intrigued by those looks, followed Gadfium by using some of the static cameras located throughout the yamen.

The chief scientist went to her own room, disrobed, washed

quickly, perfumed her stocky, grey-haired old body (good if obviously artificially maintained skin tone, the King noted, and breasts of such undeniable if assisted presence they were almost intimidating), slipped on a generously proportioned negligée, then checked the door monitor and slipped out of the room and along the darkened corridor.

Ah-*ha*, thought the King, following her to the Sortileger's own chambers.

Gadfium sat on the bed of the Sortileger Xemetrio, who had woken at her gentle knock on his door. A soft light shone from above the bed. The Sortileger sat up, took the chief scientist tenderly in his arms and kissed her. He reached behind her and undid her hair. Then he pressed her back so that her head lay near the foot of the bed, her long grey hair like veins of silver on the sheets under the footboard and her feet resting on a pillow.

– Damn! thought Adijine, who'd had to shift to a ceiling camera the instant Xemetrio had sat up and his head had left the pillow with the receptor net.

The Sortileger smiled down at Gadfium, then pulled the sheet up and over, covering both of them. The light went out.

The King cut away again, disappointed. He could have watched in IR from a concealed chamber camera but all he'd have seen was lumps moving under a sheet. It was a lot less fun than being in somebody's head.

Back in his own bed, Adijine looked down at his own hesitant tumescence, wondering if the Sortileger was simply making up the glitches in his forecasting department just to conduct these trysts with the chief scientist. Cause for concern. Perhaps dereliction of duty, especially in these straitened times. He'd let it pass this time but have Security keep an eye on the man. As for Gadfium, if anything she worked too hard and the King reckoned a little recreational fornication would do her no harm whatsoever.

He stroked his erection. He looked at the curvaceous shapes lying to either side of him.

Hmm; he was still a *little* tired.

Perhaps if he woke just one of the Luge twins . . .

*   *   *

The pen left lines of coolly luminous ink on the tiny pad Xemetrio had hidden under the sheets.

Good to see you again. Sometime we must do this for real!

You always say that.

Always mean it. What IS that perfume?

Enough. To business.

Funny name for a . . . No tickling!

There's been a signal from the tower.

I guessed: why I called.

She pulled the tiny tube that was the copied message from the hem of her nightdress. She handed it to him; he unrolled the flimsy and stared at the glowing letters.

3

Sessine walked through the darkened town, uphill and away from the direction of the ocean tunnel. A few people passed him in the quiet streets, but all avoided his eye. He reached the walls of the cavern – not rock but small glazed white tiles with networks of crazed cracks in them like little burst blood-vessels of black – where he turned left and walked until he reached the spill-sluice. It was a huge tunnel sloped at forty-five degrees or so, and from it, cascading down a series of steeply banked terraces, tipped a dirty froth of water which disappeared under a bridge and then wound away in a culvert towards the centre of the town and the docks beyond.

The tunnel was shaped like an inverted U and was perhaps ten metres across; steps led up the near side, separated from the rushing water only by a thin iron rail supported by spindly, rusting rods. Weak yellow lamps lit the tunnel roof sporadically, disappearing into the distance with no hint of any further light.

He started up the slope, and soon lost count of the steps and the time. He passed one man coming down, crying, and another lying snoring on the steps.

He came to the smoking-tavern called the Half-way House. It was just a door in the wall of the tunnel and a sign. He opened the door and found a quiet place scarcely lighter than the tunnel outside. A few people sat in booths and at tables; some looked up at him as he came in, then looked away again. A steady murmuring filled the air.

The circular bar held open shelves stacked with miniature braziers, smoking funnels and ornamental narghiles. It was tended by a hopfgeist in the shape of a tall, thin woman dressed all in black, with black, tied-back hair and dark, hooded eyes.

He walked towards the woman. She watched him, then beckoned him round to the rear of the bar, where there was a hatch cut out of the circle.

'Sir, I was told long ago you might stop by,' she said quietly. Her voice was flat and weary. 'Have you anything to say to me?'

'Yes, I have,' he said. '*Nosce teipsum.*'

It was his most-secret code, the one he had thought of once, a long time ago, in his first ever life, in case he ever needed some already-remembered code quickly one day. It was one he had never committed to any other form of storage other than his own memory and never told to anybody else, except this woman, assuming his previous self had been telling the truth in the note he'd found in the hotel room in Oubliette.

The tall woman nodded. 'That's as it should be,' she said, and sounded almost disappointed. She took a key from a chain round her neck and opened a small drawer set into the thickness of the bar counter. 'Here.' She handed him a small clay pipe, already charged. 'I think this is what you desire.' She put her hands on the counter, looking downwards.

'Thank you,' he told her. She nodded, not looking up.

He retreated to a dark, secluded booth lit by a small oil lamp set into the rock wall. He took a twisted paper spill from a nook to the side of the lamp and lit the pipe, drawing deeply on the thick, pungent smoke.

The bar faded slowly as though filling with smoke from the pipe. The murmuring rose to an ignorable roar; his head felt like a revolving planet, speeding up and shaking off its wrapping of atmosphere as if it was some excess piece of clothing, before disintegrating entirely and throwing him into space.

It was the day of the great curtain-wall road-race, held every year at the summer solstice. The race started from the western barbican, where the pits were housed and the majority of the great cars were garaged between race days. Banners and pennants flew from tents and caravans, temporary garage structures and anchored airships. A great crowd of people filled the network of scaffolded stands, bridges, stalls and viewing towers; cheers rang out across the marshalling areas and the smells of food drifted on the hot wind.

Sessine donned a light leather helmet and a pair of goggles and rolled down the sleeves of his shirt, fastening the cuffs to his sandskin gloves.

'Best of luck, sir!' the chief mechanic shouted, grinning. Sessine slapped her on the shoulder, then grasped the ladder and climbed, up through the damp smell of steam hissing from some venting valve, past the linking rods and the man-tall wheels, past the web of hydrogen pipes and hydraulic conduits webbing the main tank and on up to the curved top of the car. He waved down and the foot of the ladder was clipped up and secured.

He looked around, surveying the fifty or so cars and the barely controlled pandemonium of both the pits area and the stands beyond. Each of the mighty cars was fashioned after a particular model of steam railway engine from the Middle Ages; his was one of the first-marque machines, the largest and most powerful class in the race, created in the image of a 4–8–8–4 Mallet type used by the Union Pacific Railroad of North America, back in the twentieth century.

Sessine dropped into the Mallet's cramped cockpit, offset to the left at the rear of the huge locomotive, above where the engineer's cab would have been on the real thing. He strapped himself in, then ran through the instrument check. That done, he sat back for a while, breathing deeply and gazing round the stands and viewing towers, looking for where his wife would be sitting in the clan's own tower and wondering if his latest lover was watching from one of the old airships. The voice pipe whistled; he uncorked it. 'Ready, sir?' said the muffled voice of the chief engineer.

'Ready,' he said.

'All yours, sir. You have control.'

'I have control,' he confirmed, and recorked the voice pipe. His heart beat faster and he wiped sweat from his top lip with his shirt sleeve. He undid one glove and fished in a breast pocket for his ear plugs.

His hands were shaking, just a little.

The marshals' airship hovered pregnantly over the tall, flag-bedecked archway leading to the starting grid. After what seemed like an eternity the flags hanging under the dirigible changed from red to yellow and the crowd cheered wildly.

Sessine slipped the brake, eased the regulator on and fed power to the Mallet's wheels. The hydrogen engine shot a great detonating pulse of steam from its stack – easily twenty metres forward of where Sessine sat – hissed yet more clouds from the pistons below, and, with a great metallic groan and a crumping series of explosive steam-bursts within a cacophonous range of oiled clanking noises, the huge vehicle crept slowly forward, keeping station with the rest of the cars, all jetting steam and blasting whistles, spasmodically interspersing this symphonic din with the sudden racing solo of an engine briefly losing traction, sets of rubber-rimmed wheels slipping together on patches of oil, hydraulic fluid or water.

The race began half an hour later after various delays – every one of which seemed interminable – and much sweating and steaming and sweltering on the starting grid.

The huge cars started their charge round the wall-top roadway of Serehfa's curtain-wall, a half-kilometre wide surface of smooth roadway behind the semi-cylindrical towers. Each lap was a hundred and eighty kilometres in length, a distance the leading vehicles would complete in an hour; each race was three laps. The cars were accompanied by the marshals' airship and by a small cloud of camera platforms like swarming insects, feeding the spectacle to the implant and screen networks and the crowds watching from the viewing stands and towers.

Sessine took the lead when the clan Genetics' Beyer-Garratt burst a series of tyres and skidded off into the outer parapet in a great long articulated explosion of steam, metal and stone (and Sessine thought coldly, Well, that's old Werrieth out of the party tonight, and him onto his last life); debris spattered across the roadway in front of the Mallet but Sessine took the three hundred tonnes of car within metres of the flimsy inside wall, and missed the wreckage entirely.

He was in front! He screamed with delight, and was grateful

that the noise was inaudible within the staggering racket of the racing car; the wide roadway spread out in a gentle curve before him, empty and welcoming and sublime. The marshals' airship would be well behind the Mallet and the cloud of camera platforms just level with him. There were cameras and spectators on each of the towers, too, and more people – castlians and Xtremadurians – gathered in clumps on the outer walls, but they were blurs, irrelevant. He was alone; exulting and alone and free!

. . . He recognised the point, and was able to leave then, and so left his old self to drive, and slipped out of the seat, like a ghost, down through the hatch into the bellowing heart of the quivering machine where valves chattered and gases hissed and water gurgled and sweat popped from the skin in the oven-heat of the shrieking, vibrating engine.

And as he walked through the hammering din of the motor, he started to remember a little of what he had left here.

In a cramped corridor, on an open-work metal floor between great rods and levers darting back and forward like vast metallic tendons, he found his old first self, dressed in engineer's overalls and squatting hunched over a small table on which sat a chess board set in mid-game.

He squatted down too. His younger self did not look up. He was staring at the white pieces, the tip of one thumb in his mouth.

'Silician defence,' the young man said after a while, nodding at the board.

Sessine nodded, outwardly calm but thinking furiously. He knew he was faced with some sort of test but he had no predetermined code to cover this meeting, only the fact that, once, he and this young man had been the same person.

Silician? Not Sicilian?

Silician; Silicia; Cilicia. It meant something. Somebody he'd heard of had been Silician. An ancient.

He searched his memories, willing some connection. Tarzan? Tarsus? Then he remembered some lines from an ancient poem:

Me Tarsan, you Jesus.
And the Silician never really changed.

Ah, yes.

'Professor Sauli played it often,' he said. 'While working on the exclusion principle.'

The young man looked up and smiled briefly. He rose and put out his hand. Sessine shook it.

'Good to meet you, Alandre,' the young man said.

'And you,' Sessine said, hesitating. '. . . Alandre?'

'Oh, call me Alan,' his younger self said. 'I'm only an abbreviated version of who you are now, though I've developed on my own in here.'

'Having recently been abbreviated myself, I sympathise, Alan.'

'Hmm,' the other man said. 'Well, the first thing to do is to get you out of where you are now. Let's see . . .' He looked down at the chess board and turned both the white castles upside down.

The board blossomed with a semi-transparent holo of Serehfa. Alan studied it for a moment, then reached into and beneath it – and Sessine saw the projection of the castle's fabric bulge and swell around the young man's hand as with an infinitesimal articulation of his fingers he plucked something out of the bowels of the model fastness – Sessine experienced a fleeting sense of vertigo – and deposited it at the side of the chequered surface. Then Alan folded up the chess board and the castle projection vanished.

'Was that me?' Sessine asked casually, leaning to glance at the board.

'It was.'

'So where am I now?'

'Your construct now inhabits hardware situated within the curtain-walls.'

'Is that good?'

Alan shrugged. 'It's safer.'

'Well, thank you.'

'You're welcome,' his younger self said. 'So.' He clapped his hands on his knees. 'You're my last incarnation.'

Sessine looked into his eyes. It was true; as the self aged, and grew to awareness, filtered and downloaded into a new version of the old body, a meta-aging took place over the lives: a serial, cumulative maturing that was visible in the face unless you strove by further tampering to eradicate it. How fresh and innocent this earlier face of his appeared, and yet this seeming youth had been forty years old when he'd recorded this construct and left it free – almost forgotten and just-short-of-unreachable – to flit between the interstices of his personal lives and his clan's concerns: monitoring, collating, reviewing and evaluating.

'Yes, I'm the very last,' Sessine agreed. 'And you are the ghost in the machine.'

He smiled, and wondered as he did so what possible point there was in the gesture. 'So. What do you have to tell me?'

'Well, for one thing, Count,' Alan said, 'I know who is trying to kill you.'

4

Av got a very good view ov thi fass-towr from heer. Am $1/2$ lying & $1/2$ sittin craidled by thi babil branchis & am lookin up fru a gap in thi foleyidje @ thi dirti grate hoojness ov thi cassils centril towr.

U forget thi towrs thare a lot ov thi time coz (a) itz usyuly bhind u· if yoor lookin out thi way from thi cassil & (b) iss obskyurd by cloud moar than $1/2$ thi time nway.

According 2 Mr Zoliparia thi fass-towr is whare thi spays elivaitr woz ankird 2 Erf.

Thass y iss cald a fassness, Mr Zoliparia sez; in Inglish fassness means a stronghold, & also bcoz when fings r tied hard agenst eech othir they r sed 2 b tyed fast 2 eech othir like thi spays elivaitr woz tyed fast 2 Erf, & in a sens tyed 2 thi Erfs surfis & spays togethir, 2 (I sed; + thi spays elivaitr woz a way ov gettin in2 spaice fast; but Mr Z sed no actuly it woz slower than a rokit or whotevir but mutch moar efishint). Mr Zoliparia thot thi spayce elivaitr woz a grate idear & it woz a shame weed got rid ov it & if we hadnt then we wooden b in thi pickl we r, i e about 2 get clobberd by thi enkroachment.

But I thot spaice woz juss ful ov nufink I sed 2 Mr Zoliparia. Whats thi point ov goan thare?

Bascule, he sed, u r so fik sumtimes.

He tole me thi fass towr led 2 thi planetz & thi starz; 1nce u were in spaice u had limitles enirgy & raw mateeryls & after that branepowir took u wharevir u wantid but weed throne ol that away.

Mr Zoliparia sez thi fass towr reprisentz sumfin ov a nigma, on account that we doan striktly speekin no whot's actuly in thi top ov it; iss bin xploard up 2 about thi 10th or 11th levils but aftir that u cant get no hyer, so they say. Blokd on thi inside & nuthin 2 hold on2 on thi outside & 2 hi up 4 a balune or a aircraft 2 go. Thi nolidje ov whot's up thare's bin loss long ago in thi kaos ov thi kript, sez Mr Z.

U heer roomers that ther r peeple up thare in thi top ov thi towr but thas got 2 b nonsins; howd they breev?

Mr Zoliparia iznt thi onli persin 2 1/2 feeries concernin thi big towr; Ergates thi ant told me ther used 2 b 3 spaice elevaitrs; 1 heer, 1 in Afrika neer a place calld Kilomenjaro & 1 in Kalimantan. According 2 hir, thayve ol been dismantled long sinse ov coarse but weev got thi biggist stump on acount ov hooever disined thi American Kontinent spays elivaitr had thi wizird idear ov makin thi terminus particularly spektaklier & so desined it 2 luke like a hooj cassil, viz thi vastniss ov thi fastniss (which she claymd used 2 b calld Acsets, which wos anuthir ov them nacronyms, aparrintly).

I thot this ol soundid a bit iffy & askd Mr Z if heed evir herd ov ther bin uthir fass towrs & he sed nope, not as far as he new, & shurenuf when I serchd thi kript 4 info ther woznt eny on no othir elevaters & when u actuly luke in2 it ther dozen seem 2 b enywhare whare it sez strate out 'Thi fass-towr usd 2 b 1 end ov a spaice elivaitor,' tho iss not a secret. Nway, Kilomenjaro is a lake & Kalimantan is a big island (itz got a Crater Lake 2) & I think Ergates imajinayshin wos runnin away wif hir a bit thare & bsides if her feery wos rite thi name ov this plaice wood bgin wif a K not a S or a A, stands 2 reesin.

Poor Ergates. I stil wundir whot happind 2 that deer litl ant, evin tho Ive got plenty ov othir things 2 wury about now.

I turn ovir in thi litl nest Ive made 4 myself in thi babil branchis & luke down thi curvd trunk 2 thi wall. Nobodi els aroun. Lukes like I gaiv thi bastirds thi slip.

My sholdir stil hurts. So do my rists & my nees.

O whot a sorry state weer in, yung Bascule, I sez 2 myself.

I juss no that soonir or later am goan 2 1/2 2 go bak in2 thi kript 2 find out what on erfs goan on, evin tho thi last fing thi big bat sed woz not 2. Doan think iss goan b much fun.

Am fritend.

U c, Ive bcome a outcast.

I 1/2 2 say I had a very plesint lunch wif Mr Zoliparia & a good game ov Go which he 1 ov coarse (like he alwiz duz) in this travelin restront. Thi restront starts in a verticil vilij in thi babil neer thi top ov thi grate hol gaybil & sloely dessends 2 flore levil ovir thi next cupl ov ours. Good food & vews. Nway, I had a ver nice time & almost toatly 4got abowt Dartlin & thi jiant brane in bird space & orribl skind heds & fings whot go gididibibibigididibigigi & so on.

Me & Mr Zoliparia tokd about loads ov stuf.

Eventuly tho it woz time 4 me 2 go bcoz I stil had evenin callz 2 do 4 thi Little Big Bruthirs & they like u 2 b thare in thi monastry 2 do them & Id alredy dun 1 lot on thi hoof as it wer that mornin in thi hydrovater so I thot 4 thi evenin 1s I ot 2 actuly b thare wifin thi preesinkts.

Mr Z saw me 2 thi west wol toob trane.

U promis u woan go bak in2 that kript until u 1/2 2? Until yor bak wit de bruders? Mr Z sed 2 me, & I sed, O ol rite then Mr Zoliparia.

Good boy, he sed.

Evrifin went as per normil til I got 2 thi othir end whare ther woz a long wait @ thi hydrovater. I thot ov a betir idear & took a travelater acros thi alure 2 a fewnikuler line up a flyin buttriss; Id get 2 thi monastry by dropin from abuv.

Ther wer a cupl ov noviss bruthirs in thi fewnikuler car wif me; they wer a bit drunk, & singin loudly. I thot 1 ov them seemd 2 rekognise me but I juss lookt away & he ignoard me 2.

They kept singin as thi car wen slowly up thi curve ov thi buttris. I wooden 1/2 minded, but they woz out ov tune.

Little-Big, Little-Big, Little-Big!
We're thi Mediums who don't give a fig!

Wel, heerza fine 2-do, I sed 2 myself, cyan & starin out thi window & tryin 2 ignore thi noyse & ther beery brefs. I lookt out thi windo; it woz dusk by this time & thi lites wer on in thi fewnikular car's cabin & thi sky outside lookt pretti & ver culirfil.

When you're dead, when you're dead, when you're dead,
We'll happily live inside your heh – ehd!

O, whot thi hek, I thot.

In a way whot I woz goan 2 do wude make thi trip longer not shorter but @ least Id ½ sum respite from ol this cheeri-drunkin shit, & evin if I forgot my return code agen theez noizi prats wude wake me up soon enuf. I dipt in2 thi kript, intendin 2 spend mayb ½ a sekind in thare.

Les than that woz qwite enuf.

Ther wos sumthin goin on.

Thi furst place u go from transport is in2 a representayshin ov thi cassils transport sistim, a transparint holo ov thi fastniss with thi toob, train & fewnikuler lines, lift shafts, roads, hydrovater lines & clifter slots ol highlited. Then u moov on 2 whare u want 2 go elsewhare in thi kript. Moast bags doan evin spare this setup a passin glanse, but if yoor sumthin ov a conasewer ov thi kript's states, like I am, then u juss alwiz swing pass this sort ov fing & chek it out & do a qwik comparisun wif actule movemints 2 c if Transports on its bols or not. Upshot is, if thers anythin amiss u spot it, like I spottd thi transport setup woznt qwite rite.

It lookd like ther woz a odd kinda hole aroun thi monastry; nuthin movin out, juss stuff in-goin. Ver strainj, I thot. I didn go no furthir in2 thi kript. I chekd thi monastrys kript-biz durin thi afternoon. Definit faze-chainj in thi trafic aroun a our ago. Sumbodi tryin 2 make thing luke normil when they wernt.

Whare woz bro Scalopins usual col 2 thi *Marshin Daze* storyline, 4 exampil? Or sis Ecropé's t-time interlope wif hir luvir in thi Uitlandir embassy? Ol replaicd by makin-up-numbers trafic, thats whare.

I new I woz probly bin paranoid, but I woried ol thi saim.

Thi fewnikuler woz dew 2 make 1 more stop b4 thi stayshin Id normaly get off @. I told it 2 stop asap.

A minit later it did, & I got off @ this litl sily halt ¾ ov thi way up thi butris which served a cupl ov clan-execs luv nests, a old babil farm & a glider club, all ov them desertid. Thi 2 bros

I left on thi fewnikuler lookd puzzld but waivd by-by & kept singin as thi car trundld away agen.

Then ther woz a thump in mi hed. Thi fewnikular car stopt, then reversd & clunked & whird bak down 2wards me.

Thi thump in mi hed woz sum bastird tryin 2 nok me out wif a bit ov feedbak from thi kript; fearetikly imposibl & teknikly diffcult but it can b dun & thi jolt Id juss got wude $1/2$ nokd out moast peepil, only Ive got thi eqwivalent ov shok absorbers coz Im a tellir & ther4 used 2 gettin a ruf ride from thi kript.

Thi fewnikewlar car woz comin glowing bak down thi curvd track, its cabin lites reflectin off thi babil plants festoonin thi broad archd bak ov thi butris. Thi 2 bros inside wer @ thi bak windo, starin @ me. They din luke so drunk now, & they wos each holdin fings in ther hands that could $1/2$ bin guns.

O shit, I fot.

I ran down a spiral stareway @ thi side ov thi butriss. I herd thi car stop abuv me. Thi stairway went on & on & on & on spiralin all thi time & I thot when it levils out am not goan b able 2 stop goan roun; theyl find me whirlin roun in a tite litl circl unabil 2 go strate. I hit thi botom & sheer terrir proovd a ver iffishint coarse-stratener. I raced across a gantry slung underneaf thi stonewurk & went down anothir stairway set agenst a metil-frame bildin on thi far side ov thi butress. Footsteps clanged behind me.

I caim out on a brod balcony & dodjed thru a doarway & down sum moar steps in2 a sort ov hanger whare old gliders sat tilted like grate goastly stif-wingd burdz & a bunch ov litl bats startid chatterin & flying roun my hed. Footsteps abuv, then behind. O shit o shit o shit. Thi bats wer kikin up a heluva rakit.

I spottid a ladir agenst 1 wol leedin down thru thi floor & I ran 4 it. Sumbody shouted bhind me; thi footsteps slappd loud. Sumthin went, Bang! & a glider next 2 me explodid wif flame & loss a wing; thi blast ov air woz warm & almost nokd me off ma feet.

I thru myself @ thi ladir, held thi sides & dropt, sliding down without usin ma feet @ ol, hitin thi floor & twistin ma ankil.

I wos in sum kinda circular platform slung undir thi glider bildin. Nufin but air underneaf & nowhare 2 go. I lookd bak @ thi ladir. Thi footsteps were rite abuv me.

I herd a noise like qwuik, distant surf, & a huge blak shape lifted from under thi platform on wings longir than Im tol. It waverd in thi air alongside then graspd @ thi thin metil rale roun thi platform on thi far side from thi ladir, its talins gripin thi rale while its wings beat qwickly & almost silent bak & ford.

I cude heer sumbody cumin down thi ladir, breevin hard.

Here! shoutid thi blak shape @ thi othir side ov thi platform. Id fot it woz a bird but it woz more like a giant bat. Its wings clapped in & out in & out.

Qwickly! it sed.

I fink if thi bros cumin down thi ladir hadnt shot @ me in thi hanger I wooden ½ gon, but they had so I did.

I ran 4 thi big bat. It held its feet out. I grabd its ankils & it wrapt its talins roun ma rists makin me shout with thi bone-crunchin pane while it poold me off thi platform, crakin my nees off thi rale.

We twisted & dropt like thi thing cuden cary me & I screemd, then it spred its wings wif a snap & I neerly loss my grip as we curvd out & away. Light sparkld abuv me & I herd thi bat cry out but I woz 2 bizy lookin down @ thi dark fields in thi alure, 5 or 600 metres blow & thinking wel, if I die, thers still anuthir 7 lives 2 go. Xcept I didn fink that woz rite sumhow, I rekind whotevir trubil I woz in went beyond this life & I woznt garanteed anuthir 7 lives or evin 1.

I held on tite, but thi light crackled agen & thi bat thing judderd in thi air & cried out agen & I smeld smoke. We lurched & side-slipped 2wards thi wol ov thi grate hol, then fel like thi proverbyal, & in a screem ov air & a screem from me dippd blow thi alure & thi parapet & went on down til we wer levil wif thi lowir bretasche, whare thi bat wheeld roun so hard I lost my grip on its scaly legs & only its steel-like clasp on my rists stopt me from falin 2 thi roof ov thi 2nd level towr underneef.

Felt like my arms were about 2 pop out ma sokets. Id ½ screemed but thi bref woz gon from me.

Thi air shreiked roun ma ears as we plumitid btween thi grate towr & thi 2nd level wall, down in2 a layer ov cloud whare I cooden c a dam fing & it woz freezin cold, then we turnd in what I thot woz thi direcshin ov thi towr & outa thi mist loomd this bleedin grate rock wall. I closd mi Is.

We twisted 1ce, twice & I went – few – 2 myself but when I opend mi Is we woz stil hedin strate 4 nakid stonewurk. O fuk, I fot, but by then Id decidid Id rathir die wif ma Is opin. @ thi last momint we liftid, I saw hangin bunchis ov foleyidje strung from thi machicolation abuv & a instant later we crashd in2 thi babil; my sholder woz renched & I woz thrown off thi bat & in2 thi babil, grabbin @ leevs & twigs & branchis & slippin & fallin down thru it.

Thi bat beat fewriously, shoutin, Hold on! Hold on! while I tryd 2 get a hold on thi dam stuf.

Hold on! it shouted agen.

Am bludy tryin 2! I yelld.

U safe?

Juss about, I sed, huggin a big strand ov babil like it wos a long-loss mum or sumthin, not abil 2 look behind but stil heerin thi big bat flap & beet @ my bak.

Am sorri I cuden help u moar, thi bat sez. U mus saiv uself now. Thare lookin 4 u. Bware thi kript. Keep *outa* things! Erch! Erch! I mus go. Farewell, hoomin.

Yeh, & 2 u, I shoutid, turnin roun 2 luke @ it. & fanks!

Then thi big bat dropt, & I saw it disapeer in thi mist, fallin away strate down, traylin smoak & then juss b4 I loss site ov it curvin away followin thi circumferince ov thi towr, beetin hard but lookin week & still follin.

Disappeered.

I crolld in2 thi darkniss ov thi babil, nursin ma aiks.

O deer Bascule, I sed 2 myself. O deer o deer o deer.

I spent thi nite in thi foleyidje, constintly dreemin ov flyin thru thi air wif Ergates in ma hand but then droppin hir & hir tumblin away & me not bein abil 2 catch hir & mi wings cumin off & me follin 2 & screemin thru thi air, then wakin clutchin thi branchiz, shiverin & cuverd in swet.

So heer I am, lookin up @ thi fass-tower & Ive spent sum time so far this mornin tryin 2 pluk up thi curidje 2 go strate bak in2 thi kript 2 find out whots goan on & look 4 poor litil Ergates & this time tak no nonsins . . . & Ive also spent sum time vowin nevir 2 evin fink ov thi bleedin kript agen & desidin not 2 deside about it 4 now & so insted am juss sitin heer wonderin whot am 2 do in jeneril & not abil 2 cum 2 a disishin on that scoar nevir.

I turn ovir in ma litl nest agen & luke down thru thi branchis & this time I freez & stair, coz I can c this big animil cumin climin up thru thi babil; iss bleedin hooj, thi size ov a bare & iss got thik blak fur with streeks ov green on it & iss got big shiny blak claws & iss lukin @ me wif 2 litl beedy Is & a funy pointid hed & iss cumin up thi branch am on, strate 2words me.

O shit, I heer myself say, lukin roun 2 c if thers a way 2 escape.

Ther isnt. O shit.

Thi animil opins its mouf. Its teef r thi size ov ma fingirs.

. . . Shtay whare u r! it hissis.

FIVE

1

'In those days the world was not a garden and the people were not idle as they are now. Then on the face of the world there was real wilderness, empty of humanity, and the wilderness that humanity created, the wilderness that it packed with itself and which it called City. People toiled and people idled and the toilers worked for themselves and yet not for themselves and the idle did no work or little work and what they did, did only for themselves; money was all-powerful then and people said they made it work for them but money cannot work, only people and machines can work.'

Asura listened, fascinated but confused. The speaker was a thin middle-aged woman dressed in a plain ivory-coloured smock. Her feet were hobbled with a half-metre-long iron rod attached to wood-lined cuffs whose internal surfaces had been polished smooth and bright by friction with her skin. Her hands were similarly secured. She stood in the centre of the open gondola, chanting more than talking, her gaze raised to the belly-bulging underside of the airship above and her voice raised to cope with the noise of the craft's engines and the slipstream swirling over the gondola's semi-transparent bulwarks. Asura looked around, wondering at the effect this strange, declaiming woman must be having on her fellow travellers. She was surprised to find that she seemed to be the only person paying the woman any attention.

Asura had been standing at the airship's deck rail watching the plain roll past beneath and had seen the first line of blue hills appear through the haze. She had been waiting for her first glimpse of the great castle, but the woman's steady voice and odd words had intrigued her.

She left the rail to find a seat close to the woman. As she moved between the tables and chairs, she looked towards the bow of the gondola, where the upper deck's round transparent nose bulged out, part of a huge sunstruck circle veined with the dark lines of struts, and suddenly she was reminded of something she'd seen in her dreams last night.

She sat down, feeling dizzy.

In a great dark space there was a huge circle, subdivided into smaller circles by thin dark lines like rings of ripples in a disturbed pool, and further subdivided by similarly fine lines radiating from the very centre of the circle. The circle was an enormous window; stars shone beyond it.

She could hear a clock ticking.

Something moved at one edge of the great circle. Looking closely she could see it was a figure; somebody walking along the horizontal ray-line from the edge to the centre of the circular window. She looked more closely still, and saw that the person was herself.

She walked along until she stood in the very centre of the vast aperture, looking out through a central pane of some substance she knew was more hard and clear and strong than glass. Far below, there was a landscape of luminous grey; a circular depression of shallow, undulating hills surrounded by cliffs and mountains, lit from one side and full of deep, black shadows. The clock still ticked. She stood for a while, admiring the stars, and thinking that the circle of the great window mirrored the shape of the circular plain it overlooked.

Then the clock-sound speeded up, ticking faster and faster until it was a ripping, buzzing noise in her ears; the shadows swung across the landscape and the bright orb of the sun tore across the sky, then abruptly the sun vanished and the noise of the clock changed, took on a kind of rhythm until the noise speeded up again and became the buzz it had been before. She could barely see the landscape below. The stars blazed.

Then the stars started to disappear. They went out slowly at first, in a single region of the sky off to her right and near the dark horizon, then more quickly, until the stain of darkness was eating up a quarter of the sky, rising like a vast curtain thrown up from the ghostly grey mountains. Now a third of the sky was utterly dark, the stars going out one by one or in groups; shining, then dimming, then flickering and disappearing altogether as the darkness consumed half the sky, then two thirds.

She stared, open-mouthed, choosing brighter stars in the path of the blackness and watching them as they vanished.

Finally almost the whole sky was black; just a few stars shone steadily above the distant mountains to her right, while to her left the darkness had touched the horizon, where the sun had shone earlier.

Abruptly the clock was back to normal, and the sun blazed again – from a different angle now, but still just within the region of the darkness – sending a cold, steady light across the crater floor to the grey cliffs and crags of the rim-wall.

Earth. Cradle. Very old. There are many ages. Age within age. Age of nothingness comes first, then age/instant of infinitesimal/ infinite explosion, then age of shining, then age of heaviness, of different air/fluids, then the tiny but long ages of stone/fluid and fire, then the age of life, smaller still, and living with and in all the other ages, then the age/moment of thought-life: here we are, and all goes very quickly and at the same time all other types/sizes of ages go on but then there is next age/moment of the new life that the old life makes, and that is much faster again, and that is where we are now too. And yet.

The old ape-man looked sad. He had grey hair and grey sagging skin on a skinny frame and he was dressed in a strange costume of yellow and red diamonds topped by a pointed hat with a bell on the end. His soft shoes were pointed too, and also had bells at their tips. The only noise he could produce was a chattering laugh; he was the size of a child but his eyes looked wise and sad. He sat on the steps that led up to a big chair; the large room was empty except for her and the ape-man and one wall of the room was window, double-skinned and curved and ribbed with a fine tracery of dark lines, though much smaller than the circular window she had seen earlier. This window too looked out onto a landscape of shining grey.

The beautiful globe hanging in the black sky above the shining grey hills was Earth, the ape-man had told her. He talked by sign, using his arms and fingers. She found that she could understand him but not reply, though just by nodding, frowning or raising her eyebrows it was possible to express herself well enough, it seemed.

Eyebrows? she signalled.

And yet, the ape-man sighed, expression still downcast. Ages are in conflict, he told her. Each move, own pace, not often come together, fight. But now: happens. Age of air/fluids and age of life fight. Two ages of life, too. For all who feel sadness sometimes, there comes sadness now. For all those who die sometimes, there comes death now, perhaps.

She frowned. She was standing, still dressed in her night-blue gown, in front of the wide window. Every now and again, during pauses in the ape-man's signing, she glanced at the Earth and the steady stars hanging visible beyond its brightness. Her gown was the colour of the barren, ghostly landscape outside.

She shrugged.

People/humans made much; big things on Earth. Biggest thing, smallest thing too. Everywhere. Then inside this thing, fight. Then peace but not peace; peace for a while, short now. Now the age of air/fluids comes, threat to all. All must act. Most danger if biggest/smallest thing not act. Biggest/smallest thing fight with self, cannot talk to all of self; bad. Other ways of talking; good. Most special good if self talk to self.

The ape-man looked almost happy for a moment, and she smiled to show she understood.

You.

She pointed at herself. Me?

You.

She shook her head, then shrugged, spreading her arms.

Yes, you. I tell you now. You forget in future, but you also know still, too. Is good. Perhaps all safe.

She smiled uncertainly.

'Ah, there you are,' Pieter Velteseri said, appearing from the steps leading to the gondola's lower decks. He parted the tails of his coat and sat beside Asura, planting his silver-topped cane between his feet. He looked at her.

She blinked rapidly for a few seconds and then shook her head, as though just waking up.

Pieter glanced at the woman standing speaking in the middle of the gondola's floor. He smiled. 'Ah; our Resiler has found her voice, has she? I didn't think she would stay silent for long.' He placed his hands on top of the cane and rested his chin on top of his hands.

'She is ... Resisla?' Asura said, glancing at Pieter and frowning as she tried to pick up the thread of the woman's speech again.

'She is a Resiler; one who resiles, or recoils,' he said in a low voice. 'In a sense we all are, or our ancestors were, I suppose, but she is of a sect who believes we need to resile further.'

'No one else listens,' Asura whispered. She looked around the others on the gondola's open deck. They were all talking among themselves, or watching the view, or sitting or lying with their eyes closed, either snoozing or experientially elsewhere.

'They will have heard all this before,' Pieter said quietly. 'Not word for word, but ...'

'We are guilty,' said the Resiler. 'We have treasured our comfort and our vanity by giving shelter to the beasts of chaos which infest the crypt so that humanity's part of it now is barely one part in a hundredth, and that wasted, that turned over to the worship of self and vanity and dreams of sovereignty over what we claim to have renounced ...'

'Is all she says true?' Asura whispered.

'Ah,' Pieter said, smiling. 'Now, that is a question. Let's say it is all based on truth, but the facts are open to different interpretations from the one she supplies.'

'... The King is no King and all know this; well and good, but neither is what appears to be our good work good, but only a disguise for the face of our foolish ignorance and ill-fitness.'

'The King?' Asura said, looking puzzled.

'Our ruler,' Pieter supplied. 'I've always thought Dalai Llama would have been a better description, though the King has more power and less ... holiness. In any event, the royal term is preferred. It's complicated.'

'Why is she in irons?' Asura asked.

'It's a symbol,' Pieter said, a teasing, mischievous look on his face. Asura nodded, her expression serious, and Pieter smiled again.

'She seems very sincere,' Asura told Pieter.

'A word with oddly positive connotations,' Pieter said, nodding. 'In my experience those who are most sincere are also the most morally suspect, as well as being incapable of producing or appreciating wit.'

'What happens happens,' continued the Resiler, 'and cannot

be made to unhappen. We are the equation; we cannot deny the algebra of the universe or the result it brings us. Die peacefully or in hysterics, with grace or with despair; it matters not. Prepare or ignore; it matters not. Very little matters very much and almost nothing matters greatly. Shanti.'

'I find myself half drawn to that last statement,' Pieter told Asura as the Resiler sat down. Nearby there was a group of people who had been laughing and joking among themselves during the course of her speech; a highly dressed woman rose from among them and went over and placed some sweetmeats in the plain wooden bowl at the Resiler's side. The Resiler thanked her and ate with awkward grace. She smiled thinly at Asura as the other woman sashayed back to her friends, laughing.

'Come, my dear,' Pieter said pleasantly, rising and taking the girl's elbow. 'We'll take the air on the lower viewing deck, shall we?' They rose. 'Ma'am,' he said, nodding to the Resiler as they passed.

'Don't worry,' Asura said to the Resiler as Pieter led her to the stairs. 'It's going to be all right.' She winked at her.

The woman looked briefly baffled, then shook her head and continued to eat, her movements made strange by the iron rod linking her wrists.

Asura's smooth brow furrowed into a frown as she and Pieter descended to the main lounge. 'She eats,' she said, glancing back up. 'How does she clean herself after toilet?'

Pieter laughed lightly. 'You know, I never thought of that. The alternatives are all unpleasant, aren't they?'

Below, from the promenade deck, they saw the forested hills stretching out around them and, from the tiers of seats facing the lower section of the round transparent nose, the first hazy hints of the towers and battlements of Serehfa.

Asura clapped her hands.

That morning, over breakfast, she had told them something of her dreams and Pieter had looked at first alarmed and then resigned. She had not told them all the details; just that she had seen the tunnel of light and been in an enchanted carriage journeying across the dusty plain towards the great castle beyond the hills.

'Lucky you,' Lucia Chimbers had told her. 'Most of us

have to concentrate quite hard to have dreams that interesting.'

'Sounds like she might have implants after all,' Gil said,
helping himself to more ortanique juice.

Pieter shook his head. 'I think not.' He frowned. 'And I do
wish people would stop calling them implants; they're not,
if you're born with them and they're part of your genetic
inheritance, reversible or not.'

Gil and Lucia smiled at him with practised indulgence.

Pieter dabbed a napkin at his lips and sat back, surveying their
young guest, who sat very upright with her hands in her lap and
her eyes sparkling.

'Do I take it then that you wish to leave, young lady?'

'Please call me Asura,' she said. She nodded vigorously. 'I
think I go to castle.'

'Bit touristy, going so soon,' Lucia said. Pieter glanced
wearily at her.

'Everyone should see Serehfa,' Gil said, drinking noisily.

'Do you wish to go today?' Pieter asked.

'As soon as possible, please,' the girl said.

'Well,' Pieter said, 'I suppose one of us ought to go with
you, really.'

'Don't look at me— ' Lucia began.

'I merely wondered if we might prevail upon you to lend the
young lady— '

'Asura!' she said, happily.

'– to lend Asura,' Pieter said with a sigh, 'your clothes on a
rather longer term— '

'Take them.' Lucia waved one hand, then took Gil's in hers.

'I shall want to be back in time for the others returning,' Pieter
told Asura. 'I may have to dump you at the gates, even assuming
we can find a flight in time.'

'As soon as possible, please,' Asura repeated.

'Book her into a sisters' hostel in the place or something,' Gil
said. 'Or get a clan member to look after her.'

'I may do both,' Pieter said, then sat back and closed his eyes.
'Excuse me,' he murmured.

Lucia Chimbers and Gil poured each other coffee. Asura
looked intently at the older man, who presently opened his
eyes again and said, 'Yes, we're booked on a flight from SF

del Apure, leaving at noon. I can be back on the return service a little after midnight. The jalop claims to be charged up, so I'll drive us to the rail station. I've left a message for Cousin Ucubulaire in Serehfa. I dare say you two will manage to keep yourselves occupied without me?' he said to Gil and Lucia, who both smiled.

'Between you and me, my dear,' Pieter shouted an hour later as he drove the whirring battery car along the dusty road from the house to Cazoria, the nearest town, 'I put you in the blue room on purpose last night; the bed's headboard is fitted with a receptor system.' He smiled over at her.

They had the sunlight-powered car's top off; the wind whistled round their ears. ('Ruins the efficiency,' Pieter had told her, 'but it's much more fun.' He wore goggles and a tie-down hat, and had given her similar equipment. She wore loose trousers, a blouse and a light jacket.) 'I thought you might be able to avail yourself of the facilities. If you hadn't, well then, no harm done.'

Asura held onto her hat and smiled broadly at him. Then she frowned, and said, 'The bed made me dream?'

'Not exactly, but it let you dream . . . in concert, shall we say? Though you must have a remarkable gift to adapt so quickly and so easily.'

They drove on through the morning, between wild fruit-forests of banana and orange. Asura was enjoying the drive.

'Ah, Asura?' Pieter said.

'Yes?'

'That is not regarded as acceptable in polite society. Or, come to think of it, in almost any society, normally.'

'What? This?'

'Yes. That.'

'No? But it feels good. It is beginning with car shaking.'

'I don't doubt. Nevertheless. One does that sort of thing in private, I think you'll find.'

'Oh, all right.' Asura looked mildly puzzled, then adjusted her hands and sat with them clasped demurely in her lap.

'There's the town,' Pieter said, nodding ahead to where a collection of white spires and towers were rising above the greenery. He glanced at his young passenger and shook his head. 'Serehfa. Good grief. I hope I'm doing the right thing . . .'

2

Chief Scientist Gadfium sat in the whirlbath with the High Sortileger Xemetrio; the pumps hummed, water frothed and bubbled, steam hissed from wall pipes and wrapped them in its hot, dense fog, and music played loudly.

They sat side by side facing each other, each whispering into the other's ear.

'They sound half mad, or *it* sounds half mad,' Xemetrio said, snorting. 'What is all this nonsense about "Love is god" and the "Hallowed centre"?'

'It sounds formalised,' Gadfium whispered. 'I don't think it really means anything.'

Xemetrio drew back a little in the swirling steam; it was so thick Gadfium could not see the walls of the bathroom. 'My dear,' Xemetrio whispered urbanely once his mouth was alongside her ear again. 'I am the High Sortileger; *everything* means something.'

'You see; that is your faith, even though you wouldn't call it such; theirs is expressed in this quasi-religious— '

'It isn't *quasi*-religious, it's *completely* religious.'

'Even so.'

'And Sortilegy boils down to a matter of statistics,' Xemetrio said, sounding genuinely offended. 'Anything less spiritual is difficult to— '

'We're moving off the point. If we ignore the religious trappings and concentrate on the information itself— '

'Context matters,' the Sortileger insisted.

'Let us assume the rest of the signal is true.'

'If you insist.'

'Abstract: they confirm our fears concerning the cloud and the lack of any communication from the Diaspora, and they know of our attempt to construct rockets. They know about this idiotic war between Adijine and the Engineers and that it isn't going to lead anywhere, and they seem concerned about some "workings" going on in the level-five south-western solar affecting the fabric – we assume they mean the fabric of the castle mega-structure itself.' Gadfium wiped beads of moisture from her brow. 'Do we know any more about what's going on there?'

'There's a full Army unit there and they have a lot of heavy equipment, including something they dug out of the southern revetment last year,' Xemetrio told her. 'It's all being kept very quiet.' He leant back and adjusted a control by the side of the tub. 'They built a new hydrovator into the Southern Volcano Room just to supply the garrison. That was where Sessine was heading when he was killed.'

'Sessine was always reckoned one of those who might have been sympathetic to us; do you think—?'

'Impossible to say. There was nothing to link us and him, though it is feasible he was assassinated for political reasons.' Xemetrio shrugged. 'Or personal ones.'

'The signal spoke of "workings",' Gadfium said. 'Mine workings, perhaps? What is beneath that room?'

'The floor is unpierced; it cannot signify.'

'But if the device found in the southern revetment . . .'

'*If* somebody had finally found a machine able to create new holes in the mega-structure and made it work and dragged it all the way up here, they'd be burrowing into the ceiling of the sacristy, in no-man's land between the King's forces and the Engineers of the Chapel.'

'But the signal spoke of their concern over the fabric. If that is what they meant— '

'Then,' the Sortileger said, sounding exasperated, 'there's nothing we can do for now, unless we are to confess all to the King and his Security people. What else have you decided we can tell from your mysterious signal, assuming it's not all some bizarre self-delusion on the part of the mad people who watch stones slide and call it science?'

'I trust them.'

'Like you trust the signal itself,' Xemetrio said sourly. 'We are conspirators, Gadfium; we cannot afford so much trust.'

'We are not yet acting upon such trust and so risk nothing.'

'*Yet*,' scoffed the Sortileger, cupping water over his shoulders.

'Whoever sent the signal,' Gadfium went on, 'believes the answer lies in the Cryptosphere.'

'I'm sure the true answer does, along with every possible false answer and no way to distinguish between them.'

'They appear to believe that, as we have always suspected, there is a conspiracy to thwart all efforts to avoid the catastrophe.'

'Though why the King and his cronies should particularly want to die when the sun blows up is of course a trifle difficult to fathom. We're back to speculating about ultra-secret survival projects or some bizarre fatalism.'

'Neither of which is utterly unfeasible, but the act of the conspiracy is all that matters for now, not its origin. Lastly, the signal-senders confirm both that there is, or may be, an already designed-in method of escape— '

'What, though? Switch on some galactic vacuum-cleaner? Move the planet?'

'You're the Sortileger, Xemetrio . . .'

'Huh. We daren't run *that* question through the system, but if I had to guess, I'd stick with the obvious answer; there's some part of Serehfa which conceals an escape device. That may be what the war with the Chapel is really about. Maybe the Engineers have access to it and Adijine doesn't.'

'Whatever. The signal also suggests that the data corpus itself may hold the solution and be attempting to access it.'

'The mythical asura,' the Sortileger said, shaking his head.

'Such a method would make sense, given the chaotic nature of the crypt,' Gadfium whispered. 'The possibility of the data corpus' corruption may have been foreseen— '

'Amazing Sortilegy,' Xemetrio muttered.

'– just as was the possibility of a threat to the Earth that could not be dealt with by automatic space defence mechanisms. Physical separation of the information required to activate the escape device would ensure that no matter the delay it could never be corrupted by the crypt.'

'Though it still has to be initiated,' Xemetrio said. 'But let's not lose sight of the fact that all this supposition is built on the word of some historically, how shall I put it? . . . *eccentric* observers of sliding stones, and that even if they are to be trusted, what we've actually got is an intellectually suspect, semi-garbled message originating from somewhere within the top ten kilometres of the fast-tower; we still have no idea who or what is up there and what their motives are.'

'We also have little time to squander, Xemetrio. We have to decide what to do and how to reply. You're sure you can get this signal and our appraisal to the others safely?'

'Yes, yes,' the High Sortileger snapped; Gadfium asked this question virtually every time they had information they had to spread around their network, and each time Xemetrio had to reassure that as High Sortileger he could move data within the data corpus without Security knowing all about it.

'Good,' Gadfium said, apparently relieved afresh. 'Clispeir is going to heliograph an acknowledgment to the fast-tower's signal and a request for more information, but we must make up our minds; do we act now, merely get ready to act, or go on as before, waiting?'

The High Sortileger looked sadly at the glistening mountains of foam bobbing around him. 'I vote we wait for more information. Meantime, I'll start a quiet search for your asura.' He shook his head. 'Besides, what could we do?'

'We could find out what's going on in the fifth-level south-western solar; that would be a start.'

'I've tried that; most of the military don't know.'

'Perhaps the shade of Count Sessine could answer the question,' Gadfium suggested.

Xemetrio looked sceptical. 'I doubt it. And what if he remains loyal to the King? Quite possibly he is part of their big bad conspiracy and would report our little one to Security.'

'A way might be found to talk to him without giving too much away.'

'I suppose so,' Xemetrio said, looking uncomfortable, 'but I'm not doing it.'

'I'll do it,' Gadfium told him.

Uris Tenblen raised his face to the cold, thin wind cutting across the frozen plain, blinked red-rimmed eyes, cocked his grey-skinned shaven head to one side and listened to the song in his skull.

It was different again today. It was different every day, if he remembered correctly. He wasn't at all sure that he did remember everything correctly. He wasn't sure he remembered anything correctly. But the song in his heart said that it didn't matter.

The wind blew in through the vast windows two kilometres away across the plain. The windows were floor-to-ceiling, and broad; sometimes it seemed to Tenblen that it was better to think of three skinny pillars holding up that side of the next storey, not four broad windows in a wall. Above here there was only a broad piazza, open to the skies. Tenblen turned round and looked towards the other wall, where four similar apertures, also two kilometres away, let the wind straight back out again. Both sets of windows looked out onto a sea of white cloud.

He turned back; the wind brought hard powdery snow with it, probably not fresh but dislodged from part of the castle above here. The wind-blown granules stung the exposed skin of his face, neck, wrists and hands. He forced the visor and helmet over his head, fumbling raw-fingered with the straps. Chill weather, he told himself, but the song in his head kept him warm, or told him it did, which was just as good.

His dorm was at the edge of the camp; it was a shining aluminium box almost identical to the forty or so others which ringed the workings. This close, the workings themselves were just a huge sloped wall of rubble; from further away across the frozen marshes and low hills of the plain they appeared as a small, steep-sided crater.

From above they would just look like a hole; a dark pit, usually filled with yellow-grey mists, like a giant weeping wound.

Tenblen trudged through the rimed puddles on the rutted path leading towards the workings, fastening his tunic. His boots crunched through brittle white surfaces of ice into the hard brown hollows of the puddles.

The song in his head rose to a sweet crescendo just then and he gave a thin, grim smile, then made a small, involuntary ducking motion and looked nervously up at the ceiling a thousand metres above him.

He passed the bomb caissons, great closed iron cylinders coated with snow, their wheels sunk a little way into the cracked surface of frozen mud. Thus far, they had only two caissons, six small bombs and one large one. A new convoy was on its way, bringing fresh matériel. He saluted an officer who passed him on the path. He knew he ought to know the officer's name, but he could not remember it. That didn't matter; if he needed to talk to the officer or take him some message or order, the song in his head would remind him of his name. The officer nodded as he walked past, his gaze fastened straight ahead and his expression fixed in a broad and somehow desperate grin.

Tenblen climbed the steps by the side of the inclined plain. He ascended them in time to the song, and as he climbed he imagined that the King was looking through his eyes.

(Adijine, who was doing exactly that, experienced only very mild surprise at this point, and almost immediately felt oddly cheated that he hadn't sustained some profound sense of alienation or momentary loss-of-identity.)

The King would look through his eyes and hear the song in his head; the song of loyalty, of obedience, of joy to have this part to play, and know that he was glad to be loyal, glad to be obedient and glad to be joyful. He could think of nothing more pleasant than to be transparent in exactly that manner, and to be seen to be the King's loyal soldier. He got to the top of the crater-wall of rubble and started down the other side, towards the pit.

The fumes were already quite bad. The steam came drifting up the brecciated slope from the hole, wrapping itself around the scattered cisterns, pipes, valveheads, winches and gantries littering the incline. Sometimes the smell of the gases came with the steam, and you thought the cloud enveloping you would be pure fume and you almost panicked with only the song in your head telling you it was all right; other times the steam was far away when you picked up the stink and your eyes watered and your nose and the back of your throat felt rasped and burned.

He stopped at the quartermaster's office. There was a ghost outside.

The ghost was dressed as some ancient judge or holy man. He tried to get in Tenblen's way and shout something at him, but Uris just put his hand through the ghost and made as though to wave it out of the way as he stepped through it. The song in his head drowned out the ghost's voice.

'Bit nippy today,' he shouted to the quartermaster. It helped to shout, over the noise of the song. The quartermaster was a large, red-faced man. He nodded as he issued Tenblen with his gloves, mask and respirator.

'Wind's shifted,' he said loudly, coughing. 'I've asked them to move me further up the slope but of course they haven't done anything yet.'

'Perhaps you should be right at the top.'

'Perhaps I should. Or even on the far slope.'

'You might be better off at the bottom of the slope on the other side.'

'Yes, I might.'

'Well, see you later.'

'Goodbye.'

Tenblen put his mask and respirator on before he left the quartermaster's office. He felt hoarse and his throat was sore already. He could remember being able to talk without talking; being able to think something and somebody else understanding what it was you had thought; he could remember a long time ago when the song had started, thinking how odd it felt having to physically talk any time you wanted to tell somebody something. Promotion, people had joked at the time, at first.

The song had been young then and they had all been charmed by it. He could remember even longer ago when he'd not been a soldier and had been able to talk to anybody. He felt sad about that, sometimes. The song lifted his spirits, though. It could turn the sadness to joy. After all, you cried when you were happy sometimes, too.

He stepped outside into the slow whorls of drifting, rising steam, and continued down into the workings. His own breath sounded loud within the mask and he could hear valves clicking and hissing. He could feel the fumes on his neck, already chafing against his collar. A little of the fume-smell leaked in round the edges of the mask, and he tried to clamp the mask down harder. He tramped deeper into the steam, down a concrete path lit by tall poles tipped with small lamps and strung with a hand-rope at hip level.

The song sang majestically as he descended into the darkness . . .

(The song the song the song while he seemed to pass venting pipes and arrive at a platform in a broad tunnel where a small train waited full of coughing men but the song said no no no stuck in a breath-holding loop that said time is not passing this is not happening and sang higher sweeter fuller as the train ground and screeched its way over points and into a narrow tunnel and accelerated in utter darkness the wind in his face journeying for a time then passing through a dimly lit hole where guards with fixed stares stood then another tunnel and then the fume smell again and the steam and he started to relax as though he'd been holding his breath all that time and then out of the train with the others and down the steps relieved and even glad to be here while the song sang resuming.)

... The workings surface was a chaotic ballet from some primitive's hell; it was filled with a loud, fume-laden darkness pierced sporadically by flashes of intense, scarifying light, and permeated with a furious hissing sound punctuated by sudden screams and explosions. Through this havoc drifted a population of terrifying beasts, monstrously deformed human shapes wielding strange instruments designed to puncture, flay and burn, and the wailing, beseeching figures of ghosts.

Tenblen pulled on a harness and hitched himself to the roof struts. An officer came up to him and told him to return to his quarters, but the song in his head told him this wasn't a real officer; it was a ghost and to be ignored.

Tenblen found a pair of boots that didn't look too badly scarred and started down the steps to the mine surface. A chimeric oxephant hauling a vat of acid loomed out of the mist, making him pause. He found himself automatically checking its harness and restrainer straps; they all seemed to be in place, the harness tight and the straps disappearing up into the steam clouds towards the grid of struts barely visible against the dark roof above (and some part of him looked at that darkness above thinking, *But*— ... but then the song swelled, drowning out the sound of his recalcitrant thoughts).

He walked towards the eastern part of the floor. He glanced down as he walked. The surface. The song in his head welled up again, telling him to rejoice at the task they had undertaken, at its daring, its technological sophistication, at its audacity and its uniqueness. It was a wonderful and beautiful thing they were doing; they were reclaiming the structure, the whole castle, not just for their cause and the King but for all people. They were no longer at its mercy, it was at theirs.

A beautiful woman appeared out of the mists, her skin black, her clothes whiter and wispier than the mists, her body full and firm and voluptuous. Tenblen knew she was a ghost but he stood and stared for a while as she walked round him with a half-coy, half-welcoming smile. Then the song rose again, racketing in his head and setting his teeth on edge. It was still pleasant, like being tickled, but he could not take it for very long. He hurried on, away from the woman.

He came to the latest workings. Acid fumed, arc-light sparkled, power tools hammered. Men dressed in full protective suits stumbled round. Chimerics pawed the ground, pulled with harness hooks and bellowed.

Tenblen tried to breathe easily and shallowly through his mouth, ignoring the rasp of fumes in his throat as he walked amongst the men and beasts, checking their harness connections and restraining straps. Under his feet, the surface of the workings was smoking and peeling and blistering, constantly sprayed by the rusting agent and then further attacked with scab-hooks, welding arcs, lasers and a selection of acids, mostly sulphuric and hydrochloric. The surface was constantly attempting to repair itself, flowing back to fill holes and rearranging the large-scale fibres and scales which it was composed of. You could never be certain which sections would be susceptible to which removing agent; there was no alternative but to try everything and see what worked at that point at that time.

He stood for a moment, ignoring the ghost of a small baby at his feet, writhing and screaming on the ground amongst the acid pools. The surface here looked thin somehow. Perhaps they'd do it here (the baby looked up at him, eyes huge, while smoke curled up around its blistering skin. The song sang high and sweet while Tenblen's eyes filled with tears. He gently put his boot out, through the apparition of the baby, then when it moved out of his way, suddenly screamed in frustration and brought his boot down on it as though trying to crush the infant. It disappeared. His boot heel met the surface and the shock resounded through him, then the ground too seemed to disappear and he was looking –

– down. The circular hole started at his feet and was almost instantly ten metres wide around him.

He dropped through, screaming, in a haze of acid spray. The city was a sparkling jewel two kilometres below him. His harness tightened around him like a bony fist and the restraining straps bounced him up and down like some child in a walking yoke. The song burned in his head, exultant. He kept on screaming despite the song, and soiled himself.

On a warm marble table in the Palace baths, the King opened his eyes and looked up as the masseuse kneaded his back. He smiled broadly and said, 'Yes!'

He winked at the masseuse and lowered his head again, within range of the receptor devices buried in the marble table.

He skipped back into Uris Tenblen's head just in time to watch with him as the edges of the hole above him wobbled liquidly like grey-black circular lips, then snapped back closed with a whiplash crack, rebounding a little so that a metre-diameter hole existed for a moment before that too irised shut like an eye blinking.

The first closure had instantly severed the straps on Tenblen's harness.

He plummeted – gesticulating frantically, screaming hoarsely – towards the glittering spires of the city two thousand metres below.

The link sizzled and cut out.

Adijine raised his head. 'Shh*hit*,' he said softly.

3

'Very well, Alan, who *is* trying to kill me?' Sessine asked, smiling a little at the image of his earlier self.

The younger Sessine looked around. The engine's thrashing heart was all fury and noise; pipes roaring, connecting rods flashing to and fro. He took up the portable chess board and put it down the bib front of his engineer's overalls, then stood.

Sessine did not get up, but sat on the little stool, still smiling up at the construct of his younger self, who laughed.

'Please, Count; come with me.'

Sessine stood slowly, and nodded.

They were standing in a clearing within the high forest at the foot of the fastness walls. Sessine looked up through the sighing tops of the trees to the curtain-wall towering above. A tower a few kilometres away rose still higher, but the rest of the structure was hidden by the walls, a rosy cliff fifteen hundred metres high and festooned with variegated babilia. The wind soughed briefly in the trees, then died away.

'Here,' Alan said. Sessine turned, and the younger man took his hand.

/They stood in a vast circular space with a floor of gleaming gold, a velvet-black ceiling and what appeared to be a single all-round window looking out onto a whitely shining surface and a purple-black sky where stars shone steadily. Above them, suspended as though on nothing, hung a massive orrery; a model of the solar system with a brilliant yellow-white ball of light in the middle and the various planets shown as glassy globes of the appropriate appearance all fixed by slender poles and shafts to thin hoops of blackly shining metal like wet jet.

Under the representation of the sun, there was a brightly lit circular construction like a half-built room. They walked there across the glistening floor.

'This is a memory, of course,' his younger self said, waving one hand. 'We don't know what the upper sections of the fast-tower look like now. When Serehfa was still called Acsets, this was part of the control apparatus.'

They entered the circular area in the centre of the room; a collection of couches, seats, desks and ornately decorated wood and precious-metal consoles and dark screens of crystal.

They sat on facing seats. Alan looked up at the glaring image of the sun, his face shining. 'We're safe here,' he told Sessine. 'I've spent subjective millennia exploring, mapping and studying the structure of the Cryptosphere and this is as secure as it gets.'

Sessine glanced around. 'Very impressive. Now.' He sat forward. 'Answer my question.'

'The King. He ordered your death.'

Sessine sat very still for a moment. Then I am lost, he thought. He said, 'Are you sure?'

'Entirely.'

'And the Consistory?'

'They approved it.'

'Well,' Sessine said, running a hand round the back of his neck, 'that would appear to be that.'

'That depends on what you want to do,' the construct said.

'All I wanted was to find out why I was killed.'

'Because you have doubts about the conduct of the war, but most especially because you were starting to doubt the motives of the King and the Consistory and their dedication to the cause of saving people from the Encroachment.'

'I think others feel that way.'

Alan smiled. 'Most of the Consistory doubt the wisdom of the war, and many people think the King and his pals seem less concerned than they ought to be about the Encroachment – a lot of people suspect they have their own space-ship, though they don't. Most people can't do anything about their suspicions; you can – or could have. You have the honour of being the most highly placed and popular potential dissident, the one they felt they might benefit most from making an example of. They were still uncertain whether actually to do it – Adijine himself spoke for letting you live – but you made their minds up for them; you pulled strings to go on that supply convoy to the bomb-workings. Adijine had left strict instructions only somebody with implants could command it.'

'I know. It seemed . . . wrong.'

'You used your influence, somebody high up enough to know of the King's decree but with a grudge against you let you swing the commission, and when the King and the Consistory found out they didn't even consider trying to order you back; they just had you killed by activating a Chapel spy whose code they had already intercepted.'

Sessine considered this. 'That seems a little desperate.'

The construct shrugged. 'These are desperate times.'

'And who do I have to thank for the decision to let me go in the first place?'

'Flische. Colonel-to-the-court. He's fucking your wife.'

Sessine thought for a moment, staring at his vague reflection in the matt blackness of screen on a console opposite. After some time he sighed.

'What is happening at the workings?' he asked.

'Last year they found a mesturedo, a substance which can attack the fabric of the mega-structure. They've used it to eat through the floor of the solar. From there they built a tube track between the floor and the ceiling along to the wall between the solar and the room above the Chapel; they're currently on the last lap, burrowing through the fabric of the false ceiling directly above Chapel City. When they succeed in opening it they'll drop bombs through.

'The mega-structure fabric tries to defend itself through the crypt. It sends visions; ghosts and demons which attempt to prevent the soldiers and engineers doing the digging. The only way the Army's found to keep their personnel functional – if not sane – is to flood their minds with a loyalty signal; a song of captivity that blanks out everything else and turns the men into automatons.'

'So I would not have been susceptible to this song; so what?'

'So what they are doing there is not only destroying Army personnel, it's destroying parts of the crypt itself.'

'How so?'

'The mega-structure houses filaments of the crypt's hardware. Contrary to popular belief, the Cryptosphere is not a function of some buried horde of super-machines; the whole fastness is permeated with it. There *are* elements deep inside the structure, but the primary structure itself houses most of what we know as the crypt.

'What the bomb-workings are doing now is destroying an important nexus of that Cryptospheric structure; it's madness, and it encourages chaos. The crypt-time has slowed down locally by an appreciable additional degree. What is left of humanity is caught between the threat of the Encroachment above and the chaos within the crypt below. The course Adijine and his Consistory are following would seem to ignore one and aggravate the other. At the very least you would have been concerned, sceptical and questioning on discovering all this. They could scarcely risk that, let alone what might have been your most extreme reaction.'

Sessine gave a small, humourless laugh, and shook his head. 'And the war with the Chapel?' he asked matter-of-factly.

'Genuine enough. The Engineers do have something we need, though it's not the information on how to make spacecraft.'

'What is it?'

The construct raised his eyebrows. 'Here we reach the limits of my research. I am not certain.' He shrugged. 'But it is something Adijine and the Consistory consider to be of the utmost importance.'

Sessine shook his head and looked up at the vast orrery hanging silently overhead. It had moved, while he had been listening to the construct. Saturn hung overhead now, immense and gassy, attended by its moons.

'Madness, chaos, crypt-time slowing,' Sessine said, sighing. He stood up and walked round some of the ancient equipment, drawing a hand over the surfaces of the desks and consoles, wondering if this virtual environment included dust. He inspected the tip of his finger. It appeared it did, though only just. He rubbed his fingers together and looked back at his younger self. 'Anything else you want me to assimilate this afternoon?'

'My speculation as to the nature of the prize the Chapel and the King compete for.'

'And what would that be?'

'Can you keep a secret?' His younger self smirked.

Sessine shook his head again. 'Was I really this tiresome?'

The construct laughed. 'This is a secret you must keep even from yourself, for a time at least.'

'Go on,' Sessine said tiredly. 'What is the glittering prize we all pursue?'

The construct grinned broadly. 'A secret passage.'

Sessine looked levelly at him.

4

I stair @ thi big blak beest cumin up thi branch 2wards me.

Av got a gun! I shout (this iz a ly).

. . . Ah veri mush dout that, thi thing sez. It stops ol thi saim, smilin & showin its teef agen. But nway, it sez, shtop being shilly. Am heer 2 help u.

I'l bet, I sez, glancin roun & stil tryin 2 figir out a way 2 escape.

. . . Yesh. If ahd wantid 2 harm u ah cude 1/2 shaken u out
ov thare 5 minitsh ago.

O yeh? I sez, hangin on titer. Wel mayb u doan wan 2 kil me
mayb u juss wan 2 capture me.

. . . In whish caysh ahd 1/2 dropt on u from abuv, u
shilly boy.

O u wood, wood u?

. . . Yesh. Yoor Bashcule, arnt u?

Praps, I sez. & who or whot r u when yoor @ home then?

. . . Am a shlof, it sez proudly. U can col me Gashton.

So am bein led thru thi babil plants by a slof calld Gaston whot
has a kinda mutant lisp & takes such pride in his appeerinse heez
got fungus growin on his bak; thats whot thi green streeks r.
He ofird 2 let me ride on his bak hangin on2 his fur but I
declynde.

We clime thru thi babil, goan doun & roun thi towr.

Hoo sent u then? I ask.

. . . Shame peepil shent thi jericule lasht nite, Gaston sez, tokin
ovir hiz sholder.

Whot, that big bat?

. . . Thatsh rite.

Whot happind 2 him nway, do u no?

. . . Hir, Gaston sez. No.

O.

I follow Gaston doun thru thi babil branchiz. Followin Gaston
iznt difficult on account ov him bein a qwite remarkibly slo
moovir. If he had bin cumin 2 atak me I cude probly 1/2 juss
gon doun thi branch he woz on & climed rite ovir him b4 he
cude 1/2 startid 2 react.

Nway. Hoo woz it sent u heer then?

. . . Frenz.

U doan say.

. . . No, I do shay; frenz.

Wel fanks, thats prity enlitenin.

. . . Payshinsh, yung man.

We negoshayate a few more branchiz.

Whare u takin me nway?

. . . 2 a plaish ov shafety.

Yeh, but whare?

. . . Payshinsh, yung man, payshinsh.

I can c am not goan 2 get nuffink out ov this slof so I juss shut up & content myself wif makin sily faces @ its big blak green-streekd bak.

Iss a long slow jurny.

. . . Thers fings goan on, Mr Bascule, thass ol I can sai; thers fings goan on. Frankly I dont no xactly whot they r myself, or whethir Id b abl 2 tel u about them if I did, but as I dont I cant nway, u c?

Not reely, I sez, witch is thi troof.

Thi slof-geezir whot can onli sai, Ther's fings goan on, is calld Hombetante & heez thi cheef slof; heez got implantz & is actule considerd a bit ov a lyv wyr by slof standirds tho u cude stil go off & 1/2 a p, wosh yoor hans & brush yoor teef in thi time it taks him to blink. Heez fat & old & gray & his fungus lukes moar lyvli than he duz.

Am in a 1/2 runed bit ov thi saim towr whare thi big bat cald a jericule dropt me last nite. Me & Gaston thi slof got heer aftir about a our in thi babil, comin in thru a tol windo 1/2 ovirgroan wif babil branchiz.

This seemz 2 b Slof Sentril; iss lyk a hole room fool ov scafoldin & hangin 10ts & hamox & stuf. Thers rubbil on thi floar & no glas or anyfin in thi windos & thi wind blos in thru a windo on thi otheir syd ov thi hooj circulir room & thru thi scafoldin & makes everfin sway in thi breez & thi slofs doan seem 2 tak ver gude care ov thi plais no moar than thay do ther oan selfs, but @ leest thai gaiv me sum woter 2 drink & 1/2 a qwik wosh in & then gaiv me sum frute & nuts to eet. Id 1/2 preferd sumfing hot but I doan fink thi slofs r grate fans ov fyr so heetin stuf up mite b a problim.

Weer in a big spais in thi sentir ov thi scafoldin whare thi slofs aparently hold ther meetins. Bet thos r a bundil ov lafs.

Hombetante is hangin upside down from a bit ov scafoldin on a low staje @ 1 end ov thi meetin spais, thi floar ov which is coverd wif simla curvd lenths ov scafoldin like ver tol railins. Theyve given me a sorta sling thing 2 sit in suspendid from Hombetante's scafold pole. Thi only othir slof presint is Gaston, whose hangin from anuthir bit ov scafoldin alongside, munchin sloaly on sum particulerly un-yummy lookin leefs.

. . . U r welcom 2 stay heer, Hombetante sez, until thingz settil down.

Whot u meen, settil down? I ask. How r they settled up @ thi momint? Whot xactly is supposed 2 b goan on?

. . . Juss things, Mr Bascule. Things witch need not consern u @ thi momint.

Whot about a certin ant who goes by thi name ov Ergates? U no anyfin about hir fate?

. . . U r juss yung & doutlis hedstrong, Hombetante sez, very much like he hasnt herd whot I juss sed . . . I woz yung 1nce myself u no. Yes I no u mite find that hard 2 beleev but it is tru; I wel remember . . .

I woan bore u wif thi rest. Whot it boils doun 2 is thers trubil @ kript & sumhow Ive got mixd up in it. Mite ol b cleerd up soon, mite not. Hooevir is supposed 2 b thi good gies in ol this r bhind thi jericule pikin me up yesterday & Gaston cumin 2 find me 2day. Now am heer wif thi slofs am been told 2 lie lo, & not go neer thi kript.

& – ov coarse – 2 $^1/_2$ payshins.

Aftir my odyince wif Hombetante during which he tels me $^1/_2$ his life story & I neerly fol asleep twice Gaston takes me 2 a playce neer thi outside ov thi scaffoldin whare thers a room wif a hamok & a sling chare & a ole fashind screen workin off brodcasts. Thers a sorta cubby-hole in 1 corner with a pipe stikin up which is suposed 2 b a toylit. 2 floars abuv thers a place whare thi slofs gathir 4 food evry evenin. Also in thi room is a boal ov frute & a jug ov water. Thers a windo in 1 wol whot lukes out 2 thi big vertikil towr windo we came thru. Gaston shows me how thi screen wurx & sez if I get board I can always go frute & nut gatherin with him.

I say thangs, maybe 2morrow, & he goes & I get in2 thi hamok & pool thi cuvirs ovir & go strate 2 sleep.

I juss no am goan 2 go crazy heer, + I no that am goan 2 $^1/_2$ 2 visit thi kript sooner or later, 2 luke 4 Ergates & fynd out whots goan on, so when I wake up in thi late afternoon I splash sum water on my face, $^1/_2$ a p & 1nce Ive decided I jenerili feel awake & refreshd, I get rite down 2 it, on thi principil that thers no time like thi presint.

I try 2 cleer my mind ov ol things slof-like (cant fink ov anyfing less usefil 2 take in2 thi kript than eny semblence ov sloffoolniss) & plunje rite in.

I think I lernd a thing or 2 during ol that time I spent in thi kript as a bird so I hed bak in that direcshin onli this time am not fukin about wif wee dainty sparos or hoks or nuffin; am goan as a big bastardin burd; a simurg. Thare so big ther branes can cope wif a hoomin mind without much finessin, which meens I doan $1/2$ 2 spend moast ov my time rememberin what I am or disgysin ma wake-up code as a ring. Iss a bit ambishis but sumtimes thass thi only way 2 get nywhare.

I close ma Is.

/Check out thi immediet locality furst; nuthin out ov thi ordinary in thi neerby kript-space. $1/2$ a shufty @ thi arcitecture ov thi towr juss on jeneril principils – this ole towr iz a interestin place rite enuf – then look a bit furvir out. Thi trafic aroun thi Littl Big Bros' monastry is juss about bak 2 normil but I doan go eny neerer 2 find out moar.

Zoom in2 birdspace.

/& am a hooj wild bird floatin on thi currents slidin wifin thi driftin wind, hangin lazily loosed on ma outstretchd wings cantileverd acros thi singin air. Ma wingtip fevirs r eech thi size ov hands; they flutir like a lam's hart flutirs when ma shado folz ovir it. Ma feet r steel-tipt grapples hung on thi end ov ma hawser legs. Ma talins r unsheethd razers; onli ma Is r sharper. Ma beek is harder than bone, keener than juss-broke glass. Ma keel bone is a grate nife cozend in ma flesh & cleevin thi soft air; ma ribs r glistnin springs, ma mussils sleek bunchd fists ov oily powr, ma hart a chambir fild wif slo thunder, qwiet & unstressd; a towrin dam triklin powr, tikin ovir, hedwaters ov charjed blud pent & latent.

Wel, YES! This is moar like it! Why did I evir bothir been a hok? Why woz I so bleedin unam*bishis*? I feel feers, I feel *powerfil*.

I look about, surveying. Air evrywhare. Clouds. No groun.

Othir birds flyin in vast Vs, climin in hooj colums in thi air, gatherid in ther own dark clouds, wheelin & collin. I think 2wards roosts.

/& am in thi midst ov them; spherikil trees floatin in thi grounles blueniss like brown planets ov twigs in a universe ov air, surrounded by a sqwakin atmosphere ov birds toin & froin.

Thi parlyment ov crows, I think.

/ & am thare, in bitter air between layers ov white cloud like mirr'rd landscapes ov snow; thi grate dark winter-trees r massd 2 thi density ov blak clifs agenst thi icy billos ov frozin cloud. Thi crows' parlyment is in thi tollest, gratest biggist tree ov ol, its brown-blak twigs like thi sooty bones ov a millyin hands clutchin @ thi chil blank fayce ov hevin. Thi meetin brakes up when they c me & they cum skrawkin & screetchin out 2 mob me.

I beat, pushin down thi air, risin ovir the pesterin burds, seekin 1 who stays bak, directin.

Thi crows swarm up aroun me. A few land blows on ma hed but it dozen hurt. I laf & stretch ma nek, swivelin ma hed an rippin a few ov ther litl toyish bodies from thi air. I toss them aside; red blud beeds, pulverized white bone pushes thru ther coal blak fevirs & they tumbil torn 2 thi snow-cloud billows. Thi rest screem, pull flutrin bak a momint then mob in agen. I stroke 4wards. Air snaps swirlin undir ma wings, rollin thi pursuin birds roun like bubbles under a waterfol.

I c my prey. Heez a big grey-black fellir perchd on thi topmost twig ov thi topmost branch ov thi parlyment-tree & heez juss reelised whots goan on.

He rises, cawin & shreekin in2 thi air. Foolish; if he'd dived in2 thi branchiz he mite 1/2 had a chance.

He tries sum aerobatic stuf but heez old & stiff & I snatch him so eesily iss almost disapointin. *Snap!* & he's neetly encased in one cage ov foot, flappin & screemin & loosin fevvirs & pekin @ ma toes wif his litl blak beek & tiklin me. I slice anuthir cupil ov his fellos out ov thi air, spredin ther blood like a artist wude, paint on a white canvas, then I think *eyrie*

/ & am alone wif ma litl crowy frend abuv a tawny plane ov sand & rok, beatin 2wards a fractchird clif whare a narled fingir ov rok juts out, its summit topt wiv a jiant nest ov sunbleechd timbirs & splintered white animal & burd bones.

I land & fold thi soft clokes ov ma wings & stand upon thi brittle nest – timbers creek, branchiz burst, pikd-cleen bones snap – lookin doun @ ma bolld foot wif thi old gray-blak crow imprisind in it, flappin an beetin an hollerin.

Skreek! Skrawk! Awrk! Gerout!

O shut up, I tel it, an thi rok-crushin weight ov ma voyce stuns it 2 qwiet stilniss. I balince on that leg, compressin thi trapt crow & reechin thru thi bars ov ma talins wif a talin from thi other foot, tiklin thi bird's grey-blak frote while thi breth wheeziz out ov it.

Now then my litl chum, I say – & ma voyce iz acid on a slicin blaid, boilin led doun a opin frote – Ive a few qwestchins Id like 2 ask u.

SIX

1

She stood on the piazza of the landing tower, looking west towards the heights of the structure.

The curtain-walls – easily two kilometres high and punctuated by the tall half-cylinders of the mural towers – curved away to either side, rising and falling over the gentle undulations in the landscape to diminish and disappear into the misted distance. Within the vegetation-strung cliffs of the walls lay a broad rolling landscape of wooded hills, sparkling lakes, manicured parkland and broad fields, all dotted with the spires and towers of small villages and towns.

Beyond, still slightly blued with the distance, the fastness itself reared forever into the sky. She stared, slack-jawed.

Serehfa was a frozen turbulence of architecture beyond the merely monumental: revetments rose like cliffs topped by broad, wooded scarps, stout bastions stood like jutting bluffs, serrated ridges of parapet lay stretched hazily like squared-off mountain ranges themselves, cloud-lined walls ascended sheer or stood pierced by the vast caves of dark windows, whole forested slopes of steep-pitched roofs lay serried green beneath the warmth of the high summer sun, and soaring arches of gables and buttresses climbed to higher and higher levels piled one on top of another, all swathed in whorling patterns of colour and climbing stacked, packed, placed and lifted to where the sparkling whiteness of snow and ice sat in a broad band of collected light thrown dazzlingly against the shining sky.

Everywhere about the panoramic, sight-saturating expanse of the central structure gigantic towers of mountainous diameter forced their way into the atmosphere, piercing the few, drifting, scale-diminished clouds which left their barely moving shadows aslant along the soaring walls and were themselves thrown into shade by still higher reaches of further towers casting their own stone shadows across both the clouds and the monstrous upheaval of the edifice itself; a crescendo of form and colour filling the horizon and culminating in the stark shining column of the central tower, drawing the gaze upward like some anchored moon.

'Well, there it is, in all its glory,' Pieter Velteseri said, joining her at the balustrade. He waved his walking stick at the castle.

Asura looked at him, eyes wide. '*Big*,' she said.

Pieter smiled and took in the view of the fastness. 'Indeed. The single largest artefact on Earth. The capital of the world, I suppose. And the last city, in a sense.'

She frowned. 'There are no more cities?'

'Well, yes, most of them survive, but someone from the Age of Cities would regard them more as large towns in terms of their populations.'

She turned to stare at it again.

'Do you know yet why you had to come here?' Pieter asked her softly.

She shook her head slowly, gaze fixed upon the fastness.

'Well, I dare say you'll remember when you have to.' Pieter took a fob watch from his waistcoat, frowned, closed one eye for a second, then reset the watch. He sighed and looked around the broad piazza, where umbrellas and sun shades flapped over tables and café bars. The airship rode at anchor above them in the breeze, nose connected to the landing tower. There were still a few lingering groups of castilians greeting those who had arrived on the craft, but most of the people now were either about to embark or bidding passengers farewell.

'Cousin Ucubulaire reports she is on her way,' Pieter told her. He nodded towards the countryside of the bailey. 'She's under there somewhere, in a slow-running tube train.'

'Tube train,' she repeated.

'My dear, I think you ought to have this.' He fished in one pocket of his dress coat and handed her a small wallet containing a thin card with writing and numbers on it. She studied it. 'It makes you an honorary member of our clan,' Pieter explained. 'Ucubulaire will look after you, but in case you feel you have to move on elsewhere from Serehfa, that ought to make sure you don't have to rely on hostels for a bed or public kitchens for food; can't have you hanging onto the outside of airships or trains, now can we?'

She looked at him, uncomprehending.

'Ah well,' he said. He closed her hands over the small wallet and patted them. 'You ought not to need it, but if anybody asks you what clan you're from, just show them this.'

She nodded. 'Phremylagists and Incliometricists.'

'Not one of the more active clans, I'll grant you, but ancient, and honourable. I hope we have been of some service.'

She smiled. 'You have made me welcome, and brought me here. Thank you.'

Pieter nodded to a wooden bench behind them. 'Let's sit, shall we?'

They sat, and for a while simply contemplated the castle.

She jumped when the airship sounded its horn. Pieter looked at his watch again. 'Well, I must go. Cousin Ucubulaire ought to arrive presently. Will you be all right waiting here?'

'Yes, thank you.' She stood with him, and he took her hand and kissed it. She returned the gesture and he laughed gently.

'I don't know what your business is here, my dear, or what lies in store for you, but I do hope you will come and visit us again, when you know what all this has been about.' Pieter hesitated and a troubled expression crossed his face for a moment, then he shook his head. 'I'm sure it will all sort itself out happily. But do come back and see us.'

'I shall.'

'I'm very glad to hear it. Goodbye, Asura.'

'Goodbye, Pieter Velteseri.'

He returned to the airship. A little later he appeared on the observation deck. He waved and she waved back, flourishing the wallet he'd given her before placing it carefully in a pocket. The airship's engines hummed into life; it lifted, turned across the breeze and started back east across the hills of Xtremadur.

She watched the vessel grow slowly smaller in the sky, then turned back to feast her sight upon the castle.

'Ah, Asura?' the woman said.

She looked up. There was a tall lady standing by the bench. She wore cool blue clothes the same colour as her eyes. Her skin was pale.

'Yes, I am Asura. Are you Ucubulaire?'

'Yes.' The woman put her hand out. 'Yes, I am.' Her grip was scratchy; her hands were covered with thin net gloves made from some fine but hard filaments. 'Pleased to meet you.' She indicated a tall, square-set, powerful looking man with deep-set eyes standing a little way off. 'This is a friend; Lunce.'

The man nodded. Asura smiled. He smiled, briefly.

'Shall we go?' the woman said.

'To there, to the fastness, yes?'

The woman smiled thinly. 'Oh yes.'

She stood up and went with them.

2

Consistory member Quolier Oncaterius VI sat in the single ice-scull, pulling hard on the oars while the seat slid under him, the breath whistled out of his lungs and the claw-blades bit and chipped into the smoothly glistening surface on either side. The scull was an A-shaped tracery of carbon tubing a child could lift with one hand; it skittered across the ice on its three hair-thin blades with a nervous, rumbling, hissing noise.

The chill blast of air slid round his body-suit and licked up over the seat harness towards his face.

He pulled, slid, pulled, slid, pulled, slid, settling into a steady rhythm of heart, lung and muscle, flicking the oars back and hauling them forward, the hooked claws at the shafts' ends embedding in the ice and providing the leverage to snap himself forward on each explosive haul.

The trick with ice-rowing was to judge precisely the weight and angle of attack of the stramazon – or downward cut – of the claws, while balancing the vertical and horizontal components of the stroke, thus ensuring both that one always had a sufficiently embedded grip on the ice's skin to provide purchase while wasting as little effort as possible lifting the claw-tips out of the ice again, and that one was always just on the edge of lifting oneself and the scull partially off the ice, but never quite doing so. It was a delicate double-balance to maintain and required both finely tuned judgment and great concentration. There were many aspects of a politician's – indeed a ruler's – life which demanded exactly such equipoise.

Oncaterius was proud of the skill he had developed at the sport.

He stroked on, oblivious to the space around him save for the fuzzy black mark of the lane centre-line printed under the ice. Around him stretched kilometres of ice, lightly populated by people on skates, ice boards and ice yachts. The thin air of the level-five Great Flying Room sounded to the zizz of blades inscribing the floor-lake's frozen surface and the propeller blades of the microlights describing lazy arcs about its lofted spaces.

Something clicked in Oncaterius' mind and a display superimposed itself in his vision, giving him his time for the kilometre course.

He shipped oars and sat back, breathing hard, the scull still skidding quickly across the ice. He gazed up at the microlights circling round the ornate, suspended architecture of the central stalactite at the crux of the room's groin-vaulted ceiling.

Soon, he thought, in perhaps as little as a century, all this would be gone. The Great Flying Room, Serehfa, Earth itself. Even the sun would never again be the same.

It was a thought that filled Oncaterius with a sort of delicious gloom; a melancholic ecstasy which made the appreciation of this current life all the sweeter. To treasure each moment, to savour every experience, to evaluate individually one's multitudinous feelings and sensations with the knowledge lodged within that events were hurrying to a close, that there was no longer a seeming infinitude of time stretching ahead of one; that was truly to live.

All that they and their ancestors had known throughout the monotonous millennia of the past since the Diaspora had been a kind of elegant death, an automaton's graceful impersonation of life; the surface without the substance. Well, it was going now. The arc of humanity's purpose – that is, real humanity, the part that had chosen to stay true to the past and what it meant – was finally drawing itself back into the shade after whole long troubled ages spent in the vexatious light of day.

Fruition. Consummation. Termination . . . Closure.

Oncaterius savoured the thoughts and correlations such words evoked, drawing their meanings and associations into his mind as he drew the cool, sharp air into his lungs; arid – even sterile – and yet invigorating. Especially when one knew that one would not necessarily have to share the fate of one's fellows, or one's surroundings.

The scull skated on across the water-filmed ice, gradually slowing.

Oncaterius leant back against the seat's spindly head-rest, letting it cup his neck and scalp. He crypted for a moment, reviewing the current security condition.

They still sought Sessine, who remained loose after all this time. Probably in hiding.

Security's quasi-official leak/rumour that any asuras would actually be agents of the crypt's chaotic levels sent with the purpose of infecting the properly functioning Cryptosphere seemed to be meeting with a mixed reception; however, enough people/entities appeared to believe it for an atmosphere of satisfyingly useful paranoia to have settled over at least some sections of the data corpus.

His Majesty himself had first reported the loss of a soldier at the bomb-workings; it remained to be seen to what extent this had jeopardised the project. There had been no reaction yet from the Chapel ambassadorial mission, though they had to assume that the Engineer emissaries had been informed through their secure channel to the Palace.

Concern remained over unusual patterns within the lower crypt; some obscure species of chimeric bird appeared to have developed behaviour above its station and so was under suspicion of being an agent for the chaos; the birds would be sought out and apprehended as soon as was practical. Linked with that, perhaps, was a young Teller who'd been making a nuisance of himself and who also appeared to have a suspiciously unusual turn of mind. He too had got away, like Sessine. Oncaterius cursed the millennia of peace and prosperity which had left the Security service so unpractised in dealing with genuinely serious problems. Still, they were keeping watch; the boy would show up sooner or later.

And, at last, his fellow Consistorians had finally agreed that it was time to act against the conspiracy they had known existed for the last five years.

That . . . was being dealt with satisfactorily.

*　　*　　*

Chief Scientist Gadfium and her staff left the office of the High Sortileger with the issue of the stray crypt signals still not resolved. They returned to the Great Hall the following day and ascended to the Lantern Palace so that Gadfium could attend the weekly cabinet briefing. Gadfium found these meetings exasperating; they were supposed to keep people up to date with developments and help facilitate actions which might be of use in the current emergency, but so far all they ever seemed to do was pander to some of the attendees' feelings of self-importance and produce vast amounts of talk that substituted for deeds rather than leading to them.

Nevertheless, with that familiar feeling that she was wasting her breath on matters more easily – and far more quickly – dealt with by reference to the data corpus, she outlined her opinions on the various issues she had been involved with during the past seven days, including the progress on the oxygen works, the odd pattern formed on the Plain of Sliding Stones and the worrying irregularities in the Cryptosphere which were making the Sortileger's predictions unreliable.

The meeting – in a fair approximation of the Hall of Mirrors in ancient Versailles – was attended in person by most of the participants including the King and Pol Cserse for the Cryptographers, though Heln Austermise, the second Consistory member, was at the rocketry test site at Ogooué-Maritime and so represented at the meeting by her court attaché, and speaking through him. He was a slim, middle-aged man in a tight-fitting court uniform; Gadfium suspected Rasfline – sitting behind her along with Goscil – would look like this man when he was older.

'Nevertheless, Chief Scientist, the tests with both the direct-lift and aerofoil-assist vehicles are proceeding as planned,' the attaché said. It was his own voice; the only sign that it was not his thoughts and volition producing it was that he sat very still, with none of the usual shiftings and fidgets people tended to exhibit. Gadfium had long since ceased to find it odd talking to somebody who wasn't there through somebody who – in a sense – wasn't there either.

'I don't doubt it, ma'am,' Gadfium said. 'But some of us are a little concerned at the lack of raw data being provided. The critical nature of this project— '

'I'm sure the Chief Scientist appreciates the importance of

retaining the prophylactic distance we have been fortunate enough to achieve from the chaos of the Cryptosphere,' the attaché said.

Gadfium paused before replying. She glanced at some of the others seated around the long table; the group was made up of the King, Consistorian Cserse, Austermise's attaché, representatives of other important clans and various civil servants, technicians and scientists. Gadfium thought the King – dressed soberly in a white shirt, black hose and tunic – looked bored in a handsome and elegant way.

Probably crypting somewhere more interesting.

'Indeed, ma'am,' Gadfium said, and sighed. She was starting to lose patience. 'I'm not sure I follow. Sending us data can pose no threat to— '

'On the contrary,' the attaché said. 'If the Chief Scientist will consult with Consistory member Cserse, she will perhaps be reminded that recent cryptographic research indicates that the transmission of chaotic data virus is possible through interface-handshakes and error-checking mechanisms. Even the link through which I am talking to you now cannot be guaranteed totally proof against such contamination.'

'I thought that there were comparatively simple, fully mathematically provable programs which could deal with— '

'I think madam Chief Scien— '

'*Kindly* allow me to finish a *sentence*, madam!' Gadfium shouted. That woke the King up. Others around the table moved as though uncomfortable. The attaché appeared utterly unruffled.

'I understood,' Gadfium said icily, 'that this problem had been dealt with.'

At the end of the table, Adijine sat up a little in his seat. It was enough to turn every eye to him. 'Perhaps madam Chief Scientist would like to detail the nature of her concerns regarding the lack of raw data?' he said, smiling at her.

Gadfium felt herself blush. This often happened when she addressed Adijine. 'Sir, I'm sure those in the facility at Ogooué-Maritime are exemplary in their dedication and scrupulousness. However I do feel that an independent check on their results might ensure that this project – of potentially vital importance, as I'm sure we all agree – ' she glanced again at the others, looking for and receiving a few nods '—is beyond reproach in terms of its methodology and hence the reliability of its results.'

The King was sitting forward, pinching his lower lip between his fingers and looking absorbed by what she was saying.

'I would also suggest that regardless of their precautions it can anyway only be a matter of time before their data corpora are contaminated by nanotech chaos-carriers.'

'I think if the Chief Scientist inquires of Consistory member Csèrse— ' the attaché began.

'Thank you, Madam Consistorian,' the King said, smiling broadly and nodding as though in encouragement as he interrupted her. 'I believe Gadfium may have a point,' Adijine continued, frowning a little and looking at Cserse. 'I think perhaps if we form a sub-committee to investigate data-transmission security and viral protection . . .'

Cserse nodded and looked wise. He turned to an aide and whispered to her, and she nodded too, sitting back and closing her eyes.

Adijine smiled at Gadfium. She showed her teeth and tried to look grateful, meanwhile biting back on the urge to scream.

'Another triumph for the decision-making process,' Gadfium said as she, Rasfline and Goscil exited to the antechamber. The briefing had finished and the group was splitting up, breaking into smaller groups of people standing in the Hall of Mirrors itself or the antechamber beyond. Gadfium usually hung around at this point too – it was now, as well as before such briefings, that real decisions were occasionally arrived at – but on this occasion she doubted her ability to remain polite if she had to talk to some of those she imagined might want to speak with her.

'I thought you made your points very well, ma'am,' Rasfline said quietly as they passed between the mirrored doors.

'Maybe,' Goscil said, brushing hair from her face. 'But the rocket people hate being reminded their fancy computers are going to catch chaos too.'

'Their precautions have worked so far,' Rasfline said.

Goscil snorted. 'They've only been up and running properly for the last year, and even then with minimal real input until two months ago. I give them three months, maximum, before something gets them.'

'You seem quite an expert in data contamination,' Rasfline told her, smiling at her and then at Consistorian Austermise's attaché, who was talking to a high-rank civil servant.

Goscil ignored the insult. 'There are nanotechs you can *exhale*, Ras; chaos-carriers that can float in an aerosol or crawl out of a skin pore.'

'Still,' Rasfline said, 'Ogooué-Maritime has avoided such infection so far; perhaps it will continue to do so.'

'Three months,' Goscil said. 'Want to bet on it?'

'Thank you, no. I believe gambling to be a pastime for the weak-minded.'

Gadfium looked round the various groups of people in the antechamber, the feeling of frustration building up inside her again. 'Oh, let's just go,' she said.

Rasfline smiled. Goscil scowled.

'Madam wishes a copy of herself made?'

'That's right. A construct, for the crypt.'

Gadfium had given herself, Rasfline and Goscil the rest of the day off. Rasfline had probably gone to socialise with some of the people they'd left in the Hall of Mirrors' antechamber. Goscil was doubtless crypting fresh data on some arcane subject. Gadfium had gone to change from her court clothes into something less formal in her apartment and then made her way to the Palace's Galleria, a shopping complex modelled after part of twentieth-century Milan where the court élite could indulge themselves. She had been here only once before, five years earlier, when she had first been summoned to the Lantern Palace to be Adijine's tame white-coat. She had been slightly disgusted by the snooty opulence of the place and its too-obviously perfect clientèle then and felt no different now, but she had a plan to execute.

She sat in the subtly lit boutique – a traumparlour by any other name – sipping coffee over an antique onyx table.

'With what purpose in mind, might one ask?' asked the sales girl.

'Sex,' Gadfium told her.

'I see.' The shop assistant had called herself a sales executive and was probably the daughter of some clan chief; this would be her societal apprenticeship, Gadfium expected; the equivalent of one of the genuinely shitty jobs young people from the lower orders were expected to take on before they were allowed to enjoy themselves. The girl looked fashionably delicate and stainlessly steely at the same time. She was dressed in red, wearing what looked like a one-piece swim suit, large boots and wrist muffs. Her skin glowed like polished chestnut, her body was flawless and her ice-blue eyes looked out over cheekbones Gadfium fancied a chap might cut himself on.

'I'm too busy for a real affair,' Gadfium told her, 'and anyway the other party is also Privileged and physically distant, so we want constructs made which can have fun on our behalf and then download the rosy afterglow, or whatever.' Gadfium smiled and slurped her coffee deliberately. The girl winced, then smiled professionally and patted her tied-back black hair, held in place by a red comb which – assuming the girl was Privileged – was probably a receptor device.

'Madam does realise that there are potential recompatibility problems, over time, with constructs made from Privileged persons.'

'Yes I do, especially with the kind of full-mind construct I'd like. But I am decided, and that is what I want.'

'Full-mind constructs are particularly prone to developing independence and becoming incompatible.'

'It only has to last a few weeks in crypt-time; a couple of months, maximum.'

'The contiguity-expectancy may indeed be of that order,' the girl said, looking troubled and recrossing her long legs with what Gadfium could only think of as a flourish. 'Most people would not be happy with a self-construct becoming independent over such a time-frame, especially in a romantic context.'

Gadfium smiled. 'Most people aren't realists,' she said. She put her coffee down. 'When can we do it?'

'Madam has the permission of her clan?' the girl asked, sounding dubious.

'I'm seconded to the Palace; I think you'll find I have all necessary authorisation.'

'There is also the question of . . . discretion,' the girl said, smiling thinly. 'While of course not illegal, strictly speaking, the service madam is requesting is not one it is generally thought best to publicise widely. Madam would be requested to make an undertaking to the effect that she would restrict knowledge of her acquisition strictly to those of her own standing whom she is certain could have no objection to the process involved.'

'Discretion is the whole point of this,' Gadfium said. 'Only myself and the other party would know.'

'The process will utilise the neuro-lattice which would normally only be activated on madam's quietus. This is the device which— '

'Yes, I know what it does.'

'I see. There is some danger . . .'

'I'll risk it, dear.'

Another Gadfium woke, looking out through the eyes of the original. This must be a bit how old Austermise feels, they both thought, and experienced the other's thoughts as an echo.

The view was of a gently lit booth lined with curtains of intricate design. She was in some reclined seat, her neck and head held firmly but comfortably. There were two people standing looking down at her; a serious-looking older woman in a white coat, and the young lady in red.

'Madam's very first memory, again?' the older woman said.

'Earlier I said it was the blue swing,' she said (and heard herself say it, and thought: *oh yes, the blue swing, but what about the—*), 'but actually I think it must have been the time when my father fell off his horse into the river.' (– *horse*? Ah . . .)

The woman nodded. 'Thank you. Do you still wish your construct to be released into crypt-time now?'

'Please,' Gadfium said, trying to nod but failing.

The woman in the white coat leant forward and reached out one hand to touch something on the side of the unit restraining Gadfium's head.

The man slipped in through the curtains behind the two women as the older woman's hand disappeared from Gadfium's field of view. He was tall, slim and dressed conservatively in a light suit. His face did not look quite right. He held something thick and black and curved in his hand. Gadfium only recognised it as a gun when he brought it up towards her.

Gadfium felt her eyes widen and her mouth start to open. The

girl in the red swimsuit began to turn round. The man saw her
turn towards him; the gun moved quickly to one side so that
it was no longer pointing at Gadfium's face but at the girl. The
man shot her first.

The noise was minimal; the girl's head jerked back and she
fell instantly, a delicate fountain of blood spraying up and back
onto the tented ceiling. Gadfium watched it all in real time

/and in crypt-time, as the older woman began to turn, her
hand still somewhere behind Gadfium's neck.

Gadfium felt her other self, the construct, drop away from
her like a bomb from a plane, producing an instant of vertigo
as the girl hit the floor and the man – his face too straight, too
unmoving – turned the black tube towards the woman in the
white coat. The shot hit her in the temple, whirling her round so
that she pirouetted as she collapsed. More blood, Gadfium felt, as
she tried to move her head but still could not, still trapped, still
held, as though her neck and head had been fixed in concrete,
bored through and bolted with steel.

The man's face turned impassively to her and the gun came
up. She beat her feet on the reclined couch, brought her hands
up to scrabble over the surface of the helmet unit trapping her,
feeling desperately for some release mechanism.

He took a step forward and pointed the gun at her forehead.

/ Quickened, she fell away from the scene in the traumparlour
an instant before the man shot the woman in the white coat.

Gadfium had visited the crypt many times, through receptor
devices in helmets, chairs and pillows; she was less adept than
the average person in navigating its complexities – the sort of
natural ease that came with immersion from childhood would
never be hers – but she was no stranger to the medium.

It took her new self only a few seconds of crypt-time to realise
that she was effectively free within the system, at least for now.
Existing initially within the traumparlour's grey-zone hardware
she had not yet been given an official crypt identity.

She checked the immediate surroundings for clues to why one
woman had been murdered, another was about to be and a third
– herself – soon going to be.

Everything seemed normal; no security blanket thrown over
the local data corpus, no obvious gaps in local traffic, no

closed-off circuits. Certainly the Palace crypt-space was supposed to be completely unrestricted – once you were in, which was the hard bit – but she had half expected to find some sort of crypt presence linked to the assassin. Perhaps the Palace's private channels really were inviolable; perhaps that was why simply sending in a man with a gun was considered the best way of dealing with a problem. She wondered briefly why all this was being done, what had triggered this ghastly, murderous act, but decided to leave investigating that for later.

She looked into the hardware surrounding her head. You turned off the restrainer field ... well, just here ... but she hesitated. Perhaps she could save her base-reality self.

She glanced back through Gadfium's eyes. The view was still, like a photograph. Running her own vision round the picture in Gadfium's mind exposed both the weakness of the human sight system and its cleverness. Looked at closely from inside with an independent ability to focus and concentrate on different parts of the view, you could *see* the lack of clarity and colour at the edges of vision; the view was grey and smeared everywhere about the lucid central portion. And so slow! What torture to watch somebody being killed and know your turn was next; the woman in white was still turning, the gun in the man's hand still moving to point to where her head would be in a moment's time ...

She sucked herself away from the view. First she had to double-check the headset release mechanism, then decide what her physical self ought to *do* next, then work out the right moves to get her out of this situation, then form it into a plan that could be dropped instantly into her base-reality self's head and be acted upon without the slightest flicker of hesitation ... she had less than a second, real time; a couple of hours, in here. It might be a close run thing ...

The gun came up to point at the middle of her forehead. Gadfium watched it, helpless.

Then it was as though the bomb she had felt dropping away from herself earlier had somehow slammed straight back into the top of her head.

Move!

Her head was free and suddenly there was a whole choreographed pattern inside her head; a slotted-in four-dimensional sculpture in which all she had to do was follow the tunnel-shape her body made through that sculpture.

The lights in the booth would go out *now*. They went out.

It was almost as though the pattern moved her body for her. She ducked her head and flicked it to one side as the shot cracked into the head unit. She levered herself forward with her elbows while drawing her right leg back. She snapped it forward and up just *here* . . .

The impact was appreciably two-fold, as both the bones in the man's fore-arm broke. She added to the momentum of her still swinging leg with a two-handed push off the couch and landed already swivelling on the floor. She punched upwards but the man hadn't reacted quite as she'd expected; cloth brushed her fist as he fell away, a sudden soughing noise coming from his mouth.

Something thudded into her head and for an instant she thought he had clubbed her, but the blow was light and the thing that fell from her head and bounced off her hip was the gun; she caught it on the floor.

The lights went on again. She turned the gun towards the man. He was crouched entangled within some of the room curtains, holding his broken arm and looking at her. Then his eyes rolled back in his head and he fell over on his side.

She started over towards him.

'. . . Gadfium,' said a voice, whispering.

She turned and stared in horror at the white-coated woman on the floor. Blood was still flowing from the dark hole in her temple; her eyes stared straight up. Her jaw moved again, looking stiff and mechanical, like a puppet's. 'Gadfium!' the voice croaked.

She spared the collapsed man a glance then went over to the woman, kneeling so that she could still see the man crumpled in the corner.

'This one's still not quite dead,' said the voice. 'She's been crypted, but she's still alive. It's me; *you*,' said the voice. 'Listen; he's faking a faint; the man. He's faking it. You must kick or cosh him in the head; now. Use the gun if you must, but if you want to avoid killing him do it now.'

Gadfium felt she was going to faint. The room was spinning,

or her brain was. 'I can't,' she said to the woman, watching in horrified fascination as the rich, dark red blood oozed slower and slower and the jaws and tongue moved beneath the open, staring eyes.

'You must; now,' the soft voice said.

'But he might just have— '

'Too late,' sighed the voice.

The man was whirling round, bringing his good hand back. Gadfium reached out with the gun and squeezed, closing her eyes. The gun shuddered once in her hands.

When she opened her eyes again the man was sprawled face down in front of her, a small thin knife still clutched in one hand.

She wasn't sure she'd hit him until the blood started to well blackly from beneath his hidden face.

She dropped the gun, then started when the woman said, '... I'm losing her. The girl's comb ... quickly, Gad ...'

She could not do it immediately. Gadfium sat against the curtain-concealed wall of the room for a few minutes, shaking and staring at the three bodies in the room, watching the blood flowing slowly across the tiled floor.

When the blood from the fallen man reached the pool spilled from the woman who'd spoken after her death, something broke within Gadfium, and she cried.

She had not shed tears since she'd been a teenager.

Then she sniffed, wiped her nose and went to the girl in red. She pulled the comb from the dead girl's tied-back hair. There were flecks of blood on it. She ignored them and shoved the comb into her own hair at the back of her head.

– ... can you hear me? said her own voice.

'Yes,' Gadfium said, her voice trembling.

– Just think it, Gadfium; no need to vocalise.

– I can hear you. Are you me?

– I am. I'm the construct.

– You planned ... all that?

– Yes. Are you all right?

– Oh, far from it. But what do I do now?

– Take the knife, its sheath, which is in his pocket, the gun and any extra ammunition and equipment the man has, then leave

the shop. If you do exactly as I say I think I can get you out
of there.

– Wait. Why was he trying to kill me?

– Because the conspiracy's been betrayed and you were about
to enter the crypt. Please; there isn't much time; hurry.

Gadfium went shakily back to the young man. She fought the
urge to vomit as she caught sight of her face reflected in the dark
pool of blood. She felt in the man's pockets.

– Is he from Security? she asked her crypt-self.

– Yes.

– How did they know?

– I told you, you were betrayed. I don't know by whom.

Gadfium stopped, her hand clasping the bullet magazine.

– *Betrayed*? What about the others?

– I don't know what's happened to them. I haven't dared to
try and contact them in case I'm being watched somehow and
my movements are being traced. Look, hurry up, will you?

– Betrayed. Gadfium stared at the intricate pattern on the
curtain in front of her. Betrayed.

– Yes; now *please*; you must hurry now. Take what you can
and leave. Turn left when you leave the shop.

– Betrayed, Gadfium thought, pocketing the knife, sheath,
gun and ammunition. Betrayed.

– Yes, yes, yes; betrayed. Now *move*!

3

Sessine was dressed in plain, utilitarian clothes and carried a
light rucksack across his shoulder. He stood on the last ridge
of the hills, where the land sloped away like some huge wave
powering towards a beach. The dusty plain extended before him,
the colour of a lion; not featureless, but almost so. Hints of hills
lay upon the horizon, and patches of reflection promised water
that probably was not there. The trees behind him, above him,
made giant shushing noises.

The light came from every part of the sky, shining without a sun. The sky was light blue to the glance, darker blue then purple on closer inspection, and utterly black when stared at. On that blackness – just by willing it into existence – a network of shining lines appeared, and what looked like brightly coloured stars and fat planets shone beyond, in constellations and patterns never seen from the real Earth. He knew what these meant without having to think about it. He looked away, and the sky was light blue again.

He stared at the broad expanse of tableland, and in an eyeblink the plateau filled with a grid of tracks, roads and paths so densely packed and interlaced they created their own solid surface, overwhelming the plain. The network of trails and lines radiated away to the horizon, filling the view with blurred, flickering movement; vast broad highways buzzed and glittered with complex articulations travelling too quickly for any individual element to be discerned, but creating a conglomerative impression of streamed solidity. Elsewhere, on narrower routes, long trains of material flashed past, just glimpsed, while an unseen myriad of paths specked and sparkled with solitary packets of traffic.

In another blink, it was all gone again.

He turned to his other self.

'Well, here we are,' said the construct. 'The parting of the ways. You remember all you need to remember?'

'How would I know if I didn't?'

'Hmm-hmm. What do you remember?'

'I am going into the wilderness,' he said, looking back at the plain.

'For sanctuary?'

'For sanctuary. And to seek and be sought. To provide a container, a medium for whatever I find out there.'

'You will change.'

'I have already changed.'

'You will change forever, and may die.'

'I think you will find we have always lived with that knowledge; not all our betterments have really changed such matters.'

'I hope I've given you all you may need.'

'So do I.' He looked the other man in the eye. 'And you, now?'

Alan turned and glanced back to where a distant mural tower

was visible through the swaying trees. 'I'll be back in there,' he said. 'Doing what I've always done; watching. And waiting on your return; preparing.'

'Well, until then.' He offered his hand.

'Until then.'

They shook hands, both smiling self-consciously at the physicality of the ritual, still germane even in this translation from base-reality.

The construct nodded out at the plain, where the ghost-image of furious movement still seemed to linger.

'Sorry it will be so slow.'

'Slow is safe, in this.'

'Good luck.'

'And you.'

Then they each turned, and one headed back uphill on the path between the trees, making for the vast cliff of wall towering beyond, while the other set off down the slope towards the plain.

He walked out across the semi-desert. The paths here were so densely packed there was indeed effectively one single surface. He watched dust drift behind him on a soft breeze and wondered what aspect of the crypt's nature it signified. He stopped and looked behind him, back to where the foothills rose, sprinkled with trees. The fastness hung half-hazed in the sky beyond.

His footprints lay in the dust, leading back to the ridge.

He looked around and saw other footprints scattered here and there in lines that criss-crossed the plain. Above, the sky stayed blue, with no hint of cloud. He walked on, and when he first saw a stretch of ground where flat rocks lay like pages of stone upon the prairie, walked towards them and then upon them, changing his direction a little to follow the outcrop. When the rocks submerged beneath the dusty ground again he struck off in a different direction again.

At the next group of rocks, he sat down and held one of his shoes out to one side so that he could look at the sole. The sole was composed of simple ridges running from side to side. He thought about it changing, and the pattern changed to chevrons. He did the same with the other shoe, and felt pleased that on this scale such changes could still be effected. He hefted his rucksack, wondering what might be in it but knowing better than to look. All that mattered – he could half recall being told – was that there were useful objects within it.

He got up and continued walking.

A few times he heard the sand and rocks around him making a high-pitched keening noise, and knew he was near one of the great data highways. He would stop and stare and the highway would be there; a vast shining pipe on the surface of the plain, roaring like a waterfall, charged with pulsing, flashing movement and itself moving ponderously, writhing like an immense snake stretching from horizon to horizon, sweeping from side to side in great loops and waves and alternately raising its semi-fluid bulk up from the ground and troughing it back down.

The first time he encountered one of these gigantic, shimmering pipes, he sat and watched it. The accumulation of its sinuous movements gradually took it away, then started it moving towards him again. He inspected the surface of the plain, and saw where the ground had been scuffed clean by the paths the highway had taken. It reminded him of a river delta, where channels form, flood, silt and shift, and islands seem to move, shuffled across the flood by the ever-weaving braid of waters.

He chose his spot and – more because he wanted to check that it was possible than because he particularly wanted to proceed in that direction – ducked beneath the arched under-surface of the highway as it bowed over the sand and ran, doubled up, for the far side, the highway's great bulk a roaring shadow above him.

It was done without mishap and he looked back at the tubular rush of the highway with satisfaction.

He continued walking.

A breeze got up after a while and he was grateful for it though he was not hot; the breeze was simply something different. He felt no hunger or thirst and no fatigue; realising this he started to run, and after a while did feel tired, and his breathing became laboured. He settled back to a stroll and when he'd got his breath back he increased his speed to the pace he'd been maintaining earlier.

Darkness waxed slowly.

When the light had quite gone from the sky he was able to see a ghostly grey image of the ground in front of him, and walked on. He stared up at the black sky and it filled with the network of lines and lights again. He watched the grid shift and the constellations change, just for something to do, knowing that somewhere inside himself he knew what this silently fabulous display signified, and unworried that its import was not quite immediately available to him, but lodged in some memorative backwater he knew he could explore if he really needed to.

He stared at the plain and saw the great roads and tracks and highways again, though they looked a little more dispersed than they had been before.

Most of the time he just walked, head down, hardly thinking about anything.

After a while he felt light-headed and thought he heard voices and saw shapes that weren't there in any reality. He started to trip over rocks or roots that were not there either, each time feeling like he was back in his earlier, biological life, and was in bed, about to fall asleep, but had suffered some involuntary spasm which had wrenched him back to wakefulness. This happened again, and again and again.

He decided he needed to sleep after all. He found a hollow under a rocky outcrop, put his rucksack beneath his head and fell asleep.

4

U no whot am goan 2 do if u doan tel me whot I wan 2 no, doan u? I sez 2 thi ole crow caged in ma talinz.

Am restin in ma big nest on thi fingir ov stoan lookin out ovir thi desirt, sittin here qwite happily pullin out thi old grey-black crows fevvirs 1 by 1 wif ma free foot, hummin 2 maself & tryin 2 get sum sens out ov thi ole bird.

I doan no nuffin! thi grey-black cro shouts. Yool pay 4 this, u peece ov filf! Set me bak whare u fownd me imeedyitly & mibi we say no moar about this – eerk!

(I scrunch his beek a bit wif 2 ov my talinz.)

Zhou schwine! he blubbers.

I dcide itz time 2 fix thi old fellir wif a serius stare, so I lower

my grate-beekd head doun 2 his levil & luke in thru thi talin-bars
@ his litl black beedi Is. He trys 2 luke away but I hold his hed
roun lukin 2wards me wif a talin & put my hed closer 2 him (tho
not 2 cloas – Im not stupid). Crows cant acthurely move ther Is
very much & now he cooden move his hed neethir. They'v got
a thing cold a nicitatin membrane whot they can flik over ther
I & this old chap's nicitatin like mad tryin 2 blok me out & if
I wozen such a fine firm fleshd-out eggzampil ov a simurg he
mite blok me out (or evin takin me ovir if he woz tryin), but
I am so he cooden & I woz in thare.

I had dcided in my oan mind by this time that simurgs wer
relatid 2 lammergeiers & as eny fule wil tel u lammergeiers r
also nown as bone crushers. So thi ole crow lukes in2 ma mind
& seez whot I intend 2 do & promtly shits himself.

I luke @ thi mess on ma fine razor-sharp talons & ma nicely
decorated nest & then luke @ him agen.

O f-f-fuk, he whimpirs. Zhorry about that. His voyce is
qwivirin. Ah wil tel u enyshink u wan 2 no; jhust doan do
those shings 2 me.

Hmm, I sez, liftin him up a bit 2 luke poyntidly @ thi shit
on ma nest. Weel c.

Wot u wan 2 no? he shreeks. Jhust tel me! Whot u lookin 4?

I jab ma hed 2wards him. A ant, I tel him.

A *wot*?

U herd. But letz start wif thi lammergeiers.

Zhi lammergeiersh? Zhare gon.

Gon?

From zhe kript. Gon.

Gon whare?

Nobudi noaz! Zhey bin weerd & dishtint 4 a while & now
zhey juss aint aroun no moar. Itsh thi troof; check it out 4
yooself.

I wil, & b4 I let u go, so u *betr* b telin thi troof. Now wot
about this bleedin red-face fing goze gidibibidibigibi etc etc u
get thi idear, eh? Whots it when its @ hoam then?

Thi ole crow freeziz 4 a sekind, then he starts 2 shake & then
he – I can hardly bleev it – he lafs!

Wot? he shrieks, ol histerikil. U meen zhat shing bhind u, is
that whot u meen?

I shake my hed. What sorta bird u take me 4? I ask it, shakin it up & doun so it rattlz like a dice ina cup. Eh? Eh? Juss how stupid u fink I am? Do I *look* like a bleedin pidgin?

Gidibidibigidigibigi! screams a voyce bhind me.

(I feel ma Is go veri wide.)

I stair @ thi bedraggled blak crow trapt in thi talinz ov ma rite foot.

Anuthir time, I sez, & crush thi crow 2 thi size ov a frush.

I whirl roun & fro thi ded crow @ whare I hope thi orribil red hed fing is, pushin maself off thi nest @ thi same time.

Gidibidibigidigibigi! thi skind hed shrieks, & thi old ded crow explodes in2 flame & disappeers as it hits thi jaggd red hole ov thi thingz flayd nose. Thi hed's bigr than it woz b4 & itz got wings ov its own now; wings like thi wings ov a skind bat, ol wet & bludy & glistenin. Fukr's biggr than I am & its teeth luke sharp as hel. I beat ma wings, not turnin & flyin away but hoverin thare, starin @ it like its starin @ me.

Gidibidibigidigibigi! it screams agen & then itz xpandin, rushin 2wards me like its a planit bloatin, a sun xploadin. Am not fuled; I no its stil thi size it woz reely & this is just a feynt. I glimpse thi reel thing cumin strate @ me like a punch throan thru thi xplodin imidje.

This is ma nest. Thi hed's over thi edje ov it rite now.

I take 1 qwik flap cloaser & reach out wif a foot & slap down on a hooj white-bleechd hunk ov timber; thi timber is most ov a tree-trunk & it leevirs up in a xploashin ov smallir branchis & smaks strate in2 thi face ov thi thing goan Gidibidi-urp!

Itz wings cloase involuntirly aroun thi tent ov branchis stikin up in front ov it & it fols flappin 2 thi nest, ol tangled & shriekin & bouncin & flappin & tearin its wingz & I juss no I shude get thi hel out while thi goans good but col it instinkt, col it madnis, I jus 1/2 2 attak.

I giv 1 moar flap 2 get a bit ov hite – noatisin that thi sky seems 2 b gettin briter – then spred ma talins & start 2 drop 2wards thi orribil hed fing.

Thi sky's gon very white & brite.

I cansil thi stoop & flap 1ce more, hoverin ovir thi flappin screemin entangled hed & lookin up @ thi sky; its gon dark agen, but itz startin 2 bulje sumwot.

O-o, I fink, & say my wake-up word 2 myself.

* * *

Ther r certin fings witch wil impose themselvs on u evin when u r in thi depfs ov thi kript, & a xploashin is 1 ov them; Ither a very brite flash ov lite or a shok wave & certinly boaf, witch is whot I woz gettin heer. U doan 1/2 2 wake up & if yoor in deep enuf u woant, yool juss xplain it away 2 yoourself evin if itz blowin u apart as u fink, but am not so daft.

Thi blast rols me ovir in ma room, bouncin me off a taut-strung wall & flinging me bak in2 thi centir ov thi room agen.

I luke out thi doar thru smok & flames & c men cumin down ropes from abuv thi big window in thi tower; a handful ov gies in wing-shutes r flyin in thru thi windo, hedin 4 thi scaffoldin, shootin wif guns that send bolts ov lite thru thi smoak. A slof fols flamin past thi doorway ov ma room, makin a tearin, roarin noise as it fols & leavin a trail ov thik blak smoak. Anuthir xploashin roks thi scaffoldin aroun me & thi wols bulge. I c thi lite ov big flames shinin thru thi fabric wol 2 my rite. Outside, thi gies in thi wing-shutes swing ther guns 2 1 side & reech out 2 grab thi scafoldin as they thump in2 it; ther shutes fall away as soon as they tutch.

I rol away 2 thi bak ov ma room & bite @ thi fabric juss abuv thi floar; it holes & I hawl & pool @ it til it tares sum more then sqwirm out thru & in2 relativ darknis.

Am bhind thi wols ov thi slofs' scafold structyir, swingin from poal 2 poal like a munky, hedin downwirds. A hooj xploshin ov flame bursts out overhed, showerin me wif flamin debree; I 1/2 2 hang by 1 hand from a poal & pat out flames on ma shirt. Thi debree fols on down, litein thi way. Ther r qwite a lot ov flaims now, & gunfire.

Part ov ma mind is thinking, Blimey, can ol this reely b 4 me? & anuthir part is thinkin, No, Bascule, doan b silly! But thi first bit is goan, Then how cum ther's ol this vilence & stuf happenin aroun yures truly? This aint a vilent sosiety; bags is pretti peesfil as a rool. How cum ol this is happenin ol ov a suddin? O fuk; those poor slofs woz juss tryin 2 b frendly & how do I repay them? I wunder how fings 1/2 shakin out 4 Gaston & ole Hombetante. Then I figir mayb its best if I try not 2 fink about that sorta fing; iss dun now.

Amazin thi survivil mekanisms u bild up in times like this.

Ahed ov me I can c thi curvd innir surfis ov thi wol ov thi towr, its undressd stoan & ol blak & glistenin wif moystyir in thi lite ov flames. A few last poals 2 go, regularly spaced.

Rite hand lef hand rite hand lef hand; am in a feevir or sumthin coz I fink; juss thi time 2 kript 4 a sekind, & as I reach 4 thi next poal I fink, rite, kript until u tutch this poal, & am thare, deliberitly not finking about whare I am @ thi momint but swingin out in2 thi imeedyit locality

/only 2 find it isnt thare eny moar.

It's like ther's juss a grey fog ol aroun me; a metallic, growlin, hissin, static-ish sorta fog. I can rufly remembir whare things wer from erlyer but I doan wan 2 $^1/_2$ 2 trust 2 memry that mutch. Then thi fog semes 2 collect aroun me & its like its not fog @ ol its made up not ov water but ov metil filings, metil dust, sleetin in2 ma skin like asid, burrowing in2 ma pores & it hurts & ma Is go wide & thi metil dust is sandpaperin ma Is & makin me screem & as I opin my mouf its fillin it & nose wif metil grit & am breevin it in & its fire, like breevin flame, fillin me, roastin me from inside.

I flail out @ it, tryin 2 push it away & my hand tutches sumfink solid & I remember that means sumfing & wif a struggil I wake up.

My hand clutches thi cold bar ov thi scaffold poal & I feel thi bref whistel out ov me & I sneez & my Is watir & my skin itches evrywhare & I juss manidje 2 grab thi last poal & then fump in2 thi blak stone wol & stop thare, stil shakin & not feelin 2 good.

Thi floar is a cupil ov metirs lower down, coverd in rubish. Lukin up, thi wol disappers in2 darknis. On ither side, it curvs away, blak & barely visibil. Thi slofs' scafoldin structure fits raggedly agenst thi wol, poals stuk restin on bits whare thi ruf stone juts out & thi grey sakclof stuf flappin in thi breez. Thi channil I escaiped down rises like a naro blak canyin abuv me. Flames burn in thi distins.

I try 2 remember thi layout ov thi place from thi start ov my kriptin erlyer. Bleedin hel.

I shake my hed, then start leepin acros from poal 2 poal along thi side ov thi ruf stoan wol. Shude b this way . . .

& so I go swingin off thru thi dark space behind thi wols ov thi place whare thi slofs hang out, or @ leest did until theez gies wif thi guns & parashoots & stuf caim collin.

Am a rat bhind thi bleedin wols, I fink, skurryin abuv thi rubish lookin 4 a hole 2 disapeer down.

O deer Bascule I think 2 myself, not 4 thi furst time & Ive a orribil feelin not 4 thi last time neethir. O deer o deer o deer.

SEVEN

1

They descended through the tower by lift and went through broad, softly lit tunnels lined with pictures to a place where there were lots of trains and people and pillars which held the roof up.

Asura asked many questions about the lift and the station and the trains and the castle. The tall lady did her best to answer them. They went to the very end of one train and got on it. They had the carriage to themselves. It had lots of big seats and couches. They sat at a round wooden table; the woman who had introduced herself as Ucubulaire sat beside her and the man called Lunce sat across from them.

'What's that in your hair?' the woman said, when they were seated, and reached one hand – covered in the blue-net glove – up behind her head.

'What?' Asura asked. Then the blue glove touched the back of her head and there was a strange buzzing noise.

Darkness.

She lived in a tall tower in the forest. The tower had one large room at the top where she lived. The room had a stone floor with no holes in it; the walls had some small windows, and one door which led out onto a balcony which went all around the tower. The very top of the tower was made from a big cone of dark slates, like some huge hat.

She woke each day and went to wash her face. She washed from a bowl on a stout wooden wash-stand. Beside the bowl was a pitcher which was always full of water every morning. Several times she had tried to stay up to see how it got refilled every night but although she had been sure she'd stayed awake each time she never found out. Once she had sat up with her hand in the empty pitcher, pinching herself every now and again to stay awake, but she must have fallen asleep because she woke with a start to find her hand submerged in water. Another night she turned the pitcher upside down and slept beside it, but all that happened was that no water appeared in it that night and she went thirsty the next day.

There was a bread box on another table, and every morning there was a fresh loaf in it.

Each day she would use the pot under the bed and cover it with a cloth and each morning it would be empty and clean.

There was a beaten-metal mirror on the wash-stand. She had light brown skin and dark brown eyes and hair. She was dressed in a light brown shift that never seemed to get particularly dirty, or any cleaner. She looked at her reflection for a long time sometimes, thinking that once she had looked different, and trying to remember what she had looked like, and who she had been, and what had brought her here. But her reflection didn't appear to know any more than she did.

As well as the bed, the wash-stand table and the table with the bread box in it, the room contained another small table with two chairs set at it, a couch with some cushions, a square carpet with a geometrical pattern, and one wooden-framed painting on the wall. The painting was of a beautiful garden filled with tall trees; at the centre of the picture was a small white stone rotunda set on a grassy hillside above a shallow valley where a stream sparkled.

After she had washed and dried her face she would walk round the balcony a hundred times one way and then a hundred times the other way, occasionally looking out at the forest.

The tower stood in a roughly circular clearing about a stone's throw across. The tower was a little higher than the trees, which were broad-leaved. Sometimes she saw birds flying in the distance, but they never came close. The weather was always good; clear and breezy and warm. The sky was never free from clouds, but never covered by them either. It was a little colder at night.

There was no lamp in the circular room and the only light at night came from the stars or the moon, which waxed and waned in the usual manner. She remembered that women had a body-cycle associated with the moon, but waited in vain for its appearance.

On the very darkest nights, it rained sometimes. Once she had become familiar with the room in the darkness she began to get up and slip off her shift and go out onto the balcony into the pelting chill of the rain, standing naked under it, shivering. The rain felt good on her skin.

She watched the stars on clear nights, and noted where the sun came up and set each day. The stars appeared to revolve overhead but did not change otherwise, and there was no terrible dark stain across the face of the night.

The sun rose and set in the same place every day, as did the moon, despite its changing phases.

She used her thumb nail to make little grooves on the wooden foot board at the end of her bed, counting the days; those did not disappear overnight. She still recorded each day, but after the first thirty or so she had decided to count the moons instead, keeping the number in her head. She vaguely recalled that each moon was a month, and so knew that she had been here for six months so far.

She spent a lot of time just looking out at the forest, watching the shadows of the clouds moving over the tops of the trees. In the room, she busied herself by rearranging things, altering the position of the pieces of furniture, tidying them, cleaning things, counting things, and – after a month of doing this – by making up stories set in the garden in the painting on the wall, or in the landscape she conjured into being amongst the folds of her bedclothes, or in a maze-city she imagined within the geometric design of the carpet.

She traced the shapes of letters on the wall and knew she could write things down if only she had something to write with, but she could not find anything; she thought of using her own night soil but that seemed dirty and anyway might disappear overnight, the way it did from the pot under the bed; her own blood might work but that seemed overly desperate. She just remembered the stories instead.

She made up different people to populate her stories; at first they all involved her but later it amused her to make stories up in which she either played only a small part, or even no part at all. The people were based on the things in the room: there was a fat jolly man like the water pitcher, his broad-hipped wife who was like the bowl, their two plump daughters like the legs of the wash-stand, a beautiful but vain lady like the beaten-metal mirror, a pair of skinny men like the two chairs at the small table, a slim, languorous lady like the couch, a dark, skinny boy like the carpet, a rich man with a pointed hat who was the tower itself . . .

Gradually, though, the handsome young prince began to figure in most of her stories.

The prince came to the tower once every month. He was handsome and he would come riding out of the forest on a great dark horse. The horse was splendidly caparisoned; its bridle shone like gold. The young prince was dressed in white, purple and gold. He wore a long thin hat set with fabulous feathers. He had black hair and a trim beard and even from that distance she could tell that his eyes sparkled. He would take off his hat, make a sweeping bow, and then stand holding the reins of the great dark horse and shout up to her:

'Asura! Asura! I've come to rescue you! Let me in!'

The first time, she had seen him riding out of the forest and hidden down behind the balcony's stone parapet. She'd heard him shouting up to her and she'd scuttled away back inside the room and closed the door and burrowed under the bedclothes. After a while she'd crept outside again and listened, but heard only the sighing of the wind in the trees. She'd peeped over the balustrade and the prince had gone.

The second time, she'd watched him but hadn't said anything. He'd stood calling up to her to let him in and she'd stood, frowning, looking down at him but not replying.

He'd left his horse tied to a tree; it had grazed the nearby grass while he'd sat with his back to another tree and eaten a lunch of cheese, apples and wine. She'd watched him eat, her mouth watering as he'd crunched into an apple. He'd waved up to her.

Later, he'd called to her again but still she hadn't replied. It had started to get dark and he'd ridden away.

The third time he'd appeared she'd hidden once more. He'd stood shouting for a time, then she'd heard something metallic strike the stonework outside on the balcony. She'd crept to the door and looked out; a three-hooked piece of metal on the end of a rope had come sailing over the balustrade and clunked down onto the balcony's flagstones. It had scraped across the stones and up the wall with a rasping noise, then disappeared over the edge of the parapet. She'd heard a distant thud a few seconds later.

It had reappeared a little while later, hitting the balcony stones with a clang and leaving a mark there. Again, it had been hauled up the wall in vain; it was as though the balustrade had been designed to offer nowhere such a hook could find purchase. It had disappeared again and she'd heard the distant thud as it hit the ground far below. She'd stared in horror at the mark it had left on the flagstones.

On the fourth occasion the prince had arrived at the foot of the tower and again called out, 'Asura! Asura! Let me in!' she had already decided she would reply this time.

'Who are you?' she'd shouted to him.

'She speaks!' he'd laughed, a huge smile brightening his face. 'Why, what joy!' He'd stepped closer to the tower. 'I'm your prince, Asura! I've come to rescue you!'

'What from?'

'Why,' he'd said, laughing, 'this tower!'

She'd looked back at the room, then down at the stones of the balcony. 'Why?' she'd said.

'*Why?*' he'd repeated, looking puzzled. 'Princess Asura, what do you mean? You cannot *enjoy* being imprisoned!'

She'd frowned deeply. 'Am I really a princess?'

'Of course!'

She'd shaken her head and run back to her bed in tears, burrowing under the bedclothes again and ignoring the distant sound of his cries until it had grown dark and she'd fallen into a troubled sleep.

The next time he'd come she had hidden again, closing the door to the balcony and sitting on the couch singing to herself while she'd stared at the picture on the wall, softly singing a story about a prince coming to the white stone rotunda in the beautiful garden and leading the princess away to go with him and be his bride and live in the great castle in the hills.

It had grown dark before she'd finished the story.

She washed her face in the bowl and dried herself on the towel. She went outside for her walk round the balcony. A flock of birds flew over the forest, far in the distance. The weather was as it always was.

She stopped in the shade of the tower's roof, looking out at the shadow the tower cast, swinging imperceptibly over the canopy of forest as though together they formed some huge sundial. She was sure the prince would come today.

The prince arrived just before noon, riding out of the woods on his magnificent horse. He took off his hat and bowed deeply.

'Princess Asura!' he called. 'I have come to rescue you! Please let me in!'

'I can't!' she shouted.

'Have you no ladder? No rope? Can you not let down your hair?' he asked, laughing.

Her hair? What was he talking about? 'No,' she told him. 'I have none of those things. I have no way down.'

'Then I shall have to come up to you.'

He went to his horse and took a great slack bundle of rope from a saddle-bag. Attached to one end of the rope was the three-hooked metal thing he'd tried to scale the tower with earlier. 'I'll throw this up to you,' he shouted. 'You must tie it to something securely. Then I'll climb up to you.'

'What then?' she shouted, as he readied the rope.

'What?'

'Well, then we'll both be up here; what will we do then?'

'Why, then we'll make a sling for you; a sort of seat on the end of the rope. I'll lower you down to the ground and climb down after you. Don't you worry about that, my princess; just make sure this is tied firmly to something that won't move.'

He started to swing the hook round and round beside him.

'Wait!' she called.

'What?' he asked, letting the rope down.

'Have you an apple? I would like an apple.'

He laughed. 'Of course! Coming right up!'

He went to his saddle-bags and found a bright red shiny apple. 'Catch!' he shouted, and threw it up towards her.

She caught the apple and he started to swing the hook round and round again.

She looked at the apple; it was the brightest, reddest, shiniest apple she had ever seen.

She held it up to her ear.

'Better stand back, my dear!' the prince shouted from below. 'Don't want to hit you on the head, do we?'

She stood in the doorway, holding the apple to her ear.

There was a tiny, furtive, squirming, liquid, burrowing, writhing noise from inside it. She walked quickly round the balcony until she was on the far side of the tower from the prince and threw the apple with all her might far into the forest. She heard a distant clang as the grappling iron hit the flagstones.

She ran round and looked over the parapet.

'All right, my princess?'

'Yes! I'll tie it to the bed!' she shouted to the prince. 'Wait a moment!'

She took the grappling iron inside the room, pulled in some more rope and then untied the hooks from the rope. She left the grappling iron on the floor and then passed the end of the rope twice round one of the bed's arm-thick wooden legs, pulling on the rope to test the friction, then giving the rope another turn round the leg and testing again before walking back out to the parapet, hauling the rope after her and wrapping it once round her waist and a couple of times round her hand.

'Ready!' she called down. She pulled on the rope as the prince tugged.

'Well done, my princess!' he shouted. He began to climb. She kept tension on the rope while looking over the parapet and watching the prince climb.

When he was about two metres below the level of the parapet floor, she jerked her hand holding the rope; the prince cried out and clamped himself to the rope and looked anxiously up.

'My love!' he called. 'The rope! It might be coming loose! Make sure it's fast!'

'Stop where you are,' she told him, and raised the loose end of the rope above the parapet to show him she held it. 'The rope will stay firm as long as I let it.'

'What? But—!'

'Who are you?' she asked him. This close, she could see his short, jet-black hair, his firm, square jaw, his tanned, flawless skin and his blue, sparkling eyes.

'I'm your prince!' he cried. 'Come to rescue you. Please! My love . . .' He started to climb again and she let an arm's length more rope out with a jerk. The prince bounced on the rope and almost fell off. He grabbed it tightly again and glanced fearfully down at the ground, then looked back to her. 'Asura! What are you doing? Let me up!'

'Who are you?' she repeated. 'Tell me or you drop.'

'Your prince! I'm your prince, your rescuer!'

'What is your name?' she asked, slowly letting out a little more rope.

'Roland! Roland of Aquitaine!'

'Why does the water jug fill itself up every night, Roland of Aquitaine? Why does the moon change but not the season? Why do the birds never approach the tower?'

'A spell! All these things arise from a spell put on you by a wicked wizard! Please; Princess Asura; I'm not sure how much longer I can hold on; let me up!'

'And why was the apple you threw me poisoned?'

'It wasn't!'

'It was.'

'Then it must be the spell! The spell the wizard put on you, Asura! Please; I'm going to fall!'

'*What* wizard is this?' she asked.

'I don't know!' the prince cried. She could see his hands and arms quivering as he gripped the rope. 'Merlin!' he said. 'That was his name! I remembered. Merlin! Now, my love; please; I must come up or I'll fall. Please . . .' he said, and his gaze fixed upon her, beseeching and beautiful and tender.

She shook her head.

'You are not real,' she told him, and let the rope go.

The rope flicked across the balcony and into the room as the prince fell screaming towards the ground. She stepped back to let the end of the rope whip past her and plummet to the ground.

The prince hit with a terrible thud. She looked over the parapet. He lay, still and broken-looking on the grass at the foot of the tower; the rope fell loosely about and on top of him.

She picked up the grappling iron and dropped that on him for good measure; it missed his head and whacked into his back, bouncing off across the ground.

She looked up at the sky and said, 'Not that way, either.'

Darkness.

The young Cryptographer rose up from the couch, stretching as she rubbed her back. 'Ouch,' she said. She was small and dark and wore a disposable one-piece suit. She rubbed her eyes with her knuckles as she swung her legs off the couch and sat there for a moment. Then she looked over at the two Security people who'd brought the girl in. She shook her head.

'Your woman's fucking impregnable,' she told them.

The tall woman looked at the square-built man she'd called Lunce. The three were in a bland but comfortable staff suite in the minus-one cistern-level Security complex, deep beneath the fastness. The girl they'd called Asura was being held in a cell within the building's basement.

'Nobody's impregnable,' the woman with the blue gloves said.

'Nobody's indestructible,' the girl corrected her, getting up from the couch. 'But some people are impregnable.' She went across to the curtains and drew them open. She was still rubbing her back, and stretching. She looked out at the light-strewn darkness. A ship moved in the distance, lights glittering on the black waters at the end of the Ocean Tunnel. The port was a multi-strand necklace in the distance.

She gave a half-laugh as she rubbed her back. 'What a bitch!' she muttered, but sounded almost admiring.

'You're saying you can't get through to her?' the man said.

'Right,' the girl said. She looked back at them. 'I've tried all the obvious scenarios and I've tried a few pretty obscure ones, too.' She shrugged, looking away. 'She's wise to all of them. That last one – the princess in the tower: fairy story, legend; but it was like she'd never heard of it before, just accepted it on her own terms. And so *suspicious*! There was nothing nasty in the apple; it was a nice crunchy, scrumptious little piece of code; tasty and nutritious, dammit. If there was anything ulterior about it, it might have distracted her a bit while I climbed up, though what the hell . . . but she imagined the worm or the maggot or whatever in it; just threw it away.' The girl shook her head again, first at her reflection, then, turning, at the two Security people. 'You can keep trying, but you won't get anywhere; she's even *learning* as she goes along, she's *remembering*. Fuck knows how.'

'Clearly you don't, anyway,' the man said. The woman looked at him sharply.

The girl laughed. 'Perhaps you'd like to try, Mr Lunce?' She shook her head. 'That . . . *ingenue* you brought in could skin you alive in there, if she wanted. She's a natural. There's nothing you can give her she won't work out and exploit. You can destroy her – you can wake her up and start torturing her if you like – but it'd be strictly for your own enjoyment. Don't kid yourself you'd have any chance of getting at her core; that'll stay hidden until it's triggered. Strip her brain molecule by molecule and you still won't find out what was in there. I'd stake my life it'll destruct.' She snorted. 'Well, I'd stake your life on it.'

'But she is the asura?' the woman with the blue gloves asked.

'She's *an* asura,' the girl said, sitting back on the window sill. 'But frankly if she is this rogue piece of chaos come to infect all our precious higher functions, announcing she is an asura – using it as a name – is a pretty strange way of going about it.'

'A decoy, then?' the woman asked, looking troubled.

'Or an incredibly confident double-bluff.'

The woman nodded, looking away. 'Well, we have her now,' she said, as if to herself.

'Indeed you do,' the girl said, yawning. 'And, thankfully, she's your problem. I'm just a hired hand and I've done all I'm going to do. I need some sleep.' She pushed away from the window. 'Probably have nightmares about that vicious little bitch,' she muttered, heading for the door.

'Well, pity you failed. Thank you for your help,' the man said, sounding bored. 'We'll expect a full report; it may help your successors. Let's hope their approach is a little less negative than yours was.'

The girl stopped in front of him. She looked up at him and smiled broadly. 'Honey, you'll get your report,' she told him, 'but I'm the best there is. You're on to the *proxime accesserunt* after me and if you persist with them your new toy down there might start getting annoyed and *really* chew one of them up.' She tapped the man on his chest. 'Don't say you weren't warned, big boy.' She turned to the woman with the blue gloves. 'Charming working with you. Let me know how you get on.'

She left.

The other two exchanged looks.

'You know what I think? I think we should kill her.'

'No one cares what you think. Contact the next one on the list.'

'Oh, yes, *ma'am*.'

2

Gadfium left the traumparlour. The door clunked shut and she heard bolts snick home, locking it.

– Left.

She turned left and started walking.

– Hurry.

She walked faster.

Gadfium couldn't stop shaking. It was so bad it was affecting her eyesight and she could not believe other people weren't able to see her quivering from fifty or more metres away.

– You're breathing too quickly and too shallowly. Calm down. Take longer, deeper breaths.

– Am I this bossy with other people? she asked, taking a long, deep breath.

– Yes, you are. Turn right, here; take the lift. It'll arrive in twelve seconds.

– Where are you taking me?

– Away from here; out of the Palace.

– After that?

– Don't ask.

– Oh, grief! I'm too old to be on the lam.

– No you're not. You're only too old when you're dead, and you aren't that either, not yet.

– Yet. Oh, thanks.

– Here's the lift. Ignore the display; I've told it where to go.

– Oh, grief!

– Will you calm down? And wipe your eyes; I can hardly see when I look out of them.

She wiped her eyes while the lift zoomed. They were heading for the ceiling level.

– I know; I'm already dead, there is a hell and you're my punishment.

– Stop gibbering. I'm your guardian angel, Gadfium.

The elevator stopped at a luxuriously appointed tube station.

– Straight ahead. And try to look arrogant, and cruel, like nobody'd better interfere with you. We're taking a Security service carriage.

– Oh, grief!

– Head *up*! Arrogant! Cruel!

– If I get out of this I swear I'll never order anybody about ever again.

– Arrogant! Cruel!

She marched to the carriage with her nose in the air and a sneer on her lips, passing between potted palms standing on gleaming marble beneath a ceiling of polished hardwood. She sensed a few other people around but nobody challenged her. The carriage opened its doors, she stepped aboard and it rolled away immediately, through some points, across other tracks and into a tunnel where it accelerated quickly. She sat down on a leather couch, shaking again.

– We're out of the Palace.

Gadfium put her head between her knees.

– I feel faint.

– Yes, you do, don't you?

– That was awful, awful, awful.

– You did fine.

– I meant in the shop; those women. The man.

– Oh. Of course. I'm sorry. But you didn't have to watch it in slow motion.

– I suppose it was a long time ago, for you.

– Quite. I've been through the process.

Gadfium straightened. She sniffed and took the gun, ammunition and knife out of her pockets, holding them in shaking hands. The gun was a long, thick black flexible tube. It was weighty; it felt like metal covered by some tough, almost sticky foam. It straightened into a cosh or curved into a comfortable hand-gun shape with a finger-sculpted grip, depending on how she held it.

– Here; allow me.

Her hands and fingers moved without her willing them to; she stopped them without difficulty, making them pause poised above the gun, then let her other self – a sighing, finger-tapping presence somewhere at the back of her mind – control her again.

– It has a homing mechanism built in but I've switched it off, the construct said as she used Gadfium's fingers to click the gun open, put some of the fresh ammunition in, closed the stock again, checked the weapon's action, briefly switched on a laser-dot sight, then gave her back control.

– I very much doubt I can use this again, Gadfium told her other self, before repocketing the gun.

– So do I.

– Perhaps I ought to throw it away.

– Don't be silly. You only throw away weapons when they might get you into trouble.

– You don't say.

– And you're already in deep trouble. So deep it can't get any deeper.

– Wow. It's a good job you're here to keep my spirits up.

– Keep the gun, Gadfium.

– What about this knife? she asked, taking it from her pocket. It was flat; the blade was as long and broad as two of her fingers. It was wickedly sharp; slots in the centre of the flat of the blade guided it into the hard plastic sheath, keeping the edges away from the sides.

– Keep that, too.

Gadfium shook her head as she slid the knife back into its sheath and carefully put it in her pocket.

– I don't suppose you can tell me any more about what's going on, can you? she asked.

– Still investigating. Though I think I may now know who betrayed you.

– Who?

– . . . I'm not yet certain. Let me check.

– Oh, check away, Gadfium thought, and sat back, sighing. She held her hands up. They had almost stopped shaking.

The carriage hurtled through the tunnels, swaying and rattling as it took turns and crossed points. Lights flashed sporadically through the shaded windows. Air whistled.

– Where are you taking me?

– I suppose it can't do any harm to tell you now, her other self said crisply. The carriage started to slow down. – You'll be getting on one of Security's secret intramural microclifters very soon and descending four levels. You're going to the castle core, Gadfium; the deep dark inner rooms.

– Oh, grief! Where the outlaws are?

– That's right. The carriage drew to a halt and the nearest door hissed open to darkness; a wave of cold, damp-smelling air flowed in over Gadfium. – Where the outlaws are.

3

Sessine wandered the face of the world beyond Serehfa, journeying through its version of Xtremadur to the distant Uitland, travelling across its prairies and plains and deserts and lakes of salt, through its rolling hills, broad valleys and narrow ravines, between its tall mountains and its rolling rivers and its dark seas, amongst its scrub, grassland, forests and jungles.

He soon grew used to the perverse negativity of this world, where the empty aridity of the semi-desert indicated the greatest richness and intensity of transmitted knowledge, which yet remained untappable, and where the seeming fecundity of the jungle's congested greenery betokened impassible lifelessness, and yet radiated a kind of barren beauty.

Cliffs and mountains indicated buried fastnesses of storage and computation, rivers and seas embodied unsorted masses of chaotic but relatively harmless information, while volcanoes represented mortal danger welling from the explosively corrosive depths of the virus-infested corpus.

The wind was the half-random machine-code shiftings symbolic of the movement of languages and programs within the geographical image of the operating system, while the rain was raw data, filtering through, slowed, from base-reality, and as meaningless as static. The grid of lights available in the sky was simply another representation of the Cryptosphere, like the landscape visible around him, but mapped on a smaller scale.

The optionally visible highways, roads, trails and paths which criss-crossed the countryside were the information channels for the whole of the uncorrupted crypt. Data within them moved at close to the speed of light, which meant that viewed within the context of crypt-time their traffic appeared to move at supersonic speeds. Sometimes he stood near the great coiling highways, listening, rapt, to their eerie, hypnotic songs and staring intently at their gargantuan writhings as though trying through concentration alone to divine the meaning of their cargoes, and always failing.

The first time he saw somebody else he felt a mixture of emotions; fear, joy, expectation and a kind of disappointment that this wilderness was not his alone. He saw a light in the distance across the rocky plain he was crossing, and went, cautiously, to investigate.

An old woman sat alone, staring into a small fire. He had found no need for or way of making fire. She sensed him watching her and called out to him.

He kept his rucksack open and held in front of him and went to join her at the fire. He gave a small bow from a few metres away, uncertain what protocols might apply. She nodded; he sat a quarter-way around the fire from her.

She wore her white hair in a bun and was dressed in loose, dark clothes. Her face was deeply lined. She was sitting back against a small pack.

'You're new here?' she asked. Her voice was deep but soft.

'Forty days or so,' he told her. 'And you?'

She smiled at the fire. 'A little longer.' She looked quizzically at him. 'So, am I your Friday?'

He frowned. 'I beg your pardon?'

'Robinson Crusoe; a story. He believes he is alone on his desert island until he sees another's footprint, on the day called Friday. When he meets the other man he calls him Friday. We call the first person a new arrival meets their Friday.' She shrugged. 'Just a tradition. Silly, really.'

'Then you are, yes,' he told her.

She nodded as though to herself and said, 'Another tradition – and I think it a good one – has it that a Friday answers any questions a newcomer may have.'

He looked into her old, dark eyes.

'I have many questions,' he said. 'Probably more than I know.'

'That is not uncommon. First, though, may I ask what brings you here?'

He turned his hands palm up. 'Oh, just the passing of events.'

She nodded and looked understanding, but he felt he might have been rude. He added; 'I made enemies in the other world, and was brought near to extinction. A friend – a Virgil to my Dante, if you will – led me away from that to whatever sanctuary this represents.'

'Dante, not Orpheus, then?' she asked, smiling.

He gave a modest laugh. 'Ma'am, I am neither poet nor musician, and I don't believe I ever quite found my Eurydice, so was unable to lose her.'

She chuckled, suddenly childlike. 'Well then,' she said, 'what can I tell you?'

'Oh, let's just talk, shall we? Perhaps I'll find out anything I need to know in the course of our conversation.'

'Why not?' she nodded. She sat up a little. 'I shan't ask your name, sir; our old names can be dangerous and I doubt you have settled on a new one yet. My name here is Procopia. You are not tired?'

'I am not,' he said.

'Then I shall tell you my story. I am here because of a lost love, as are not a few of us here . . .'

She told him a little of her life before she came to be incrypted, much of the particular circumstances which led to her being in this level of the crypt, and all she thought relevant of what she had learnt since she had been here.

He talked a little in return, and she seemed content.

Mostly, though, he listened, and as he did so, learnt. He decided he liked the woman; it was very late when they bade each other goodnight and fell asleep.

He dreamt of a far castle, sweet music and a long-lost love.

In the morning when he awoke she was packed and about to depart.

'I must go,' she said. 'I had thought of offering my services as a guide, but I think you may have some point to your wanderings, and I might impose too much of my own course on yours.'

'Then you are doubly kind, and wise,' he said, rising and dusting himself down. She held out her hand, and he shook it.

'I hope we meet again, sir.'

'So do I. Travel safely.'

'And you. Fare well.'

Gradually he started to meet more travellers. He discovered, as Procopia had told him, that these fellow wanderers of the mirror-world, human and chimeric, were either exiles like him – some through choice, some through coercion – or those who were really no more than illicit tourists; adventurers come to sample the strangeness of this anomalous paradigm of base-reality.

A kind of subsidiary ecology had arisen within the fractured human community he made occasional contact with; there were those who preyed upon other wanderers – taking on the form of animals in some cases, but not all – and those who seemed to exist only to mate with others, merging from the time of their coupling to become an individual incorporating aspects of both the former lovers, usually still imbued with whatever hunger had driven them to fuse in the first place, and so seeking further unions.

Most of the people he met wanted only to absorb his story and exchange no more than information; he declined to reveal who he had once been but was happy to share what he knew of this level of the crypt. He was neither surprised nor disappointed when he realised he appeared to have lost all interest in sex.

He discovered that his rucksack contained three things: a sword, a cape and a book. The sword had a coiled metal blade which extended up to two metres and was not particularly sharp but which produced an electric charge which could stun the largest chimeric – or, at least, the largest which had ever attacked him. He thought of the cape as his chameleon coat; it took on the appearance of whatever his environment was at the time and appeared to offer almost perfect concealment. In its own way, it was more effective than the sword.

The book was like the one he'd found in the room in Oubliette; it was every book. Opening the back cover let the book function as a journal; words appeared on the page when he spoke. He made entries in the journal every few days and kept a note of each day that passed even when he didn't record anything more about it. He read a lot, at first.

The landscape of the crypt was littered with monuments, buildings and other structures, most of them well away from the shifting sum-paths of the great data highways and many of them of indefinable design. It was here, in these singular follies, usually in the evening after a long day's travel, that he tended to meet and converse with others; men, women, androgynes and chimerics. He never saw anyone who even looked like a child. They were rare enough in base-reality, but quite absent here.

He found, as his time in the crypt extended, that his dreams attained a vividity that sometimes made them seem more real than his waking hours. In those oneiric passages, when he felt that he sank beneath the surface of the land and entered a deeper underworld, he played the hero, often as not, in a landscape filled with people, cities, commotion and event: he was a dashing captain thrust by circumstance to unsought glory and fame, a poet prince compelled to take up arms, a philosopher king forced to defend his realm.

He commanded a squadron of cavalry, of ships, of tanks, of aircraft, of spacecraft; he wielded clubs, swords, pistols, lasers; he climbed to surprise an enemy cave, besieged walled cities, charged across river shallows to fall upon a vulnerable flank, planned the mining of lines zig-zagging across the swell of countryside, rode the leading missile-carrier to the smoking rubble of rail-heads, threaded a corkscrew course between black bursting clouds towards enemy capitals, slid unseen through the folds of sable space to wheel against unwarned convoys lumbering between the stars.

Gradually though, as if some part of him – the realist, the cynic, the ironist – could not accept the improbable serial triumphs of his exhausting martial adventures, the furniture of each of these aspirant dreams began to include the Encroachment, and in the midst of the bright clamour of some clash upon a dusty plain, he would find himself looking up above the joined havoc of the contesting armies to see the moon in a cloudless sky, whole face half dimmed by some fearful agent beyond precedent; or on some night mission, below radar across the darkened enemy coast, he would look up to see the stars had disappeared from half the sky; or, sling-shotting through the well of a gas-giant, the planet's ringed bulk would fall away to reveal no welcoming spatter of familiar constellations, but a dark void, glowing beyond sight with the inflamed exhalations of long-drowned stars.

Increasingly, he woke from such dreams with a sense of gnawing frustration and abject failure no amount of subsequent rationalisation could assuage.

'Let me see, let me see,' the woman said. She looked perhaps ten years younger than he, though she sported an unflatteringly tonsured scalp and had no eyebrows. Black-clad, she sat in the centre of a circle of seven travellers, on a bare floor in a bare room in a large, square-planned house which stood, stark and alone, on a dark plateau.

He sat a little way off with his back to a wall where earlier callers had left strange curlicued designs and patterns carved into the plaster. Light came from a bulb hanging above the centre of the group. He had been reading while the others had told their own stories, taking turns in the centre of the circle.

It was the seven thousand, two hundred and thirty-fifth day of his time within the crypt. He had been here for nearly twenty years. Outside, in base-reality, somewhat more than seventeen hours had passed.

'Let me see,' the woman in the centre of the circle said again, tapping her finger on her lips. She had completed her own tale and was supposed to choose the next story-teller. He had been half listening while he'd read, finding this group's compended histories more absorbing than most. 'You, sir,' the woman said, raising her voice, and he knew she was addressing him.

He looked up. The others were turned towards him.

'Yes?' he asked.

'Will you tell us your story?' the woman asked.

'I think not. Forgive me.' He smiled a little then went back to his book.

'Sir, please,' she said, pleasantly enough. 'We would count ourselves fortunate if you'd join our group. Will you not share your wisdom with us?'

'I have no wisdom,' he told her.

'Your experiences, then?'

'They have been trivial, uninteresting, and full of error.'

'So you protest,' she said evenly. She looked at one of the others in the circle. 'Great souls suffer in silence,' she said quietly, amidst laughter.

He frowned, hiding his face with the book.

He slept that night in a high bare room looking over the dark plain.

The woman came to him in the night, her presence signalled by a creak on the stairs even before the rucksack – balanced against the door – fell over.

Called from a dream – in which he heaved a cutlass, knee deep in a fly-blown salt marsh – he sat with his cloak drawn around him up to his eyes, the sword concealed beneath.

She stood in the doorway, a pale ghostly head seeming to float above her black gown. She saw his eyes, and nodded.

He swept the cloak aside to let her see the sword.

'I did not come for a duel, sir,' she said quietly.

'Then I regret there is no field in which I can give you satisfaction.'

'Nor for that,' she said, shutting the door and sitting down beside it. They sat looking at each other for a moment.

'Why, then?' he asked.

'*Absens haeres non erit*,' she told him.

He took a while to reply. 'Plainly,' he said without inflection, and waited to see which way that would be taken.

He saw the whiteness of her teeth as she smiled. 'I was told it might not be possible to tell if you are the one. That might be a further sign in itself.'

'Nonsense.'

She nodded. 'That's what I thought.'

'What "one", may I ask?'

'You may. Choose from the many rumours, myths and legends. I don't know.'

'You have disturbed your own sleep and mine merely to tell me what you don't know?'

'No; to tell you this: seek the transformation of the enemy.' She rose. 'Good night.'

Then she opened the door and left, more silently than she had arrived.

He sat, thinking.

It took him a while to work it out.

4

Am in thi lammergeiers roost, ma bref soundin loud in ma eers & mixd in wif theez hissy clikky noyses coz am wearin this mask on ma fais & a breevin botil on me bak boath ov witch I got off thi ded spier.

This is a spooki ole playce & no mistake. Thers nobodi aroun & its very coald indeed & thi lite is very wyt & intens & washd out lookin. Bein in thi lammergeiers roost is like bein insyd a jiant holy cheez; sorta interconectid bubbilz & stretchd punkchird membrains ov stoan & metil evrywheare & hi up on thi wols in plaises whare thi bubbilz mak cup & boals juttin out thers theez nests lynd wif babil plant & fevirs onli thers no birdz in them nor eggs nor nufin. Thi floar of thi roost is lyk a hoal lot ov littil craters eech ov them holdin loadsa brokin, splintird boans. Ma feet go cruntch cruntch as I wok, lookin up & aroun & tryin 2 c if thers enybodi else heer Ithir hoomin or creetch but thi plais seems 2 b dessertid.

Ther r hooj sirkils in thi outer wols lyk porthoals whare thi winds cumin whistlin thru & soundin hi & reedy & weerd; I clime up 2 1 ov thi bigir holez & luke out. Its hazy whyt clowd out thare like a lair ov fog whot extends 2 thi horyzon; u can juss about c thi lowir levils ov thi cassil showin undirneef, like sumfin trapt inside a transparint glaysier. Thers a cupil ov towrs stikin up froo thi cloud but they luke very small & far away. No sine ov no birds out thare neevir, but then thats thi fing; this is 2 far up 4 birdz 2 fly, so how cum thi lammergeiers wer evir here?

I slide doun a curv ov bubil & cruntch in2 sum boans, then hed 2wards thi centir ov thi towir, in2 thi shados whare thers a faint breez cumin from.

Thi nests fin out & disapeer as I go deeper, stil cruntchin ovir thi occaysinal boan while it gets darkir & darkir & I can hardly c whare am puttin ma feet. Av got this torch whot thi ded spyer had on him so I turn it on & juss as wel; thers a dirty grate hoal rite in front ov me. I edje closir & hold on2 thi wol & stik ma hed out ovir thi hooj sirkulir hoal. Muss b 50 metirs or moar acros. Blak deep. Goze strate up in2 thi darkniss, 2. Thers a jentil draft ov air cumin up thi shaft. Iss warm, @ leest in comparison wif thi freezin air up heer. No sine ov eny uthir entrinses aroun thi shaft, juss this 1.

Am stil not enywhare neer thi centir ov thi towir; thass way, way furthir deep, probly a cupil ov klometirs away. Am in thi fass towr, stil on thi lam & serchin 4 litl Ergates.

I leen bak from thi hoal.

Then thers a cruntchin noyse sumwhare in thi darknis bhind me. I whirl roun.

I foun Gaston thi slof peekin out ovir a stoan ledj on thi inside wol ov thi slofs' towr, neer thi sloped tunnil whot led 2 thi ole lift shafts. Accordin 2 thi glimpse Id had ov thi locality when Id criptid erlier these shafts wer abandind & unyoosd but Id fot wif eny luk theyd b thi tipe ov shaft whot has stares goan roun thi inside ov thi shaft 4 merjencies, & mayb they wooden b garded by thi bods whot wer attakin thi slofs.

Wel, that woz thi feery. In fact thi scoop ov thi tunil on thi levil blow whare Gaston woz hidin woz fool ov Security geezirs wif guns. O grate, I fot.

I'd climed along btween thi dank blak wol ov thi towr & thi framework ov scaffoldin whot woz thi slofs' hoam neyburhood, hedin 4 heer, whare thi floar dropt away in steps & thi aksess tunil woz. Lookt like old Gaston had had thi saim idear.

I didn fink Id maid a noyse but he turnd roun sloly & saw me & pushed himself bak from thi edj ov thi ledj & climed up thi scafoldin 2wards me, poyntin bhind me.

We retreetid a bit, bhind sum ov thi canvas-hung scafoldin.

. . . yung Bashkule, he sed, u r shafe; gude.

Yeh & u, I sed. But it lukes like thi Security boyz 1/2 this playce strung up gude & tite. U no eny uthir waze out ov heer?

. . . ash it happinsh, Gaston sez, I do actchirly. If yule jusht folo me . . .

Gaston set off bak froo thi scaffoldin hedin upwards @

whot woz probly a extreme sprint 4 a slof. I ambild aftir him.

We climed up about 7 floars ov thi slof scaffoldin; ther woz qwite a lot ov smoak up here & I cude c flaims in thi distins, deepir inside thi struktyir.

. . . Heer, Gaston sed, stopin @ a pritti ordnari lookin bit ov wol. He gript thi top ov a drippin blak stoan; it hinjed down 2 riveel a roun blak hoal. He moashind me in.

I muss 1/2 lookt doobeyus.

. . . I'll go firsht, then, he sed, & clambird in2 thi hoal.

I shuden 1/2 luked doobeyus bcoz I cuden lift thi stoan bak up aftir us & so Gaston had 2 sqweez past me 2 do it. I doan no if u 1/2 evir had a larj swety slof wif kopeyis qwantities ov fungis on itz pelt sqweez past u in a confined spaice . . . Cum 2 fink ov it probly u 1/2nt, but asoomin thass thi case fink uself luky thass ol I can say.

1/2in Gaston sqweez past me agen didn seem like sutch a gude idear.

Al juss leed off then if itz ol thi same 2 u Gaston ole sun, I sed.

. . . By ol meenz, yung Bashcule.

Thi tunil woz crampt & only fit 4 crollin in. Thi dam fing wen up, doun & roun this way & that way; it woz like climein around in thi intestinez ov sum hooj stoan jiant. Wif Gaston's pelt-fungis stil smeerd ol ovir me, it didn smel dissimilir neevir.

Lissin Gaston, I sed @ 1 point while he woz givin me a punt up a partikerly steep bit ov thi jiant intestin, am reely sorry if that woz me whot brot ol that thare shit down on u gies. I reely presiate whot u did, rescuin me & takin me in etc & Id hate 2 fink I woz responsibil 4 ol this.

. . . I qwite undirshtand yoor angwish, yung Bashcule, Gaston sed. But itsh not yoor folt shertin pershinsh r tryin 2 pershicute u.

U reely fink they woz aftir me? I askd.

. . . Zhat woz zhe impreshin I formed from what I overherd, Gaston sed. Zhey did not sheem 2 b intereshtid in eny ov ush. Zhey were lukin 4 shumbody elsh zhey shuspected ush ov harberin.

Blimey.

. . . In eny event, Gaston sed, Zhi reshponsibility ish thersh, not yoorsh. Whot happind ish just 1 ov thoshe thingsh I shupoashe.

Wel, fanks, Gaston, I sed.

. . . U didn . . . *kript*, did u? Gaston sed. Ish jusht that mite 1/2 led them 2 ush. But u didn, did u?

O no, I sed. No, not me; I didn. Nope. Not gilty. No sirree. Uh-uh. Wooden catch me doing a fing like that. O no.

. . . Zhare u r then, Gaston sed.

& so we wound on fru thi guts ov thi towr, me feelin lowir than a tapewurm.

Eventyooly we came 2 a bit whare thi tunil wideind out & thi floar turnd from stoan 2 wood; I moar or less fel in2 this woodin bowl whare a faint lite shon. I didn qwite get out ov thi way in time so Gaston slid down on top ov me.

Moar pelt fungis.

. . . ther shude b a trap heer shumwhare, Gaston sed, feelin aroun on thi floar . . . A, heer it is. Ther woz a sorta holo clunkin noyse & in thi 1/2-lite I cude c Gaston pullin whot lookt like a hooj plug up out ov thi floar.

. . . Itsh a holod out babil shtem, Gaston explained, settin thi plug 2 1 side. I'll go firsht, I shink.

Thi holo babil trunk heded down in a serees ov long, stretchd Ss. Ther wer rungs on thi wols; Gaston wen down them prity qwikli 4 a slof. Now & agen we passd whot mite 1/2 been doars in thi trunk whare thi okayshinal crak ov lite showd, but moastli it woz toatily dark. We seemd 2 go on doun 4evir & I neerli fel off a cupil ov tyms. Juss as wel Gaston woz beneef me; thi thot ov anuthir cloas encountir wif his pelt fungis qwikly consintraitid my mynd, I can tel u.

@ last Gaston sed, . . . Heer we r, & we stept on 2 a platform ov stoan & wen thru a doar in2 a crampt spais whare Gaston wriggld & I crold btween a stoan floar & this metil sealing witch maid a sorta blurbilurbilurbil soun. We caim out in whot luked lyk a big long kurvin servis duct hoos wols wer lynd wif pyps; weed juss crold undir a big gurglin tank ov sum sort. I cude heer whot soundid lyk a trane rumblin sumwhare neerby.

. . . Zher ish a frate tube line juncshin thru zhare, Gaston sed, poyntin @ a hatch in thi floar. Zhi tranes 1/2 2 shlo doun 2 negoshiate thi poyntsh & it ish poshibil 4 a hoomin 2 jump on bord a wagin & sho shicure a ryde. I shink I 1/2 2 retern 2 c

whot has befolin ma frendsh, but if u can maik yoor way 2 thi
sekind levil shousht-wesht buttry u wil fynd a toun zhare. Go
2 thi shentril sqware; shum1 wil b lukin 4 u & wil luke aftir u.
Im sorri 2 1/2 2 abandin u in zhish way, but it ish ol I can do.

Thass ol rite, Gaston, I sed. U dun ol u can & I doan deserv
ol thi kyndniss yoov shown me. I woz so choakd I cude 1/2
hugd him, but I didn. He just noddid his big funy pointid hed
& sed, . . . Wel, gude luk yung Bashcule, u tak care now . . . & u
promish u wil go 2 thi shousht-wesht buttry & thi toun zhare?

O yes, I sez, lyin thru ma teef.

Good. Fair wel.

Then he woz away, crolin bak undir thi big gurgli tank.

I went doun fru thi hatch in thi floar in2 a brod dark cavern
whare lots ov toob lyns converjd from singil tunnils. Ther woz
nobodi about but I hid bhynd sum hummin sorta cabinet fings
between 2 ov thi trax & wated; a whyle laitir a trane ov opin
wagins came rattlin fru, claterin acros thi points; I let thi unmand
endjinn & moast ov thi wagins go pas & then jumpd on 1 neer
thi end, hollin maself up thi side & ovir in2 its emty interier.

After a few minits during witch thi trane entird a blak-dark
tunnil & pikd up speed agen, I rekind it woz safe 2 kript.

Ther woz no horibil corrosiv fog/sleet heer. Everyfin loakily
seemd normil. Thi trane woz heddin 4 thi far end ov thi 2nd levil,
neer 2 thi Sutherin Volcano Room. It wude slo down @ a few
moar playces yet whare I cude get off. I kriptd furthir afeeld.

/Thi lammergeiers roost woz frozen. Its kript-space representation woz thare but it woz like a stil piktcher insted ov
a moovy; ther wer no birds nor enybody or enyfin thare &
u cuden interact wif nufin thare. I sensd sumfin neerby in
thi kript space & suspectid ther woz sum kinda gard on thi
playce, waitin 2 c who turnd up inarestid in thi lammergeiers.
I disconectid qwik.

Thi trane rold on. Thi lammergeiers livd – or used 2 liv – in
thi fass towr, on thi 9th levil. I rekind ther woz sumfin goan
on up thare. Thi frate trane wude pass almost undirneef thi fass
towr. Gude enuf 4 me. Thi 9th levil soundid a bit hi & cold &
inaxessibil but Id burn that bridje when I came 2 it.

I almost decapitaytid myself jumpin off thi trane when it wen
fru anuthir set ov points in a wide bit ov tunil thi lenth ov witch

I slitely overestimated, but apart from bangin a shoaldir on a wol & skinnin 1 nee I escaped unscaved. I climed a ladir, wokd a bit ov servis tunnil & took a servis elevaitir up 2 thi main floor levil. I foun maself in whot lukd like a jiant kemikil wurx, all pipes & big preshir vessils & leekin steem & funy smelz. Shurenuf, a qwik chek on thi kript & confirmd it woz a plastix rfinery.

Aftir a lot of fancy & hily teknikil kriptin, sum wokin & climein ovir pipes & ducts & avoidin thi dodjier lookin shados I foun a otomatik frate elivaitir taikin vats ov sum sorta fertilizer up thi towr & hitchd a ryde up in that.

Ma eers popt aftir 2 minits, & aftir about 5, & 10.

Sumoar fancy kriptin got thi elevaitir 2 go a floar abuv whare it woz expectid; this woz as hi as it cude go. I got out in a sorta tol opin gallery whare a feerse coal wind blu & thi vew woz ov babil plantz formin a fretwurk ov narled branchis lettin in a spare icy lite.

I let thi elevaitir tak itself bak doun a floar.

Ther woz a piller about 100 metirs away witch supportd thi roof ov thi tol gallery. Thi 1 in thi uthir directshin woz twice as far away. I set off 2wards thi neerir 1.

I woz stil only dresd in ma yewshil cloavs & this wind woz makin me shiver olredy, but then it had been fairly warm furthir down so mayb it woz juss thi suddeniss ov thi change. I wokd along thi gallery, btween thi silooetid babil & thi smoov ashlar ov thi towr's barely curvd wol. Thi floar felt coald thru my shooz & I wishd I had a hat.

Thi kript startid 2 get a bit vaig & unhelpful about thi layout ov thi fass towr @ aroun this levil. I juss had 2 hoap thi piller mite 1/2 a set ov stares in it.

It didn. It had 2 sets ov stares in it, intertwynd in a dubil heelix like deenay.

Didn seem 2 mattir whitch 1 I took. I startid climein.

I went fass @ furst 2 try & warm up but thi bref juss wissld outa me & my legs turnd 2 jelly; I had 2 sit down & poot ma poundin hed btween ma nees b4 I cude continu, moar sloly.

Thi steps went roun & roun & roun; pretti steep.

I ploddid on & up, tryin 2 settil in2 a rithim. This seemd 2 wurk but I woz gettin a hel ov a hedaik. Luky I woz fit, not 2 menshin determind. (Not 2 menshin bludy stupid, it woz startin 2 okur 2 me.)

Thi piller got 2 thi next storey – anuthir opin gallery – & didn stop; it went on up. Seemd 2 go on 4 a good ways yet so I stuk wif it. Thi stare case had no handrales & tho it woz a good cupil ov metirs wide it wude 1/2 been friteninly open & exposed on thi outir side if thi babil plants hadent bin hangin growin ol over thi outside ov thi towr. As it woz it woz stil prity friteninly exposd on thi uthir side, but thi best fing 2 do woz not 2 fink about it & sertinly not 2 luke.

I kept climein.

Anuthir levil. My hed woz hurtin lyk mad. I luked 4 thi piller but it wozent thare eny moar. Insted ther woz a hoal network ov twistid pillers, weevin this way & that wif hi-alt babil – thin weedy stuf – ol ovir it, coatin thi floar ov thi galery, nettin thi weev ov thi frettid stoan wol.

I wandird, my feet trippin ovir thi babil, lookin 4 a strand ov stonework wif steps in it or on it so that I cude go hier, my vishin gettin dark @ thi edjis, my legs feelin bouncy & strange & sumfin howlin in ma eers that mite 1/2 bin thi wind & mite not.

I doan no how long it woz b4 I foun thi spyer, fallin amungst thi babil, ded, crumplid, head shattered, skin dried, white bones pokin thru his neepads. I remember lukin up & finkin he must 1/2 follin from thi opin-wurk seelin, & I saw his mask & thi cylinder on his bak but I just wanderd off agen, feelin like I woz wokin along this tunil coz that woz ol I cude c & it seemd like ours layter while I woz stil serchin 4 anuthir stareway or @ leest a doar or sumthin that I thot, Hey, mayb I cude yoos thi spyers geer! & I startid 2 turn roun & almost tript ovir him bcoz Id wanderd in a sirkil.

Ther woz old brown blood dried on thi faice mask but it fel away like dark dandruf when I nokd it. Thi oxijin in thi tank wos coald & it felt like it waz freezin ma lungs but my hedaik startid 2 go & I wozen lukin down a tunnil ol thi time no moar.

I finishd thi watir in his canteen, took his jaket, hat & torch & left thi poor buggir lyin thare.

Thi stares wer in a reely obvyis place, just along from thi top ov thi piller Id climed.

Thi lammergeiers' roost woz on thi next levil. I got thare @ dusk & collapsed in a nest ov dry babil an hooj scratchy fevvirs.

Thi don woke me & I startid investigaytin, endin up lookin down thi big shaft.

I heer thi cruntchin njoyse.

I swing thi torch roun aimin thi beem down thi tunnil; thi warm breeze cumin up thi deep blak shaft tugs @ my jaket. Thi torch beem juss disapeers in2 thi dark, swolod up.

Sumthin cruntches agen, then thers a noyse ov sumfin cumin whisslin 2wards me.

I doan 1/2 time 2 duk & I doan c whot hits me, but it bashis in2 my chest & noks me bakwards, thi bref goan *Hoof*! outa ma lungz. I feel myself start 2 go ovir thi edj ov thi shaft & grab wif 1 hand as thi lip ov stone skates under my bum. My hand misiz.

I fol in2 thi blak frote ov thi shaft.

Thi rore ov air bilds up aroun me, tearin thi mask off ma fayce.

After a few sekinds I get my bref bak & I start screemin.

EIGHT

1

She was a closed codex within a vast dark library whose floor was a valley, whose walls were cliffs, whose alcoves were hanging valleys; she was an ancient book, rich of smell, gravid with collected knowledge, huge and heavy with ink-thick illuminated pages and a cover of embossed leather, chased with metal and fitted with a lock for which only she possessed the key.

She was a virgin wise too long now on her wedding night, wined, dined, coddled, sozzled, wished well by family and friends still revelling in distant loudness in the halls below, swept up by her handsome new husband and left to change from wedding gown to nightgown and slip into the huge wide warmed welcoming bed.

She was the only speaker in a tribe of the dumb, walking amongst them, tall and silent while they touched her and beseeched her with their sad eyes and their deferent, hesitant hands and their flowing, pleading signs to talk for them, sing for them, be their voice.

She was the captain of a ship sunk by enemy action, alone still conscious in the lifeboat while her crew died slowly around her, moaning quietly through salt-crusted lips or raving as they twitched and spasmed in the bilges. She saw another ship and knew she could signal it, but it was an enemy vessel and only her pride made her hesitate.

She was a mother watching her child suffering and dying because she was of a faith inimical to medicine. Doctors, nurses and friends all pleaded with her to allow her child to live by merely saying a word or making a gesture, the syringe there ready in the surgeon's hand.

She was a protester who'd had proved to her that her fellow dissidents had betrayed her, deserted her, lied to her. It was known beyond doubt that she was guilty; all that was required was that she acknowledge her guilt; no names were needed, nobody else had to be implicated; she merely had to accept her responsibility. She had been foolish and she owed society that. Regretfully, they showed her the instruments of torture within the place of torment.

/She allowed the book to be opened, its every word translated into a language only she knew. When it was slammed shut again, she smiled to herself.

/She fed her new husband yet more wine as she slowly undressed him, and when he had to relieve himself locked him in the latrine, donned his clothes and escaped the room on a rope made from the bed sheets, spilled wine like a proud deflowerer's trophy stain, flourished to the night.

/She sang to the tribe with her dance and her own gestures, more beautiful than speech or song, so silencing their signs.

/She signalled the ship and when she saw it turn set the lifeboat towards it, slipping into the water to swim away while her comrades were rescued.

/She would still say nothing, but took the syringe herself, went to apply it to the child's arm, looked into its blank and empty eyes, then squirted the fluid over its skin before quickly sucking air into the instrument and turning and plunging it into the horrified surgeon's chest.

/By the rack within the gory chamber she broke down and wept, squatting on her haunches, hiding her face and sobbing. When the torturer bent pityingly to hold her, she looked up with a tear-streaked face and bit his throat out.

'Fuck! Fuck! I can't let go! I can't get out! I can't let go!' the man screamed, his voice hoarse. 'She won't let me *go*!'

He sat up in the couch and pulled at his collar, his face reddening as he struggled with something at his throat that nobody else could see. The nurse tapped at her keyboard and a tiny light flickered on the head-net the man wore like a thin hat over his shaved scalp. He swayed from the waist, his hands fell from his throat, his eyelids drooped and he lay back again.

The woman waved one hand and the window into the room blanked out. 'Thank you,' she muttered to the nurse. She turned to the tall, broad-shouldered man at her side and motioned with her head. They stepped into the corridor outside.

'Do you realise what she did?' she asked him. 'She put a

mimetic virus into *his* head. Could be months before we get him back. If we get him back.'

'Evolution,' Lunce said, shrugging.

'Don't give me that shit, the guy was one of our best.'

'Well, he wasn't best enough, was he?'

'Oh, well put. But the point is, word's got out now and nobody else will touch her.'

'I'd touch her,' Lunce told her, and made a show of cracking his fingers.

'Yeah, I bet you would.'

He shrugged again. 'I mean it. Wake her up and really torture her.'

The woman sighed and shook her head. 'You really have no idea, do you?'

'So you keep telling me. I just think we're all missing something really obvious here. Maybe a bit of real physical . . . pressure might actually produce some results.'

'Lunce, we have the Consistory member with special responsibility for Security Oncaterius breathing down our necks on this; if you're tired of your work, why don't you suggest that to him? But if you do, just remember it's nothing to do with me.' She looked him up and down. 'In fact, as I haven't particularly enjoyed working with you, maybe it's not such a bad idea.'

'We haven't tried what I'm suggesting,' he pointed out. 'We have tried what you suggested and it's failed.'

The woman dismissed this with a wave of her hand. 'Well, we'll keep her in solitary for now and see if that gets any results.'

Lunce just took a deep breath and snorted.

'Come on,' the woman said. 'Let's get something to eat. I have to think what we're going to tell Oncaterius.'

Asura was left in a cell. She thought of it as a mirror cell because when she lay down on the bed and put her head on the thin pillow there was a cell in there too; that was the only place they would let her go to in her sleep.

So she was in two cells. It was a little like being in the tower in the first of the dreams she could remember, but less interesting. There was a tap for water and another tap which dispensed a sort of soup. Between the two taps was a cup chained to the wall. Also in the cell was a toilet and a bed platform and a chair platform, all parts of the wall. There was no window and no view, though there was a locked, tight-fitting door.

She slept a great deal ignoring the pretend, dead-end cell they offered her. Instead, when she dreamt, she recalled what had happened to her so far.

She remembered the view of the great castle, the journey on the airship, the train and car journey before that, the dream in the night at the big house, the things that Pieter Velteseri had asked her about, her walk through the garden from the vault and the strange dreams she had had before she'd awoken.

And it was as though there was something beyond those dreams too, something she knew was there but knew nothing else about save that it existed. The knowledge tickled her mind when she thought back to the time – instant or aeon – in the Velteseri family vault. There was something there, she knew there was, but like a dim light just sensed with the corner of the eye which disappeared when looked at directly, she could not inspect it more closely; the very act of attempting to do so had the effect of extinguishing it completely for as long as she tried.

She reviewed all that had happened to her in the short life she could remember. She wondered if there had been a degree of choice in the fact she had awoken in the Velteseri vault; most of the clan had been away and Pieter might have been chosen as somebody likely to help. She thought she had been right to trust him, and thought that the dreams she had had during the night she had spent at the house had been genuine dreams; something that had put her here had contacted her and told her what her purpose was.

She supposed she had been kidnapped by somebody who was not really Cousin Ucubulaire. These people must have recognised her name, or found out about her in some other way, and not wanted her to do whatever it was she was supposed to do here (assuming she actually had been taken to the big castle she had seen). Perhaps travelling under the name Asura had been a mistake.

And yet as soon as she'd heard Pieter Velteseri utter the word she'd known that was her name. There had been no feeling of warning, no niggling sensation that she might be doing something dangerous; instead she had recognised her true title and claimed it.

She thought about this. She had the impression that somebody or something had gone to great trouble to get her here. How silly not to realise that her name itself might bring her into danger.

But she was here (again, assuming) and she did not feel she had anywhere else she had to go. She was where she wanted to be. So perhaps she had been meant to be found by Lunce and the lady who'd called herself Ucubulaire, or by people like them. That made a kind of sense. They had her, but they had not succeeded in finding out anything she didn't want them to know . . .

She decided she would wait.

She waited.

2

Gadfium felt she was an insect crawling across the floor of a dank cellar. Everywhere she looked there was garbage, showing up grey and ghostly in the not-quite totally dark space around her.

The whole first-level room was one gigantic rubbish tip filled with the debris of millennia. From pipes, ducts and chutes high on the walls and ceiling a constant rain of refuse, tailings, junk and trash pattered down. She picked her way across a heap of what looked like doll-size plastic sanitary ware, her feet sinking and sliding through the mound of miniature baths and bidets in a slough of breaking and crackling.

– Are you sure this is going to throw people off our trail?

– Positive. Bear right here. Not too far. That's it.

Gadfium walked on, avoiding a pile of rotting babil fruit husks. She heard a series of crunches and crashes somewhere to her left, where she would have been walking if her crypt self hadn't told her to bear right. She looked around the hills of rubbish.

– I'm sure we could recycle more.

– I suppose it will be re-used, eventually. Or would have been, but for the Encroachment.

A bright stream of yellow fire burst silently from a distant wall and fell slowly in a livid arc towards the raised floor of the lumber room, its colour changing as it fell from yellow to orange to red. A sizzling sound came from that direction, and then a distant roaring noise as whatever it was hit the surface.

– That's pretty.

– Furnace smelt-slag.

– Thought it might be something like that. How are your researches going? Have you discovered anything else interesting?

– Goscil was the Security agent.

– Really? I always assumed it was Rasfline. Gadfium shook her head. You just never knew. – What else? she asked.

– I still don't know who betrayed the group, but they've all been taken into custody except Clispeir.

'*Clispeir*?' Gadfium said out loud, and stopped.

– Please don't stop here, there's a hopper full of reject cerametal vehicle parts due to land where you're standing in about a minute.

Gadfium started walking again. – You don't think it was Clispeir, do you?

– I don't know. She is due for some leave in two days; perhaps they are waiting for her to come to them. The observatory at the Plain of Sliding Stones is still cut off from normal communication so she would not have been able to find out about the others.

– If it was her, could the message we received from the fast-tower have been a Security trick, simply made up?

– Possibly, though I doubt it.

Gadfium walked on for a while across the flat bed of some long-dried tailings. Whistling noises from above and behind terminated in distant thumps which shook the dusty surface.

– Some Palace gossip, her crypt self told her. Our lot and the Chapel may be about to come to some sort of agreement.

– This is sudden.

– Apparently the Army had some supposedly war-winning scheme that didn't work. Now we have no choice but to reach terms . . . Ah.

– What?

– Security. They think they have the asura.

'What?' Gadfium said, and stopped again, feeling herself fill with despair.

– Keep going. They could be wrong.

– But . . . so soon! Is everything hopeless?

– . . . No. However, I may have a change of plan for us.

– What exactly is this plan, anyway? I'm grateful to you for getting me out of the Palace, but I would like to know where you're taking me, apart from into outlaw territory.

– Well, onward and upward from there, but first, I think now, deeper.

'*Deeper*?'

– Deeper.

The neatly folded uniform appeared to have been washed but not repaired. There were still a few rips and tears in it. On top of the pile of clothing lay a pair of Army-issue boots, a belt and some complicated webbing, a mask and forage cap. The collection was held easily in one huge white furred paw; black claws extended a little on either side, bracketing the pathetic heap of effects.

The chimeric polar bear sat at one end of the long table in the committee chamber. The Palace civil servant officially in charge of the meeting sat at the other end, on a seat in front of an empty throne. Adijine had decided to stay away when he'd discovered what had arrived earlier in the diplomatic bag. The Consistorians all seemed to have found urgent appointments elsewhere as well, though like the King most of them were probably watching the events through others' eyes, as the Chapel representatives would know.

The head of the Engineers' delegation set the pile of clothing down on the table top. Adijine, sulking alone in bed, stared through the civil servant's eyes, then switched to an overhead camera.

Looking carefully, the King could see little round holes in the grey uniform material and matching craters on the well-worn boots where acid had eaten away. He tried to feel some shock of recognition on seeing the Army-issue gear, but he hadn't been paying that much attention when he'd been in the head of – he had to search for the name – Private Uris Tenblen.

One of the boots toppled and fell over, lying on the polished surface.

'Your plan,' the ambassadorial emissary rumbled, setting the boot upright again with one massive paw, 'fell through.'

He looked round the others in his team, receiving smiles and quiet chuckles. The Palace team sat silently, though some moved uncomfortably and a deal of close table-surface inspection ensued.

'We have,' the polar bear emissary said, obviously relishing each loudly spoken word, 'taken other precautions as well, but we shall be keeping a very careful and continuous watch on the ceiling above Chapel City, and not only have powerful sensors trained on the relevant area, but various missiles as well . . .'

Adijine swore. He'd half hoped the Chapel traitors would misinterpret the body which had fallen into their midst – maybe, he'd thought, they would assume the man had fallen from a hang-glider, or some apparatus that could climb along under a ceiling. But it looked like they'd guessed correctly.

'And I must say,' the polar bear said, drawing itself up in its seat and sounding appropriately sententious, 'even though we thought ourselves by now inured to the thoroughly reckless nature of our opponents, we have been profoundly shocked and disappointed to discover the completely irresponsible and utterly senseless depths – or should I say heights?' – the ambassadorial emissary showed his teeth and glanced round his appropriately appreciative team – 'to which our previously at least ostensibly esteemed adversaries have been prepared to stoop to in their understandably increasingly desperate attempts to secure victory in this outrageously prosecuted, thoroughly unfortunate and – on our part – wholly unprovoked dispute.'

Adijine cut out there. That hairy white bastard was going to milk the situation for all it was worth, and doubtless at inordinate length.

He checked the representation of his private secretary's suite. There were calls waiting. He selected that of the Consistorian with special responsibility for Security.

Gadfium negotiated the lumber room. A flight of rungs set into the wall led her to a door and a lift shaft with spiral stairs running round it. The elevator appeared from above, stopped and opened its doors. Gadfium ducked under the stairs' safety rail and into the lift. She'd been hoping her other self had been kidding about going deeper but when the lift moved it was downwards, dropping her below ground level, deeper into the earth beneath the fastness.

– I'd better warn you there might be unexpected things ahead here.

– Such as?

– Well, people whose presence I can't warn you about.

– You mean outlaws.

– That's a little pejorative.

– We'll see.

– No, let's hope we don't see.

– You're right. Let's hope we don't.

– I'm going to put the lights out.

– Oh? Gadfium said as the elevator went dark.

– Help your eyes adjust.

'Oh, and I've always loved the dark,' Gadfium whispered to herself.

– I know. Sorry.

The elevator slowed and stopped, the doors opened and Gadfium got out into a darkness that was only just short of absolute. She could hear running water in the distance. Her feet splashed when she walked cautiously forward, arms in front of her, into what looked like a broad tunnel.

– Should be left here. Whoa. Stop. Feel forward with your right foot.

– It's a hole. Thanks.

– Look left? Yes; two steps left then walk on.

– Wait a minute; are there any cameras here?

– Not down here.

– So you're looking through my eyes—

– And I'm running an image enhancement program on what you're seeing. That's why I can see better than you can out of your own eyes.

Gadfium shook her head. – Anything I can do to help, apart from not keep my eyes open?

– Just keep looking all about, especially at the floor. Ah; here's a door. Turn right. Two steps. Right hand; feel?

– Got it.

– Careful; it's a vertical shaft. There's a ladder. Go down. And pace yourself; it's quite a way.

Gadfium groaned.

The city within the fourth-floor Chapel was formed in the shape of a magnificent chandelier which had been detached and lowered from the ceiling in the centre of the apse, above what would have been the chancel in a genuine chapel. It sat on a sheer-sided, three-hundred-metre-tall plateau which took the place of an altar, and rose in concentric circles of glowing, gleaming spires to the sharp pinnacle of the central tower. Formed from a metal framework wrapped with square kilometres of glass cladding interspersed with sheets of various highly polished stones, it looked out over the extravagantly decorated, elaborately columned length of the forest-floored Chapel and had been the monarch's traditional high-season residence for generations.

Uris Tenblen had fallen, still screaming hoarsely, onto the steep side of a tall spire in the second circle of the city, bounced once, hit a sheer wall opposite the spire, rebounded again and plummeted, still hardly slowed, into a flower bed on a stone-flagged courtyard. He had left a shallow elliptical crater in the earth and scattered blossoms like soft shrapnel as he'd bounced a third time and finally come to a halt crashing into a group of tables outside a café.

Most of Tenblen's precipitous descent and each successive part of its termination had been captured by an automatic camera on a seventh-level tower.

By the time a medic had arrived Tenblen had been quite irretrievably dead for some minutes, but the glancing nature of his first two contacts with the tower and then the wall, along with the comparative softness of his third impact in the flower bed, meant that there had been time for the alerted rebel Cryptographers to target and interrogate the dying man's bioware. The Army, as a matter of course, retro-fitted devices to its soldiers' implants to prevent this sort of thing, but – as was not unknown when an individual sustained a series of individually non-fatal impacts – these had been slow to react, and the rebel army had been furnished with recordings of what at first appeared to be merely the nightmares of a dying man but which were later realised to be accurate if still horrific records of reality. They were also, collectively, war intelligence of the first order.

Deep beneath the fastness ground level, in a tiny alcove off a larger alcove off a great arched tunnel off an even more enormous tunnel, Gadfium – exhausted after her escape and the various ensuing traverses and descents – slept.

When she awoke it was to her own voice crackling in her head and breaking up.

– – kup, will you?– – thing – – gon!– – fium!–

She opened her eyes. A blast of fetid breath rolled over her. She looked along the dust-dry floor and in the grey almost-light saw what looked like two hairy tree trunks with something resembling a furred snake dangling between them.

She looked up slowly. The tree trunks were joined at the top; a bulging hairy cliff continued up to a tusked, seemingly eyeless head which was broader than her whole body. On top of the domed head was another head, pale and hairless and half human, staring down at her. Weaving above and to either side of it was yet another head, with tiny staring eyes and a thick, curved beak, balanced on a long, scaly, snake-like neck.

A series of snorts and deep, chest-shaking breaths drew her attention to the fact that the enormous creature in front of her was only one of many, standing in a rough semi-circle around the alcove she had taken shelter in. One of the animals stamped a foot. She felt the ground shake.

Gadfium stared. She waited to faint but it would not happen.

Adijine walked to the window of his private office, shaking his head. 'You mean we might have to give those bastard Engineers in the Chapel what they want?'

'We don't appear to have very much choice,' Oncaterius said, crossing his legs and brushing one careful hand over his knee to free his robe of creases. 'It would seem the war is becoming recognised as unwinnable even by those who were originally most in favour of it.'

Adijine wrinkled his nose at this but did not rise to the bait.

'Time draws on,' Oncaterius said evenly. 'The Encroachment draws closer, and perhaps therefore so should we to our, ah,

Engineer cousins in the Chapel. We require the access they claim to have to— '

'Yes, *claim*,' the King said, staring out of the window and down into the depths of the Great Hall; rivers, roads and rail tracks threaded the landscape below in ascending orders of directness.

'Well, let's say, appear to possess,' Oncaterius continued, unruffled. 'They would appear *not* to possess our access to the necessary systems within the Cryptosphere, therefore an accommodation would appear to make sense for all concerned.'

'An accommodation in which those bastards get to call far too many fucking shots,' Adijine spat.

'I believe Your Majesty knows my opinions on the wisdom of having antagonised the clan Engineers in the first place.'

'Yes,' the King said, rolling his eyes and then turning round. 'I think you've made them clear on more occasions than I care to remember, except when it might have made a difference, right at the start.'

Adijine stood behind the imposingly heavy and ornate swivel chair on the far side of his even more imposingly heavy and ornate desk.

Oncaterius looked wounded. 'If I may say so, Your Majesty does me a disservice. I'm sure the records will show my voice was one of those raised in— '

'Oh, never mind,' the King said, turning the chair round and sitting heavily in its enveloping frame. 'If we have to compromise we have to. We can thrash it out at the Consistory meeting this evening, assuming the Chapel delegation have come up with their answer by then.' The King smiled ruefully, shaking his head once. 'At least we won't be making any concessions to some cross-clan posse of concerned scientists and mathematicians.'

Oncaterius smiled coldly. 'I accept Your Majesty's thanks on behalf of the Security service.'

Adijine narrowed his eyes. 'Is Gadfium still free?'

Oncaterius sighed. 'For now. She's an old lady scientist who got lucky, not a— '

'Couldn't we have tried to capture her? What was the point of trying to kill her?'

'On the confirmation of the existence of the conspiracy,' Oncaterius said, sounding a little as though he was reciting, 'and having received permission to proceed with its amelioration, it was she who happened to be in the position to do the most immediate damage. Rapid action was called for. Our operative took appropriate steps, considering the urgent nature of the circumstances. And I am sure Your Majesty understands that it is usually considered a great deal more straightforward to kill somebody than it is to capture them.' Oncaterius favoured the King with a thin smile. 'Given that our agent's attempt merely to murder Chief Scientist Gadfium resulted in three deaths it is perhaps just as well we did not endeavour to effect her capture.'

'*Given* the level of competence your people brought to the operation, I'm sure you're right,' the King said, taking some pleasure in the facial flinch this produced on the other man. 'Now, was there anything else?'

'Your Majesty has been informed of the capture of an asura?'

'Held for questioning,' Adijine said, waving one hand. 'Any progress?'

'We are being gentle. However, I think I may attempt to question her myself,' Oncaterius said smoothly.

'What about the child, the Teller who was under suspicion of crypt-hacking or whatever? Didn't he get away too?'

Oncaterius smiled. 'Dealt with.'

3

Sessine stood on the sloped desert sands, looking towards the tall grey tower at the end of the peninsula, cut off from the sands by a high black wall. Within, gardens formed a green triangle at the tower's base. Beyond and to either side, the sea rolled in, waves like creased bronze where they reflected the light of the network of red-orange burning in the sky. He looked away for a moment, trying to cancel the display in the heavens, but it refused to disappear.

The cliffs behind him were rosy with the same light, the sand beneath his soles strewn with shadows like wavelets. The air smelled of salt.

He felt something he had not felt for a long time, and it took a while before he admitted to himself that it was fear. He shrugged, hoisted his pack over his shoulder and continued on towards the distant tower, leaving a deep, scuffed trail of footprints behind him in the talc-fine sand. A vague, gauzy cloud of accompanying dust hung in the air.

It was the ten thousand, two hundred and seventh day of his time in the crypt. He had been here for almost twenty-eight years. Outside, in the other world, a little more than a day had passed.

The wall was obsidian; pitted in places, still highly polished in others. It met the sands and plunged into them like a black knife a kilometre long and fifty metres high at least. He stood in the silence, staring up at the almost featureless cliff, then trod down to the nearest shore. The wall extended a hundred metres or so out to sea. He turned on his heel and set off for the other end.

It was the same. He squatted by the shore and tested the water as a wave broke and rolled, pushing foam up the slope of sand. It was warm. He'd have to swim. He'd thought he might.

He started to undress.

He had not ever paid very much attention to his geographical position in the crypt, though it did roughly correspond to hardware in the base-level world. He supposed he must have wandered over much of South and North America before he had encountered the tonsured woman with her elaborately coded message; that had been, as nearly as he could make out, in a position which equated to somewhere in the North American Midwest; Iowa or Nebraska, he thought. His path since then had led him through Canada, Greenland, Iceland, Britain, Europe and Asia Minor to Arabia.

The sea crossings had been the most dangerous parts of his journey; whether they were effected by the likeness of a bridge or a tunnel, they represented choke points for travellers, and such a focusing of potential prey had in most cases produced a predatory exaggeration of the level's ecological balance. He had had to use the sword a few times, and – on occasion – opponents had attempted to best him through other levels of the crypt, imagining him into situations within which they thought he could more easily be defeated and absorbed.

He found, however, that he had little difficulty in assuming control in such situations. Much appeared to depend on one's wit; a general flexibility and quickness of mind plus an extensive and catholic knowledge-base – as long as these attributes were combined with a generous dash of ruthlessness – were all that one really needed to operate successfully within such imagined realities.

He had walked over broad bridges and within great tunnels hundreds upon hundreds of kilometres long, travelling within the spaces afforded by the slow sweeps of the writhing data highways, in something like a trance sometimes when the pace was forced and he could not afford to sleep, imagining himself to be a molecule of water trapped within the fold of some Archimedean Screw, a wave carried upon some articulation of light within a subsea cable, a fleck of sand-dust borne on the dark gurglings of a submerged water course veined beneath the baking desert.

He swam round the wall, at first attempting to keep his pack balanced on his head, then, when the waves became too rough, resorting to pushing it before him.

The waves mounted, the wind increased, and he realised that he was being blown away from the shore and the wall. He swam on as best he could but after swallowing water and being continually overwhelmed he was finally forced to surrender his heavy, waterlogged pack and all it contained to the sea; it sank quickly. He struck out with all his remaining strength for the just-glimpsed beach beyond the surf-skirted blackness of the wall.

Only his dreams had disturbed him on his journey to this place, still nagging at him with their images of slow eclipses and the death of stars all glimpsed above impressions of battle.

As he'd neared what he still only guessed and hoped was his goal, the dreams had begun to change, and instead of pan-historical images of the Encroachment, he had started to experience what appeared to be presentiments of its effects.

He'd seen the night sky, utterly black but for a twice-dimmed moon. He'd seen a cloudless day that was nevertheless dim, and a sun shining within that faded clarity that was high and full and yet dull orange, not fiery yellow-white; a sun it was possible to gaze at comfortably with the naked eye.

In his dreams he'd seen the weather change and the plants die, and later the people.

By virtue of its location Serehfa did not have a four-season year, alternating between seasons of dry and wet heat whose external effects were moderated by the construction's altitude as well as the carefully altered geography of its surroundings, but he remembered the spring and later the summer coming to Seattle and to Kuybyshev in the year that he had left base-reality behind, and in his dreams that summer did not last as long as the one before, and winter came earlier. The pattern was repeated more intensely in the southern hemisphere.

The following winter lasted throughout the spring before finally delivering a summer hardly warmer than the autumn it quickly lapsed into, and after that there was nothing but winter; winter with the dim face of thee sun high in the sky, or a winter set within a winter when the sun dipped nearer the horizon.

The pack ice grew continually, permafrost buckled the ground and thrust blisters of ice through what had been temperate soils, the currents of the air and of the sea changed as lakes and rivers froze and the hearts of the continents and the upper levels of the oceans cooled.

Plants died back, creating new deserts where vegetation used to copious heat and light had withered and plants better suited to the colder conditions had not yet had time to colonise, while those plants themselves succumbed to the sudden, smothering weight of the advancing snow and ice.

Animals of all descriptions found themselves being concentrated in a smaller and smaller band around the waist of the world, raising the contest to survive to new levels of ferocity, while even in the comparative warmth of the oceans life became gradually less abundant as the white shutters of freezing sea irised slowly closed over the brash-ice waves, and the trickling streams of sunlight energising the top of the food chain were reduced almost to nothing.

As though in mocking compensation for the shaded sun, great storms of light played about the heavens at night, flickering like aurorae, cold and vast, inhuman and numbing.

Still in those dreams he saw people crouched round fires, struggling through snow drifts with packs and possessions, taking refuge in mines and tunnels as the snow piled and the glaciers advanced and the icebergs crunched aground off equatorial shores and the pack ice spread from either pole like crystals in some drying solution.

No spears of fire or engines of more sophisticated energies lifted exiles into space, but for all the corpses abandoned at roadsides, for all the men, women and children left to die or freezing together in cars, carriages, houses, villages, towns and cities, still people persevered; retreating, stocking up, burrowing down, sealing up.

The fastness that had been Serehfa fell slowly, surrendering to aggregated megatonnes of ice until only the fast-tower itself remained, a listing cenotaph to human hubris. Then the glaciers swept down from the mountains to north and south and scoured even that from the surface of the world; the fast-tower's only memorial was a brief volcanic eruption wrenched from the earth by the thermonuclear-level energies its final fall created.

And so humanity left the surface of the world to the ice, wind and snow, and sheltered, reduced and impoverished, within the stony depths of the planet's skin, finally coming to resemble nothing more than parasites in the cooling pelt of some huge dying animal.

With it it took all its knowledge of the universe and all the memories of its achievements and all the coded information defining the animals and plants that had survived the vicissitudes of time and evolution and – especially – the pressure of the human species' own until then remorseless rise.

Those buried citadels became whole small worlds of refugee communities and spawned still smaller worlds as new machines took over the job of maintaining the levels of the crypt, until gradually more and more of what was in any sense humanity came to reside not simply in the created world of its tunnels, caverns and shafts but within those worlds in the generated realities produced by its computers.

Then the sun began to swell. The Earth shucked off its mummifying cocoon of ice, passed quickly through a feverish spring full of flood and storm, then wrapped itself in deeper and deeper cloud and more torrential rain. The atmosphere thickened and the heat and pressure built up while lightning played across the boiling clouds; the oceans shrank; the swollen bulk of the invisible sun poured energy into the deepening cauldron of gases around the planet, transforming it into a vast caustic foundry of chemical reactions and precipitating a welter of corrosive agents to pour upon the razed, enfumed surface of the Earth.

Earth turned into what Venus had once been, Venus began to resemble Mercury and Mercury ruptured, flowed and disintegrated to become a ring of molten slag spiralling in through the livid darkness towards the surface of the sun.

Still, what was left of humanity persisted, retreating further from the open oven of the surface until it became trapped between it and the heat of the planet's own molten sub-surface. It was then that the species finally gave up the struggle to remain in macrohuman form, pulling back fully into a virtual environment and resorted to storing its ancient biochemical inheritance as information only, in the hope that one day such fragile concoctions of water and minerals could exist again upon the face of the Earth.

Its time from then was long as people reckoned it from that point, short as they would have before. The sun's photosphere continued to expand until it swallowed Venus, and Earth did not survive much longer; the last humans on Earth perished together in a crumbling machine core as its cooling circuits failed, the half-finished life-boat spaceship they had been attempting to construct already melted to a hollow husk beside them.

. . . He suffered with each child abandoned to the snow; with every old man or woman left – too exhausted to shiver any more – under piles of ice-hard rags; with all the people swept away by the howling, fire-storm winds; with each consciousness extinguished – its ordered information reduced to random meaninglessness – by the increasing heat.

And he woke from such dreams sometimes wondering whether all that he was being shown could possibly be true, and on other occasions so convinced that it had been real that he would have faithfully believed what he had seen was the inescapable future, rather than some mere possibility, projection or warning.

He crawled ashore at dusk, collapsing onto the golden slope of the beach, the perfumes of the lush gardens beyond washing over his naked skin while his body shook and trembled with the after-effects of exertion.

He stared ahead, panting, while the surf washed at his feet, then rose unsteadily and staggered up the smooth stretch of beach towards a low white stone wall separating the strand from the gardens. Steps led up. He stood, then sat, shivering a little on the stone parapet, just looking.

Brightly coloured birds flitted through moss-hung trees, fountains played tinkling on shaded pools, paths meandered between plump lawns, and gaudy banks and beds of flowers offered up their bells and mouths to a lazy buzz of late-gathering insects.

The grey tower towards the apex of the gardens looked dark and deserted against the deep bruised hues of the sky.

He got his breath back and when he started to shiver again stood up and walked smartly towards the tower.

He walked out from under the sheltering trees.

The tower's dark grey surface had the rough-smooth texture of eggshell. It stood on a plinth of veined porphyry surrounded by a shallow moat where lilies floated and over which bowed an ornamental bridge of red-painted wood.

As he watched, something caught the faint light in the sky at the top of the tower and flashed, and floating down towards him there came an angel.

He laughed out loud.

4

I get tired screemin. Evin moar I get tired ov gettin bashed on thi hed wif thi mask whot has cum off ma faice; itz stil atatched 2 thi air tank on my bak & itz slipt roun bhind ma nek & is goan fump fump fump on thi bak ov my bonce.

I feel bhind me & tare it away.

Ma eers r goan pop pop pop. Thi air iz blastin roun me so hard therz harly eny poynt in me screemin nway. Its olmost totily dark; Ive got a sorta gray sensation ov thi wols rushin past aroun me, & if I twist roun I can luke up & c a vaig impreshin ov a tiny patch ov dark gray on thi blakniss.

Downwirds, thers jus blakniss.

I try 2 kript but I cant; doan no if itz coz Im movin 2 fass or coz thi shaft is sheeldid or coz Im 2 terrifyd 2 consintrate proprly. I start screemin agen, then stop, gulpin 4 bref.

Id 1/2 shat my pants by now but itz been so long sins I 8 I cant.

Thi air is coald & am shiverin but its not freezin. I setil in2 a sorta floppi X-shape aftir a while, like Ive scene skydivirs do; I drift 2wards 1 wol, then manoovir myself away agen. I 1/2 2 keep swaloin 2 keep my eers from burstin. I try 2 fink how far up I woz & how long itz goan 2 taik me 2 fol 2 thi botim, if its thi botim thats goan 2 brake ma fol. I reelize that ther mite b sumthin btween me & thi botim & I cude hit @ eny momint & I start screemin agen.

I stop aftir a while. Teers get whipt off ma faice but itz not me cryin itz juss thi feercniss ov thi wind tearin @ ma Is.

Ive nevir dyed b4. I doan no whot itz like. Ive herd from uthir peepil & Ive bin in thi minds ov bags whot 1/2 dyed & got ther impreshins but thay say itz difrint 4 evrybodi & I doan no whot itil b like 4 me & I woz hoapin not 2 find out 4 a while yet thanx very mutch but thare we go.

I start wunderin if thayl resusitate me @ oll. O fuk; whot if Im in sutch big trubil thayl juss looz my ident from thi kript? Whot if thay catch ma dyin fots & then juss interogate me, or doan bothir sayvin me @ oll?

I feel like am goan 2 b sik.

Thi roarin aroun me goze on forevir. My Is r dry & soar. My eers hurt 2.

O fuk I doan wan 2 dy.

I cant bleev how long this is takin. I feel like Im in kript-time. It okurs 2 me mayb I am, mayb I kriptid without noin about it. But I cant b. Im obveyisly not. I'm heer, follin down this shaft, damit. I try kriptin agen.

It wurx. Im on thi sekind basemint levil, praktikly @ c levil.

How mutch furthir down can this bleedin shaft go?

/ I port acros in2 thi kript; @ leest I can avoid thi momint ov impact. My implants will pool me bak when I dy, so ther woant b 2 ov me, but @ leest . . . wait a bleedin minit.

Accordin 2 thi loakil hardware Im stil on thi saim levil. Thi kript finks Im staishinry. Wots goan on heer?

I dubil chek, trebil chek, kwadroopil chek. Yep; thi kriptosfeer finks Ive stopt.

I giv a sorta mentil gulp, then port bak acros 2 my bod.

/Thi air iz stil screemin up roun me. Itz stil totily blak but wif thi thermil bit ov my vizhin I can stil make out thi wols 2 ither side. Shurenuf, they do luke a bit difrint; no impreshin ov them hurtlin past no moar. I stare down.

I doan c nuthin but blakniss but now I fink about it thi sound is diffrint sumhow; evin moar ov a roar.

Then suddenli thers lites evriwhare, blindin me.

I cloas my Is. I fink; blimey, I nevir felt a fing. Thass me ded & this is thi long tunnil wif thi lite @ thi end whot evribody getz 2 c & I muss 1/2 hit thi botim & not evin felt it.

Xsept thi roarins stil thare & thi wind is stil pushin in2 ma face. I opin my Is agen.

Im stairin strate down @ a sorta a hexagonil grid ov wires or metil or sumfin, & beyond thi grid, a few metirs furvir down, thers ol these big propelir fings, 7 ov them, ol whirlin away & roarin & sendin thi air screemin up past me.

I luke 2 thi side.

Thers a doar in thi wol levil wif me & a cupil ov big black meen lookin birdz wif skaley nex perchd thare, lookin @ me, beedy-Id, ther fevirs rufflin in thi draft.

I cant fink whot else 2 do. So I wave 2 them.

That woz how we used 2 reech our hoam, 1 ov thi birdz tells me.

Am wokin along a brod britely lit tunnil. Thi 2 lammergeiers r keepin pace wif me by sorta 1/2 hoverin in thi air 1 on ither side ov me, ther wings goan whuf whuf, whuf whuf. I didn evin no they cude do this.

Am wokin kinda funy coz I think I did crap my pants juss a litil, but they doan seem 2 notis, or thayr 2 polite.

U meen u got blastid up thare by thoaz fans? I say, suriptishisly poolin @ thi seet ov ma pants.

Krect, sez thi bird (½in 2 shout abuv thi noise ov its wings goan whuf whuf).

So whyd u leev? I shout. & who woz that up thare pooshd me down?

We left bcoz it woz no longir safe, & we wer needid down heer, yelz thi bird. As 2 who pooshd u in2 thi shaft, I imajin it woz probly a state employee.

Whot, a Security geezir or sumfing? But—?

Pleez; I cant tel u eny moar. Our comandir may b abil 2 ansir eny uthir qwestions u ½. Luke; wude u mind runnin?

Runnin? I sez, Why, is ther sumbidy aftir us? I glans bhind expectin 2 c Security peepil pursooin us but thers juss thi long brite tunil stretchin way in2 thi distins.

No, shouts thi bird, itz juss this pace is very tyrin 4 us.

Sorry, I sez, & braik in2 a run. Dozent do my chafed bum no gude but it keeps thi 2 lammergeiers happy, beetin alongside.

& so that woz how I arrivd @ thi lammergeiers HQ; brefliss, on thi dubil & wif my pants spottid wif kak.

Thi hed lammergeier iz a feerce big bugir ov a burd; tolir than me when heez perchd & wings longir than Im tol. He iznt no ole gie neevir, heez in hiz prime wif sleek blak & wite fevvirs, steely lookin talins, a naykid nek that lukes oild & brite, & jet-blak Is. I doan no if heez got a naim; we ½nt bin propirly introdoosed.

Heez sittin on a perch, Im sat on thi floar. Thi room iz funnil shaped & thi brod sirkulir roof has a imidje ov a blu sky wif litil flufy clouds in it. Thers anuthir ½ dozen or so uthir lammergeiers perchd aroun thi room 2.

U ½ been a propir pest 2 sertin peepil, mastir Bascule, thi big bird sez, stairin @ me & rokin from side 2 side & sorta stampin itz feet on thi perch. A moast persistent pest.

Thang u very mutch, I sez.

That woz not a complimint! thi bird screetchiz, flapin.

I sit bak, blinkin (my Is r stil a bit soar aftir ol that wind roarin past me when I fel). Whot do u meen? I ask.

Itz qwite possibil that we ½ givin away our noo posishin heer by turnin on thi lift fans so we cude save yoor miserabil hide! thi bird shouts.

Wel, sory Im shure, but I woz toald u mite ½ sum informayshin about thi whareabouts ov a frend ov mine.

What? thi hed bird sez, soundin puzzld. Who?

Itz a ant. Hir name is Ergates.

Thi bird starez @ me. Yoor lookin 4 a *ant*? he sqwaks, & sounz increduliss.

A ver speshil ant. (I naro my Is.) Whot woz taikin by a *lammergeier*.

Thi bird shaiks itz hed. Wel, it woznt dun by 1 ov us, it sez, shakin its fevirs.

O yeh? I sez.

We r chimerix, mastir Bascule. This . . . ant muss $1/2$ bin taikin by a wild lammergeier.

& whare r they then? I ask. (Dam, fot I woz on thi rite trak @ last!)

Ded, thi hed bird sez.

I blink my Is. Ded?

Thi state had them kild during yesterday evening when it reelized we opoasd it; moast ov them wer mobbed by chimeric crows & brot down. We bleev we wer thi reel targets. 2 ov us wer cot & distructid. Ol thi wild lammergeiers r ded.

O, I sed. O deer, I thot.

Hmm, I sed, I doan supoase u no if eny ov them sed anythin about—?

Wait a minit, thi bird sez, waivin 1 wing @ me. It cloases its Is 4 a momint. It opinz them agen.

It lukes stedily @ me 4 a momint, then sorta $1/2$ shaiks its hed. Wel, mastir Bascule, it sez. As I sed, u $1/2$ been nuthing if not persistint. & u $1/2$ not been fritind 2 risk yoor life. It stamps its feet agen. Ther is sumthin u mite do.

Do 4 what, 4 who?

I cant tel u 2 mutch, yung sir; itz best 4 u if u doant no 2 mutch, beleev me; but ther r sum very importint things happening rite now, things whitch affect – & whitch wil affect – ol ov us. Thi state – thi peepil who $1/2$ atakd owr frends thi sloths & $1/2$ tried 2 kil u – r tryin 2 prevent sumthing happening. Wil u giv us yoor help in making it happin?

Whot happenin? I ask, suspishiss. They say thers a emisiry from thi kaotic bits ov thi kript aroun, wantin 2 infect thi uppir layers.

Thi big bird shayks its wings impayshintly. Thi emisiry, it sez, is kold an asoora & it is from 1 ov thi few parts ov thi kript whitch haz *not* bin tutched by thi kaos. It carrys within it thi meens ov our salvayshin, but its mishin is in jeperdy; the state oposes it 2 bcoz thi fulfilment ov its mishin wude – conseevibly – meen thi end ov thi presint power structyoor. Ov coarse thi state has used thi bogey ov thi kaos 2 atemt 2 turn uthirs agenst thi asoora & those who wude aid it. Thi fact remanes it iz our only hoap. If it duz not sukseed we r ol lost.

I shift my bum a bit. I reely shude 1/2 askd 2 cleen up a bit b4 ol this. Not that a playce whare lammergeiers r iz likely 2 b big on washrooms, judjin from thi state ov sum ov thi floars Ive seen aroun her. Im finkin fru whot thi hed geezirs juss toal me. It mite b tru, but I ver mutch dout am been toald thi hoal trufe heer.

& whot am I suposed 2 do? I ask.

Thi hed bird lukes distinkly uncumfortabil, & flaps itz wings a bit. Itz danegeris, it sez.

Id kinda gessd that, I sez urbainly, feelin pritti groan-up, thangu ver mutch. Whot did u 1/2 in mind? I ask.

Thi lammergeier fixiz me wif its ice-blak Is. Goan bak up thi fass-towr, it sez. Only hi-er this time. (It stamps its feet, 1 aftir anuthir, & thi uthir burdz do thi saim thing.) Mutch hi-er.

I sit bak. Frotes gon a bit dry.

U got a toilit I cude yooz? I ask.

Lukes like thi hoal bleedin fass-towrs juss pakd wif shafts. Weer heer @ thi foot ov anuthir 1. Itz biggir than thi 1 I fel down; a lot bigir. This is thi 1 in thi centir ov thi towr & it muss b eesily 1/2 a kilometir acros. Very faynt lite filtirs down from . . . blimey, I doan no; helluva far up, thas 4 shure.

We r heer curtisy ov thi war, thi hed bird telz me. Both sides think thi uthir controlz this space.

O reely.

Yes; thi fact they may b about 2 reech an acomadayshin shortly is anuthir reezin 4 ther bein a degree ov urjinsy about thi presint sityooayshin.

Thi hed bird is perchd wif his 1/2 dozen pals on whot lukes like a peece ov crumpild, soot-blakind missile rekidje neer thi centir ov thi shaft base. Uthir lammergeiers r flittin about thi place fru thi shados. Thi rok floar ov thi shaft lukes like it used 2 b smooth but itz ol chipt & skard now & literd wif bits ov broakin mashines. Thers a dubil set ov rales leedin in from thi side ov thi shaft whitch is whare we came from; thers a big cavern thare whot lukes like a mooseum ov rokit flite or sumfing; fool ov big sheds & misteeryus bits ov eqwuipmint & rustin missiles & big sferikil tanx & telescopes & radar dishis & deflatid silvir baloons like discardid bolgounz.

I luke strate up. Didn no u cude get vertigo lukin up.

This iz thi mane shaft, thi hed bird sez, & poziz. 1nce it led 2 thi stars.

I luke up agen & I can bleev it. My hed spins @ thi thot & I olmost fol ovir.

Thi top ov thi fass-towr has bin inaxessibil 4 as long as enybodi or anything can remember, thi lammergeier telz me. Meny atemts 1/2 bin made, moastly in secrit, 2 reetch its hites. Ol 1/2 fayled, as far as we no. It lifts up 1 foot & lukes down @ thi bit ov missile itz perchd on. U c sum ov thi rekidje around u.

Uh-huh, I sez. Sumfin up thare keeps shootin them down, yeh?

No; but ther apeers 2 b an armurd conical base 2 thi towrs upir reetches @ about 20 kilometirs whitch nobody has bin abil 2 penitrate.

I luke roun @ ol thi missile rekidje. Thi offorities doan yoozhily let airplanes operate wifin thi cassil 4 feer ov a crash weekinin thi struktyir, let aloan missiles. U cant help wunderin whot sorta damidje has bin dun up thare by ol this rekd hardware.

So? I sez.

We 1/2 a final vacyoom baloon, thi lammergeier sez.

A whot?

A vacyoom baloon, it repeets. Teknikly, a very strong impermeebil membrane encloasin a hi vacyoom & fitid wif a harnis.

A harnis, I sed.

+, we 1/2 sum hi-altitood breevin eqwipmint.

U 1/2, 1/2 u? I sez. (& am finkin, 0–0 . . .)

Yes, mastir Bascule. We r askin u 2 take thi baloon up as far as u can & then clime sum way beyond thi levil thi baloon attanes.

Iż that posibil? How far up we tokin?

It is sertinly posibil, tho not without risk. Thi altitood is aproximitly 20 kilometirs.

Haz enybudy els bin up that hi?

They 1/2.

They get bak down agen?

Yes, thi lammergeier sez, stampin from side 2 side agen & flappin its wings out a bit. Sevril mishins 1/2 ataned sutch hites in thi past.

Whot am I suposed 2 do up thare?

U wil b givin a pakidje 2 tak wif u. Ol u 1/2 2 do is diliver it.

Whare? Who 2?

U wil c when u get thare. I cant tel u eny moar.

If this is so urjint, how cum u gies cant do it? I ask, lukin roun @ thi othir birdz.

1 ov our numbir tryd, thi hed bird sez. We beleev he is ded. Anuthir woz about 2 mount a sekind atempt juss b4 u apperd but we wer not veri hoapful ov suxess. Thi problem is that we canot fly 2 a 1/2 ov thi altitood reqwired, & 1ce thi baloon wil rise no moar simply woking up steps apeers 2 b thi best meens ov gainin hite. We r not bilt for wokin. U r.

I fink about ol this.

It is a simpl task in a sens, thi hed lammergeier sez, but without it thi asooras mishin wil shurely fale. Howevir, this is a danejiris undertaikin. If u lak thi curidje 2 taik it on then b shure that moast hoomins wood feel thi saim way. Probly thi sensibil fing 2 do is 2 turn it doun. U r bairly an adolesint, aftir ol.

Thi hed bird lowirs his nek a litil & lukes roun @ his 2 neereist pals.

We ask 2 mutch, he sez, soundin sorofool. Cum – & he starts 2 opin his wings as if 2 fly away.

I swolo hard.

Il do it, I sez.

NINE

1

The cell was dark. She had been troubled by strange dreams and awoke, restless and disturbed in her narrow cot. She tried to get back to sleep but could not. She lay on her back, trying in vain to remember what she had been dreaming about. She opened her eyes to the darkness, and when she rolled over again noticed a tiny glow of pale light coming from the floor. She gazed down at it. It was like a pearl, lit from inside, and so faint she could only see it when she didn't look straight at it. She put her hand out to touch it. It felt cold. It was stuck to the floor. She caught a hint of movement inside, and got out of the bed, kneeling on the floor and putting one eye up to the tiny glowing pearl.

Inside the pearl she saw ice and snow and cloud and somebody standing dressed in furs.

Without hesitating, she plucked the pearl from the floor. It was damp and cold in her fingers, like ice. The tiny hole in the floor glowed more brightly now; the scene below was clearer. She wished she could slip through into that other place, and found herself shrinking – or the hole and the cell around her expanding – until she was able to do just that.

She awoke on a frozen lake; a huge sheet of ice stretching smoothly away in every direction to a pale grey horizon. Above was a roof of white cloud.

It was very cold. She was dressed in a fur hat and a calf-length coat. Her boots were long and her hands were clasped together inside a fur muff. Her breath smoked in front of her.

In the distance she saw a black dot. It gradually enlarged until eventually it resolved into a man rowing a kind of spindly frame across the ice. He didn't turn round to look at her, but stopped rowing some distance away and coasted to a halt level with her and about a stone's throw distant. He wore a thin, tight-fitting one-piece suit and a thin cap. He sat, still not looking at her, breathing hard and leaning forwards to rest on the claw-oars he held.

She looked down at her boots, which became ice skates. She glided over and stopped neatly, facing him.

He was middle-aged but fit-looking in a stocky, compact sort of way. There was a sculpted leanness hinted at in his face and his hair was thick and black. He looked slightly surprised. 'Who the hell are you?' he asked.

'Asura,' she said, nodding. 'And you?'

'Hortis,' he said. He turned and looked around and behind him. 'I thought I was alone here. They don't usually . . .' his voice trailed off as he looked back at her, eyes narrowed in suspicion. 'What do you want here?' he asked her.

'Nothing,' she said.

'They all want something,' he said, sounding bitter. 'You must, too. What is it?'

She shook her head. 'I don't know what I want,' she admitted. 'I wanted to be here, and I'm here.' She thought. 'I can't go anywhere else. They keep trying to make me answer questions. Apart from— '

'And you're not ill or sick or needing to be rescued?' he asked, a sneer on his face.

'No,' she told him, puzzled. 'Are you?'

'Only from this nonsense,' he said, not looking at her, but checking the angle of the claw-oars. He levered them back and flicked them down into the ice. 'Tell them nice try; at least they're getting more subtle.' He pulled on the claw-oars and the A-shaped frame rumbled off across the ice, gaining speed with each sweep of the oars the man made.

She hesitated, then set off after him, skating smoothly in his wake. He looked annoyed. He lengthened his stroke, trying to outdistance her, but she kept up with him. She loved the feel of the ice under the blades on her feet and the cold air on her face. Warmth spread from her legs as she pushed after the man in his strange, spindly craft. He was pulling quite hard now and she was struggling to keep up, but he didn't look comfortable with the pace he'd set either. His face grew more angry-looking.

She wanted to laugh, but did not.

'How long have you been here?' she asked him.

She thought he wasn't going to answer, but then he said, 'Too damn long.' He gave one explosive sigh and settled back to a more steady rowing rhythm, seemingly giving up his attempt to pull away from her.

'Why are you here?' she asked.

'I'll show you mine if you'll show me yours,' he said, smiling humourlessly, and shook his head as he watched his claw-oars flick and bite.

'Where did you come from?' she asked patiently.

Again, she thought he wasn't going to answer. It looked like he was thinking hard. Finally he said – suddenly looking straight at her – 'The tower.'

She ceased to push after him and glided on for some time, skates parallel, then felt herself brake gently. The man had stopped rowing, though his own momentum was still drawing him further away over the ice from her. He was frowning.

She came to a stop.

'The tower,' she whispered to herself.

The man who had called himself Hortis slowed and stopped the fragile-looking ice-boat, some distance off. He was looking at her strangely, his head tipped to one side. Then he angled one oar behind him and the other in front and pulled them together to turn the craft and come back to her.

The small craft rumbled a length past her and stopped. He shipped the claw-oars, leaning forward and looking intently at her. He gazed at her for a while, then appeared to come to a decision.

'All right, then,' he said. 'Maybe I've been in here too long, or maybe I just can't resist a pretty face, but I suppose it can't do any harm.' He gave a small smile. 'I was one of a small group of scientists and mathematicians who opposed the Consistory. We believed their desire to hold on to power had entirely superseded any duty to govern for the general good; our conspiracy – which had started at university and never really been more than a secret club – became more serious when the Encroachment was discovered and we began to suspect that the Consistory – with the King as its puppet – was doing less than it might to find a solution to the emergency.

'We pursued many different courses. We tried to contact the Cryptosphere's chaotic levels, believing that at least part of the so-called chaos was in fact an AI nexus at odds with the Consistory's philosophy. We set up secret transmitters in an attempt to contact the deep-space monitoring system the Diaspora was supposed to have left in watch over us, and we tried to elicit some sort of response from the fast-tower, where rumours had it that either an uncorrupted crypt core existed, or, again, elements remained which were still in touch with the Diaspora.

'A couple of days ago, in base-time, we apparently received a signal from the heights of the fast-tower. It was . . . couched in slightly eccentric terms, but appeared to be genuine.

'The signal confirmed some of our suspicions concerning the Consistory's lack of sincerity in finding a way to defeat the Encroachment. It did not seem to indicate that it was in touch with whatever remains of our space-going ancestors, though it did talk of some system left behind by the Diaspora which might ensure the survival of all of us. The message – or at least its ramifications – led . . .' the man sighed, and looked sad, 'to our conspiracy being betrayed and me ending up here, and,' he said, looking straight into her eyes, 'it talked of another part of the crypt, some uncorrupted section which contained the key to the Diaspora-donated survival system. This key would be sent here, to Serehfa, and it would come in the form of something called an asura . . .' – he smiled, and in that smile she saw a kind of sadness, some defensive cynicism, and an unspoken hope – '. . . Asura,' he finished. He shrugged. 'Your turn.'

She looked down at him, while inside her mind what felt like great slabs of ice slipped and slotted, colliding, joining, fusing and interconnecting.

She took a deep breath.

2

'Chief Scientist Gadfia?'

The voice had come from the scrawny-necked bird squatting on the shoulders of the ape-human who in turn sat behind the head of the chimeric mammoth. The ape-human glared down at her, grinning inanely. The other mammoths to either side shuffled a little in the darkness, pale human faces looking down from each of them as well. She gulped. 'Well, sort of,' she said.

– Hello? she said, inside, trying to find her own voice, but within was only silence.

'All praise,' the bird said, its voice echoing in the complex of hidden tunnels and galleries around them. The creature hopped to and fro from one foot to the other. 'Love is god. Well met by darkness, truth-seeker Gadfia. For darkness gives birth to light. All here are hallowed, hallowed in hollow, the hollowness that supports, the centre that is the absence that gives strength, the hollow darkness that underlies supporting light, seeker-after-illumination Gadfia. Please (Hiddier: trunk!); come with us. There is work to do.'

The mammoth extended its trunk towards her; a giant, tapered hairy snake with a naked, glistening double orifice at the end from which a damp, subtly fetid gust of air issued.

She stared.

– Back.

– Thank goodness. Where did you—?

– I was snooping where I shouldn't have been and I was almost caught by Security. Cut me off for a while.

– Good grief. Do you know where—?

– You're riding through vast dark dripping tunnels on the back of a chimeric mammoth with a dumb, naked and deformed semi-human and a lammergeier that talks like some ancient preacher and reminds you of the message from the fast-tower.

– Correct. And I can't get sense out of anybody. The bird spouts religious balderdash and the humanoid just grins, hoots and dribbles. I was thinking of asking the mammoth what was going on next.

– At least you went with them.

– Did I have a choice?

– I suppose you forgot about the gun.

– Oh.

– It doesn't matter. You did the right thing. Never mind; guess who I've been talking to.

– Surprise me.

– The fast-tower.

– *What*?

– Well, an emissary thereof; it can't get back in touch with the tower for fear of chaotic contamination, but it represents it.

– How? Where? What's—?

– The representation just appeared in the crypt; an old white man with white hair and flowing white robes. The thing proliferated illegally – set off system crashes everywhere; everybody thought it was some vast attack from the chaos until they found how easy it was to trap and kill; I don't think the tower is very good with humans. Anyway, the copies all started trying to talk to anybody who'd listen. The Cryptographers mopped most of them up and they're tracking down the others but I was able to find one of the copies and quiz it.

– And?

– There is an asura and it's here, it's in Serehfa, it's on its way, but it's being held up. The tower seems pretty confused itself about who and what it is, but it believes it's here somewhere and it needs help.

– Are you sure this isn't some Security or Cryptographers' trick?

– Fairly. There is another aspect to all this.

– What?

– We have an ally.

– Who?

– Myself, ma'am, said another voice, a male voice, in her head, startling her. – How do you do.

– Oh. Hello, she thought, and felt flustered. Who are you?

– Call me Alan. Pleased to meet you, madam Chief Scientist, though in fact we have met before, in a sense. Whatever; I dare say we shall communicate again.

– Ah, right, yes, she thought, still not sure how to respond.

– That was him, said her own voice again.

– I guessed that, but who—?

– Another *planētēs*, Gadfium, another wanderer in the system, though this one's been here a lot longer than I. He's kind of cagey about revealing who he really is but I get the impression his human original was pretty powerful and important. His current self is extremely well informed and knows his way about the crypt better than the Cryptographers. It would seem he came to the same conclusion the tower did about the efficacy of using chimeric agents rather than humans to slip past Security.

– I hate to sound a note of caution again, but—

– No, I don't think he's a plant for Security. He found me, lurking around where they're holding the asura. If it hadn't been for him Security would have got me.

– So you think.

– I know. Look, it was he who put me on to the chimerics you're with.

Gadfium looked at the back of the half-human thing in front of her. It was dark and matted and she suspected if the light had been better she'd have seen things crawling in the creature's hair. The giant bird which had been perched on the thing's shoulders had flown off down the black tunnel, cackling. Below her, the mammoth swayed from side to side with a surprisingly rapid motion as it led the twenty-strong herd down the huge tunnel. The other humanoids riding, legs clenched behind the heads of the mammoths, grinned widely and made excited fist-clenching gestures at her when she turned to look at them.

Gadfium scratched and tried not to think how far down the ground was.

– Well, tell him thanks for that, I think, she told her crypt self. But where exactly are we going and what precisely are we supposed to do?

– You're the cavalry; we're riding to the rescue, Gadfium! her other self said, excited.

– I thought I was the one needing to be rescued.

– Well, you've become the rescuer, Gad. We're going to free the asura.

– We're what?

– You're on your way to Oubliette, the sea-port under the fastness. That's where Security are holding the asura. Alan and I can do most of it, but physically, to rescue the girl, we may need you. And the chimerics, of course. The mammoths and the semi-humans seem to be under the influence of our friend, the lammergeier . . . Well, I'm still trying to work it out. Could be connected with the tower.'

Gadfium couldn't think what to say for a while. She stared into the darkness ahead, where she could just make out the heat signature of the returning lammergeier. She imagined the dark, buried city of Oubliette coming closer ahead, and herself riding with a preaching bird, twenty cretinous semi-humans and as many house-high mammoths to do battle with the élite of Security and probably the Cryptographers too.

The scaly-necked bird flapped and settled on the broad hairy shoulders of the creature ahead of her.

'Have faith in the nothing,' it said in a quiet screech. 'Faith is the eye that sees nothing and rejoices in it. Unknowingness absolves the future path of danger. The eye sees, sees nothing, and so has faith. Fair set, all are hallowed. Shanti.'

Gadfium shook her head and looked down at the matted fur of the huge animal she bestrode, feeling its damp, rank heat welling up around her like doubt.

– Are we both mad? she asked her crypt self, – Or is it just you?

3

The angel was tall and sleek and sensually asexual; its eyes and hair were gold, its skin shone like liquid bronze. Its clothes were confined to a loincloth and a small waistcoat. Its wings varied from the coppery tint of its body at their roots through every shade of blue to white at the very tips of the feathers. It flew with an elegant effortlessness and landed lightly in front of him.

He had stopped laughing, not wanting to appear impolite.

The angel bowed slowly and deeply to him.

When it spoke its voice was like something beyond music, each phoneme, syllable and word at once utterly clear and yet setting off a symphony of tones which fanned instantly out from the primary expression like an avalanche down a pristine slope.

'Welcome, sir. You have travelled a long way to be here with us at last.'

He nodded. 'Thank you. Had we met during any other day of my journey I would have greeted you somewhat better dressed.'

The angel smiled, but did not look at his nakedness. 'Please, sir,' it said, and like a conjurer flourished one hand, and was suddenly holding a large black cape, which it held out to him.

'I'm grateful for the gesture,' he said, not taking the cape. 'But if its utility is restricted to saving my blushes, I'd prefer to remain as I am.'

'As you wish,' the angel said, and the cape was gone.

'Tell me,' he said. 'Did I misinterpret something, or was I summoned here?'

'You were, sir. We would ask something of you.'

'Who is this "we"?'

'A one-time part of the data corpus charged with overseeing the functioning of the rest, and with the monitoring of our world's welfare.'

'No small brief. And your current intentions?'

'We will attempt to contact a system set up long ago which may help deliver us from what has been called the Encroachment.'

'And how exactly is it supposed to do that?'

The angel smiled dazzlingly. 'We have no idea.'

He could not help but smile too. 'And what part may I play?'

The angel lowered its head, its gaze still fastened on him. 'You can give us your soul, Alandre,' it said, and Sessine felt something quail within him.

'What?' he said, crossing his arms. 'Aren't we being rather metaphysical?'

'It is the most meaningful way to express what we'd ask of you.'

'My soul,' he said, hoping he sounded sceptical.

The angel nodded slowly. 'Yes; the essence of who you are. If you are to help us you must surrender that.'

'Such things may be copied.'

'They may. But is that what you want?'

He looked into the angel's eyes for some time. He sighed. 'Will I still be me?'

The angel shook its head. 'No.'

'Then whom?'

'What will exist is what we create from you, and with you.' The angel shrugged; a magnificent and beautiful flutter of shoulders and wings. 'Another person, with aspects of yourself within them, and more you than anybody else, but not you.'

'But will something of me remain that will remember this, and my time here, and who I was, and so know what became of me from this point, and whether I . . . did any good?'

'Perhaps.'

'You can put it no more strongly than that?'

'I cannot. Partly, that aspect would depend on you, but I'd lie if I told you the chances are good.'

'And if I refuse to help you?'

'Then you may walk away. We can furnish you with items to replace those you lost in the water and you may resume your travels. On your funeral, in another fifty or so years of crypt-time, I assume you will have the usual courtesies accorded you and so take your place within the Cryptosphere. Twenty thousand years of crypt-time await even before the Encroachment is complete; there will be far, far longer than that before matters become desperate in the physical world.'

He felt he had to insist, even though he listened to himself speak and felt ashamed: 'There is a chance of some continuity though; some element of me might survive which will remember this and know the connection, know what I did?'

'Indeed,' the angel said, with what was almost a bow. 'A chance.'

'Hmm,' he said. 'Oh well, it's been a long life.' He gave a small laugh. 'Lives.' He smiled at the angel, but it looked sad.

Strangely, he felt sad for it, too. 'What do I do?'

'Come with me,' the angel said, and was suddenly a small dark-haired, white-skinned man dapperly dressed in a three-piece suit and carrying a hat, cane and gloves. He flourished the hand holding his pair of spotless white gloves, indicating the path back through the garden.

Sessine went with him, walking side by side along the path to where a rotunda set on a small hill was revolving slowly and rising; its revealed base was in the shape of a huge cylindrical screw, and gradually an aperture came into view, rotating with the rotunda, its full size being revealed after a few more revolutions.

They climbed the path to the now motionless rotunda. The doorway faced them. It was dark at first, then it began to glow with a warm orange-yellow light, like side-lit fog.

'Merely enter, and you will have done all we ask of you. If you carry something of your being through what awaits here, you may do what you ask of yourself.'

He took a step forward. The doorway shone like hazy sunlight. He smelled the sea again. He hesitated and turned to the little man who had been in the form of an angel.

'And you?'

The little man smiled wryly and looked back over the trees at the grey heights of the quiet tower, proud against the sky's last dusky light. 'I cannot go back,' he said, and sounded resigned. 'I shall probably stay here, in the garden, to tend it.' He looked around. 'I have often thought it exhibits too perfect an elegance. It could do with some . . . love.' He turned back, grinning self-consciously. 'Or I may wander the level, as you have done. Perhaps both, consecutively.'

He put his hand on the small man's shoulder and nodded at the beautiful tower. 'I'm sorry you can't go back.'

'Thank you for having asked, and for saying so.' The small man frowned and seemed to hesitate. 'Perhaps,' he said, 'my "perhaps" earlier was overly pessimistic.'

'We'll see. Fare well.'

'And you, sir.'

They shook hands, and then Sessine turned and walked through the doorway into the glowing mist.

4

Hoo-wee! Am probly hier than nbody els in thi hole wyde wurld rite now, xeptin onli thi peepil in thi fass-towr assoomin thers nbody up thare ov coarse.

Thi baloon is a grate enormis shado abuv me. Am hangin undir it by whot lukes lyk a pair ov freds from a wispy net ov moar freds whot loop ovir thi big sfeer. Thi lammergeiers strapt theez 3 oxijin tanx 2 my chest & gaiv me this lite litil pakidje 2 put on my bak. Av got anuthir mask on now, 2.

   & a botil ov wotir.

   & wormir cloves.

   & a torch,

   & a nife.

& a hedake, tho thats probly thi leest ov my problims, but nevermind.

& av got a parashoot 2, tho that mite $1/2$ 2 go when I get a bit hier up.

Thi birdz @ thi botim ov thi shaft seemd 2 b in a bit ov a hury & I only got about 10 minits ov instruxin on how 2 control thi baloon while I woz getin kittid out wif thi hi-alt clovin & stuf, but it boils down 2 yoosin a cupil ov pairs ov lines 2 pool hinjd flaps like airbrayks whitch shude steer me a bit, + (2 control my speed ov assent) waitin 4 thi baloon 2 slo down & then cuttin off lenfs ov plastic tyoobin sikyoord 2 thi same freds holdin me.

Thi lammergeiers brot thi baloon out ov a big shed in thi cavern @ thi foot ov thi shaft; it ran on rales atatchd 2 thi seelin. Thi baloon is juss a big sfeer fool ov vacyoom; iss as simpil as that. It lukes greyish & akordin 2 thi birds iss made ov sum sorta stuf simla 2 thi fabric ov thi cassil, so it muss b prity strong. Thi freds wer olredy draped ovir thi baloon.

Whot if busts? I askd, jokin reely, but thi hed bird luked kind ov awkwird & sed sumfin about uthir modils wif litlr baloons inside them not bein up 2 thi job & if it was goan 2 burst it wude b low down probly & they wude giv me a parashoot 4 lowir altitoods.

Nway, not 2 wury I sed, kinda wishin I hadnt askd in thi 1st place.

I got my flyin lessin, they wayd me, then they gave me thi vayrayis bits ov stuf, strapt me in, pooshd thi baloon – wif me hangin undir it – along thi rales out in2 thi botim ov thi shaft & along 2 juss b4 whare thi rales endid. They atatchd thi lenfs ov plastic toobin 2 thi harnis in frunt ov me & that was us redy.

Gude luk, mastir Bascule, thi hed bird sed. We wish u ol thi best.

Me 2, I sed, witch mite not $1/2$ been very grayshis, but @ leest it was tru. O, & fanks 4 ol yoor help, I sed.

U r welcum, thi hed lammergeier sed. It seemd 2 stifin, then sed, We'd betir get on wif it; things apeer 2 b cumin 2 a hed. It went qwiet 4 a moment, then seemd 2 nod 2 itself. I wude advise u not 2 yoose thi kript 4 thi momint, it told me.

Ritey-ho, I sed, & gave thi fums up sine.

They poold sum leevirs & thi rales abuv me swung up & opin; thi baloon took off with a whoosh ov air, draggin me & thi lenfs ov plastic toobin up wif it. It was like follin upwirds. Felt like my stumik was poold down 2 ma boots.

They ithir cloasd thi doars 2 thi caverin alongside thi botim ov thi shaft or poot thi lites out, bcoz it ol went dark down thare & I was left wif juss thi dark greyness ov thi shaft wols. Thi slipstreme wind tugd @ my cloves.

Thi baloon seemd 2 go up prity strate, tho I poold on thi control lines conectid 2 thi hinjd flaps juss 2 make shure they wurkd.

Evin wif ol that toobin & stuf we fairly shot up & I had 2 keep yawnin 2 cleer ma eers. Sum ov thi lammergeiers had floan up inside thi shaft, & I wayvd 2 ther shadoy shapes as I wen past. Thi hoal hooj sirkil ov thi shaft botim seemed 2 shrink like sum cloasin shuttir as me & thi baloon wissild upwirds; prity soon thi birds wheelin roun inside thi shaft had groan 2 smol 2 c, & thi botim ov thi shaft was juss a blak sirkil gettin sloly smolir.

I doan no how meny minits it took 2 get 2 whare I needed oxijin, but it had got prity bleedin coald by then, I can tel u. I woz glad ov thi fermils & stuf they'd givin me. My hed was a bit soar by this time.

I turnd on thi furst oxijin tank & took a bref. Thi baloon had sloed down a lot & I didn want 2 yoose eny moar oxijin than I had 2, so I cut a lenf ov thi toobin off; it was fik stuf like yood make a drane or sumfink out ov & it fel away like a big stiff wurm; thi baloon pikt up speed agen & thi fin air hissd past me.

Thi wols ov thi dark shaft wer plane & boarin, juss lines & rales & okayshinil sirkulir outlines that mite $1/2$ been doars but witch were nevir opin.

Id let 5 ov thi 8 bits ov plastic toobin go when I saw flashes down below, in thi depfs ov thi shaft. A bit later I herd sum muffild bangs.

Ther wer moar breef flashiz, & then I saw a litil wayverin spark ov lite whot didn fade; in fact thi bugir seemd 2 be gettin briter & cloasir.

O fuk, I thot, & cut thi strings holdin thi uthir 3 lenfs ov plastic toobin. Thi baloon whooshd up thi shaft; thi harnis bit in2 my fys & my arms wer dragd down 2 my sides. Thi air roard distintly aroun me & my hedake got wurse.

I wotchd thi 3 bits ov toobin folin away, hopin theyd hit

whotevir it woz wos cumin up aftir me, but they didn. Thi rokit – witch is whot I woz assoomin it was – climed on aftir me. I didn want 2 cut my parashoot free & I didn think that wude make mutch difrinse nway + ther woz juss a chanse if thi rokit destroyd thi baloon Id survive & b abil 2 yoose thi parashoot (Ha! Who woz I kidin?). I felt my bladir gettin redy 2 liten me a bit.

Wotir, I thot. I got my wotir botil out & woz about 2 chuk it away when thi fire aroun thi tale ov thi rokit went out. It stil kept cumin 4 bleedin ages mind u, & I woz 1/2 waytin 4 sum sekind stage or sumfin 2 ignite, & stil hesitaytin about chukin away thi watir botil.

Nevir hapind; thi rokit got 2 wifin about 1/2 a kilomitir or so & then juss sorta topild ovir & sloly startid 2 fol away, tumblin end ovir end bak in2 thi darkniss & eventyooly disapperin.

I breevd a si ov releef that mistid up my fayce playt. Thi baloon almost scraypd thi side ov thi shaft but wif a bit ov dextriss poolin & a modicum ov swayrin & panikin I got thi dam fing bak on thi crect coarse.

Ther woz a xploshin @ thi botim ov thi shaft.

No moar rokits.

I cuden c upwirds natchirily, but thi base ov thi shaft woz a ofil long way away & I fot I had 2 b neer thi top ov thi fing by now. On thi uthir hand, thi baloon woz stil farely rayssin upwirds, so I gesd I was wrong. Shurenuf, thi clime went on 4 sum time aftir that. My feet & fingirs was startin 2 get reely coald. My hed was aykin fit 2 burst.

I didn feel I woz breevin rite, but cuden remember whot u were supposed 2 do 2 breev rite. I startid 2 wury about whot wude happin if they'd taken thi top off thi tower or I driftid out thi side thru a hoal & went on up in2 spaice. Whot'd I do then? I wunnerd. I luked down; my gluvd fingers wer fiddlin about wif thi valvs on top ov thi litil botils strapt 2 my chest. I shuke my hed. Doin this hurt a lot.

I think I muss 1/2 blakd out 4 a bit coz when I awoke I was stayshiniry.

My hed stil hurts like hel but @ leest Im alive. Thi baloon iz floatin agenst 1 wol ov thi shaft wif & sorta bobbin me up & down very gently. Its a bit liter @ last. I can c thi traks goan up thi side ov thi shaft in grate detayl, but no doors. I try 2 fink whot I can throw away. A oxijin tank; thers 1 empty. I muss 1/2 chaynjed ovir 2 thi sekind 1 aftir ol.

I unscrew thi tank wif very coald gluvd fingerz & let it drop.

Thi baloon floats up very sloly.

My hed feels tite & buzzy like itz goan 2 burst & my hoal body feels bloatid like am a baloon maself. Lites sparkin in frunt ov my Is & roarin in ma hed.

Thi baloon stopz, bobbin agen.

Stil no sine ov a doar.

I rok bak & forward as if Im on a swing; this scrapes thi baloon agenst thi side ov thi shaft, but it cant b helped. Swinging qwite hard, I can c a doar – a opin doar! – a bit furthir up thi shaft.

I take a drink from thi watir botil, then let it drop in2 thi darkniss. Thi baloon bobs a bit hier ovir thi next few minits. Neerly thare but not qwite.

I mite need thi nife; cant thro that away. I luke @ my boots & my gluvs, but I suspect it wude be crazy 2 thro them away. I cude throw away thi parashoot but then Id 1/2 no chanse @ ol ov gettin bak down.

It lukes prity lite up heer; I take thi torch out & throw it downwirds as hard as I can.

I keep thi baloon goan from side 2 side as it floats up a bit hier. I'm levil wif thi doar; its hoomin sized & like a sorta sqware O shape. Lukes dark inside there. I can olmost reech thi doar but I need 2 make thi baloon rok sum moar. Thi baloon floats down a bit & I shout & curse but I keep swingin & swingin & eventyooly I'm whippin bak & forward in a olmost complete 1/2 sircil & the doars juss about in ranje; I fling out 1 leg & hook on2 thi sill ov thi doarway, then pool myself in wif my legz.

I dunno; I muss b dopey wif thi altitood or sumfin coz I juss undo thi harnis & ov coarse thi baloon races off up thi shaft, neerly draggin me out ov thi doorway @ thi same time; I staggir wif 1 hand flailin out ov thi doar while thi uthir gluv slides along thi flanj inside thi doarway.

I pool maself bak in, gaspin 4 bref. I luke up thi shaft. Thers a big blak coan hangin down filin thi top ov thi shaft, & thers big long hoals like sorta upwirdly-sloapd gill slits lettin in sum lite aroun thi wols ov thi shaft oposit thi coan. Thi lite looks like daylite, tho it must be cumin from a fayr distins as this is thi centir ov thi towr & evribody nose it doan taypir mutch.

Ther's anuthir cupil ov baloons up thare whare thi 1 that brot me up is heddin. I watch mine fump agenst thi side ov thi black coan. It goze on up, neerly disappers out ov 1 ov thi big long slits, then cums 2 a stop @ thi top ov thi shaft, between thi coan & thi shaft side, bobbin like a baloon lost 2 thi seelin @ a kids party.

O u silly fool Bascule, I fink 2 maself. I luke down thi shaft. How am I goan 2 get bak down now? Stil got thi parashoot but wifout thi baloon 2 slo me down inishily thi lammergeiers rekin thi parashoots neerly yoosless. O wel, mite as wel leev thi dam fing heer. I take it off & dump it by thi doarway.

Blimey its coald. I peer in2 thi darkniss beyond thi doar.

Thers anuthir doar & a sorta control-panil lookin thing. Cude b a lift I supose but I shude b so luky. Shurenuf, nuffink hapins when I press thi simbols. I try kriptin, very carefily & short-rainje, so it's reely not like kriptin @ ol. Blimey; ther's nuffink here! Not evin eny lectrix neerby! I never been so far away from thi kript, from sivilizayshin.

Nway, thi poynt is, this elivaiters ded.

Thers anuthir doar 2 1 side. It isnt qwite cloasd. I poosh it opin. Very dark, but thers steps thare ol rite. Ver dark indeed. Wish I stil had that torch. Spyril steps. Bludy big deep steps, 2; muss b only 3 2 a metir. O wel, I fink, tryin 2 encuridje myself; I didn ½ eny uthir plans 4 2day.

I start climein.

I count thi steps in hundreds, tryin 2 keep 2 a stedy rithim. It dozent get eny darkir or eny briter.

I try not 2 think about how hi I am, evin tho thers a kind ov pride in me that Ive got this far. I also try not 2 think about how Im goan 2 get down, or about thi peepil who shot thi rokit @ me & whithir they wil stil b thare if I am abil 2 find a way bak down. I pass anuthir side doar; its lokt. 500 steps. & anuthir doar. Its lokt 2. I also try not 2 fink ov ol thi fings u heer about thi fass towr; about reel ghosts or monstirs from b4 thi Diaspora or from thi depfs ov spaice or juss poot here 2 gard it & stop silly bags from attemptin 2 xploar it. I spend qwite a lot ov my time tryin not 2 fink about ol these fings.

Anuthir doarway. Thi doars r spaiced every 256 steps. Ol lokt so far.

1000 steps.

Suddenly thers sumthin ahed ov me, roun thi turn ov the stare; sumthin that lukes like its alive & waitin & crouchd lukein @ me.

Its stil olmost pitch blak but this things blakir, + its hooj & its poysd ovir me like sum avenjin ainjil ov darkniss. I feel 4 my nife. Thi fing abuv me on thi steps dozent moov. Id like 2 kid myself it iznt reely thare but it is. Cant find my nife. Itz hangin on a bit ov string sumwhare heer but I cant find it; o blimey, o fuk.

I find thi nife & hoald it out in front ov me wif 1 shakin hand. Thi blak thing stil dozent moov. I glanse bhind me. I *cant* go bak. I stare @ thi motionless thing blokin my way.

It takes a few moar moments 4 me to reelize.

Its thi frozin ded body ov thi lammergeier they sent up b4. I breev a bit eesier (if u can b sed 2 b breevin eesier when yoor lungz feel like thare about 2 cum out down yoor nose & yoor skin feels tot & about 2 split like a ripe froot), but when I go up past thi bird I try not 2 tutch it.

I keep goan.

Thers a doar @ 1024 steps, blokin thi way up. I try kriptin but thi doars lectricly ded. Thers a big sorta wheel thing on thi front so I spin it & aftir stikin @ furst, it turns. Aftir a offil lot ov wheel whirlin thers a clik. Thi doar stiks 2 but it opins eventchirly, hissin & skraypin.

On & up.

1500 steps.

I $1/2$ 2 switch 2 thi furd & last oxijin botil @ 1540 steps.

Keep goan, keep goan, keep goan. Round & roun & roun & roun 4evir & evir & evir . . .

2000. Keep climein. Roarin ears, flashin Is, sikniss in ma stumik, coppery tayst ov blud in ma mouf.

Am xpectin sumthin @ 2048 steps but I cant remember whot it is. I get thare & its a cloasd doar. I remembit thi last 1. Saim performins heer xept this 1 stiks wurse & can hardly moov thi bugir.

2200. 2202. 2222. I want 2 stop here, I keep bashin in2 thi wols & am fritind ov follin ol thi way bak down 2 wharevir it woz I startid from. Its so coald. I cant feel ma feet or ma hands. Tutch my nose wif ma gluv & cant feel that neevir. Hak & spit. Spit goze *krik* in mid-air. That meenz sumfin but I cant remember whot. Sumfin bad, I fink. 2300. 2303. 2333. Not sutch a good playce 2 stop. Fink Il keep goan.

2444. 2555. 2666.

I doan no whare Im goan nor barely whare I am eny moar. Im in a hooj screw fing what is windin down in2 thi erf as I clime up inside it.

2777. 2888. 2999, 3000.

Then thers a emptiness in ma lungz. I try hard 2 fink.

Im in thi fass towr, in a stareway. 3000 steps. I can c sum lites, but thare juss in ma Is. Nufink in thi tank, nufink in my lungz, nufink in my hed.

256, sumfin keeps tellin me. 256. 256. 256. I doan no whot it is but it keeps bleedin bangin on about 256 256 256 ol thi dam time. 2560; ther woznt enythin thare woz ther? I stand thare, swayin, suddnly finking, O no! Whot if I missd a opin doar? Whot if Ive gon past wharevir it wos I wos suposed 2 b goan?

256 256 256.

O shut up.

256 256 256.

O hel, ol rite; 256; whot's 12 tyms 256?

Bugird if I no. 2 dificult 2 work out.

256 256 256.

Fukin hel Im goan 2 keep goan juss 2 get away from this dam noyse in ma hed.

256 256 256.

3050. Tunil vishin. No noyse but roar. 3055. Sparks gon. Not shure if Im stil climin or not. 3060. Hiest corps in thi cassil miby. Shit, am goan 2 dy & am outa reech ov thi bleedin kript; am goan 2 reely reely dy, 4evir.

Try kriptin but its hard, juss like keepin ma Is opin is hard. Get a hint ov a reply tho. A wee tiny smol voyse goin:

Bascule! Keep going! Keep going! We're almost thare!

O, its Ergates. Ergates thi litil ant. Cum bak 2 me now.

Thass nice. But I ½ 2 brake thi conexin, iss 2 hard 2 mayntayn.

3065. Taykin off thi harnis now; iss yoosless, like thi kript. I can c 2 do it tho. Very coald now. Very very coald.

3070. Moar lite.

3071. Lite; doarway. Doarway 2 thi side. Doan bleev it. Juss anuthir haloosinayshin.

3072. Opin doarway, brite & warm. Lungz on fire. Goan 2 keep goan.

Fol.

Fol in2 thi doarway. Hit thi floar.

Iss gude 2 ly down.

Lites lite up, sounds sound.

Flash!-flash!-flash! Hiss. Vhoot!-vhoot!-vhoot! Clunk. Flash!-flash!-flash! Hiss. Vhoot!-vhoot!-vhoot!

Blimey, I fink, cloasin my Is, I didn no dyin involvd such a bleedin comoshin . . .

TEN

1

The girl looked down at him. Her brown face, framed by the white fur of her hat, looked open and honest. Her eyes held an expression somewhere between naïvety and innocence. She gave a little sigh, and her shoulders, arms and muffed hands all rose a fraction. She looked, smiling, away over his head and with those calm, regarding eyes half closed as though in recollection, said:

'I did not know who I was; only that I might be able to help. I was born in the clan vault of the family Velteseri. They brought me here at my request. I was taken by— '

'*Did* not know, Asura?' he asked gently.

' – by people who wish to hold me and so try to stop me from doing what I am supposed to do.'

'Asura,' he asked, 'do you know who you really are now?'

She looked down at him, eyes glittering. 'Yes,' she said. 'Yes I do, Quolier.' She showed her teeth and took one gliding step forward, so that she was between the open end of the A-shaped ice-craft.

Quolier? he thought.

'Oncaterius,' the girl said, and there was something new and un-girl-like in her voice that set his heart racing. 'You slug; is this really the best you can do, impersonating an old lady scientist?'

He grabbed the right claw-oar and swung it at her.

She doubled up, dodging beneath the blow. He leapt from the ice-scull. The girl swung at him with one leg, but he cancelled the skates; this arena was within his control, and he had only ever allowed her to specify those rather than boots. The slicing kick brushed past his face and he felt the wind of it on his cheek. The girl staggered as the blade beneath her foot disappeared, but she did not fall.

The ice-scull trundled off a little way behind him; he lunged at the girl to force her back, then retreated two steps to the scull; he grasped the remaining oar and threw it away behind him, skittering and whirling across the ice.

The girl grinned at him, throwing away the hand muff with a similar gesture.

'Ah,' she said, glancing in the direction of the oar. 'It's to be a fair fight, then.'

He jabbed forward and swung the oar. The seven claw blades were needle-tipped and razor sharp; they hissed through the air in front of her face as she jinked back and side-stepped.

'Well, you still have the advantage of me in terms of names,' he told her, keeping himself between the girl and the other claw-oar, still sliding away across the ice.

'As in so much else, Oncaterius,' she laughed, dodging one way, then the other, as if trying to get past him. He was ready for the bluff, but not the double-bluff; the claw-oar slammed into the ice where the girl would have been as she slipped and skidded past behind him. He twisted, levering himself on the embedded oar to perform a sort of stunted vault and landing kneeling with the oar held out in front of him.

She had not attacked, and she had not attempted to run for the other oar, fifty metres or more away across the ice; instead she'd picked up the ice-scull, brandishing its thin A-frame in front of her now like a shield, and advancing.

'We *have* met before, haven't we?' Oncaterius said, rising and hefting the claw-oar as he moved forward too.

'Once or twice,' she agreed.

'Thought so,' he said, thinking furiously, certain he knew this person in some other guise. He cancelled the image he'd taken on, removing any trace of Gadfium from his appearance. There was just a hint of a delay as this took effect, almost as though the alteration had had to be approved, which ought not to be the case.

He watched the girl's tensed, intense face, framed by the ice-scull, edge closer to him.

He'd had enough of this. He attempted to cut out, back to base-reality, but the command failed. He was stuck here.

Now that *was* interesting, he thought. He tried thinking the girl unconscious, then imagined that the claw-oar was a gun, but neither worked. He attempted to summon help; that oaf Lunce was supposed to be waiting in the wings . . . No reply. The Serotin, then: . . . again, nothing.

Alone, then, as well as trapped.

'Problems, Quolier?' the girl asked, still advancing warily towards him. One of the ice-scull's rear blades caught the light and glinted, and for the first time Oncaterius realised that the spindly craft might be pressed into use as a weapon as well as a defence, and that he was just a little afraid. So this was how it felt.

He laughed. 'No, not really,' he said, then swung furiously at the girl. She fended the blow with the ice-scull; he was already swinging back, but that slice too was parried. He anticipated a counter attack and saw her moving as though to comply; he used his own momentum to whirl round and then brought the claw-oar up and then down where he expected her to move.

The claws ripped through the left arm of her coat, encountering some resistance, then slammed into the ice. He hauled the claws back out as fast as he could and ducked and twisted, but the A-frame of the little ice-craft came whistling through the air and a blade bit into his shoulder.

They separated a few metres, each carried across the ice by their own momentum. She bled from the left arm, tattered fur hanging dripping red onto the ice, her face still set in a strange, eager grin. His own shoulder felt numb and suddenly stiff. There was blood on the ice at his feet.

He advanced again, feinted and swung; the claw locked into the ice-scull's frame; she twisted it and the oar was almost torn from his grasp. He pulled, skidded on both feet, and suddenly they were face-to-face through the A-frame of the craft, him pulling one way on the locked blades, her hauling in the other direction on the warping frame of the little ice-boat. Their breaths met in a single cloud amongst the carbon tubing.

Oncaterius tugged, feeling his feet start to slip, and planted them further apart. At least the shaft of the claw-oar was between them, preventing her kicking him in the balls. She was sweating. Blood was dripping from the elbow of her left arm. He felt the A-frame and the oar start to tremble as the girl's strength began to give out. She grunted, her mouth set in a compressed line. He was sweating too and his shoulder hurt abominably, but he could feel her gradually yielding to him.

Her breathing was laboured now; their faces were less than half a metre apart and he felt her breath on his face, smelling of nothing. He wondered – with a sort of furious idleness that allowed his real concentration to focus on the physical struggle – how far down the reality-base the parameters here extended. They were each modelled for muscles, skeleton, cardiovascular system and appearance, but was there some sub-routine running which impersonated their intestinal flora? He really ought to look into these things more closely. Meanwhile, all that mattered was that he was physically stronger than this girl, and the trembling he was feeling through the ice-craft's A-frame and the claw shaft was increasing as he forced the oar round.

He laughed, conscious of his breath clouding around her, enveloping her face. She frowned, and he knew he had won. He glanced, grinning, round the A-frame as he twisted it slowly round. 'Use my own scull against me, eh?'

Her eyes flashed. Her head came thudding forward and her forehead smacked into his nose. He heard a crunch and his face went numb. He dropped back and heard a great bell tolling inside him, as though his bones were metal and hollow and just struck. Something whacked into the back of his head, sounding another toll within his reverberating bones.

He lay, spread upon the ice. He tried to draw breath through the warm liquid bubbling up in his mouth and nose.

Then she was on top of him, her knees on either side of his chest, the front blade of the ice-scull cutting into the skin over his Adam's apple.

'All right, all right,' he said, spitting and spluttering through the blood. 'Tell you what; we'll call it a draw.'

She didn't reply. She was staring off to one side.

The ice beneath them trembled. Then – thirty metres or so away – the surface bulged and split; great wall-sized plates of ice tipped over and slammed back, breaking and splitting and spreading out across the water-filmed surface as from the middle of the spreading, creaking breach, in a blast of steam and smoke, a huge animal covered in thick, knotted hair appeared, the size of a house, the sweeping yellow brackets of its tusks as tall as a man, its trunk longer still, thicker than a man's leg and hoisted to the cold skies, blasting an ear-splitting bellow on a cloud of mist. On its back an ape-like thing screeched and punched the air while a giant black bird screamed and spread its broad wings. An elderly woman – clinging onto the beast behind the gibbering ape-man – glanced nervously under the bird's wings as the mammoth roared again and trod with surprising delicacy over the ice towards them.

She took a handful of the material at the neck of Oncaterius' one-piece suit and hauled him to his feet; he was unsteady and almost fell; blood poured from his face and he held both hands to his mouth and nose, trying to staunch the flow. He blinked at the sight of the approaching mammoth.

'Good grief,' he said, sniffing. 'Well, I hope they're your friends, because I haven't got a *thing* in.' He snorted back some blood, coughing. 'And the hairy one looks hungry.'

'Shut up, Quolier.'

'This is terribly amusing, but I'd make the most of it if I were you.' He snorted again, throwing his head back. She still held him by the neck of his suit. 'Fuck,' he said, 'did we really have to make pain so realistic here?' He coughed again.

The mammoth stopped five metres away. The beast's trunk swung, pendulous and heavy. The ape-thing chuckled, the great bird flapped once. The elderly lady looked down at them. She glanced at Oncaterius and looked rather shocked.

'Madam Chief Scientist Gadfium, I presume,' the girl said.

'Yes, hello,' she said. 'Are you the asura?'

She nodded. 'Apparently.'

'Well then,' Gadfium said, 'apparently we're here to rescue you.' She looked at Oncaterius again. 'Isn't that Consistorian Oncaterius?'

'Delighted, ma'am,' Quolier said, bowing. Blood splattered on the ice. He threw his head back once more and sniffed mightily. 'Actually, I'd been hoping we'd meet again. This is not quite how I'd imagined it, but— '

The girl shook him, quieting him. 'Shall we go?' she asked.

2

Gadfium – swung so violently through all three axes of motion that she feared both biting her tongue and losing her breakfast – clung desperately with both hands to the tangled fur on the back of the bellowing, charging mammoth. The ape-man in front of her whooped and screamed and waved both arms wildly in the air, only the grip of his legs on the animal's thick neck and a generous measure of luck preventing him from being thrown off. The lammergeier flapped overhead, cackling.

The troop of galloping beasts thundered through the streets of the dark city-port of Oubliette, scattering startled people to left and right.

They had exited the tunnels by a series of ramps leading to a huge dark hall full of neatly stacked railway wagons, then crashed through a partition wall of flimsy plastic boarding into an empty warehouse. Sweating and trumpeting, the mammoths had swept down the aisles in a half-dozen hairy streams, their humanoid riders whooping and clamouring.

The warehouse doors had given way; they let out onto a dock-side where black water stretched away under the dark sky of the vast cavern which housed Oubliette and the end of the tunnel which led to the distant sea. The mammoths had wheeled and headed along the dock between warehouses and ships for the city itself, their riders hollering and making faces at a few astonished container-crane operators and sailors.

A broad boulevard led up from the docks to the centre of the quiet city; there were some vehicles on the road but they had all stopped. The Security building was plain and undistinguished and formed one corner of a square. The other mammoths came to a stop outside; the one Gadfium was on thumped on up broad steps, turned at the top, kicked in the tall closed double doors with its rear legs and then turned and shouldered its way through. Gadfium had to duck. The lammergeier clung to the animal's rump behind her.

There were no obvious guards, just one man at a desk who sat staring straight ahead and did not react when they charged into the reception area, but sat immobile and unblinking.

– What's wrong with him?

– Our new friend, her own voice said. He's jamming the Security people's implants. We should be safe here for a while.

The ape-man hopped off the mammoth and bounced easily on the floor. He scampered for a door, which hissed open in front of him. He disappeared; the door seemed continually to be trying to close, but could not, and so oscillated fractionally back and forth with a series of clicks and hisses.

The lammergeier flew over to the receptionist's desk and settled there, folding its wings and stamping from foot to foot, making an S of its long, naked neck and staring quizzically up at the face of the unmoving man.

The ape-man reappeared at the hesitating door. He beckoned her. The mammoth settled, kneeling.

Gadfium sighed and clambered down off the mammoth. At least its knotted fur provided ample foot- and hand-holds.

– Get the receptionist's keys, her other self said.

She did. The ape-man took her hand and led her by corridors and stairs to a door with a complicated mechanical combination lock. The ape-man screamed and leapt up and down, hitting the lock with one fist.

– 6120394003462992, the voice in her said.

– One at a time, please.

– 6...

The room beyond held a woman and a very large man, both of them sitting at a table holding cups and staring straight ahead.

The ape-man pulled her onwards.

The room led to another combination-locked door and then a corridor where her crypt self led her to a distant door; this door had an electronic lock – already winking green for Open – a combination lock and two key-locks.

The girl was inside, sitting on a small bed. She nodded when she saw Gadfium, and took the ape-man's hand when he ran to her, chuckling happily.

She came up to Gadfium.

'I am somewhere else as well,' she said. 'Come and see.' And she reached out and gently touched Gadfium's neck.

– Woa, here we go—

/ And Gadfium was back on the great mammoth but this time in a crypt reality, where the great animal rose like a furry fist through a white glowing ceiling of ice. The little ape-man was seated in front of her again and the lammergeier flapped above.

They burst out onto the frozen surface, where a man with a bloody face lay on the ice, straddled by a slim girl in a fur coat who was holding the blade of an ice-scull to his neck and who had just turned to stare at them.

3

The mist was the world was the data corpus was the Crypto-sphere was the history of the world was the future of the world was the guardian of un-done things was the summation of intel-ligent purpose was chaos was pure thought was the untouched was the utterly corrupted was the end and the beginning was the exiled and the resiled, was the creature and the machine was the life and the inanimate was the evil and the good was the hate and the love was the compassion and the indifference was everything and nothing and nothing and nothing.

He dived within, becoming part of it, surrendering completely to it to accept it into him and dissolve himself within it.

He was a flake within the fall, an insect sucked up into the whirlwind, a bacterium caught within a water droplet forced whirling within the hurricane's howl. He was a particle of dust from the plain thrown up by the hoof of one horse within the charging line, a grain of sand upon the storm-besieged beach, a fleck of ash from the eruption's endless detonations, a mote of soot from the continent afire, a molecule within the encroaching dust, an atom from the star's heart thrown out in its last, majestic, exhaustive blast.

Here was the meaning at the core of meaninglessness and the meaninglessness at the centre of meaning. Here every action, every thought, each nuance of every least important mental event within any creature mattered utterly and fun-damentally; here, too, the fates of stars, galaxies, universes and realities were as nothing; less than ephemera, beneath triviality.

He swam through it all as it coursed through him. He saw backwards and forwards throughout time forever, seeing everything that had happened and everything that would happen and knew it was all perfectly true and completely false at once, without contradiction.

Here the chaos sang songs of sweet pure reason and reserve,

here the loftiest aims and finest achievements of humans and machines were articulations of psychopathic insanity.

Here the data winds howled, dissociated as plasma, abrading as blown sand. Here the lost souls of a billion lives had poured and shattered and tattered and dissolved and mixed with a trillion extracted, excerpted strings and sequences and cycles of mutated programs, evolved virus and garbled instructions, themselves irretrievably compounded with uncountable irrelevant facts, raw figures and scrambled signals.

He saw, heard, tasted and felt it all, and was submerged within it and borne over it; he carried within him, always there and just collected, the seed of something else, something at once supersessant and insignificant, and foolish, wise and innocent all together.

He stepped ashore from a molten ocean of chaos, walked calmly from the belching volcano mouth, floated comfortably on the supernova's radiation wave-front to the dust-rich depths, always holding his charge.

. . . When he got to the garden he recognised it, and wondered if his future self would, but thought probably not. The rotunda was on the side of a small hill, surrounded by tall trees, manicured bushes and rounded, well-kempt lawns. A stream ran through the small valley, and a path led towards the towered house in the distance, through the formal hedge-garden.

He got to the vault and found that he held nothing in his arms after all, that his own naked self had been all there ever was, and knew he had always known that. There would be no other, no remainder or survivor who would walk away again afterwards.

He stood a while at the doorway to the rotunda, drinking in the place where he would lie down to die and something else would rise. It was not his home, not his clan's territory, not really part of anything or anywhere that he knew except that it was upon Earth, and fashioned by and for his own species, and so was part of his own and his ancestors and his descendants' aesthetic and intellectual inheritance.

It would, he told himself, have to do.

He wondered again what it was he was supposed to do, what message he was supposed to carry; he had hoped that at some point during all that had passed he might have discovered what the signal he was supposed to act as carrier for actually was, but in this he had been disappointed, if mildly; he had not really expected that to be part of the process. Still, it would have been nice to have known.

He looked around again, knowing that he had lived many lives, and each of them well beyond the term the vast majority of his forbears would have called a natural span, and knowing that he lived on, in a sense, elsewhere, but for all that he still experienced a feeling of regret at leaving the world, however foolish and ultimately trivial it all was, and could not help but let that reluctance detain him, just a few moments longer, to gaze upon the represented face of this small, pleasant garden, and still know that for now, for this moment – which whatever happened in the future always would have happened and always would have contained him – he was alive.

Then he approached the vault and entered it, stepping through the neat wall of cabinets and into one where something – he had no idea what or whom, but hoped they had the best of him, somehow, and that that would help them fulfil whatever their purpose was – would soon be born.

And so he fell asleep, to wake.

4

'Shall we go?' the girl asked, shaking the man with the bloody nose. Gadfium started to nod, but the ape-man jumped down from the mammoth, ran to its trunk, took the end of it and then led the mammoth over to the girl. He squatted in front of her and looked up into her eyes. He extended the hairy hand holding the tip of the beast's trunk towards her.

'Relative of yours?' Oncaterius asked, snorting blood.

The girl said nothing. She stared into the ape-man's eyes as he whimpered and made little nodding motions and continued to offer his hand and the mammoth's trunk.

Slowly, the girl put out her hand.

When their hands touched, the little ape-man and the mammoth both disappeared and Gadfium found herself sitting on the ice, looking around, unhurt but still stunned. The girl shivered once. Then she blinked and turned to the man whose collar she held.

'Come on, Quolier, we have a meeting to attend.'

Adijine stared at the desk screen. 'What,' he said, slowly and calmly, 'the fuck is going on?'

The Security colonel's face looked grey. He winced a little. 'Ah, well, sir, we're not entirely sure. There seems to be some sort of, ah, problem associated with the Cryptosphere's error-checking protocols. We are in the process of switching to back-up electronic systems where possible but the interfaces are exhibiting crash tendencies under apparent parity contradictions. Ah . . .'

'Again, colonel,' the King said, drumming his fingers on the table top. 'In Clear.'

'Well, sir, the situation is somewhat uncertain, but there does appear to be some sort of violent, and, ah, virulent localised contamination centred around the Security unit in Oubliette but which has spread within the fabric of the main structure as far as the outer wall and intermittently elsewhere. We did conjecture that these phenomena might represent some sort of post-armistice sneak attack by the Chapel but they would appear to be having similar and related problems and therefore this hypothesis has been abandoned.'

'I see, I think,' Adijine said, looking around the state room as the lights flickered and the desk screen display wavered. 'And what was the last we heard from Oubliette?'

'Consistorian Oncaterius was in projected attendance interviewing the asura suspect. Then a disturbance was reported, first in the Cryptosphere and then in base-reality. Back-up Security units are on their way to the focus of the disturbance, though we are experiencing a degree of difficulty in maintaining contact with them. Reports are confused, sir.'

'As are we all, it would seem,' the King said, sitting back in his chair. 'Any further news from the fast-tower?'

'The situation was under control, last we heard, sir.'

'And you were fighting – let me get this clear – birds?'

'Chimeric lammergeiers, sir. The sub-species believed respon-sible for and certainly associated with some of the Cryptospheric anomalies over the last few days. A number of them were successfully eliminated.'

'There was talk of a balloon.'

'An antique vacuum balloon appears to have been released.'

'Manned?'

'We are not certain, sir. Reports— '

'– are confused,' Adijine sighed. 'Thank you, colonel. Keep me informed.'

'Sir.'

Adijine left the screen on. He removed his crown and put it back on again, then tried to crypt.

Nothing.

He placed the crown on the desk and leant his head back against the top of the chair, closing his eyes.

Nothing.

He got up and walked to the far end of the room, looking out through the broad windows and down into the depths of the Great Hall. Threads of smoke trailed into the air from the carpet of landscape. Airships floated against the ceiling, rolling helplessly. Then the room's lights went out and the windows polarised to black.

The King sighed into the darkness.

'Ah, Adijine, here you are,' said a half-familiar voice, immediately behind him. He froze.

They stood in a vast circular space with a floor of gleaming gold, a velvet-black ceiling and what appeared to be a single all-round window looking out onto a whitely shining surface and a purple-black sky where stars shone steadily. Above them, suspended as though on nothing, hung a massive orrery; a model of the solar system with a brilliant yellow-white ball of light in the middle and the various planets shown as glassy globes of the appropriate appearance all fixed by slender poles and shafts to thin hoops of blackly shining metal like wet jet.

Under the representation of the sun, there was a brightly lit circular construction like some half-built room. A group of perhaps two dozen people sat on couches and seats within the circle, blinking and looking up and around and at each other. Some looked surprised, some nervous and some gave the impression of trying strenuously to look neither.

The girl, Gadfium and Oncaterius walked across the glistening floor towards the group in the centre. The girl had exchanged her furs for an old-fashioned-looking boiler suit. Oncaterius looked uninjured now but his hands were bound together, as were his feet, with Resiler shackles, forcing him to adopt a shuffling gait. There was a piece of tape across his mouth. He looked quietly furious.

The girl walked into the centre of the group. Gadfium stood with Oncaterius on the circumference. She looked round the people. She recognised all of them; Adijine, the twelve Consistorians, the three most senior Army generals and the heads of the most important clans, with the exception of Aerospace but including Zabel Tuturis, head of the Engineers and leader of the Chapel rebels. They were all bound hand and foot with Resiler spancels and had their mouths taped over like Oncaterius. Also like him, none of them looked particularly pleased with their situation.

Gadfium stared at the slight figure of the young girl, who stood under the model sun, looking round the others, an expression of satisfaction on her face. If what she was seeing was a true representation of this group's current status ... Gadfium thought about it, and found herself gulping.

'Thank you all for being able to attend at such short notice,' the girl said, smiling.

Brows furrowed, eyes glared, expressions darkened. Gadfium wondered what it must feel like to be the focus of such concentrated – and potentially potent – wrath. The girl seemed to be revelling in it.

She snapped her fingers. The rest of the vast circular room around them filled instantly with a mass of people, all standing looking in at the group in the centre. Gadfium inspected the nearest faces. All different; just people. They looked real enough, but frozen somehow, as though they were watching in base-level time. Perspective, or the angle of the floor, seemed to have changed; it was as if the whole huge space was now a shallow cone, giving everybody in the room, even those with their backs to the distant windows, a clear view of the group in the centre.

'We're going live to whoever wants to watch,' the girl explained to the seated group.

She clasped her hands behind her back. 'Think of me as Asura, if you like,' she announced, pacing slowly in a small circle, her gaze sweeping around each member of the group. 'Firstly, some background.

'We are here because of the Encroachment and the inappropriate response to it exhibited by those in power. The facts concerning the dust cloud and the effects it will have on Earth unless checked have been neither exaggerated nor down-played. At least one of the rumours concerning it is also true; there may indeed be a system which can deliver us all from the Encroachment. If there is, we ought to know soon. Again, if there is, access to it may be through the heights of the fast-tower, part of which this is a representation of.'

(And, in a distant province, Pieter Velteseri watched, like millions of others.

He had been gossiping with one of his sisters and dandling a grandchild when one of his nephews had walked into the conservatory complaining his implants weren't working properly and he was getting some weird live broadcast swamping everything.

Pieter had worried that it might be something to do with the attention they'd been getting from the Security people – tapped communications, interviews through the crypt and in person – all of which seemed to be linked to Asura, who'd disappeared at the airport tower before cousin Ucubulaire could find her. Pieter had crypted to see what was happening, and there she was!

He watched, fascinated.)

'There certainly is a potential escape route for a few,' the girl said, standing beneath the model of the sun and looking around the represented crowd, 'a secret passage, if you like. It is in the shape of a wormhole; a hole through the fabric of space-time. One end is contained within the Altar Massif, in the Chapel, here in Serehfa; the other end is located either in a space ship of the Diaspora or on a planet which one of the ships reached.'

She paused, glancing at Gadfium.

Gadfium was aware that her mouth was hanging open. She closed it. The seated people looked mostly bitter, resentful or angry, though one or two appeared as surprised as she felt.

'The recent dispute amongst our rulers was over control of the wormhole portal,' Asura went on. 'The Chapel commands access to the portal but cannot operate it; the Cryptographers may or may not be able to do so, depending on whether they can design and run the appropriate programs. In any event, the wormhole is physically small, and even if it is brought to an operational state in the next few months – an unlikely and optimistic time scale – it could only ever be used to save a tiny fraction of Earth's human population.'

The girl looked over the heads of the seated group to the ranks of people standing behind. 'Hence the struggle for power, the war, and the secrecy. Of course, the wormhole might save many more of us – perhaps all – if we were transmitted in an uploaded form, but that solution does not appear to have appealed to our rulers, who took the decision on everybody else's behalf that it would be unacceptable.

'There is another reason for their reluctance to commit themselves to a purely non-biological form, and that involves the chaos.'

The girl paused, gazing again round the seated group before addressing the silent crowds beyond.

'What we choose to call the chaos is in fact an entire ecology of AIs; a civilisation existing within our own which is enormously more complex than ours and supports immensely greater numbers of individuals, as well as being, by the most meaningful standards of mensuration, vastly older.

'When the Diaspora occurred the humans who chose to remain on Earth also chose to renounce both space and Artificial Intelligence; in that sense, we are all Resilers, or at least the descendants of Resilers. The world data network of the time was swept almost completely free of virus; it had, of course, already exported all its AIs. Nevertheless, the corpus could not be freed entirely of non-controllable entities and the inevitable process of selection and evolution took place within the niches available within it, and so the chaos grew. Our rulers have chosen to ignore the full implications of the chaos for all these generations because its very existence fails to accord with their philosophy, their faith, if you like; that humanity is supreme, and that not only does it not need to cooperate with what it calls the chaos, but must actively oppose it.

'However, for all this supposed supremacy, there can be no doubt that in the war our ancestors chose to instigate and we have blindly continued to wage, the chaos is winning. Consider;

the speed-up factor between base-reality and the crypt is only ten thousand. It ought to be closer to a million. The discrepancy is accounted for by the ludicrously complicated error-checking systems required to prevent the further proliferation of the chaos. Still, the chaos advances, taking up a little more of the data corpus with each generation and slowing the crypt down further. And the chaos always and only advances, never retreats. We can build new hardware, but eventually it too becomes contaminated, either through direct data intrusion or through nanotechs – also, naturally, ignored, banned and persecuted – acting as carriers. Our war upon the nanotechs is equally doomed, of course, though we have had a little more success in limiting their spread and forcing them to assume forms we find more acceptable.' The girl smiled broadly. 'Babilia is their most successful strain, I think you'll find.'

Gadfium nodded. Well, that made sense. Babil research had been an arcane and paranoically secretive area for as long as she could remember.

'So,' the girl said, lifting her head and looking round the crowd again. 'How do I know all this?' She gestured at the seated people. 'Because part of what I am was once like these people, and part has travelled the crypt and part has swum within the chaos.' She glanced at Oncaterius, then settled her gaze on Adijine and spoke as though to him. 'Base-reality years ago, the man who became Count Sessine made a data copy of himself; the construct was left to roam the upper levels of the crypt and provide an ally there should Sessine ever need one. One day, he did. The construct helped Sessine's final iteration to escape those trying to destroy him and sent him in search of further help; not for himself, but for us all. That ultimate Sessine wandered the Uitland limits of the crypt until he was contacted by one of the systems the Encroachment's approach has activated; he allowed his mind to be used as the framework for the personality of a human asura the system created. The construct he'd left behind in the main data corpus prepared for the hoped-for arrival of the asura, attempting to contact both the chaos and anybody or anything in the fast-tower.'

The girl looked away from the King, looking around the rest of the seated group and the surrounding crowd with a kind of defiance.

'I am both that construct and that human asura. I am all that remains of Alandre, Count Sessine. I have had the cooperation of what we call the chaos in arranging this . . . presentation, and while the chaos has shown no interest in using this opportunity to extend its grip on the data corpus, it could give no guarantee in that regard. Doubtless I shall anyway be cursed as a traitor to my species, at least initially and perhaps in the longer term as well. However, I believe that the units of the ancient planetary defence systems still residing in the fast-tower have now awoken, and that they await the asura.

'And be assured that the asura is our very last chance; there was never any need for our salvation to rely on so fragile a method of deliverance, but our forbears, like our present rulers, did everything in their power both to locate and destroy any information pertaining to the defence systems and to attack and corrupt the automated systems themselves within the fast-tower; they have always known that these might save us, but long ago chose – again, on our unknowing behalf – to attempt to extinguish even that link with the Diaspora. Luckily for all of us, they have failed. It is only through the patience and tenacity of exactly the sort of Artificial Intelligences our rulers so despise that even this last slim chance has been preserved, and we can only hope that it will be successful.'

The girl bowed, slowly and formally.

Suddenly the bonds restraining the seated people vanished, as did their gags. Gadfium staggered back as they rose and rushed shouting in towards the girl. Oncaterius, who'd been standing rather than sitting, had a one-pace start. Something appeared in the air above him, red and glistening and twisting violently; it fell upon the girl, screaming:

'Gidibibigibidibibidibi!'

The girl looked exasperated. She plucked the thing from her hair with one hand and crushed it; first it and then she vanished, an instant before Oncaterius' grabbing hand would have clamped onto her arm.

The room, all the people in it and the fabric of sensation itself seemed to waver and haze then, and Gadfium felt a moment of sickening dizziness before everything seemed to snap back into focus again.

Adijine whirled to Oncaterius. 'Check the distribution on

this,' he said, then – as the others in the group started to disappear, some of them together, already talking urgently – the King looked round the crowd of watching people and raised his magnificently leonine head, frowning. 'Fellow citizens,' he intoned. 'Obviously most of what you have heard is untrue. What can be confirmed is that an act of war has been committed upon us; an attempt had been made to extend the chaotic levels to include the crypt's higher functions. That attack is being resisted vigorously. What you have witnessed here has been a bid to spread confusion, despair and contempt for the rule of law amongst all loyal subjects. I know that it will not have succeeded. Please, do not panic. We shall keep you informed on the progress being made to combat this despicable and treacherous attack. Thank you, and remain vigilant.' Adijine glanced at Oncaterius, then he disappeared. The crowds vanished an instant later. The huge room was almost empty.

Oncaterius turned to glare at Gadfium. They were the only people left in the representation for a second or two, then the place filled with Security personnel. Most of them levelled weapons at her. Two of them pinned her arms.

'You,' Oncaterius spat, pointing at her, 'are under arrest.'

– Oh no you're not, laughed her own voice.

The room vanished.

She staggered, unsure of both where she was and where she was supposed to be. She was sitting. The girl who'd called herself Asura stood in front of her. Gadfium looked around; she was in what looked like some sort of small lobby. It was pleasantly if rather old-fashionedly furnished. The air was warm and smelled odd; stuffy, somehow, even stale. Two sets of double doors faced each other across the room. The lammergeier was perched on a table beside her, gazing levelly at her.

'Now where are we?' Gadfium asked.

'Not far from where we were,' Asura said.

– Near Oubliette, her own voice told her.

Asura looked at one of the sets of doors. 'We're waiting,' she announced.

– For the elevator, to take her to the top of the fast-tower, said the voice in Gadfium's head.

– How did—?

– The *presentation* as she called it took place in base-level time, with a half-hour hiatus immediately afterwards when the whole upper crypt became chaotic. All of that gave her time to get herself and you back into the tunnels. The mammoth troop is either standing guard or leading any pursuit away in the wrong direction.

– What did she do, carry me?

– No; you walked the last bit. You just weren't really here, that's all. But it means you don't know where you are, which is what she wanted. Oh, and I'm only in your implants now; I had to leave the data corpus or Security might have been able to trace our movements through me. Only temporary, though; I can download again.

– I see. Well, welcome back aboard.

– Thank you.

Asura was looking down and smiling at a ring on one of her hands. It appeared to be silver with a small red stone.

– What about the bird? Gadfium asked, smiling uncertainly at the animal.

– It isn't under Asura's control. It is some sort of ally though and it may be the birds are avatars of whatever is in the fast-tower. They get instructions from somewhere and they seem to have their own agenda, but nobody has been able to work out what it is yet. Well, I haven't and Asura says she hasn't either.

– Why has she brought me?

– You're a waif, Gadfium; a stray. You've been picked up for your own good. But don't worry about it.

– What about you? Does she *know* about you?

– Yes, of course she does. There isn't much she doesn't know about.

Gadfium looked over at the girl. Every now and again she would look down at the ring she wore, and smile.

– So, is this lift on its way?

– Not yet, I think.

– Shall I ask her how long she intends to wait?

– If you like.

'Until the elevator arrives,' the girl told her before Gadfium could say anything. 'Or until we are captured or some different circumstance otherwise determines our course of action.' She smiled. 'We must be patient, Hortis,' she said. 'This place is not recorded on the plans that Security use, and it took me a very long time to find it, even with help. It ought to remain undiscovered and so safe for some time, though doubtless Security – and especially Consistorian Oncaterius – will be doing all they can to find us. I imagine we ought not to have to wait more than a few hours. Would you like to sleep again in the meantime?'

'No, thank you,' Gadfium said, quickly holding up one hand. 'No, I'll stay awake, thanks.'

'Good,' the girl said, and sat down, her hands clasped on her lap and her gaze fixed on the double doors across the room.

– Oh. So she can hear what we're saying.

– Yes.

Asura turned to her and smiled as though coy, then turned her attention to the double doors again.

Gadfium took a deep breath and watched them as well.

5

Itz a very strainje feelin wakin up alive when u wer fooly expectin 2 b ded. Speshily when u fot u wer reely reely ded, like compleetly uttirly & finely. U sorta cum roun sloly thinkin; I muss b ded, but Im finkin, so I cant b, so whots goan on heer then? U r evin a bit fritind about wakin up eny moar in case thers sum sorta unplesint surprise in stoar, but then u fink, wel, Im never goan no whots goan on unless I do wake up, & so u do.

I opin my Is.

Gloari bleedin b, its brite & warm. Im lyin on ma bak lookin up @ sum sorta sculptchir or mobil or sumfin; a bludy hooj 1, 2. Thers this grate big planit fing suspendid rite abuv me & ol theese uthirs suspendid from thi seelin & conectid wif hoops & stuf. I sit up. Im in sum kinda big sirculir room with dark windos; stars outa 1 side, thi Encroachment on thi uthir. Thi thing abuv me seems 2 b a modil ov thi solar sistim & it takes up most ov thi space in thi room. In thi midil ov thi room, undir

thi big gloab ov thi sun, thers a buncha cowches, seets & desks
& stuf. Thers a gy thare, standin on a desk, holdin his hand up
2 thi modil sun. He sez sumthin, nods, then gets down & cums
ovir 2 me. Heez got blond hare & goldin Is & skin like dark
polishd wood. Heez wayrin a pare ov shorts & a litl waystcoat.
He waves 2 me.

O helo, he sez, r u ol rite?

Not 2 bad, I say, witch is tru. My soar hed's a lot betir &
thi rest ov me isnt aykin 2 mutch Ither but if I had 2 pik 1
improovmint abuv ol thi uthirs it wude 1/2 2 b thi fact I doan
feel like Im juss abowt 2 dy eny moar.

Welcum 2 thi hi Grate Towr, thi holo blossim ov thi fastniss,
he sez. This iz thi Orrery Room. May i help u up?

Thanx, I sez, akseptin his hand & getin 2 ma feet.

Thi lites in thi room flikir. Thi man lukes up & smilez.

Ah, he sez. He lukes bak @ thi centir ov thi room, goze stil
4 a sekind, then lukes @ me & wif a grate big smyle on his fayce
sez, Fayth moovs mownitins. From our holoniss is discharjed
owr sentril purpis; *it* is sent that *we* may b deliverd.

Padin? I sed.

Cum; let me find u sumthin 2 eet & drink.

Wel, I wen wif thi gy, but I doan mind sayin I woz givin him
a funy luke bhind his bak. He got me 2 sit in a chare in thi centir
ov thi rume & startid fiddlin wif sum sorta control fings on 1 ov
thi desks.

It's bin so long, he sez, scratchin his hed. Whot wude u like?
he asks.

Frankly chum, I sed, am parcht. I fancy a cup ov t but enyfin
wet wude do.

T, he sez, scratchin @ hiz nodil agen. T; let me c. He punchiz
sum moar controals.

I luke up @ thi modil ov thi sun hangin ovir my hed. I stil
doan feel 2 brliyint but Im a lot betir than I woz. I 1/2 a stretch
& luke aroun. Lyin on a neerby desk thers thi pakidje I woz
supoasd 2 delivir heer.

O I sez. Scuse me, is that pakidje 4 u then? & poynt @
it.

Whot? he sez, turnin & lukein @ it. O, i spose so, if u like,
he sez, & turns bak 2 thi controls.

Ahem, I sez. I doan wan 2 apeer ungratfil or nuffin but I did neerli dy getin that pakidje up heer; wude u mind telin me whot woz in it?

In it? thi gy sez, frownin @ me. O, ther woznt actchooli enythin in it. He goze bak 2 thi screen. T, he sez, t t t. Hmm.

I stare @ him.

Wel then, hulo? am saying scuse me, but wel then; whot thi bleedin hel woz thi poynt ove me cumin up heer then?

Thi gy turnz & smiles @ me, then turnz away agen.

I juss sit thare shakin ma hed & feelin lyk a pryz idyit.

Thi chap wif thi goldin lox muttirs 2 himself & eventyerli gets a sorta silindir 2 apeer up outa thi desk. He reetchis inside & brings outa a cup ov stuf witch he shos me.

T? he sez.

I snif thi cup & shak ma hed. Cola, I sez. But itil do. Cheers.

Frangly its crap cola but begirs cant b choosirz.

Sumfin to eet? thi gy sez, lukin hoapfil.

I fink about this. Whot wude u rekomend? I ask.

I drink anuthir few cups ov soda – its getin betir wif eech cup – whyle thi gy trys 2 get sum cakes 2gethir but wifout mutch suksess. Hes starin @ a pyl ov steemin pink goo thi desks just prodoosed when he straitins & luks @ me, smilin & lukin ded hapy.

Then sumfin drops onto ma sholdir from abuv.

Its time to stare agen. So I stare.

Bascule; helo agen. Wel dun. Mishin akumplished. U no, I lost count ov thi times I cursed u 4 yoor damd persistins ovir thi past cupil ov days, when far 2 mutch ov ma time seemd 2 b spent makin arrainjmints 4 yoor saifti witch u seemd 2 dvote ol yoor efirts 2 frustraytin, but in thi end I needid help & u wer thare 2 provyd it. I thang u. Wel, sumfin 2 tel yoor grandchilrin, I supoas. Don't u fink? . . . Bascule? Bascule, can u heer me?

I stare @ thi tiny litil thing sitin on ma sholdir.

Ergates? I sez hoarsly.

Hoo els?

Is it reely u?

U no eny uthir tokin ants?

Whot thi bleedin hel u doin up heer?

Deliverin a mesidje.

Thass whot they toal *me*, I sez, glansin @ thi blond gy, hooz stil mutterin & punchin butins.

A nesisery fabrikation. Whot u wer reely deliverin woz me. U?

Me. Aftir I abandind my baloon I had got so far up thi steps from thi sentril shaft, but then it becaim obvyis I cude go no furthir bcoz ov thi doar – doars in thi plooril as it turnd owt – blokin ma way. Very frustraytin. I woz abil 2 contact thi lammergeiers but thi burd they sent 2 help me cude not evin reech me b4 thi por creetchir dyd. U wer lyk thi ansir 2 owr prayrz. I juss hopt on u as u pasd & hitchd a lift.

So I did heer u wen I tryd 2 kript! I fot I woz dyin!

Actyerli i think u wer, Bascule, but u also did heer me.

Nyway, I sez, poyntin @ thi blond puntir struglin wif thi food-desk thing, y cuden this gy $1/2$ cum & helpt u?

He did not no I woz on ma way. Thi fass-towr is not thi eesiest ov plaisis 2 comyoonicate wif evin if we had wantid 2 anownse I woz on ma way. He onli new we wer heer wen I woz abil 2 activayt thi doar 2 thi botim-most live floar.

I juss luke @ that dam ant 4 a wile.

So r *u* this asoora evribod's bin tokin about?

No, Ergates sez, laffin. Tho i woz creatid in a simla mannir. My task woz 2 act as a kee 4 thi towr axess sistims; they wer kept seperit from thi rest of the towrs funksins so that if thi towr AIs wer evir infectid wif thi kaos they cude not fasilitayt a fizikil invayzhin ov thi towrs upir reechis. I supose am a sorta micro-asoora if u lyk, tho ol ive reely dun is press a lift butin.

But whot abowt that bleedin lammergeier whot snatchd u from Mr Zoliparias; that woz ol a set-up, woz it?

Ov coars.

But u shoutid ma naim & went Eek!

Had 2 mak it luke convinsin.

U mite $1/2$ sed gudeby.

I wayvd ma anteni; whot moar u wont?

Bludy hel. I stare in2 thi distins, then luke up @ thi mobile. So whots goan hapin now? I ask. Whot were u doin up thare?

I woz deliverin a messidje 2 a receptor chip berrid in thi modil erth. Thi coad itself is meeningless but its supoasd 2 activayt thi relivint sistims. Evrything seems 2 b wurkin, tho ther r reportz we may not $1/2$ tym 2 test thi elivaytirs. I $1/2$ 2 say I didn xpect my arivil & that ov thi asoora 2 okur in qwite sutch close proximiti.

Cake! thi gy sez, & brings ovir a plate cuverd wif smol steemin brown lumps. I snif them.

Miby sumfin in thi savery line mite be moar apopryit, I sujest. Thi gy lukes like his crest juss fel.

O! # browns; my fayvrit! Ergates sez. Let me @ them.

Thi gy lukes hapier & ofirs thi playt 2 Ergates, who climes on2 it & lifts a crum bigir than she is & then returns 2 my sholdir.

Yoor Is r bigir than yoor stumik, I tel hir.

Im a ant; my Is r bigir than my stumik.

Smart ass.

Then thi goldin-Id geezir straytins, lukes unfocussd 4 a bit & sez, Ah, we $1/2$ sumbodi reqwestin 2 join us. Elivater WesNorWes.

Am abowt 2 say, So? Whot u telin me 4? when Ergates speeks;

Is it hir? she sez.

Yes, thi gy replyz. (I giv him a funy luke; I fot only I cude heer Ergates speek.) & 1 ov thi wingd emiserys, thi gy continuse, + anuthir she wil vowch 4.

I wude sujest we alow them 2 assend, sez Ergates.

Very wel, thi gy sez.

Weer goan $2^1/_2$ cumpany, Ergates telz me.

There were three sets of doors; they hissed open in sequence, revealing a small cylindrical elevator with couches similar to those in the waiting room. A wave of cold air spilled from the lift's opened doors. Gadfium and Asura walked into the chilly interior. The lammergeier hopped in after them, cackling excitedly.

The doors closed, one after another.

The elevator lifted quickly; Gadfium sat down along with Asura, who wore an expression that seemed both relaxed and concentrated at the same time. She glanced once at her ring.

The lammergeier looked uncomfortable under the vertical acceleration.

It went on for some time.

6

Wel heer we r, us exiles trapt in thi towr. Iss bin a hoal munf so far sins we tuk refuje up heer. Evribodi seems hapi enuf so far.

Thers me, Asoora, Madam Gadfyum & lots ov lammergeiers. Weev got a hoal bludy flok ov them birds up heer; a lode ov them manidjed 2 get 2 thi lift whot brot up Asoora & Madam Gadfyum, b4 thi Security geezirs found it. Now they cant get up & we cant get doun but I no whare Id rathir b. Asoora sez it doan matir nway as thers uthir lifts they ½nt fownd, tho we shuden b in eny hury 2 yoos thoas juss yet.

. . . Whot happind wen Asoora & Madam Gadfyum got heer woz ded simpil; Asoora went strate up 2 thi big globe ov thi sun & put hir hand up & tutched it & stayd that way 4 a minit or so wyle thi rest ov us luked on, then she sat down & cloasd hir Is.

Whot happins now? I askd thi golden-Id gy.

Weel no if its wurkd in 16 minits, he sed.

16 minits, I fot.

Rang a bel, sumhow, but I cooden fink qwite witch 1.

Let me mak sum introdukshins, I herd Ergates say . . .

Thi fass-towrs branes got thi kaos but it didn seem 2 b botherd. Thi golden hare-and-Is bloak dozen seem 2½ chainjed sins thi kaos got in2 thi towrs computirs but then frangli he woz a few fevvirs shot ov a fool wing 2 start wif so no chainje thare.

Asoora sez thi hoal naytchir ov thi kaos may b abowt 2 chainje soon nway, or @ leest thi way we luke @ it mai b abowt 2 chainje, witch wude amownt 2 thi saim thing. Furst we got 2 stop fitein it tho.

Al bleev it when I c it.

Thi ole fass-towr's a fassinaytin playse; thers a lot moar 2 it than juss thi big rume wif thi orrery; thass like juss 1 litil rume out ov 100s. Bits r a bit dilapidaytid & 1 or 2 bits r off limits bcoz they wer punkchird by metirites & byond repare & so coodint b re-presserized & heetid when thi towr woak up, but moast ov itz up & runin agen & itz juss a totil hoot. Amazin vews, 4 a start.

Thers loada fassinaytin mashines up heer; grate big hooj ls like spaice guns & stuf but also lots ov litil robots. Thi robots wer tryin 2 fix sum ov thi big mashinery theyv got up heer. They moastly broke down when thi towr got thi kaos & a lot ov thi ls that didn had 2 b deactivatid, but sum ov them stil run on thare own on-board computers, whitch rnt very clevir but let them moov & do stuf.

Its a bleedin edyercayshin livin up heer, I tel u; thers telescopes & a mooseum ov space flite wif wurkin simyerlaters & 000s ov hotel rumes & swimin bafs & flooms & ice rinx & a hooj & totily brilyint spyril skee sloap & a hoal bludy sqwadron ov space planes tho thayr far 2 old 2 b yoosd & wude certinly blo u 2 smivereens if u tryd 2 fly them, whitch is a pity. Thers also rokits & satelites & ol sortsa stuf & as Asoora poyntid out when she woz negoshiatin wif this gy Oncoterrerist & thi uthir bags downstares, sum ov thi stuf we got up heer cude make a reely nasty mess ov thi cassil if we woz 2 start dropin it or lonchin it on them. She sed they bcame grately less agresiv when she sent them pictchirs.

Nway, thi roolirs 1/2 got enuf on thare playts @ thi momint as it is wifout wurryin about us; ol sortsa shaykups happenin down thare. Thi Kriptografers & Endjineers 1/2 got 2gethir & r tryin 2 get thi wurmhoal operayshinil, evin tho it lukes like we woant need it 4 escaypin. Old Adijine is stil King but heez ½in 2 fite increesin cols 4 his abdicayshin + ol thi clans 1/2 demandid & got reprisentayshin on thi Consistery but evin so bags stil rnt hapy & feel thayv bin missled & want moar info & say. Aparintly thi fastist groan politikil moovmint @ thi momint is 1 colin 4 Asoora 2 b made Qween or President or sumfin. Watch that spaice, like they say.

Weev got axess 2 thi kript now 2, & Ive bin in tutch wif Mr Zoliparia, hoo woz moast releevd I woz ol rite & is currintly in a triky posishin in owr Go game. I also contactid thi Littil Big Bros. Doan fink Il b doin eny Tellin 4 a while; we didn looz mutch 2 thi kaos but in thi curint State Ov Emerjency Im not thi sorta persin thi Littil Bigs want 2 assosyate wif, whitch is fare enuf; plenty 2 do up heer & I cude always go freelans if I misd it, whitch I doant.

Asoora muss $1/2$ mistaykinly thot I woz upset @ getin nokd bak by thi Bros bcoz juss aftirwurds she made me a presint ov hir ring. I woz reely pleesd enyway but evin moar so when I reelised whot it actcherly is. Itz got a litil red stone in it & if u luke reely cloasly u can c sumfin moovin abowt in thare sumtimes & if u try 2 kript in2 it u can heer sumfin way way in thi distins goan gidibibibigidi (etc), very tiny & smol & far away & playntiv.

Har har har, I sez.

Nope, am prity hapy heer & so r thi uthirs I fink. Asoora & Madam Gadfyum tok a lot & do lotsa studyin & thers anuthir Madam Gadfyum whot livs in thi fass-towrs branes & is helpin Asoora tok wif thi kaos. Ergates makes me lern lotsa stuf 2, claymin my edyoocashin isn ovir yet & sheez probly rite I supoas Iv stil got fings 2 lern.

As 4 thi hoal reesin Asoora woz sent heer in thi 1st place, 2 delivir thi messidje whitch woz suppoasd 2 poot everyfin in moshin in jeneril & Do Sumfin abowt thi Encroachmint, wel that appears 2 $1/2$ gon smoovly, aftir a iffy start.

Thi furst sine ov whot woz goan on woz a badun; thi amownt ov lite from thi sun dropt by a 8th, ovirnite. Evrybudy, evin thi cyantists, got in a bit ov a blu funk abowt this. Ther wer ryits in thi cassil & elswhare & I myself remembir finkin, O fuk, & Whot $1/2$ we dun? & Whot is 2 bcum ov us? That sorta fing. But then from that day on thi lite startid 2 increes agen, very sloly but continyerly.

Thi sun shon down, thi moon did likewyse, thi planits continyood on ther alotid pafs, but it woz like thi big ole nasty Encroachmint had gon in2 revers, howevir unlikely that mite sound.

It woz sum time b4 thi astronimers spotid whot woz reely happinin & it woz a evin longir time b4 they convinsd themselvs it woz tru, but it woz & it is & now we no xactly whot thi bags ov thi Diaspora left us wif 2 get us outa trubil, & itz a feersum endjinn indeed.

Thi sun shines a teeny bit strongir evry day, & tho itil b a long time b4 nybody can c it wif thi naykid I, thi starz $1/2$ moovd.

Thi End.

EXCESSION

Iain M. Banks

A novel set in the universe of the Culture

Two and a half millennia ago, the artifact appeared in a remote corner of space, beside a trillion-year-old dying sun from a different universe. It was a perfect black-body sphere, and it did nothing. Then it disappeared. Now it is back.

'Staggering imaginative energy'
Independent

'Banks has rewritten the libretto for the whole space-opera genre'
The Times

'A dizzying adventure'
Daily Mail

'Gripping, touching and funny'
TLS

'The story is vital and urgent and has a brilliantly subtle resolution . . . wildly enjoyable'
Interzone

'Explosive but tender'
Sunday Times

'Thrilling, affecting and comic . . . probably the finest science fiction he has written to date'
New Scientist

A novel of extraordinary imagination, richness and energy, *Excession* is Iain M. Banks at his magnificent best.

INVERSIONS

Iain M. Banks

In the winter palace, the King's new physician has more enemies than she at first realises. But then she also has more remedies to hand than those who wish her ill can know about.

In another palace across the mountains, in the service of the regicidal Protector General, the chief bodyguard too has his enemies. But his enemies strike more swiftly, and his means of combating them are more traditional.

Spiralling around a central core of secrecy, deceit, love and betrayal, Inversions is a spectacular work of science fiction, brilliantly told and wildly imaginative, from an author who has set genre fiction alight.

'A fantastic, awe-inspiring book … I can't imagine anyone not being won over by this deeply entertaining, thought-provoking and humane story'
Express

'Taut, hilarious and wicked'
Mail on Sunday

'Compulsive Banksian reading … thoughtful, intelligently bloody stuff'
SFX

'Captivating … incisive … as sublime as ever'
Time Out